Zane

The Halversons: Book #8

by

KIMBERLY RAE
JORDAN

THREE**STRAND**
P R E S S

A CORD OF THREE STRANDS IS NOT EASILY BROKEN.

A man, a woman & their God.
Three Strand Press publishes Christian Romance stories
that intertwine love, faith and family. Always clean.
Always heartwarming. Always uplifting.

ZANE/ Kimberly Rae Jordan. -- 1st ed.
ISBN-13: 978-1-988409-83-2

A man's heart plans his way,
But the Lord directs his steps.
Proverbs 16:9 (NKJV)

CHAPTER ONE

As his shift ended, Zane Halverson took a moment to speak with the two people who had come into the restaurant to clean it now that it had closed for the day.

"I've left food for you in the warmer drawer," he told Carlos, the man who worked there with his wife.

"What did you make for us today?" the man asked, his words heavily accented.

The food the restaurant served was high-end cuisine, which often meant smaller serving sizes, immaculate presentation, and ingredients that not everyone enjoyed. The first few times he'd left meals for the couple, when he'd asked how they'd enjoyed the food, they'd exchanged a glance, then confessed that it wasn't quite what they were used to.

From that point on, Zane took the time at the end of his day to make a simpler, more substantial meal for Carlos and his wife. It was a nice way to unwind while he waited for the kitchen staff to finish their cleanup and sometimes their prep for the next day.

He made the meals with the blessing of the head chef—and restaurant owner—which made him appreciate the man even more. And it was like cooking for his family, all of whom—except for maybe Kayleigh and Hudson—preferred simpler fare.

"Roasted chicken and rice pilaf with some vegetables."

"*Gracias,*" Carlos said with a smile and a bob of his head.

After removing his chef jacket and saying goodbye, Zane left the restaurant and stepped out into the warm, late Florida night air. He quickly crossed the parking lot to where he'd left his car earlier, when he'd arrived for his shift as sous chef at the one Michelin star restaurant.

He was eager to get home to the apartment he shared with his wife.

His *wife...*

Even after six weeks, the word was still new to him. But every time he thought about Kelsey, he smiled.

The late-night traffic was lighter than when he'd driven to work earlier that afternoon, which meant it didn't take him long to get to the building where he and Kelsey were currently renting an apartment.

After parking his car in its assigned spot, Zane made his way inside the building to the elevator. Though it was nearly one in the morning, Kelsey would still be up. They'd adjusted their schedules so that even though he worked late, they still had time together at the end of the workday.

He'd no sooner stepped into the apartment than Kelsey appeared from the kitchen. Smiling, she approached him and stepped into his embrace. After sharing a kiss, she drew back enough to gaze up at him. Her eyes, which were a lovely blue-green shade, shone with love.

"I missed you," he said, pressing his forehead to hers. "I wish we still worked at the same place."

"Me, too," Kelsey replied.

Stepping apart, Zane took her hand and together they walked to their bedroom, then through to the attached bathroom which sported a rainfall shower. When they'd been looking at apartments, this shower had weighed heavily in their ultimate decision to rent this particular unit. The shower was large, with multiple showerheads, and they both loved it.

Since they'd only been married six weeks, they were still in the honeymoon stage and enjoyed the times they were able to spend together, which had ended up including taking a shower together.

It was the perfect way to unwind and reconnect after being apart for most of the day, which was kind of new for them.

They'd met when Kelsey had been hired as a hostess at the restaurant where Zane had been working as a chef. So, most days, they'd seen each other at work, even before they'd started dating.

When they moved to Tampa, there hadn't been a position available for Kelsey where Zane had been hired so she had had to find work at a different restaurant. Still, he wasn't going to complain about it because at least he had her there with him.

There had definitely been adjustments in the move from Chicago to Tampa, but having Kelsey with him had made it so much more enjoyable. More like an adventure. A new start to the new chapter in their lives.

Zane had never thought he'd find a connection that rivaled what he'd had with Sarah, his most serious relationship. The end of that relationship had left him devastated, and he'd been convinced that Sarah had been his one and only shot at a deep and meaningful love in his life.

He hadn't been looking for love—in fact, he'd been actively avoiding any opportunity for it—when he'd first met Kelsey. Becoming friends first had made the transition to a romantic relationship fairly easy when it had happened.

His feelings for Kelsey had snuck up on him, and the realization that he loved her had been such a subtle thing that he hadn't had time to reject it or distance himself from her. She'd been so sweet, and she had a very steady personality, which he really appreciated since life could be so chaotic in the kitchens where he worked.

The way their lives fit together so well had been just one more thing that had made their relationship work. His hope for his personal future was so much brighter than it had been in a very long time, and a lot of that was because of Kelsey's presence in his life and the way she loved him.

After their shower, they dressed in pajamas, then went to the kitchen. Sometimes, Zane was in the mood to cook, even after he got home from work. But that day, they'd both eaten their main meals at the restaurants where they worked.

"Sandwich, love?" Zane asked as he pulled some artisan grain bread from the bread box on the counter.

"That would be nice." Kelsey opened the fridge and removed the turkey breast deli meat, cheese, and tomatoes they'd picked up earlier in the week.

Working side by side, they built their sandwiches. Zane also added onions to his, but Kelsey wasn't a fan of them.

At one point, he wrapped his arm around her and pressed a kiss to the top of her head. "Yum. You smell like a cookie."

Kelsey laughed as she leaned against him. "I'm that sweet, am I?"

"Oh, you know you are." He took the time to kiss her and show her how much he appreciated her sweetness.

Finally, they returned to the task at hand and finished putting their sandwiches together. Zane carried the plates with their sandwiches over to the small table set in front of the window that looked out over the city. Kelsey followed with their drinks.

As Kelsey gazed out the window at the dark night, Zane gazed at her. She hadn't bothered to do more than towel dry her hair with his help, so it was darker than normal, and curled slightly in damp strands on her shoulders.

Her face was bare of the makeup she usually wore in her role as hostess, but to him, she was more beautiful that way. She didn't wear much makeup when she wasn't working, and none when they were at home.

Looking away from the window, her eyes widened briefly when she realized he was watching her, then a shy smile curved her lips. When he winked at her, a blush filled her cheeks.

"You look beautiful."

Kelsey's gaze dropped to her sandwich, but the smile didn't leave her face. "Thank you." She looked back up at him. "You're rather handsome yourself."

"Do tell," he said, leaning forward a bit.

Their flirty banter lasted the duration of the meal, and Zane felt any lingering stress of the day drop away as he and Kelsey enjoyed being in their own little world without phone calls or text messages to draw their attention away from each other.

It was one of the things he liked most about these late-night hours when it was just the two of them awake. Even though his family was a couple of hours behind them, pretty much none of them were awake at this point, so there were no interruptions to their time together.

It wasn't until they'd finished their meal that Kelsey asked, "Did you hear from your parents today?"

Zane grimaced. "No. Nothing. Wilder did text me, though."

"What did he have to say?" Kelsey's voice was low, like she was afraid to ask.

"He said that he thought it was *his* role in the family to make out-of-the-blue decisions."

Kelsey gave a soft huff of laughter. "From what you've said, he gave up that role when he and Lexi started dating."

"That's true," Zane agreed. "He even proposed in a pretty conventional way, and their wedding was fairly traditional."

When he'd gotten the job in Tampa, Zane had known he didn't want to leave Kelsey behind in Chicago or have to juggle a long-distance relationship. But getting her to move to a new city, only to live on her own, hadn't seemed right.

And even though he hadn't been active with his faith in recent years, he hadn't been comfortable asking her to move there and live with him without being married.

So in the end, he'd proposed, and when she'd said yes, he'd proposed something else... that they elope.

Unfortunately, his parents hadn't been happy with his decision to get engaged and then elope, especially since he hadn't told them until after it had happened. In fact, they'd been married for a month before Zane had let his family know. It hadn't gone over well at all.

Zane didn't think it was because they disliked Kelsey, but he couldn't say that with one hundred percent certainty since he hadn't had a long conversation with any of them about her. They'd warmed up to Sarah really quickly, so he'd hoped they'd do the same with Kelsey once they had the chance to spend more time with her.

They'd all met her since he'd taken her to Serenity the previous Christmas. That should have been an indication to them of how seriously Zane felt about her. And following that visit, no one had shared any concerns they had about them dating.

If they were unhappy about the situation now, there wasn't anything Zane could do about it. And even there was, he wouldn't do anything. He and Kelsey had made a decision that worked for them, and he didn't regret it.

"They'll come around," Zane said, trying to reassure Kelsey. "We just have to give them some time."

Kelsey nodded, then gathered up their plates and took them into the kitchen. Zane followed her, helping her clean up before they went to the living room with mugs of decaf coffee and some chocolate chip cookies they'd picked up from a nearby bakery they'd discovered.

Over the course of their dating, Kelsey had revealed that she wasn't close with her family, so it was no surprise that she hadn't been worried about their reaction to an elopement. If only he could have said the same about his family. The tense situation with them was the only thing marring these first few weeks of their married life.

"So, have you come up with what we're going to do on our days off this week?" Zane asked.

They hadn't really had a honeymoon, unless he counted the three days following their elopement when they'd come to Tampa to find an apartment before returning to Chicago to pack up all their belongings. Which he didn't because it had been a super stressful and busy time.

Even during the drive down almost four weeks ago, they hadn't had a lot of time together. They'd had to travel in separate vehicles, since Kelsey had driven Zane's car, while Zane drove the moving van they'd packed with their personal belongings and used to tow Kelsey's smaller car. So they'd only had a few hours together at the hotels where they'd overnighted during the trip.

Since arriving in Tampa, Zane had jumped right into his job, while Kelsey had spent the first week going to interviews and finally landing a new job. Thankfully, Kelsey's new place of employment had been willing to work with her so that she and Zane had the same days off each week.

So far, their days off had been filled with unpacking and buying the things they needed to set up their new home together. They hadn't had a lot of time to explore their new city, though they had gone to the beach one day because they'd really just needed a break. But now that they were more settled, they were hoping to do more sight-seeing.

After a brief discussion, they decided that on their days off that week, they had better take care of a few other necessities—like switching over their driver's licenses before the thirty days were up—and then spend some time just relaxing and seeing what else Tampa had to offer.

They'd both decided that one visit to the beach was probably going to be enough for now, so they had to figure out what else was of interest to them around the area.

Zane was glad to leave the touchy subject of his family behind, and from the appearance of Kelsey's dimples as they talked about something more enjoyable, so was she.

Once they'd finished their coffee and cookies, they cleaned up together, then made their way to the bedroom. He'd always had a fairly practical décor aesthetic, but Kelsey had brought warmth and coziness to their apartment.

Their bedroom was dominated by the queen size bed, but Kelsey had picked colors and styles that made it feel like their own private oasis. Which it really was. They made a practice of not discussing difficult things once they were in bed, unless it pertained to their relationship. So far, that hadn't been necessary.

Kelsey went into the bathroom to do her nighttime skin routine and brush her teeth, while Zane got his clothes ready for the next day. Once she was done, Zane took his turn in the bathroom, then he crawled into bed next to Kelsey.

He was so grateful for Kelsey's presence in his life, and though things might seem a little rough with his family at the moment, he was confident it would smooth out. His parents had only ever wanted what was best for their children, and Zane was sure that in time, they'd see that his marriage to Kelsey was what was best for him.

"Want to read a chapter?" he asked, holding up the paperback they'd been reading together at night before going to sleep.

Though he wasn't sure that Dean Koontz was the best before sleep reading. This particular book had some vivid descriptions of some scary situations. Still, he and Kelsey had had fun reading it. She was better at reading out loud, and after a long day at work, it was a relaxing way to end their day.

Nodding, Kelsey moved over next to him. She leaned back against him, her head resting on his shoulder. Zane slipped his arm around her waist and listened as she started the next chapter.

When his relationship with Sarah had ended, he'd really struggled. He'd also been convinced that he'd never feel about anyone else, the way he'd felt about Sarah.

He'd been filled with so much hurt and anger, with cooking being the only thing that brought him any sort of joy. To fill the empty hours, he'd cooked. At work and at home, he'd cooked.

He'd made huge advances in his recipe development, though he'd abandoned his original plan to create dishes that might appeal to children or people who were intimidated by the idea of fine dining. That change had garnered him a better position at a better restaurant, which had eventually led him to the job at the one Michelin star restaurant in Tampa.

Eventually, though, he'd come out of his fog of hurt and anger and once again began to socialize, mostly with his co-workers at the restaurant where he'd gotten a job a year or so after his breakup with Sarah. One of those co-workers had been Kelsey, and the rest was history.

Not wanting to ever revisit that time before meeting Kelsey, he had initially closed the door firmly on Sarah and had refused to talk about her, their relationship, or the breakup with anyone. Even to Kelsey. He hadn't wanted his future with Kelsey to be tainted by the knowledge of the emotional wreck he'd been following that breakup.

But three months ago, he'd reached out to Sarah once again, wanting to apologize for his behavior following the breakup. He'd even met up with her and her husband, and his plan was to tell Kelsey about Sarah and to hopefully introduce them.

However, that plan had changed with the job offer in Tampa, plus Sarah and her husband had moved to Washington state. Zane had put off telling Kelsey about Sarah for so long, he now wasn't sure how to broach the subject with her. Especially since they'd had a discussion about previous relationships, and he hadn't mentioned Sarah.

It was hard for him to share with Kelsey just how off the rails he'd gone when faced with Sarah's rejection of him and the future they'd planned together. That was his pride, really. He needed to get over it and be transparent with Kelsey, telling her about everything that had happened with Sarah.

Because as difficult a time as that had been, he'd learned and grown from it, and he believed it had prepared him for this next phase of his life with Kelsey and as a sous-chef at a one Michelin star restaurant.

But that could wait for another time. The sanctuary of their bedroom wasn't the place to have that conversation.

CHAPTER TWO

Even though she always got home well before Zane, Kelsey didn't tend to linger at the restaurant where she worked. That night, however, she took her time since he was probably going to be at least an hour later than he usually was.

"Did you and your hubby have a fight?" Tanya asked.

"What?" Kelsey looked up from the menus she was straightening at the hostess stand.

Tanya was the manager of the restaurant, and she'd been the one who had hired Kelsey three weeks earlier.

"Most days, you're out of here as soon as your shift is over," Tanya said, her brown eyes holding concern. "Is the honeymoon over already?"

Kelsey gave a short laugh. "No. Zane's working later than usual, so there's no rush for me to get home."

"Ah... for the days of young love. Feels like forever since I've had that with my hubby."

"How long have you been married?"

"Twenty-five years."

That surprised Kelsey. She'd thought Tanya was somewhere in her early thirties. The woman was striking, with high cheekbones and flawless brown skin. Her curly black hair was pulled smoothly back from her face, accentuating her beautiful features.

"That's wonderful." Kelsey hoped that she and Zane could do whatever it took to make it that far in their marriage. Or even further.

"It hasn't all been sunshine and roses," Tanya said. "But the good times we've had together are an incentive to fight through the rough times to get back to the good."

Kelsey hoped that she could keep that mindset if she and Zane ever ran into struggles in their relationship. Given that they hadn't been married all that long, they hadn't had many disagreements. Even things that might have caused conflict for other couples—wanting to elope and making a major move—hadn't in their situation because she hadn't had an issue with either.

"Just keep the lines of communication open," Tanya advised. "If you both keep talking, it's less likely that small issues will become big ones."

Kelsey appreciated the advice because she had no one in her family that had set a good example in a relationship, let alone a marriage. Even her best friend had had trouble keeping a boyfriend.

She had also been adamantly opposed to Kelsey marrying Zane and moving away. They hadn't spoken since Cheryl had called her a desperate idiot for agreeing to elope and move away with Zane. Cheryl had never liked Zane, though she'd never voiced why.

Kelsey suspected it was because he treated her so well, and Cheryl had never experienced that kindness with any of her boyfriends.

Still, it was sad, but perhaps not surprising, that her friend hadn't wanted her to have something good in her life. No one had ever wanted that for her.

No one except Zane.

The man had proven himself to be a cheerleader as she'd shared about her dreams, and Kelsey knew that when she finally took and passed the nursing exam, he'd be thrilled for her. And even though she was working hard for her own sake, his belief in her made her want to work even harder for him.

Finally, she said goodbye to Tanya and headed home. She had two days off, which she was really looking forward to. Especially since she would be spending them with Zane.

They had plans to run a few errands because there were some things they hadn't sorted out from their move to Tampa yet. The nitty-gritty things that were necessary when moving to a new place. They'd been putting them off, and they needed to stop doing that.

The dark apartment was quiet as she walked in, but that was the norm these days.

After turning on some lights, she went to the bedroom and changed out of her work clothes. She either wore a black pencil skirt or black slacks with a white blouse and heels. It was a simple but elegant outfit which was appropriate for the restaurant since it was a popular date night destination.

Once dressed in a pair of loose cotton shorts and a T-shirt, Kelsey carried the hamper of dirty clothes from their room into the short hallway leading to the main living area and opened the doors of the closet that contained their washer and dryer. She quickly moved the clothes from the hamper to the washer and started it up, grateful that they could do laundry in their apartment whenever it was convenient for them.

After she was done with that, Kelsey grabbed a glass of water, then went to the comfiest chair they had in the apartment and picked up her tablet to do some studying. It had taken her years to complete nursing school, and she was hoping to finally be able to sit for the nursing exam soon.

The move to Tampa had postponed her initial plan to take the test in Chicago, but she didn't mind. It was a small price to pay in order to be with Zane.

When he'd first told her that he'd been accepted for the sous chef position at a one Michelin star restaurant in Tampa, Kelsey had been sure that he'd leave her behind. Her heart had broken at the thought, and she'd readied herself for the inevitable.

When he'd told her they needed to talk, she'd been braced for the breakup. Instead, she'd gotten a proposal. She hadn't hesitated even a second before saying yes, and when, soon after, he'd posed the idea of eloping, she'd jumped on board.

Her dream for her wedding had never been for a fancy one. No, it had been for her groom to be a good man who loved and cherished her. Which Zane certainly seemed to be and do.

There had been no way she'd let him go, even if it meant moving across the country and postponing taking the nursing exam. It had already taken her longer than usual to make it to this point in her quest to become a nurse, so what was a few more months?

Most days, she used the hours between when she got home from work until Zane got home to study and prepare for the exam. Though school had never come super easy to her, she'd always worked hard to get good grades, realizing she was going to need them if she wanted to achieve her goals. So she was studying hard in order to not just pass, but to excel as a nurse.

It felt like all parts of her life were finally falling into place. And while Kelsey had always figured that with hard work, she could attain her goal of becoming a nurse, she hadn't been so sure she'd end up with the type of man she wanted.

But for whatever reason, Zane had walked into her life, and after first becoming friends, they'd become something so much more. She was determined to do whatever she had to in order to make sure that their life together lasted forever.

As time clicked by, Kelsey kept an eye on her phone, watching for when Zane left the restaurant. When she finally saw his indicator move, she smiled. It would probably take him about half an hour to get home, since the late-night traffic would be light.

Occasionally, he'd call her once he was in the car, but he told her that more often, he liked to use the drive to the apartment to think back over his shift so he could let it go when he got home to her.

While Kelsey waited for him, she got up and switched the laundry over to the dryer, then went to the kitchen. She got a couple of plates from the cupboard, along with a couple of glasses.

Since he was getting home later than usual, they'd probably have sandwiches for dinner again. Which wasn't a problem. She'd eaten at the restaurant, so she wasn't too hungry.

When a half hour had passed with no notification that he was at the building, Kelsey picked her phone up to check where he was. She frowned when she saw that his location was still twenty minutes away, but then she noticed that it hadn't been updated since then, either.

It seemed like maybe his battery had died on him again. That had happened a couple of times, but he'd gotten better about checking and plugging his phone in if it was too low.

Trying to distract herself, she sat back down and picked up her tablet. However, minutes ticked by, and soon, Kelsey had to set aside her tablet, unable to focus on the material as her worries mounted. She tried calling Zane, but it went straight to his voicemail.

Getting up from her chair, she went to the balcony of their apartment. When she slid open the door, warm, humid air greeted her. She stepped out onto the empty balcony. They hadn't bought any furniture for it yet. Neither of them were quite able to find it appealing to relax while sweating to death.

Though it was night, she could see cars approaching with their headlights. A couple of cars went by, but neither turned in.

She stood there for several minutes, watching for any more cars on the road, hoping just one would turn into the parking lot of the building. But none did. Just a smattering of vehicles driving past.

Worry and anxiety crept up her spine, and Kelsey couldn't stay still. After pacing a bit on the balcony, she went inside, but then she turned right back around and returned to the balcony.

What was she supposed to do?

How was she supposed to know what was going on?

It was now almost an hour past when he should have been home, and her thoughts and worries were in overdrive.

Kelsey's heart raced, and she struggled to take a breath. Her shallow breaths left her feeling a little lightheaded and like she was going to suffocate if she couldn't take a deep inhale.

She tried to count in her head, but her focus was shot.

Finally, she had enough presence of mind to pull up the voice note on her phone that she'd made years ago to help her when she had a panic attack. It had been a long time since she'd last needed it, but as her own voice counted for her, Kelsey was grateful she still had it.

Inhale, two, three, four.

Hold, two, three, four.

Exhale, two, three, four.

Hold, two, three, four.

Kelsey sank down on the rough cement of the balcony floor and struggled to bring her breathing under control. It felt like it took forever. It had been so long since she'd last had a panic attack that she was out of practice in dealing with them.

And what was she panicking over, anyway? She didn't even know if the situation warranted her reaction.

But that was the problem. It was the not knowing that was ramping up her anxiety.

Right then, everything was out of her control.

She didn't know what was going on, and she had no idea how to find out, especially since her calls to Zane were still going directly to his voicemail.

Though her anxiety wasn't gone, her breathing eventually settled. Unfortunately, that allowed her thoughts to once again start to stress as she thought back over what she knew.

Which, quite simply, wasn't enough.

All she knew for sure was that Zane had left the restaurant in his car.

Then... nothing.

Kelsey leaned against the wrought-iron railing, peering down once again at the parking lot. She thumped her head on the rail, trying to figure out what to do.

Should she get in her car and try to trace the route that Zane was likely to take to get home? Unfortunately, she wasn't that familiar with Tampa yet to know for sure which way he might take to get home. If she was still in Chicago, she wouldn't be as hesitant.

Still, it was tempting because it meant she'd be doing something and not just sitting around worrying. But what if Zane came home while she was out? Would he think she'd severely overreacted?

Maybe she should call the cops? But would that make him mad?

Or should she call someone in his family? Would *that* make him mad?

Besides, what could they do since they were all the way across the country?

And then they'd think she was overreacting, too. It wasn't the impression she wanted to give them, especially since they apparently already didn't think too highly of her.

Please, God, help me out.

Appealing to God for help wasn't something she'd done in a very long time. Mainly because the last time she had, nothing had happened.

Her anxiety faded into the background, and a numbness settled in. She stayed slumped against the balcony railing, immobile because she just didn't know what to do. Periodically, she checked the tracking program to see if Zane's phone had come back online.

But there was nothing beyond the last location that had registered, which was coming up on two hours ago. Only two hours? It felt like a lifetime.

What if he'd been in an accident? What if he was…?

"No!" Kelsey spoke the word loudly. She wasn't going to contemplate that. There was no way she could even let herself consider that the man she loved was anything but alive.

"I need to do something," she muttered, her gaze back on the parking lot. "I need to do something."

But still she just sat there, tears blurring her gaze.

She had no one to call to ask what she should do. Being in Tampa meant her support system—small though it had been before they moved—wasn't there for her. If she and Cheryl had been talking following their fight over Kelsey's elopement and move to Tampa, she would have called her, regardless of how late it was.

But she was alone, the one person she could count on, nowhere to be found.

The sudden ping of her phone jerked Kelsey out of her stupor, and she blinked rapidly to clear her gaze before looking at her phone. It was a Messenger notification, but she couldn't see who it was from.

Hoping it was Zane—though that didn't make much sense—she quickly swiped with a shaking finger to activate the screen. Confusion filled her as she took in the message from Lee, Zane's brother.

Hi Kelsey ~ Can you call me? I need to talk to you for a minute.

The second message from him contained his phone number. It was all very weird, but it seemed fortuitous that he'd called her when she'd thought about calling one of them. Maybe he'd been trying to contact Zane as well.

She copied the number into a contact and then placed the call, clearing her throat as it rang to make sure she could talk past the tightness of her throat.

"Kelsey?"

"Yes. Yes, it's me."

There was a moment of silence before Lee said, "Listen, I have no other way to tell you this but to just say it. Zane's been in a car accident and is in the hospital."

"What?" Shock coursed through her, though there wasn't any surprise, really. She'd known this was a possibility. She just hadn't thought she'd hear the news from one of her brothers-in-law.

"I got a phone call just a bit ago from the police there in Tampa to let me know what had happened."

"I don't understand," she said, still frozen in place at the railing, her hand tightly gripping the iron railing

"The police found my name as his emergency contact in his wallet, so they called me. I didn't have your number or address to give them."

Kelsey dragged herself to her feet. She had to get to Zane.

"How bad is he hurt?"

"It seemed like he's in pretty bad shape," Lee said. "He had to be extracted from his car with the jaws of life."

"No..." The word came out on a sob. "No..."

"Listen, you need to get to the hospital. Can you do that?"

"Yes. Of course." Anxiety was threatening to overtake her again, but now she had something to focus on. She had a purpose. She had to get to Zane.

"We're going to be there as soon as possible," Lee said. "Hudson's been in New York, and he's heading back here as soon as he can with his dad's private jet, and then we'll be on it to fly to Tampa."

"Okay." Though she knew they didn't think much of her, Kelsey was grateful that she wouldn't have to deal with everything on her own. She just hoped they'd let her have some say in any decisions that might have to be made. Especially since she might not be listed as his next of kin on anything. Just another one of those things they hadn't gotten around to changing yet.

"We'll be praying for you both," Lee said after he gave her the name of the hospital. "Please let me know as soon as you get any information. I won't be going to sleep."

After promising she would, Kelsey said goodbye and stood for a moment, gathering her thoughts. Then she was on the move, going back into the apartment. She closed and locked the balcony door before heading to their bedroom.

It felt like she was moving on autopilot. But now that she had a direction in which to proceed, her anxiety had moved to the back of her mind. The news that Zane had been in an accident wasn't good, but at least he was alive, and she knew where he was.

Though she wasn't sure about calling for a rideshare, she also wasn't sure about driving in a still-unfamiliar city. In the end, she decided on the rideshare. While she waited for the car to arrive, she changed into a pair of jeans and a shirt, since the clothes she'd been wearing were only for around home.

Her thoughts were a jumbled mess, but she had the presence of mind to grab their wedding certificate, just in case they questioned her about being his wife. Given she wasn't listed as his next of kin, it was a possibility.

The driver ended up being an older man, with a kind face and sympathetic words when he learned where she was going and why.

"I'll get you there as quickly as possible," he assured her as they pulled away from the curb in front of the building. Kelsey had a feeling that no matter how quickly they arrived, the trip would still feel like forever.

Indeed, by the time the driver came to a stop at the entrance to the ER, it felt like hours had passed.

"Thank you," she said as she opened the door.

"I'll be praying for you and your husband," he told her as she climbed out.

Pausing, she leaned back inside the car and said, "We appreciate that."

After closing the door, Kelsey hurried through the doors and looked around for someone to help her. Approaching a woman seated behind a desk, Kelsey gave her name as well as Zane's, along with the details Lee had given her.

"Please have a seat," the woman said. "I'll have someone come and get you."

"Is he okay?" Kelsey couldn't help but ask, even though she knew it wasn't likely that she'd give her any information.

"I'm sorry. You'll have to wait to speak to the doctor."

Kelsey nodded, then went to sit down in a chair not far from the desk. She couldn't relax as she waited for someone to come and tell her what was going on. There were plenty of people in the waiting room, but she tuned all their noise out, not wanting to interact with anyone there.

Finally, she opened her phone and sent Lee a message. Even though she had no news yet, she had to do something. She needed to keep a connection with someone.

Arrived at the hospital a couple of minutes ago. Waiting for someone to tell me what's going on.

Lee's reply came right away.

Lee: *Hope they don't make you wait too long. Praying it's good news.*

Kelsey hoped it was too, but she was preparing herself for the worst. Her anxiety was rising again, and she began to count her breaths right away, before it got too out of hand.

"Mrs. Halverson?"

It took Kelsey a moment to register the woman was talking to her. Looking up, she got to her feet.

"I'm Kelsey Halverson," she said as she approached her.

"Please come with me." The woman turned and led her away from the waiting room.

Kelsey hurried to catch up to her. "Can I see him?"

"I'm afraid not yet," the woman said. "He's currently in surgery. After that, he'll be in the ICU. I'm going to take you to the waiting room on the floor where he'll go when he's out of surgery. Is there anyone with you?"

Kelsey didn't want to think about why they might not want her to be alone. "Not at the moment. My husband's family is flying in from Idaho. They'll be here later today. Do you have any news about him I can pass on to them?"

"When we get to the waiting room, I'll see if there's an update for you."

The waiting room the woman led Kelsey to was empty and fairly non-descript but not sterile, with warmly painted walls and generic framed art. The chairs looked like they would be comfortable, but Kelsey really hoped she didn't have to wait too long in them.

Five minutes after she chose one of the chairs to sit in, she started to fidget.

Was she just supposed to sit there? There was no way her anxiety wasn't going to eat her alive as she waited for someone to come tell her that Zane was okay. Remembering that her earbuds were in her purse, she dug them out and put just one in. She didn't want to completely block the room noise out since she needed to hear when the doctor came to speak with her.

Kelsey pulled up her voice note again, breathing in rhythm with the counting. Closing her eyes, she tried to just concentrate on that, but images flashed through her mind. Images of Zane injured in his car. Of him on an operating table.

She felt alone and so weak, incapable of being the strong person she had to be. Her anxiety was making her question her ability to deal with what was to come.

But her love was stronger than her anxiety. It had to be. Zane needed her in a way he never had before.

He had always been the strong one. The organized one. The one who took care of everything. But for the next little while, that was going to have to be her.

"Mrs. Halverson?"

CHAPTER THREE

Kelsey shot to her feet, pulling the earbud out of her ear. "That's me."

A young woman in scrubs approached her, then guided her to a small room down the hall a short distance from the waiting room. She introduced herself as a resident and said the surgeon had sent her out with an update after the nurse had passed on her request for one.

Kelsey didn't know if that was the norm for this doctor or not. But if it wasn't, she appreciated they'd made the exception for her.

"How is Zane?" she asked, clutching her purse to her chest.

"He was critical when they brought him in," the resident said. "He'd lost a lot of blood, so we had to replace that. The scan we did revealed swelling on the brain and internal bleeding. He also has some cracked ribs, and his left tibia is broken."

"But he's going to be okay?" Even as she asked the question, Kelsey knew they wouldn't give her that reassurance.

"We're continuing to monitor him," the woman said, her expression sympathetic. "He's having to deal with a lot physically, and there's a possibility he'll have to be sedated for a while to allow the swelling in his brain to lessen. Keeping him immobile for a bit will help with the healing of his other injuries as well."

"He's still in surgery?"

"Yes, but they should be finished with him in the next hour or so, then he'll go to the ICU, which is on this floor."

"And I can see him then?"

The woman nodded. "Once he's settled in his room."

"How long might that be?"

The woman gave her an understanding smile. "I know you're eager to see him, but it's important that we take our time to make sure he has the best chance of a full recovery."

Kelsey's shoulders slumped. She knew that, but it was like all her training and common sense had disappeared beneath the weight of her desire to see for herself that Zane was still alive. "Thank you for the update."

"You're welcome." The woman reached out and touched her arm, her brown gaze gentle. "He's in the best of hands here."

Kelsey appreciated her assurance that Zane was in good hands, but it did little to settle the mess of nerves in her stomach.

Once she was back in her seat in the waiting room, Kelsey opened up her messaging app and typed out a message to Lee, giving him the information that the doctor had shared with her.

She hoped that the medical professionals in Zane's family would make better use of their own knowledge and expertise than she was of hers. It was like all her training had gone out the window, the moment someone she loved became a patient. Somehow, she didn't know how to be a wife and a nurse when the patient was her husband.

Lee: *Thank you for the update. We continue to pray for Zane, and for the doctors as they work on Zane and for you as you wait to see him.*

Kelsey appreciated Lee's words, and she hoped that meant that they weren't still upset by her presence in Zane's life. Perhaps this would be the thing that drew them together. Zane would need all the support he could get. He'd need all the people who loved him to be there as he worked to recover from his accident.

It was almost two tortuous hours before they came to get her. Just inside the door of the ICU area, a doctor waited to speak with her.

After introducing himself, he reiterated much of what the resident had shared with her. He also confirmed that, for the time being, Zane was sedated.

Once he'd finished giving her the update, he led her to the room where Zane had been taken and left her there with a nurse. Kelsey hesitated outside the open doorway, suddenly feeling again like she couldn't catch her breath.

"Just breathe." As the woman spoke, a hand landed gently on her back.

Clearly realizing what was going on, the woman guided her through some breathing exercises. Once again, that kept the panic attack at bay, but Kelsey didn't know how long that would be the case.

"Feeling better?" the nurse asked once Kelsey looked up and met her gaze.

Kelsey nodded. "Thank you for helping me."

The nurse's smile was warm. "I understand that this is a highly stressful situation for you. It's understandable that you'd be dealing with some anxiety." She tipped her head toward the open door. "Let's go see your husband."

Knowing she had a sympathetic person at her side made it a little easier for Kelsey to walk through the door.

Though the room's lights weren't bright, she could still clearly see Zane on the bed. There were tubes and wires running to and from his body, but Kelsey's relief at finally seeing him nearly brought her to her knees.

"We'll just have you wash your hands, then you can get closer to him." The nurse showed her where the sink was and waited as Kelsey carefully washed her hands, soaping them up twice before drying them on the paper towel the nurse handed her.

"Why don't you come to this side of him?" the nurse said when she was done, laying a hand on Kelsey's back to guide her.

When she got her first clear look at Zane's battered and swollen face, Kelsey began to cry. The nurse pulled a chair over next to the bed and helped her sit down.

"Here. Hold his hand." With the nurse's guidance, Kelsey wrapped her fingers around his. As she did so, she realized his ring was missing.

"What happened to his ring?"

"I believe it's with his other items. I'll get them for you."

"Thank you."

Before leaving them alone, the nurse took a few minutes to explain what was causing all the beeps and what the various tubes and wires were for. If she'd put her mind to it, Kelsey could have figured it all out for herself, but she was relieved she didn't have to.

In that moment, she was glad that precious few people knew that she had training as a nurse. She didn't want to be a medical professional right then. She just wanted to be a wife.

After sitting there for a few minutes, whispering softly to Zane, Kelsey took a picture and video of him. It wasn't that she wanted to preserve this memory, but she thought that his family might want to see him. Especially the ones who weren't on their way there. Lee could use his judgement in passing on the pictures and videos she took.

Lee had texted her when they were preparing to board the private jet, letting her know approximately when they'd be arriving in Tampa and when they hoped to be at the hospital.

Once she'd sent the heartbreaking images to Lee, along with the little bit of extra info the doctor had given her, she took Zane's hand again and began to talk to him. She reminded him of their plans, of all the life they had left to live together, then pleaded with him to fight.

The nurse came in periodically to check on Zane, bringing a water bottle with her for Kelsey after she'd been there for over an hour.

Kelsey hadn't been sure that they'd let her stay, but so far, there'd been no mention of her having to leave. It was possible that once the others were there, she'd have to go to make space for them, even though she didn't want to ever leave Zane's side.

In the end, Kelsey was forced to leave Zane's bedside a few times to use the bathroom and to get some coffee. Though she didn't really feel much like eating, she did pick up a packaged sandwich in the cafeteria.

She knew it was important to keep her strength up. Zane didn't need her to be physically or mentally weak. And she knew from experience that the surest way to weaken herself further mentally was to not take care of herself physically.

What she needed most, though, was sleep. She was almost twenty-four hours without sleep, and she was struggling to stay awake.

Finally, Kelsey laid her head down on her arm next to Zane's, keeping their hands clasped. Though the room was far from quiet, her body demanded the rest it needed.

She didn't know how long she'd been sleeping when a touch on her back woke her. Blinking, she sat up, feeling like she'd just closed her eyes.

"Hello, Kelsey. How are you doing?"

Kelsey stared at the couple standing next to her, then got to her feet, keeping hold of Zane's hand. "I'm fine."

"That was rather a dumb question, wasn't it?" Zane's mom gave her a small smile. "I'm sure you're not doing too great, and you're probably exhausted."

"I'm okay." Kelsey didn't want them to have any reason to doubt her ability to be there for Zane when he needed her. "Did you have a chance to speak with anyone about Zane?"

"We did," Dan Halverson said. "The doctor happened to be at the nurse's station when we arrived. It seems they're doing all they can for him right now."

"Though I understand why he's sedated, I wish they hadn't had to do it," Cathy said, her gaze going to her son. "It's hard to see him like this."

"I can go to the waiting room so that you can spend some time with Zane," Kelsey said.

"Thank you," Dan said. "We'd appreciate that. Could you tell Lee to come in?"

Kelsey nodded, then turned to lean over Zane, pressing a gentle kiss to his swollen cheek. Keeping her voice low and soft, she whispered, "I love you. I'll be back."

Blinking back tears, Kelsey left Zane with his parents. She didn't want to leave him, but they needed to be with their son. She knew that.

In the waiting room, she found not only Lee, but his wife, Rori.

"How are you doing, Kelsey?" Rori asked as she got up and approached her.

Kelsey was surprised when the woman wrapped her arms around her and gave her a tight squeeze. She froze for a moment, then returned the hug. Rori was the first person, aside from Zane, who had hugged her in ages.

Even when the hug ended, Rori kept hold of her hands, concern in her gaze.

"I think I'm doing as well as can be expected," Kelsey said. "Tired. Worried."

For some reason, Rori's obvious concern for her made it easier for Kelsey to be more honest. Lee approached them then, his expression also concerned.

"Your mom and dad said you should go be with them," Kelsey said.

Lee nodded as he glanced at his wife. "Okay. I won't stay there too long so you can go back to him."

It seemed that perhaps Lee and Rori were more willing to accept her relationship to Zane, even if his parents were reluctant to.

Once Lee had left, Kelsey sank down on a chair, tucking her hands under her thighs as she stared at the floor. She was so tired, but she couldn't leave. All she wanted was to be with Zane.

She felt movement beside her, then a hand slipped through her arm. "Can I pray for you?"

Kelsey glanced at Rori, then nodded. Surely it couldn't hurt.

"Heavenly Father, we are so thankful that You spared Zane's life in the accident he had. We ask that You would place Your healing hand upon Zane's body so that he'll recover quickly from his injuries. I pray for Kelsey as she deals with someone she loves being injured in this way. Please give her strength and wisdom in the days to come. In all of this, we pray that You are glorified. In Jesus' name. Amen."

Kelsey couldn't recall anyone ever praying for her. For all that Zane's family seemed to take their faith seriously, Zane never had in the time she'd known him. Would this brush with death change that?

"Thank you," Kelsey said as Rori straightened.

"You're welcome."

"I didn't know that you were coming too," Kelsey said. "But I'm glad you did."

Rori gave her a smile that lit up her eyes. "Lee thought maybe it would be good for me to be here. For him, and for you."

Kelsey had always assumed that Lee was the sibling that Zane was closest to, and it appeared that assumption was correct. She and Rori hadn't had much chance to get to know each other, but apparently that didn't matter to the other woman.

Suddenly, she didn't feel quite so alone.

"Do all Zane's siblings know what's happened?"

Rori frowned. "Lee sent messages to everyone, but not all of them have responded. His youngest brother and sister are notorious for not getting back to people in a timely manner."

"Why's that?"

"I guess they're just too busy. Skylar hasn't been home in ages. I've only met her once, actually. Cole is playing professional basketball, but even though it's the off-season, he hasn't come home."

"Are any of the others coming?"

"I don't think they've decided. They're waiting to hear what Mom and Dad have to say."

Kelsey found it interesting that Rori referred to the Halverson parents as Mom and Dad. She wasn't sure she could, but beyond that, she wasn't sure they would want her to.

"I think perhaps Gareth will come, and maybe Wilder or Jay. I'm sure they'd all like to come, but it's just more difficult for most of them because of kids and jobs."

Though Zane hadn't talked a lot about his siblings, she knew he cared about them. Maybe he assumed she wouldn't want to know about them.

She'd only met them once, when she'd gone home with Zane the previous Christmas, and they'd seemed friendly enough. But perhaps they thought she was okay as his girlfriend, but they weren't on board with her as his wife.

What had it been about her that they objected to?

She hadn't told them anything about her family, so it couldn't be that. Over the years, she'd worked hard to smooth out any rough edges she had because of how she'd been raised, realizing that they might prevent her from getting what she wanted in her life.

But maybe it hadn't been enough. Maybe Zane's family—which was full of successful professionals—had still been able to sense what she'd tried to rid herself of. Although Rori didn't seem to hold anything against Kelsey.

Kelsey was glad for the distraction the woman offered her as they waited for Lee to return. She doubted that Mr. and Mrs. Halverson would leave Zane's side any time soon.

Sure enough, when Lee returned a short time later, he was alone. His expression revealed just how upset he was, and Rori got up and hurried over to him, wrapping her arms around him. The pair stood there for a moment, wrapped up in each other in a way that made Kelsey's heart ache.

It had been barely a day that she'd been without his hugs and kisses, but already she missed that with Zane. Hopefully, he'd wake up soon, so that even if he wasn't in a position to hug her, they could share their love through words and kisses.

Ending their embrace, Lee took Rori's hand and headed over to where Kelsey sat. He sank down heavily into the chair beside her and let out a long sigh.

"That was rough," he said.

Kelsey couldn't help but agree. All of it had been very rough. But as long as it meant Zane was still alive, she would take all the roughness in the world.

"Mom and Dad said that Rori and I should take you home to your apartment so that you can get some rest."

Kelsey pulled back like she'd been slapped. They wanted her to leave Zane's side? It was bad enough she'd had to come to the waiting room, and now they wanted her to leave the hospital?

"No. I need to be here."

Lee's expression firmed. "What you need is to take care of yourself. It's what Zane would want. For now, he's sedated, so he's not aware of whether you're here or not. Now is the best time for you to make sure you're getting adequate rest. Let us take you home so you can sleep in your own bed, then you can come back in the morning."

What he said made sense, but Kelsey really struggled with feeling like she wouldn't be a good wife if she left the hospital. And there was a small kernel of fear that if she left, the family might make decisions for Zane's care that didn't include her.

"It really is what Zane would want," Lee said again.

Kelsey stared at her hands. "How do you know?"

"Because it would be what I'd want for Rori. Zane will need you more when he wakes up, so now is the time for you to rest. Take care of yourself so you're able to take care of him."

"Okay. But I want to see him again before we go."

"Of course."

When Kelsey returned to Zane's room, his parents said they'd leave her with him for a bit. Relieved to finally be back with Zane, Kelsey sat down in the chair and took his hand.

"I'm going to go home for a bit," she said. "They're telling me that's what you would want. I hope they're right because I really don't want to leave you, but I'm so tired."

She sat in silence for a moment, feeling emotion rise within her. This would be the first time she slept in their bed without him since their marriage.

"I need you to get better. I need you so much, Zane. You got me used to being an us. I don't want to go back to being just me. I love you. Fight. Please fight."

Tears slipped down her cheeks as she lifted his hand to press her cheek to it. Her anxiety was pulsing again at the thought of leaving him. What if something happened while she was gone?

Finally, when she felt herself falling asleep again, Kelsey got to her feet and leaned over to press a kiss to Zane's lips. She rested her forehead against his for a moment, then straightened.

"Goodnight, love. I'll be back in the morning."

The hardest thing in the world was to walk away from Zane and leave his room. Anxiety swelled inside her, but Kelsey breathed steadily, forcing herself to put one foot in front of the other. The sooner she left, the sooner she could come back.

In the waiting room, she found Lee huddled in conversation with his parents. Rori spotted her first and smiled.

"Ready to go?" Lee asked as he got to his feet.

"Not really," Kelsey said. "But I'm not sure I'll ever be ready, so I might as well go now."

"We'll call if anything develops," Mrs. Halverson said.

"Thank you."

Kelsey wasn't sure what would happen if a major decision needed to be made for Zane while he was still unconscious. Would they let her have any input?

"We've booked a nearby hotel, so we'll go there to check in once we've dropped Kelsey off, then we'll come back to get you guys," Lee said, then the three of them headed out of the hospital.

The ache in her heart grew the further away they got, but Kelsey managed to hold her composure. Total privacy was within reach. Then she wouldn't have to contain her emotions any longer.

But was that actually a good thing?

Kelsey wasn't sure.

She gave Lee the address of the apartment building, which he then put into the GPS in the car that they'd rented.

When they reached the building, he pulled to a stop at the curb in front of the door. "We'll come back and pick you up in the morning. Just text me when you're ready to go."

"You don't have to do that," Kelsey said. "I might end up wanting to go in fairly early."

"Okay. Just let me know if you need a ride."

"Thank you for everything today." Kelsey opened the door. "I'll see you tomorrow."

"We'll be praying for you," Rori said. "I hope you sleep well."

Kelsey wasn't sure that would be the case, but she didn't argue with her. Just said goodnight and got out of the car.

Once she reached the apartment, the silence was oppressive, but she tried not to dwell on it. Though it was still quite early, not even six o'clock, Kelsey decided to take a shower, maybe eat something, then go to bed.

As she stood in front of the shower a few minutes later, waiting for the water to warm up, the tears began to fall. She didn't know how it had happened, but they'd gotten into the habit of showering together, and now she was going to have to do it alone.

Sobbing, she stepped into the warm spray and let it pound down on her and wash away her tears. But nothing could stem the emotion that rushed out of her, so she didn't even try.

The shower ended up being so emotionally draining that Kelsey was in no mood to eat anything. Instead, she fell into bed, her hair still wrapped in a towel.

How long was she going to be doing all the things they'd done together, alone?

As Kelsey curled up under the covers, Zane's pillow clutched in her arms, exhaustion dragged her toward sleep. Unfortunately, her thoughts were still going a mile a minute, clutching tightly to the edge of consciousness.

There were things she needed to do the next day, in addition to being with Zane. She had to call his workplace and hers, since neither of them would be able to work for awhile.

It seemed wrong to focus on the practical things while Zane's condition was still so perilous, but he'd expect her to do it in his absence. So she would.

That next day set the pattern for the days to come.

Each morning, she went to the hospital to spend the day with Zane. His parents were there as well, though they didn't talk much to her. They spent a lot of time on the phone, giving updates on Zane to a variety of people. Some family members, but also what sounded like people from their church.

After a few days, Lee and Rori had gone back to Serenity, and Gareth and Wilder had arrived. Wilder had brought his wife as well, but Gareth's had stayed home with their kids.

Kelsey missed Rori, who had ended up being a great support for her. Lexi was nice, but she wasn't as warm and friendly as Rori.

With Lee and Rori gone, Kelsey felt very much on the outside as they all waited for the day when Zane would wake up.

It took several days, but finally everything looked good enough to the Halverson parents and Zane's doctors to bring him out of the sedation. She'd hoped that he'd wake up immediately, but that didn't happen.

All she wanted was for him to open his eyes so they could move into the next phase of healing from his accident. Kelsey knew it wouldn't be easy because there were so many parts of his body that needed to heal, and with his broken leg, he wouldn't be able to work for a while.

But they could handle all of that.

He just needed to open his eyes.

CHAPTER FOUR

Pain... pain... pain...

There was no escaping it, and Zane couldn't seem to pinpoint exactly where it was coming from. His torso hurt. His leg hurt. His whole body ached. But of it all, the pain in his head hurt the most. Like the worst headache he'd ever had.

Was this a nightmare?

It felt far too real to be a bad dream, though. But what had happened? It felt like he'd taken a tumble down the stairs and hit every single step with every part of his body. Twice.

He tried to shift, moaning as pain shot from the top of his head down to his toes.

"Zane? Son?" His dad's voice broke through the cloud of pain in his mind. "Don't move too much. Can you open your eyes?"

As he struggled to do as his dad had asked, Zane heard his mom say, "Wilder, go get Kelsey. I'll let the nurses know."

Slowly, Zane opened his eyes to a dimly lit room, though it still made him blink. He was very thankful for the lack of light, because he had a feeling that if the lights in the room had been fully on, the pain in his head would have felt like an explosion.

He blinked a couple more times and lifted his hand to touch his head.

"Careful, son," his dad said. "You're hooked up to a few things."

"What—" He stopped talking when the word made his throat hurt.

"Here." His dad lifted something to his mouth, wetting his lips and adding moisture to his dry mouth.

"Water." The word still hurt, but he needed more than a wet sponge.

"The nurse will be here in a minute."

Before he could say anything more, there was motion at the door, and three people came into the room.

"Zane!" A woman with blonde hair and a worried look approached the bed, leaning down to press her cheek to his. When she pulled back, there were tears in her blue-green eyes. "Finally! I've been so worried."

Frowning, Zane stared at the woman for a long moment. "Who are you?"

The woman's eyes widened as shock and then devastation crossed her face. Letting go of where she held onto his hand, she took a step back, away from the bed.

"Zane, darling." This time it was his mom who spoke and approached him to give him a kiss.

"What happened?"

"You were in a car accident. You're in a hospital in Tampa."

"Was I down here for Spring Break?" He looked around the room. "Where's Sarah?"

His mom frowned and glanced over at his dad before focusing on Zane again. "What's the last thing you remember, darling?"

Before he could answer, the nurse, who had been checking the machines beside his bed, said, "The doctor should be here in a couple of minutes. How is your pain?"

"Terrible," he managed. "I hurt everywhere."

"Let me get something for you."

Zane closed his eyes, struggling to take in everything. Clearly, he'd forgotten a few things. Like who the blonde woman was. And what he'd been doing in Tampa. And where was Sarah? The more he tried to think about all of it, the more his head hurt.

What was the last thing he remembered? Nothing immediately came to mind.

"Zane?" A deep voice broke into his thoughts. "Can you open your eyes?"

Zane opened his eyes to find a tall man with a white coat standing where the nurse had been. He had silver hair that was professionally styled, and his smile was warm as he asked Zane a series of questions.

The man's expression didn't change with Zane's answers. However, he could hear whispered discussions in the room that told him the others weren't happy with what he was saying.

"It would seem that we're dealing with a case of amnesia here," the doctor said.

"Amnesia?" Zane asked, words coming easier now that he'd had a bit of water from the nurse.

"Temporary?" his mom asked.

"For the moment, we don't know," the doctor replied. "We'll have to do some additional scans."

"What have I forgotten?" Zane asked. "What don't I know?"

Looks were exchanged. Even in the dimness of the room, he could see that.

"Just tell me."

"Perhaps we should wait until after we have a better idea of what's going on," his dad said, caution in his tone.

"Just *tell* me," Zane demanded, then gritted his teeth as that brought on a pulse of pain in his head. He squeezed his eyes shut for a moment.

After a stretch of silence, his mom took his hand. "It appears that you've lost about four years."

Four *years!?* How was that possible?

When he asked that question, it was the doctor who answered. "There's never a set amount of memories that are lost in situations like this. The complete workings of the brain are still beyond our understanding. We know a lot, but not everything. I have no idea why your brain has lost four years and not six or two."

"But I'll get them back, right?" Zane desperately needed him to say yes. So much must have happened in four years' time.

"I'm sorry, but I can't give you that guarantee. There is a possibility as your brain heals from this injury that your memories will return. Maybe all of them. Maybe just some of them. I'm afraid there is no definitive answer I can offer you."

"What did I miss?" Zane asked. "Why am I here in Tampa?"

He was desperate for answers. Desperate to know what had happened in the years since his last memory.

"You moved here about a month ago to work at a restaurant."

Why had he done that? He'd been planning to stick around Chicago to work and save enough money to start up a restaurant of his own. Had he somehow abandoned those plans?

Suddenly, he recalled the woman who had approached him earlier. "Did I move here on my own?"

Another look was exchanged between his parents before his dad said, "No. You moved here with your wife."

"My wife?" Zane asked. "Sarah and I got married?"

Someone in the room gasped, but Zane wasn't sure who it was.

"You got married about six weeks ago, but not to Sarah."

That news was shocking. He'd always hoped that he and Sarah would get married at some point in the future, and Sarah had felt the same way. The love they shared far exceeded anything he'd ever felt for a woman before. Why wasn't she the one he'd married?

"Why not to Sarah? Did we breakup or something?" He shook his head, then winced from the pain. "I never would have broken up with Sarah. I love her so much."

Movement caught his eye, and he saw the woman from earlier rush from the room.

"Who was that?" he asked.

His mom frowned at him. "That's Kelsey. Your wife."

He felt nothing at the revelation. Sarah was the woman he'd always assumed he would one day call his wife. "I don't recognize her at all."

"Hopefully you will after your brain has had a chance to recover more."

He better remember, because he felt like they were talking about someone else. A stranger.

Zane couldn't imagine having a wife that he had no memory of. No feelings for. But how could he have feelings for her if he couldn't remember her or any part of their relationship?

"You need to get some rest," the doctor said. "Real rest. Not the sedation you've been under for the past few days."

As soon as the doctor suggested rest, Zane felt a wave of exhaustion sweep over him. "Yeah. I could probably use some."

"We're here to stay as long as you need us," his dad said. "Though Gareth has to get back to Aria and the kids."

"Kids?"

"Yes. Do you remember Timothy?" Zane considered his mom's question before shaking his head. "Aria must have been pregnant with him around the time you last remember. They also have a daughter who is just a year old. Her name is Emily, but we call her Emmy."

"Wow." Obviously he was missing the details of more than just his life. He wanted to ask about all his siblings but decided not to. He was too tired to deal with more information.

"Don't worry about anything more tonight," his mom said. "Get some rest."

"Do you want us to stay?"

Zane shook his head at his dad. "There's no need. I'll probably just be sleeping."

"Okay. We'll come back tomorrow."

His mom bent over to kiss his forehead. "We're so glad you've woken up. And we're with you through all of this."

"Don't worry about anything that has happened." His dad rested a hand on his arm. "We'll be praying for you."

"Thanks, Dad."

"In fact, why don't we pray before we leave?"

As he listened to his dad pray, Zane felt himself drift. Now that the pain in most of his body had been taken care of, courtesy of the nurse, he could feel sleep calling to him.

"We love you, darling. Sleep well," his mom said as she pressed one more kiss to his forehead. "We'll see you in the morning."

He heard some murmured conversation and was briefly aware of the nurse at his bedside before he fell asleep, hoping and praying that the morning would bring less pain, more clarity, and the return of his missing memories.

~ * ~

Kelsey stared at herself in the mirror of the women's bathroom. Her skin looked sallow under the bright fluorescent lights, and the dark circles under her eyes spoke to the sleepless nights she'd endured lately. But none of that matched the devastation in her heart.

She'd been so certain that once Zane woke up, everything would be okay. He'd still need healing, of course, but her worry over his physical state would have lessened a lot. No one had warned her that he might have memory issues.

Although maybe she should have realized it was a possibility.

Or that he'd think he was in love with another woman. One named Sarah... that Kelsey knew nothing about. The pain she'd felt as she'd heard him say he loved Sarah hadn't lessened at all.

She wanted to believe that his memories would return in full, but she could no longer allow herself to be that hopeful. Hope was the reason she was hurting so badly right then.

She'd hoped that all would be well when Zane finally opened his eyes. She hadn't realized that—for her—things would go from bad to worse.

Still, it had been good to see him awake and interacting. While he might not remember her or the love he once had for her, he was still the man she loved. So seeing him take this step forward in his recovery by waking up was still a good thing.

Bracing her hands on the counter, she took several deep breaths, wondering if there was any way she could leave the hospital without having to deal with the Halversons.

Hoping to keep her emotions under control, Kelsey took several deep breaths. She could do this. She'd stayed strong through these new developments, just like she'd stayed strong since the accident.

She had no choice.

Returning to the waiting room, she saw that all the family members currently in Tampa were gathered there. Wilder spotted her first and left the group to approach her.

"Are you doing okay?"

"I'm fine." She could tell he didn't believe her, but that was too bad. She wasn't going to parade the hurt she was feeling out for them to see.

"I know it must have been difficult to hear that Zane had lost his memory," Wilder said, glancing over at Lexi as she joined them. If Rori had been there, she would absolutely have wrapped Kelsey in a tight hug. "But we're all very hopeful that it's just temporary."

"As am I," she said.

The others had moved over to where they stood, and Cathy said, "Zane has fallen asleep."

"I'm going to go see him, then I'm going home."

"But he's asleep," Cathy repeated.

"Mom." Gareth's voice was firm as he spoke. "It's probably easier for Kelsey to see him while he's sleeping, and I doubt her intentions are to wake him. But regardless of all that, she's his wife. She has the right to see him whenever she wants."

Kelsey appreciated Gareth coming to her defense, especially when she hadn't expected it.

"He's right," Dan said. "We need to be going as well."

Once Lee and Rori had returned to Serenity, Kelsey had brought her own vehicle to the hospital, so she didn't have to spend any time trapped in awkward silence with members of Zane's family.

"We'll see you tomorrow, Kelsey," Gareth said. "We'll be praying for you."

Kelsey appreciated his words, since, given his defense of her, he might just be as sincere as Rori and Lee had been in their prayers for her. "Thank you."

Turning, she headed for the doors that led to the ICU. A nurse was in Zane's room when Kelsey stepped through the door. She looked up and gave her a smile.

"He's just fallen asleep," the woman said.

"That's fine," Kelsey said as she approached the bed. "Probably for the better, since he doesn't remember me."

The woman reached out to lay a hand on her arm. "I'm sure that must be difficult for you, but don't give up hope."

"I love him too much to do that," Kelsey said.

"That's the spirit."

"Is everything else okay?"

Keeping her voice low, the nurse took a couple of minutes to review everything, giving updates on how his other injuries were, as well as his head. "He's definitely in a better position than he was when he was first brought in. His body is healing."

"Will he be leaving the hospital soon?" And if he did, where would he go?

"Since he's awake and stable, they'll probably move him to a regular unit tomorrow or the day after," the nurse said. "And then his doctor will determine when he's ready to leave from there."

Kelsey thanked her for the information, then stepped closer to Zane's bed. She wanted to take his hand, and to bend and give him a kiss, but she restrained herself. Though she'd been eager for him to open his eyes, she didn't want to wake him right then. Not when her emotions were still so raw.

She didn't plan to stay long with him, so after the nurse left them alone, Kelsey bent close. "I love you, Zane. You might not remember me or the love we share, but I do. And it's worth fighting for. I will stay by your side until you tell me to walk away."

Though she didn't want that to ever happen, she was no longer going to delude herself into thinking that things couldn't get worse.

"Goodnight, my love." She gently brushed her fingers across the back of his hand, but he didn't stir.

Finally, Kelsey tore herself away from his bedside and left the room. She waved at the nurse who'd been in his room earlier, then went through the doors leading out of the ICU. The waiting room was empty of the Halversons, so she was able to head right out of the building.

The air was muggy as she left the hospital, so she cranked the air conditioner in her car before she left the parking lot and headed home.

When she finally pulled into her parking spot at the apartment, Kelsey breathed a sigh of relief. That relief didn't last long, however. As she stepped into the apartment, she was reminded that along with her, Zane didn't remember the apartment and the home they'd been building together.

He wouldn't remember the time they'd spent searching for an apartment that would suit their needs. He wouldn't remember the things they'd purchased together to make the apartment their home. He wouldn't remember the moments they'd captured, then had printed out and hung on the wall, including a couple of pictures from their wedding day.

Kelsey wanted to just wallow in her hurt and fear, but there were some practical issues to consider. Something told her that if Zane's memory didn't come back soon, the Halversons would want him to return to Serenity to continue his recovery.

In losing four years' worth of memories, he'd lost the experience that had helped him gain his position at the restaurant there in Tampa. Which would mean he'd lose his job, and there was no way that she could afford to keep this apartment on her salary alone.

When they'd gotten married, Zane had said he'd take on three-quarters of the expenses, leaving just one-quarter for her, since his salary as a chef was about three times what hers was as a hostess. That plan had been working for them until the accident.

Now she needed to figure out what she was going to do.

If the Halversons did take Zane back to Serenity, should she follow him?

She wanted to. She'd meant what she'd told him in his room before she left earlier. He needed to tell her to leave him alone, not his family. So she'd empty her savings account to follow him to Serenity if she had to.

As it was, she needed to make a decision about returning to her job there in Tampa. They needed an income, especially since there were going to be some medical bills coming in. Even with good health insurance—which they had—they were still going to owe something for his hospitalization.

Focusing on the practical, even though it wasn't encouraging, was easier than dwelling on what had happened with Zane earlier.

After making herself something to eat, Kelsey took a shower, then pulled on a T-shirt of Zane's. It reached her mid-thigh and past her elbows, making her feel like she was wrapped in his arms.

The night after the accident, she'd taken one of his clean T-shirts and spritzed it with his cologne, since it made her feel like he was with her in their bed.

Before she crawled into bed, Kelsey went to her side of the walk-in closet and dug through a box of stuff she hadn't unpacked yet. It held an assortment of stationery products, including a journal she'd bought but never used. Taking it and a gel pen from the box, she went back to the bed.

After the events of the day, there was even more in her heart and mind that she had no one to talk to about. Rori had told Kelsey she could call her if she needed to talk, but it felt like her disconnect with the Halversons had only increased over the past few hours.

This has become the second worst day of my life. The first was the day of the accident when I wasn't sure if you would live. Now, I'm not sure you will ever remember me. Or remember the love we shared.

Her phone beeped with a message, and though she wished she could ignore it, Kelsey knew she shouldn't be ignoring any messages these days.

Rori: *We just heard what happened when Zane woke up today. I'm so, so sorry. You must feel heartbroken. Don't give up hope, though. Lee and I are praying for you and Zane, and we're here for anything you need. I know you don't know us well, but we do care about you and Zane. He told Lee how much he loved you, so just hang in there.*

Kelsey's eyes pricked with tears. Maybe it wouldn't be the worst thing if she had to go to Serenity. At least she'd have one friend there. Two, if she counted Lee.

Yes, it was a horrible day, but I'm doing my best to stay strong. Not sure where we go from here, but I appreciate your prayers.

She had no idea if those prayers were working or not. They'd been praying for Zane to regain consciousness and for healing. Both of those prayers had been answered, but not in the way they'd expected.

As much as she was upset about the memory loss, she was sure it was hard on all of Zane's family, too. It wouldn't be easy for them to accept that the memories they shared with him over the last four years were lost.

But at least he remembered his family.

It was more than she had at the moment.

CHAPTER FIVE

Just leave me alone!

It was what Zane wanted to yell at everyone, but he bit his tongue.

He knew they meant well, but their hovering was starting to aggravate him. Or perhaps it was the ache he constantly dealt with in his head that was making him more irritable than usual. The pain would lessen with the meds, but it always came back.

He'd been moved to a room on a regular unit, which was good. But what he wanted most—his memory back—just wasn't happening. How was he supposed to get back to his life when he had no idea what his life had been before his accident?

Also, he was apparently not allowed to make any decisions for himself. His family was busy trying to figure out what should happen to him when he left the hospital. They weren't consulting him, however.

The one person he'd thought would be there was the woman they said was his wife. So far, he hadn't seen her since that first day he'd woken up.

"I really think he needs to come home to Serenity to heal," his mom said. "He can't go back to his job here. Not until he gets his memory back. The best place for him is with us."

Gareth had been quiet through most of the conversation so far, but now he spoke up. "Mom, Kelsey needs to be part of this discussion."

"Well, then where is she?" his mom demanded.

"From what the nurses have said, she comes by once Zane's asleep and spends time with him then."

"Why wouldn't she come by during the day?" Wilder asked.

"I think she feels it would be upsetting for Zane since he doesn't remember her."

Right then, Zane felt like he'd rather deal with his stranger wife than with his family.

Gareth crossed his arms. "But at the end of the day, as his wife, she needs to have a say in his on-going care."

"They've only been married for a few weeks," his mom protested. "I think we know what's best for him."

"Zane has been on his own for years, and though he doesn't remember the past few years, he knows what he wants for his life."

Zane appreciated Gareth's voice of reason. If Lee couldn't be there to help him, Gareth appeared to be the second best. Even so, there was something appealing about returning to a familiar place when he was feeling very unmoored. He could return to the familiarity of Chicago, but he wouldn't have the support he'd have in Serenity if he couldn't work for awhile.

"Let me see if Kelsey can come to be a part of this discussion," Gareth said as he headed for the door.

"Why don't you like Kelsey?" Zane asked once Gareth had left.

He'd picked up on the tension they had, especially his mom, whenever Kelsey was around or was being discussed. It was hard to imagine he'd married someone his family didn't like.

His parents exchanged yet another look. Their ability to communicate without saying a word had apparently only gotten better with time.

"We just don't think she's the best woman for you," his mom said.

"Not that we know her all that well," Wilder added.

"We know she isn't a Christian," his dad said. "And you know that we wanted a Christian spouse for each of you kids."

"And yet the way she's been treated is probably not exactly endearing her to Christians," Wilder said with a tilt of his head.

"Wilder!"

"It's true, Mom. We haven't been nearly as welcoming to her as we should have been."

What on earth had gone on in his life that he'd decided to marry someone who didn't share his faith? With every hour that passed, the number of questions he had about what had transpired over the past four years seemed to grow.

When Gareth returned, he actually had Kelsey with him. "I found her in the waiting room."

"I didn't have anywhere else to be," Kelsey said with a shrug as she stopped just inside the door, her arms crossed. She glanced at Zane, but then looked away.

Zane took a moment to observe her. She had medium length blonde hair with a sweep of bangs. She was on the curvier side and looked to be four or so inches shorter than him, given where she came up to on Gareth. From the day he woke up, Zane recalled that her eyes had been a light blue-green shade.

"We're discussing where Zane should go when he gets out of the hospital," his dad said. "And we'd like your input."

Kelsey's brows rose, like she didn't quite believe him.

"Would you be willing to come to Serenity?" his mom said. "Or would you prefer to stay here while he comes home with us to recover?"

Kelsey frowned. "I would prefer to be where Zane is."

"Of course," Gareth said. "And that's completely understandable."

"We'll have to let our apartment here go."

"Do you think that will be a problem?" his dad asked.

"I don't know. All I can do is speak to the landlord and explain the situation."

"Maybe we should ask Lee to come back to help Kelsey pack up," Wilder suggested. "And then he and I can drive a moving truck back to Serenity."

Zane was listening to the discussion, but his attention was still on Kelsey. He noticed that she avoided looking at him, and he wondered why.

It took less time than it should have to sort everything out, and all of it decided with no input at all from him and little from Kelsey. Once he'd agreed to return to Serenity, they hadn't asked his opinion about anything else.

The final plan was that they'd get Lee to come back to Tampa, and they'd pack up the apartment. While Zane, Kelsey, and his folks flew back on Remington's plane, Wilder and Lee would drive the moving van across the country from Tampa to Serenity.

Zane appreciated all the efforts on his behalf, though he really wished none of it was necessary.

"Now that that's all settled," Gareth said. "How about we give Zane and Kelsey a few minutes together?"

The look Kelsey gave Gareth could only be described as panicked, and it kind of matched what Zane was feeling.

"We'll go grab some coffee, then we'll be back," Wilder said, letting them know without saying it that they wouldn't be left alone indefinitely.

Though his parents didn't look thrilled at being essentially forced out of the room, they followed without protest.

When it was just the two of them, Kelsey finally looked at him, but her gaze was wary. "How has your pain been?"

"It's better, I guess," Zane said. "Though I'm sure that's because of the drugs they're giving me."

"No doubt."

Silence stretched between them, making Zane wonder how their communication had been prior to the accident. Finally, he said, "So where am I working here? What made it worth the move away from Chicago?"

When she named a one Michelin star restaurant and told him he was sous chef there, Zane was surprised. His plan had never been to attain a lofty position in a famous restaurant. He had been happy with where he'd been working in Chicago, and he'd been able to save quite a bit of money in hopes of opening his own restaurant some day.

For some reason that had changed. He'd clearly worked hard and progressed to the point where an esteemed chef had been willing to give him a position in their restaurant.

And now all that experience was gone.

Or at least it felt like it was. Right then, his body didn't feel anywhere near ready to take on the rigors of a kitchen in a Michelin star restaurant. He worried he'd never get it back.

"Have you been in contact with the restaurant since the accident?"

She nodded. "I spoke with the head chef, who is also the owner, and explained what happened. I wish I could say they were willing to hold your position, but unfortunately, that isn't the case. They can't afford to have the kitchen down a sous chef."

He understood that, but it was aggravating. Even though he didn't remember any of it, he'd clearly worked hard to get that job, only for it to be taken away from him.

"He did say that once you're feeling back to where you were prior to the accident, you're welcome to contact him."

"So in other words, once my memory comes back."

"Probably, yes."

Again, he understood why they wouldn't want him when he'd lost the knowledge and experience of the past few years that had helped him gain the position.

He turned to stare out the window that was next to his bed. "It's ridiculous that I've lost so much of my memory. Who knows what else I've lost along with my job?"

Kelsey didn't say anything, and Zane wondered what it was about her that had drawn him to her. What was it about her that had made him fall in love with her, when he'd only imagined loving Sarah?

And what was he supposed to do about the fact that the feelings he had in his heart were, unfortunately, not for the woman everyone said was his wife?

"I suppose I'd better head home to the apartment to start packing," she said finally, shifting on her feet. "I'll bring back some clothes for you for whenever they release you."

"The doctor will have to clear me to fly before I can go, so I might need to remain in Tampa for a week or so."

"Will you want to stay at the apartment?"

Zane wasn't sure that would work, given they were virtual strangers. "I have a feeling that Mom and Dad will want me with them so they can keep an eye on me."

That would probably be the case in Serenity as well. He didn't know what Kelsey would do or where she would stay. Would his parents let her stay at their home? Or could she stay at Charli's house? If it was still Charli's house. Or maybe she'd want an apartment of her own?

Zane wasn't sure what he wanted her to do. It was hard to have a strong feeling about any of it considering that she was a stranger. Even though they'd told him he was Kelsey's husband, he didn't feel like he had any right to have a say in what would happen with her.

"I guess I'll see you... soon."

Even though he didn't know her well, he could see the strain on her face. It dawned on him then that she was also in an incredibly difficult situation. Her plans for the future had also been impacted by his memory loss.

"Thanks for talking to my boss and taking care of that."

"You're welcome." With a nod of her head, she turned and disappeared out the door into the hallway.

Silence fell in the room, and Zane relished it. He just needed some quiet to process everything.

He found that he was having difficulty focusing on what people said. Especially if there was more than one person talking at a time. Even now, he couldn't recall all the details of what had been planned for the upcoming days. Fortunately, it didn't seem he was responsible for anything, so if he didn't remember it all, no one would care.

Pressing his fingers to his eyebrows, he categorized the pain he still felt in his body. Dull ache in his head. Sharper pain in his ribs that they said were cracked but not broken. Pain in his stomach and leg.

Alone, he was able to acknowledge just how daunted he was by his situation and his unknown past and future. Anger. Fear. Confusion. It was the worst possible quagmire of emotions. A mixture of negativity that he just couldn't get out of.

Why on earth had God allowed this to happen?

"Zane?"

Hearing his brother's voice had Zane lowering his hands. Gareth approached the bed, snagging a chair and sinking down into it. His brother's brown gaze was serious as he regarded him.

"How are you doing?" he asked.

"Is this brother Gareth asking, or doctor Gareth?"

"Does it matter?"

"I suppose not."

"So?" Gareth prompted. "How are you doing?"

"As well as can be expected, I suppose."

"Pain?"

Zane gave him an honest assessment of his aches and pains.

"And how are you feeling about the plans to go to Serenity?"

"It's the best place, I guess. I'm going to need the support."

Gareth nodded. "You are. But you could have that here with Kelsey."

Zane frowned. "I can't stay here just with her."

"She's your wife, and whatever else we might feel about your relationship, I'm sure she loves you."

"I'm so confused by the family's reaction to her."

"I think it has less to do with her specifically, though clearly Mom and Dad have concerns about her not being a Christian, and more about how your relationship and marriage unfolded."

"What do you mean?"

"We met her for the first time at Christmas, and she was only with us for three days. We didn't have much chance to get to know her in all the hustle and bustle of the holiday. The next thing we know, a few weeks ago, you announce that you and Kelsey had eloped and moved together to Tampa. It was a... shock."

"So Mom's upset that she didn't get a wedding?"

Gareth shook his head. "I doubt it's that. Mom's upset that you married someone that the family doesn't know at all. She's worried about you. That's how she is. You know that."

"I guess."

"Mom will come around, especially if she gets to spend more time with Kelsey. I don't think you would have married someone who wasn't a decent person."

"I'm just surprised that I'm married to... uh... to someone who isn't Sarah," Zane confessed. "I'm having a hard time accepting that. As far as my memory goes, we're still together, and I love her."

There was a long stretch of silence as Gareth frowned at the floor. "I can't imagine how that would be. If I woke up and Aria and I weren't together anymore, but in my memory, we were, I think I'd lose my mind."

It definitely was something that Zane was struggling with. He tried not to think about it, which was only doable when Kelsey wasn't there, and no one was talking about her.

"It's a bit of a brain scrambler, to be sure," Zane said. "And I really struggle with just not knowing how I've ended up with someone else. I need to understand."

"I don't know the details," Gareth said with a shake of his head. "Just that Sarah broke up with you three or so years ago. I never heard anything more."

"She broke up with *me*?" That didn't clarify anything. But it did cause pain when he realized that she'd rejected him.

"You could try talking to Lee to see if he has more details. Or maybe you need to have a conversation with Kelsey about it. She might know."

"I'm not sure about that. The conversation we just had was plenty awkward, and we weren't discussing anything so touchy as my previous relationship and the current state of things between us."

"You've got time. Once we're in Serenity, you'll have the chance to talk more with her."

"Where am I going to be staying?"

Gareth let out a bark of laughter. "You have to ask that?"

"Okay. Yeah. I'm sure I'm staying with Mom and Dad."

"Yep. Mom wouldn't even consider any other plan."

"And Kelsey?"

"We're going to present her with some options to see what she's most comfortable with."

There was a large part of Zane that wished she'd just stay in Tampa. It would be one less thing he'd have to deal with while he was trying to recover. Hopefully, his memory would come back and then they could pick up where they'd left off before his accident.

"Any chance she might want to stay here?"

"Zane, she's your *wife*," Gareth said with a frown.

"She's a *stranger*. I have no memory whatsoever of her. None. All I remember is my relationship with Sarah. So forgive me if I'm a little stressed at the idea of having to deal with my marriage to a woman I don't know, on top of everything else."

Gareth let out a heavy sigh. "I honestly don't know what to say. What I do know is that if Aria had lost her memory of me, I'd still want to be with her. To help her, however I could. You can't just shut love off." He paused, his brow furrowing. "I guess it applies to both you and Kelsey in this particular situation. Since you have feelings for Sarah. Still, I think you need to accept Kelsey's role in your life and not try to leave her behind."

Zane knew he was right, but it was just so hard.

"I'm pretty sure your vows said in sickness and in health," Gareth continued. "I was going to say that you should be honest with Kelsey about how you feel. However, considering your feelings for Sarah, I think I've changed my mind. Hearing that you'd rather her just disappear would be excruciating for Kelsey."

"I just don't want people forcing something on me. What if I never remember her? Am I just supposed to stay married to a woman I don't love?"

"Let's cross that bridge when we get to it," Gareth suggested. "It's possible that the same things about her that you fell in love with the first time around will be what makes you fall in love with her again."

Zane supposed it might happen that way, but it was impossible to imagine when he still felt the way he did about Sarah.

"Just keep an open mind about things with Kelsey, and remember that she's also going through a difficult time."

"I will."

It wasn't like him to be so selfish and... unsympathetic. Gareth was right to remind him that he wasn't alone in the tragedy of the situation.

"Remember that you can talk to me about anything, and it will just be between you and me."

"Thanks." Lee had always been his confidante when it came to his siblings, but he knew there might be instances where Gareth was the better choice.

"Wilder and I are going to try to organize the move," Gareth said as he got to his feet. "Are you okay with Mom and Dad coming back in?"

"Sure."

He watched his brother leave, then leaned back against his pillows, tipping his head to stare up at the ceiling. Maybe he should have told Gareth he was going to take a nap, because suddenly, he felt exhausted.

"How are you doing, darling?" his mom asked as she came to his bedside, resting her hand on his arm.

"I'm okay. Tired, though."

"If you'd like to take a nap, go ahead," his dad said. "We can entertain ourselves."

"I think I will."

"We'll go for a walk, then we'll come check on you in a little while."

"Would you like us to bring anything back for you?" his mom asked.

"I wouldn't mind something sweet. A cookie?"

"We'll see what we can find."

After his parents left, the nurse came in and spoke with him for a few minutes, then left him to sleep.

He'd hoped that his exhaustion would keep his worrisome thoughts at bay, but he laid there far longer than he wanted to before he finally fell asleep.

His last thought was a prayer that he'd wake up with his memory restored.

CHAPTER SIX

Kelsey stood in the living room, looking around at the dismantled home she and Zane had shared for such a short time. All their things were now packed away in boxes, ready to load into the moving truck.

It hadn't taken a lot of time to get everything packed. Neither of them had had much beyond the basics when they'd moved, figuring they'd pick up what they needed as time went on.

While Zane's brothers tackled the kitchen and living room, Kelsey had taken care of packing away all their clothes and personal effects. It had been decided that most of their things would go into storage at first. So all the furniture they'd purchased—including their brand new bed—would sit unused until their life together could continue.

If it continued.

As she'd packed away their things, Kelsey had shed many tears, wondering if their lives would ever be closely entwined again. Would she ever be able to sleep in his arms again? Or slow dance in their living room? Or share all the little moments in a day that she'd never shared with anyone else?

Would their plans for a family ever become a reality?

Or was all of it lost to Zane's amnesia?

It hurt to know that when he looked at her, he didn't see the friend he'd made as they'd gotten to know each other at the restaurant. He didn't see the woman he'd fallen in love with. And he definitely didn't see the woman he'd vowed to love and cherish for the rest of their lives.

All he saw was a stranger. Someone he didn't know. And maybe someone he didn't want to know.

Someone who wasn't Sarah.

Swallowing hard, Kelsey blinked away tears. She'd shed so many lately that there should be none left. And yet, here she was, wanting to cry yet again.

A knock on the door had her taking a deep breath, hoping to contain her emotions as she blinked rapidly to clear her eyes. She opened the door to find Gareth, Wilder, and Lee there.

After greeting them, Kelsey stepped back to let them into the apartment. She clenched a hand against her stomach, knowing their arrival signaled a huge change in the direction of her life.

She was leaving behind the first home she and Zane had shared. Would they have a second one together? Or would this apartment also be their last?

"Good morning. Friendly old man let us in," Wilder told her as he walked through the door.

Glancing around, Lee asked, "Everything ready to go?"

"Yes. I think so."

"While Gareth and Wilder load the truck, I'm going to run you and the others to the airport," Lee said. "The van is parked downstairs."

"Thank you for doing all of this, and for bringing my car to Serenity."

"You're welcome," Gareth said with a smile. "We'll see you in a few days."

With one last look around the apartment they'd never return to, Kelsey walked out the door with Lee by her side, pulling the suitcases with her and Zane's clothing and personal effects. This time around, Lee had rented a van since there was more luggage and people to transport.

Rori had returned with Lee, but she'd fly back with them in the private jet, while Lexi would go with the guys as another driver.

There would be two drivers per vehicle, so hopefully they'd be able to drive long stretches to get through the forty-plus hour trip from Tampa to Serenity.

Once the bags were loaded in the back of the van, Kelsey climbed into the front passenger seat, though she'd give it up once they got to the hotel.

"Did you manage to get all the loose ends tied up here?" Lee asked as he guided the van out onto the road.

"Yes. The landlord was sympathetic and let us out of the lease. Even gave us back our deposit. Everyone has been very understanding as I've explained the situation."

"How's the insurance going for Zane's car?"

"It was written off, so I think he'll just get a check in the mail."

"That's a shame. He loved that car."

"Hopefully he can get another one he likes as much."

"And did the police give you an update?"

"They've arrested the drunk driver, but I don't know anything beyond that."

"That's good news. I suppose there's not much need for them to talk to Zane when he can't remember anything."

Kelsey shook her head. "No. But there were some witnesses, apparently, who've given statements."

It had actually been easier than she'd thought it would be to close out their lives in Tampa. They'd had a few things still needing to be done to cement their lives in Florida—like switching their driver's licenses—but now those things wouldn't matter.

"This is the second serious car accident we've had in our family," Lee said as he steered the van toward the hotel.

"Really? Another drunk driver?"

Lee shook his head. "Icy roads. Janessa and Will were in an accident when they were dating. Will had injuries similar to Zane's, and it just about ended their relationship."

"Did he have memory loss, too?"

"No, but Janessa had experienced a lot of loss in her life, and I think it scared her to think she might lose someone else she loved. Her dad died in a car accident, and her mom died of cancer."

Zane hadn't spoken much about the details of his siblings' lives. Of course, she hadn't talked much about her family either. He'd never met her parents because she just couldn't even begin to imagine how that would have gone. Introducing Zane to her parents had been the last thing she wanted to do.

And it was still the last thing she wanted. She didn't want questions about her family from his family, either. Hopefully, there were enough distractions going on at the moment that the subject wouldn't come up.

In a family where the parents were loving, and the siblings genuinely cared for each other, parents and siblings like hers would be incomprehensible.

"Do you want to just wait here?" Lee asked as he pulled up in front of the hotel.

"Yes. I'll keep an eye on the van."

"Sounds good."

She decided to wait in the front seat until they came back down, and then she'd climb into the back. Most likely with Rori.

When she'd realized that Rori was going to be traveling back with them on the plane, she'd felt a huge sense of relief. Hopefully, the other woman would be a buffer between Kelsey and the Halverson parents for the duration of the trip.

It wasn't long before Lee reappeared with a cart holding some bags, Rori at his side. Kelsey slid out of her seat and went to greet the woman.

Once the bags were in the back of the van, Kelsey climbed into the third row of seats with Rori. Zane appeared on a pair of crutches, with his parents hovering close behind. He wore a pair of loose basketball shorts and a T-shirt. He hadn't styled his hair like he usually did, and he had a bit of scruff on his face, which was also unusual.

She could see pain on his face, and it took everything within her to keep from going to him and offering her help. There would have been no hesitation if he remembered her, but Kelsey was fairly certain that her offer wouldn't be well received in the current circumstances.

After a quick greeting, Cathy climbed into the middle row, then Dan helped Zane in next to her, handing off the crutches once he was seated. Dan and Lee took the seats in the front and soon they were off to the airport, where the private jet waited to whisk them to Serenity.

Kelsey was a mess of nerves as she thought of what was to come. Lee and Rori had a large home that had once been Charli and Janessa's, and they had offered for Kelsey and Zane to stay with them. It was a good option for Kelsey, so she'd agreed right away. Zane had also wanted to stay there, but his mom had protested.

In the end, they'd compromised. Zane would stay with his parents for a week, then he'd move into Lee and Rori's. Though Kelsey hated the idea of being separated for even longer from Zane, it might be for the best.

Zane hadn't outright rejected her yet, and Kelsey wasn't going to give him any reason to, if she could help it. So if he wanted to stay with his parents for a bit, she wasn't going to argue with him about it.

As they climbed onto the jet a short time later, a flight attendant in a sleek uniform greeted them with a smile. The Halversons and Zane had boarded first, and once Zane had settled into a seat, he'd propped his crutches on the seat next to him. Kelsey took that as a sign that he didn't want anyone sitting beside him.

Kelsey kept going further toward the back of the jet and took a seat that was a part of four seats facing each other. Rori took one of the other ones. The Halversons ended up taking seats near Zane.

Lee had come on board after making sure their bags were safely stowed. He spoke briefly with his parents before coming to where Rori sat. She got to her feet and stepped into his arms.

"I'll see you in a few days, sweetheart," Lee said, his words soft but still audible to Kelsey. She looked away. The intimacy of the pair was a poignant reminder of what she'd lost. "Love you."

"Love you too. Please drive safely."

"I will do my best."

After they shared a kiss, Lee said goodbye to everyone, then left the jet.

Kelsey had only ever flown economy, so the private jet was a luxury. This would definitely spoil her for any future flights.

Her gaze went to Zane, who she could just see in slight profile, wishing they could have shared this experience together. She had some nerves about flying, so being able to hold his hand would have been nice.

Soon the attendant came into the cabin to ask if they'd like anything to drink. Kelsey requested a coffee, as did Rori. The woman said she'd return with their drinks once they'd reached altitude, then she asked for them to make sure they were buckled in because they'd be taking off soon.

Kelsey was seated by the window, and she turned to look out of it as the plane began to move.

"Is this your first time flying?" Rori asked from her seat across from Kelsey.

"No. Just the first time on a private jet."

Rori grinned. "Yeah. Flying commercial isn't bad for someone like you or me who isn't very tall, but it's definitely harder on the guys. It was a blessing that Alexander allowed us to use his jet."

"Especially with Zane on crutches."

Rori nodded. "I hope the guys and Lexi have a smooth trip."

Feeling the plane pick up speed, Kelsey took a deep breath, her gaze going to Zane again. He seemed relaxed, with his head resting back on his seat.

As the plane lifted off the runway, it felt like her stomach was being left behind. Kelsey pressed a hand against it and gazed out the window as the ground dropped away.

She had no real emotions about leaving Tampa behind. Because they'd been there for such a short time, she hadn't had a chance to feel like Tampa was home.

What did cause some emotion within her was the thought of what this departure represented. Tampa was supposed to have been where Zane finally cemented his place as a haute cuisine chef, and where she finally started her nursing career. The career that had taken her years of hard work to achieve.

Now, Zane had had a possibly permanent setback to his plans, and she was once again having to put hers aside for the time being.

The plane continued to climb, and the city below grew smaller and smaller. Until finally, they veered away from it as they headed north and then a bit west along the coastline.

It felt like another chapter—a brief chapter—was closing, but there was no excitement for this new one. In the back of her mind was the thought that this one was going to hold more heartache for her.

Once the plane had leveled out, the attendant returned with their drinks and some pastries. Kelsey wasn't overly hungry, but she still took a chocolate croissant. Rori settled for a cinnamon roll. It looked like Zane waved away the offerings, making his mom give him a worried look.

It worried Kelsey too, because Zane liked his pastries. He wasn't a pastry chef, so they weren't something he made himself, though she was sure he could if he wanted to. Instead, he just enjoyed other people's efforts. Except he wasn't that day.

"I need to speak with you about paying my share at the house," Kelsey said as she sipped her coffee.

"Oh. You don't need to worry about that."

Kelsey frowned. "I don't want to take advantage."

She couldn't afford a lot, especially if she wasn't working. Her savings were going to dwindle pretty quickly.

"You aren't, but if you feel strongly about it, speak with Lee. As soon as we got married, I told him he could take care of the finances. I never liked doing that."

"So you combine your money?"

"Yep. I know a lot of people don't like to do that, but it works for us. Everything goes into one account, and Lee takes care of paying all the bills from that."

"You don't mind not having control of your money?"

"I do have control over it," Rori said. "Lee doesn't tell me I can't buy things I want or need. We have some guidelines in place, but they apply to both of us. We decided on a dollar amount that would require discussion, but anything below that, we're free to buy on our own. I completely trust Lee to take care of us, but he wants me to know what's going on, so at the end of each month, he goes over the finances with me."

Kelsey hadn't thought much about the fact that she and Zane hadn't combined their finances. Was it a big deal? She didn't think it was, especially since he had made an effort to make things fair, taking into account the differences in their incomes.

Now, because she had no access to or knowledge of any accounts that belonged to Zane, she was on her own once again when it came to finances.

Rori gave her a smile. "Every couple has to figure out what works for them. I wouldn't presume to say what works for Lee and I would work for anyone else. It's what we've discussed and decided on based on our own needs and desires."

Kelsey hoped that she and Zane would have another chance to set up a life together. But with her husband loving someone else, her hopes weren't too high for that.

A couple of hours into the flight, the attendant once again came around offering food. Kelsey thought they might get sandwiches or something, but no, apparently on a private jet, you got a full-fledged meal with dessert.

"I just need to move around, Mom," Zane said, his voice raised.

Kelsey noticed that, while both her and Rori's attention went to Zane, the attendant didn't turn around. She was truly a professional.

"Uh, sure, I'll have the chicken."

"Me, too," Rori said, giving the woman a smile.

"I'll have that out in a few minutes."

The woman turned, keeping to the side so that Zane had space to move toward the bathroom at the rear of the plane. Kelsey tracked his progress, but he never looked in her direction. Slowly, he made his way past where she and Rori sat, and as he did, Kelsey could see the tension and pain on his face.

She wanted to go to him, to see if there was anything she could do. However, if he was rejecting his mom's help, he would surely reject hers. At some point, she might not be able to keep from offering her help. Her heart longed to help her husband through this rough time.

Kelsey's gaze went to her mother-in-law, and her sympathy was triggered by the pain she saw on the woman's face as she stared at where her son had disappeared. Even from her seat, Kelsey could see the deep breath Cathy took as she leaned her head against her husband's arm.

Dan lifted his hand and cupped his wife's cheek, his lips moving, forming words that Kelsey wasn't privy to. Being surrounded by loving couples was going to be a hard part of being in Serenity.

When Zane came out of the bathroom, rather than going back to his seat near his parents, he went to a couch on the opposite side of the plane to the cluster of seats where Kelsey and Rori sat. With an audible sigh, he laid down, lifting his leg to elevate it on the armrest.

He crooked his arm over his eyes, then went still. Kelsey doubted he was asleep, however. On a good day, Zane needed time to fall asleep, and that day definitely wasn't a good day.

After their wedding, they'd fallen into the habit of reading together, then talking a bit to help wind down enough to sleep. Though there were times that Kelsey fell asleep mid-conversation, it was rare that Zane did.

Zane didn't eat anything when the attendant brought the rest of them their meals. He stayed on the couch until the announcement was made that they were preparing to land in Coeur d'Alene. Then he sat up and buckled himself in without moving back to his original seat.

"How are we going to get to Serenity?" Kelsey asked, then yawned, trying to relieve the pressure in her ears.

"Blake is going to come get us," Rori said. "Since he and Charli have four kids, they've got a van, which is what we need."

"That was nice of him to agree to do that for us."

"Blake is always good at helping out. They all are, actually."

"Do you have family in Serenity?"

Rori grimaced. "Yes. My mom lives here with her husband, but I hardly ever see her."

"You don't get along?"

"Not really." Rori paused. "You know how there are some parents who, when they split up, fight over who gets to keep the kid?" Kelsey nodded. "Well, in my case, they fought over who *had* to take me."

That hadn't been Kelsey's experience, but she understood not having a relationship with parents. "I don't have much communication with my mom, either."

"It was hard for a lot of years, but God has brought other mother-figures into my life, for which I'm grateful."

The descent of the plane drew Kelsey's attention to the window once again. She glanced at Zane and saw that he was also looking out the window, but she could tell from his profile that he was frowning.

She knew it had never been his desire to return to Serenity, and yet, there they were. Preparing to call Serenity their home for the foreseeable future.

Once the plane was on the ground and stopped, they were allowed to disembark. Blake was there to meet them, and soon they were loading everything into his van. Kelsey and Rori once again climbed into the back, then Zane and his mom took the middle row.

"I'm glad you'll be here to keep me company," Rori said. "The house would be big and lonely if I were here by myself."

Her words were a reminder of how different everything would be for the time being. She was a wife without a husband. Like Rori, she was lonely without her husband, but at least Rori's separation had an end in sight.

CHAPTER SEVEN

"Are you sure you want to move?" his mom asked, worry lacing her tone. Worry always laced her tone these days.

"Yes, Mom," Zane said. "We agreed that I'd stay with you a week, then move to Lee's. It's been a week. I'm doing better, so I think it's time."

"You're still not remembering anything, though."

It wasn't a reminder he needed or wanted, but his lack of memory wasn't physically impairing him the way his broken leg did. Thankfully, he'd gotten used to using the crutches, and his ribs didn't hurt as much as they had when he'd first started using them to get around.

"Staying here isn't necessarily going to help with my memory," Zane said. At that point, he wasn't sure that anything would.

"Is it because of Kelsey?"

For some reason, she was still really struggling with Kelsey's presence in his life and in Serenity. Zane hadn't spent any time with Kelsey since their arrival in Serenity. His mom had been insistent that he rest since he was still having pain and headaches.

He hadn't even been able to help when Lee and the others had returned with the moving van full of his and Kelsey's stuff. Aside from the suitcase she'd packed for him in Florida, they'd put everything else in storage, and Zane wasn't sure when it would ever be needed again.

"It's not because of Kelsey." And it really wasn't. He'd want to make the move even if she wasn't there. He just needed to feel like he had some control over his life, and living with his parents didn't really give him that option. "I appreciate your help, but I need some space. It's not like I'm leaving town."

"I'm just worried about you."

"I understand, but I'm getting better every day. More able to do stuff for myself."

"You always were an independent one."

He gave her a quick smile. "You raised me to be that way."

"I know," she said with a sigh as his dad slipped his arm around her shoulder. "I just wish you weren't exerting that independence right now."

"I'm not going far. We're still in the same town."

A knock on the front door, then the sound of it opening, interrupted their conversation.

"Hey, Lee," his dad said as Lee walked into the kitchen.

Lee greeted each of his parents with a hug. "I'm surprised you're not handcuffed to something, Zane."

"I'm not that bad," his mom said with a huff of laughter. "But I *am* reluctant to let him go."

"We'll take good care of him," Lee assured her. "And you know that you can drop by whenever you want."

"But we're not going to move in," his dad added quickly, as if he thought that his wife might suggest that.

"I know."

"Is your stuff packed?" Lee asked. "Or do you still need to do that?"

"It's all packed. The suitcase is at the bottom of the stairs."

"I'm going to go put it in the car. I told Rori I wouldn't be gone long."

Zane was happy that Lee had told Rori that, so there wouldn't be a big delay leaving his parents' home.

As soon as his bag was in the car, they all went outside, and Zane carefully made his way down the steps on his crutches. It had taken him some time to get the hang of stairs, but he'd gotten plenty of practice since his room was on the second floor, requiring him to go up and down the steps at least once a day.

His mom wrapped her arms around Zane, squeezing him tightly. "Take care of yourself, and if anything comes up that is concerning, call us."

"I will, Mom."

After a hug from his dad, Zane maneuvered his way into the front seat of the van. He let out a long sigh as he pulled the door closed.

"Ready for some freedom, bro?" Lee asked with a laugh as he slid behind the wheel.

Zane groaned. "I love Mom and Dad so much, but their hovering has tested my patience. I'm hoping that you and Rori will just leave me be."

"That's the plan," Lee said as he circled the car around the driveway and headed away from the house. "You know that I don't hover, and Rori would never do that to you."

Zane noticed he didn't mention Kelsey. Of course, he probably didn't know her well enough to know if she would hover or not. Zane hoped she didn't. He really just needed a chance to take a breath.

"How did you guys end up with the big house?" Zane asked.

Last he remembered, Charli and Janessa still owned it and lived there with their husbands, and in Charli's case, her three kids.

"After Janessa had her baby, it got a bit more crowded in the house, then Charli got pregnant. Will and Janessa moved out with their little guy first, then when Rori and I got married, she moved in with me there. Though the house size might have been good for Charli and Blake, they decided to move to a smaller, cheaper place because Charli wanted to be able to stay at home with the kids."

"Wilder didn't want to stay with you guys?"

"He might have," Lee said. "But Lexi didn't seem to be on board with that, so when they got married, Wilder moved into Lexi's place."

"So that left you two?"

"Yep. We bought the house from the girls."

"Do you plan to fill it with kids or something?"

"Well, I don't know about filling it, but we do hope to have two or three kids if it's God's will. Both of us just felt like we should keep the house in the family. We also are both open to having people stay with us. We want that, actually."

"Like me?"

Lee gave him a grin. "Yep. Like you."

However it came about, he was grateful for a place to stay and recover without people hovering over him. Even if it was with a wife he didn't know.

Lee pulled the vehicle into the driveway of the house, then parked in front of the garage. As Zane angled himself out, Lee got his suitcase out of the back of the car. Zane wished he could offer to help, but he needed both hands on the crutches.

Leading the way up to the front door, Lee moved with ease, leaving Zane in the dust. It was frustrating because Zane was used to being able to move around quickly.

Working in a professional kitchen in a busy restaurant had required high energy. And if there was one thing Zane was lacking in his current situation—aside from his memory—it was definitely his energy.

"Hey!" Rori greeted them with a big smile as she came into the foyer. "Glad you made it, Zane."

"Me too," he said as he maneuvered himself away from the door so Lee could close it. "Mom tried her best to convince me to stay. But finally, she let me go."

"Did you want to go up to your bedroom?" Lee asked as his dog, Elsa, came to greet Zane with a curious sniff of his cast. "Are you able to do stairs?"

"Yep. I've been practicing at Mom and Dad's. I'm slow though."

"We put you in one of the rear facing rooms. Kelsey is in the other one on that side of the house."

"Sounds good." He'd never stayed in the house before. When he'd visited in the past, he'd usually just gone to his parents' place since he was never home for very long.

"Would you like something to drink?" Rori asked as she waved him to follow her into the kitchen. "I've made supper, but it won't be ready for a little while yet. It's probably nothing like what you cook, but hopefully it will be tasty."

"Well, that's the most important thing for food to be." It smelled delicious, so he was sure it would taste fine.

As he settled on a stool at the island counter, Rori asked him again about a drink.

"Water would be great. Thank you."

She filled a glass from the water dispenser, then placed it in front of him on the counter. "How is your leg doing?"

Zane appreciated that she didn't ask him about his memory. "Pain is pretty much gone. I'm hoping that Gareth will approve me for a boot soon so I can ditch the crutches."

"Is that an option?" Rori asked.

"I don't know, but I sure hope it is. These crutches are horrible."

"You'll be a pro on them soon."

"Haven't really had a choice. Either I learned to use them, or I'd have to sit on my butt all day."

"Have you ever had a broken bone before?" she asked as she stirred a pot on the stove.

"Yep. Broke my arm when I was in middle school. I was more upset about the fact that I hadn't broken my dominant hand than I was about having a broken arm. I thought it would have gotten me out of school."

Lee walked into the kitchen and went immediately to where his wife stood. He wrapped his arms around her and bent to rest his chin on her shoulder. "Smells good."

"Hopefully it tastes good as well."

"Well, I was talking about you, but the food smells good, too."

Rori's laugh was soft as she reached up to touch his cheek.

Zane shifted his gaze down to his glass of water. Seeing his brother and Rori so casually affectionate made him wonder about his own marriage. Had he and Kelsey been like that?

He pulled out his new phone, searching for a distraction from his brother and Rori's affectionate behavior. Over the past week, in addition to getting a new phone to replace the one destroyed in the accident, he'd managed to get into all his accounts, thanks to a password file on his laptop.

He'd discovered that over the past four years, he'd saved up a considerable amount of money. Also, his salary at his latest job had been fairly impressive. He had definitely been moving in the right direction, career-wise.

Even though he'd replaced his phone, he still needed to get another car. He didn't have a settlement from the insurance company yet, but he had enough in his savings to cover the cost of a vehicle until the check arrived. It was just a matter of deciding which car he wanted.

He heard the front door open and shifted so he could see the entrance to the kitchen. Lee stepped away from Rori as Kelsey appeared. Her gaze met Zane's, and for a moment, a warm smile came to her face. But then it faded away, as if she recalled that he didn't remember her.

"Hey, Kelsey," Rori said with a smile. "How did it go?"

Kelsey bent to pet Elsa. "They said they'll let me know next week."

"What's going on?" Zane asked when no one gave more details.

"Kelsey is applying for work," Rori said. "She had an interview this afternoon."

"You need to get a job so soon?"

"Yeah. My savings are pretty much depleted after two moves. Plus, I don't really want to sit around doing nothing when I'm perfectly capable of working."

Zane frowned, thinking of the size of his own savings account. How was Kelsey's so small? Did she have a problem handling her finances?

He didn't want to ask her about it right then since they had an audience, plus, he wasn't sure it was any of his business. Delving into how their marriage had been might open a door he wasn't ready to walk through just yet.

"It's too bad Kayleigh doesn't need a hostess at the resort," Rori said.

"It's what I have the most experience with," Kelsey said, then glanced at the stove. "Do I have time to run upstairs for a minute?"

"Yep. We'll be ready to eat in about twenty minutes."

Kelsey nodded, then left the kitchen. Zane watched her go, then continued to stare at the empty doorway. He knew that Lee and Rori probably hoped that having them both under the same roof would help their relationship. However, Zane wasn't so sure.

Though every day he went to bed and woke up with the prayer that his memory would return and that his feelings for Sarah would disappear, neither had happened. He knew he needed God's help with both, and he prayed that God wouldn't abandon him in his time of need.

At Rori's request, Lee got dishes from the cupboard. He took them to the breakfast nook and set them out. Just four place settings.

Zane was now being faced with the thing he'd been ignoring in his eagerness to get out from under his parents' hovering. It was going to be awkward with just the four of them in the house.

In his desire to escape his parents, he'd landed in another situation that he wasn't entirely comfortable with. But where else could he go?

Rori finished up with the food on the stove, draining the pasta and putting it in a bowl. By the time Kelsey reappeared, all the food was on the table.

None of the others took their seats until Zane had shifted himself over from the counter. Lee ended up sitting next to him while the ladies sat on the opposite side of the table.

Lee said a prayer for the food, then they began to eat.

"This is good, Rori," Kelsey said. "Thank you for making dinner."

Zane wondered how much cooking he'd done during their marriage. When he'd lived on his own, he'd spent a lot of time at the restaurant, so he rarely cooked when he was home.

Rori's pasta wasn't made fresh, and her sauce probably came out of a jar, but it still tasted pretty good. She also had breadsticks and a salad. All in all, it was a tasty and filling meal. Better than his mom's, if he was honest. Although that was rather a low bar.

"It's as tasty as you promised," Zane said.

Rori smiled, her eyes lighting up. "Thank you."

"See, sweetheart," Lee said. "I told you you didn't have to worry. Zane isn't going to judge you on your food."

Zane wasn't going to say he never judged the food he ate. However, that only happened if someone really hyped up what they'd made and then it didn't measure up. Even in those circumstances, though, he rarely voiced his opinion.

He hadn't tried cooking since the accident. It was too hard with a broken leg and sore ribs. Not to mention the frequent headaches he still had off and on. More on than off, but hopefully that would change as time went on and his brain continued to heal.

"How was the vet clinic today?" Kelsey asked. "Any new animals?"

"Not today," Rori said. "But the kittens we got last week are soooo cute. If I thought Elsa might like a kitten friend, I'd bring one home."

Lee gave a huff of laughter. "I think Elsa would be fine. It's me you have to convince."

"Have you ever had a pet, Kelsey?" Rori asked. "Could we interest you in one?"

"Nope. Never had a pet. My mom had a dog while I was growing up, but it was her pet, not ours."

"I think everyone has adopted Elsa as theirs," Lee said. "I was surprised that she was still here after Charli and Blake moved out. I half expected Amelia to have smuggled her into her suitcase."

Zane silently ate his meal as the others at the table chatted. Listening to them, he picked up more info on what had happened over the years that were a black hole in his memory.

His parents had dumped a lot of information on him over the week he'd been with them. He'd managed to retain most of what they'd told them, aside from what they'd told him while he'd had a bad headache and couldn't focus well. It gave him hope that his memory wasn't impacted in retaining new memories.

What he wasn't sure about was if he'd think he was remembering things because he was being told so much. It was one of the reasons he'd held back on asking Kelsey for information about their marriage. If he recalled any details, he'd know they were really him remembering and not just knowledge someone else had passed on to him.

Unfortunately, he was pretty sure that sooner rather than later, his curiosity about his marriage would get the better of him and he'd start asking questions.

"Do you have a doctor's appointment coming up?" Lee asked.

"I'm going to see Gareth on Monday. I have a neurologist appointment next week, following up on my initial visit when we first got here."

"Probably better if you're not going to a relative," Lee said. "I mean, is Gareth even allowed to treat you?"

"I don't know. But he's just keeping an eye on me."

"If you need a ride somewhere, I can take you," Kelsey said. "Since I don't have a job yet, my schedule is pretty open."

"Okay. Thanks."

He appreciated that she was willing to help him, but he didn't want her inserting herself into his care. It was hard enough that his parents had done that.

"Are you feeling up to going to church on Sunday?" Lee asked. "Then we often have a barbecue in the afternoon."

"No more Friday night pizzas?" Zane asked. He hadn't attended many of those gatherings, but he'd heard plenty about them.

"We found out that with the growing number of kids in the family, it was simpler to do a Sunday afternoon event, which is usually a barbecue."

"The pizza oven is still in the backyard, so we do pizza sometimes," Rori said. "But most of the time we barbecue because it's a bit easier for so many people."

"I don't know for sure how I'll feel on Sunday," Zane said. "But if I'm feeling okay, I suppose I'm up for church and a barbecue."

"That's great," Rori said, then turned to Kelsey. "Will you join us too?"

She glanced between each of them, then shrugged. "I suppose I could." Her gaze darted to Zane again. "We never went to church, so it'll be something new to me."

"Did I mention why I'd stopped?"

She shook her head. "We never really talked about it."

Zane turned to Lee. "Did I discuss it with you?"

"You had a period of time when you were really struggling with stuff in your life." Lee paused, then said, "You started working more and attending church less. I also got busier and found it easier to avoid all things related to our faith."

"But you're back to church now."

Lee nodded as he smiled at Rori. "As part of our vows, we committed to our faith together."

Zane looked at Kelsey. Was it weird for her to hear about this part of his life that he hadn't discussed with her?

Was it possible that if he re-committed to his faith, that Kelsey would see that as something she didn't want in a husband?

Zane still had a hard time believing that he would walk away from a faith that had been part of his life for so long. He thought there were more details that Lee was leaving out. Had it been because of his breakup with Sarah?

"I wasn't a Christian when Lee and I first met," Rori said. "But when I started to attend church, I found something that I hadn't realized I was missing in my life. I believe that sharing a faith with Lee has strengthened our relationship."

Lee smiled at Rori. "I believe that too."

Zane glanced at Kelsey to find her watching the pair, sadness on her face. Was she missing what they had?

He gave himself a mental shake. Of course she was. They had basically been newlyweds when the accident had happened. He might not know what he was missing, but she certainly did.

It sank into him then.

She was his *wife*.

He had a *wife*.

Even though it wasn't Sarah, he'd taken on that responsibility with Kelsey. Willingly. So eventually, he'd have to figure out how to deal with her and their relationship.

There was no way he could just jump right back into the marriage with a virtual stranger. However, maybe it was time to take it seriously. Perhaps the first place to start was with the photos that he'd downloaded from the cloud when he set up his new phone.

He'd avoided looking at them, but perhaps they would help him understand a bit about their marriage and how he felt about Kelsey.

But there was a knot in his stomach at the thought, and his head started to ache.

Maybe it could wait for another day or three.

CHAPTER EIGHT

Kelsey followed Lee and Rori to a row about midway down the aisle in the large sanctuary of their church. Zane was behind her on his crutches.

They'd been stopped by a few people as they'd entered the foyer, but many had seemed to realize that Zane wasn't comfortable standing to chat with them for too long. Most had just assured him that they were praying for him.

Kelsey wasn't sure why she'd decided to go to church with them that day, except for the fact that she wanted to be with Zane. It had been a bit like water being poured on her parched heart when she'd seen him again after nearly a week apart.

It had taken everything inside her to not protest them living separately for the past week. However, it was important that they move things along at his speed. And now they were back under the same roof, so she was happy. Well, as happy as she could be given their current circumstances.

When they reached a nearly empty row, Lee went in first, followed by Rori and Kelsey. As they settled into their seats, Zane propped his crutches beside him. He shifted around a few times, clearly trying to get comfortable on the padded pew.

It was a bit of a surprise to Kelsey that Zane had wanted to come to church. Never in all their time of dating had he mentioned wanting to attend any services. They had gone to church together once, back when they'd come to Serenity for Christmas. The whole family had attended the Christmas Eve service, so they'd gone with them.

Her world had been turned upside down in the recent weeks, and at times, it felt like she was living in a nightmare. To go from their happy life in Tampa, to living in Zane's hometown—a place he'd never planned to return to—with a husband who didn't remember her... It felt like too much for one person to have to endure.

As the pews around them filled, Kelsey spotted other Halverson family members taking their seats. Charli and her husband and kids slid into the row in front of them. Well, two of their kids. The two youngest ones weren't with them.

"Hey, Uncle Zane." Charli's oldest daughter Layla greeted her uncle with a smile.

The girl had dark hair and brown eyes like her mom and looked to be maybe thirteen or fourteen years old. Amelia, who sat next to her, had blonde hair and was younger than Layla. Her smile was a little more reserved than her sister's.

"Hey, girls," Zane said, reaching out to bump fists with Layla then Amelia. "How's it going?"

"Good," Layla said. "How's your leg?"

"Still attached, so that's a good thing."

"Definitely," Amelia agreed with a nod.

Before they could talk more, music began to play. The girls turned around, and Kelsey looked toward the stage where the musicians stood. She recognized Gareth on the drums, but he was the only family member up there.

Kelsey had no idea what to expect of the service, so she hoped she didn't flub anything up. Rori had explained that there was nothing she needed to do to participate, which Kelsey had appreciated. Going into new situations wasn't anything new for Kelsey, but she preferred familiarity.

After a man had welcomed the congregation, he invited them to stand. Kelsey glanced at Zane, thinking he might stay sitting, but he grabbed his crutches and managed to get to his feet. His arm brushed hers as he adjusted the crutches once he was up.

He might have lost four years of his memories, but apparently, he remembered all the songs they sang that morning. Though Kelsey had heard him sing before, this seemed different. *He* seemed different.

After the service had gone on for about twenty minutes, a middle-aged man took his place behind the podium. He smiled as his gaze swept the congregation, before landing on Zane.

"I just want to say how happy I am to see Zane and his wife Kelsey here with us today. I won't ask you to stand, son. However, I want you to know that since word of your accident reached us, we've been praying for you. And we will continue to pray for your healing."

Out of the corner of her eye, Kelsey saw Zane smile and nod. She was aware of people turning to look at them, offering smiles. It took everything within her not to shift in her seat.

Did they know about Zane's memory loss? Did they know that he didn't remember his wife?

Her thoughts continued to churn as the pastor spoke, so she heard very little of his sermon. When he asked the congregation to stand for the final song, she breathed a sigh of relief.

For the next several minutes, they made their way up the aisle and into the foyer. Unlike their arrival before the service, it was slow going because they were stopped repeatedly by people wanting to talk to Zane. They all greeted her with smiles, and Kelsey tried her best to return their friendliness, but it was a struggle.

Finally, they made it out of the church. She waited with Zane and Rori while Lee went to get the car. They'd all come together, though Kelsey had considered bringing her own vehicle so that she could escape if need be.

"Ready for some barbecue?" Rori asked as Lee turned out of the parking lot onto the street.

"Who's cooking?" Zane asked in response.

Lee laughed. "Will that determine whether or not you're ready for barbecue?"

"Maybe?"

For the first time, Kelsey heard a lilt of humor in Zane's voice, something she'd always loved.

"It's a potluck barbecue. Misha said her mom made ribs for her and Jay to bring. We're contributing chicken breasts, and Charli is bringing hotdogs for the kids. We're also having potato salad, and some raw veggies and dip. Oh, and Charli said Layla and Amelia made some buns, along with cookies and brownies for dessert."

"Sounds good," Zane said. "I guess I'm looking forward to it now."

Kelsey stared out the car window as they drove through the town, trying to psych herself up for the afternoon. The food all sounded wonderful. However, she didn't have much of an appetite. Hadn't had much of one since the accident.

When they reached the house, Zane sat down on a stool at the counter. While Rori and Lee sorted out the chicken for Lee to throw on the barbecue, Kelsey washed her hands and set to the task of putting cut-up veggies on a platter.

They hadn't been home long when people began to arrive. Even though Rori had said that Dan and Cathy didn't attend the Sunday afternoon barbecues very often, they showed up that day. Which didn't surprise Kelsey at all. Zane had mentioned the day before how much his mom had wanted him to continue to stay with them.

People greeted Kelsey with smiles, but no one approached her to talk. Well, except for Rori. She also kept giving Kelsey things to do, which Kelsey appreciated more than words could say.

Soon, they were all gathered out in the backyard to eat. Mr. Halverson prayed for the meal, then pandemonium broke out as adults and children approached the food tables. Kelsey took advantage of the commotion to slip into the house and up to her room.

She switched out the clothes she'd worn to church for a pair of leggings and a T-shirt. Finding a pair of her runners in the closet, she slid her feet into them, then pulled her hair back into a pony-tail.

Before leaving her room, Kelsey slipped her driver's license and debit card into the pocket of her leggings. Then she grabbed her earbuds and phone and stepped out onto the landing of the second floor.

Pausing, she listened to see if she could hear anyone in the house. When there was no noise coming from the main floor, she made her way down the stairs with light steps, then hurried to the front door and carefully opened it.

Once on the porch, she pulled the door closed behind her and set off down the stairs to the sidewalk. After looking both ways, she headed off in the direction that appeared most residential.

For a moment, she thought that perhaps she should have let someone know that she was leaving. But honestly, she wasn't sure they'd even notice she was gone in the chaos of so many people.

"You're having a pity party, Kelsey Lynn Paine... Halverson," she muttered to herself. "You've got to pull yourself out of this."

It was true. She definitely was having a pity party of an epic mag-nitude.

But wasn't she entitled to one?

After all, she'd lost her husband, her job, her new life... all in one fell swoop. She was running out of money and still hadn't found a job. And then there was the anxiety over her unknown future and the panic attacks that threatened on a daily basis.

Kelsey felt a bit like she was living in hostile territory. Her one connection to this family had disappeared, and Zane didn't even seem to care about her at all.

Hurt filled her heart at that thought. It had been hard to fully trust Zane back when they'd started dating, and it had taken time to get to that point with him. She hadn't known why Zane would actually care enough about her to establish a friendship when her own parents had kicked her out of the house the minute she turned eighteen, leaving her all on her own.

But she'd eventually seen that his care for her was genuine and not something that would come and go, depending on his mood. Unfortunately, that care had disappeared along with his memory, and that was terribly hard to accept.

When she saw Zane, her heart swelled with her love for him. But she could see that he didn't feel the same way. She was nothing to him. Nothing.

How long did she hold on, hoping that he'd remember? She'd married him with the intention of sticking with him through the good and bad, but she'd never ever considered that the bad would involve him forgetting her.

She wanted to run away. To take her broken heart and try to start her life over yet again.

She'd done it at eighteen when she'd been kicked out by her parents and had to find a way to put a roof over her head and food in her belly. It had been very hard, but she'd done it, and she could do it again, if she felt like it was the only option left to her.

Though she'd been nearly broke back then and survived, she'd rather not have to do it again. So she had no choice for the moment but to stay and have her heart broken over and over and over again.

She felt moisture on her cheeks and reached up to brush away the tears that had slipped free. How did she still have tears left to shed?

Putting her earbuds in, Kelsey strove to escape her thoughts, even if it was for just a few minutes. After starting up an audio book, she began to jog, nodding as she passed people out walking with their kids and their dogs.

There were lots of quaint looking houses on the street. Most of them had colorful flowers planted in garden beds along their fronts. Someone was mowing, filling the air with the scent of freshly cut grass.

All in all, Serenity wasn't a bad place. It looked like it might even be a good place to raise a family.

However, it wouldn't work for either her or Zane, which was why there had never been any discussion between them about returning to live in Serenity. And yet, here they were. Forced by circumstances to come back.

She kept jogging, not really paying attention to where she was going. It wasn't a big worry. She knew the address to the house, and she had the GPS on her phone to guide her if she got lost.

Running was something she'd only done periodically, so she couldn't keep up a steady pace. That meant she slowed to a walk at times, which allowed her to take in more of the town. At one point, she saw a sign for a park and didn't hesitate to veer in that direction.

The park had a walking path beside the road, and the further she got into the park, the more company she had on it.

Big trees towered over the walkway, and there were lots of people of all ages enjoying the nice weather. Many sat at picnic tables. Others had blankets laid out on the grass while kids played nearby. There were some people playing volleyball, while others tossed a football around.

It was idyllic, and even soothing in a way. She stopped her audio book and pulled her earbuds out so she could enjoy it.

The longer she was away from the house, the more the fog of grief and hurt thinned. For the first time in what felt like forever, she felt like she could breathe. She was away from people she barely knew, some of whom didn't seem to like her very much. Who only tolerated her because she'd married someone they loved.

The grief and hurt didn't completely go away. But enough of it did to give her a chance to view the situation with a little more clarity.

She had a decision to make: stay or go.

Was the love she'd had with Zane prior to him losing his memory worth enduring the hurt and rejection she felt on a daily basis?

There was no guarantee that the love he'd had for her would ever return. It was possible that Zane would never regain his memory, and they'd never share that love again.

Maybe if she left, he'd come find her if his memory returned.

However, what would happen if she moved on with her life, and he showed up in that new life with his memory intact? It could lead to even more heartache.

So many scenarios ran through her mind, and she gave each one due consideration as she continued to wander through the park. It quickly became apparent that the only path she saw to happiness was with Zane regaining his memory and remembering their love.

And she wanted that more than anything else.

So she wasn't going to leave. Not yet. Not unless Zane asked her to.

By coming to Serenity with Zane, she'd sort of made that decision already. However, this time, she really meant it. If she wanted to get through this with her mental health intact, she had to stick to that resolution.

There might be people who didn't want her there, but she knew that pre-accident Zane would have. If the roles were reversed, he would have stuck beside her. She knew that with one hundred percent certainty.

Of course, she didn't have a serious boyfriend in her past that she'd be in love with, had she lost four years of her memory. It was hard to ignore that revelation from Zane, but she was trying her hardest to do just that.

Give me a chance to either remember you or fall in love with you all over again.

It was like Zane was there, whispering in her ear. Asking her to give them a chance. To give *him* a chance.

He might not currently be the person she'd married, but that man was in there somewhere. She just needed to find him again.

She thought of how the pastor had said they were praying for her and Zane. Maybe it was time that she tried to pray, too. But would God hear her since she didn't have the same faith that Zane and his family did?

All she knew was that she had no answers and no direction, and she desperately wanted both.

Along the path, she stumbled upon a structured garden area, which, thankfully, offered some places to rest. As she sat on a cement bench, Kelsey rotated her ankles, realizing that perhaps she hadn't taken into account the possibility of sore feet when she'd set out. Also, she was thirsty and hadn't thought to bring a water bottle.

She'd have to keep an eye out for a water fountain on the way back. Or stop somewhere to buy some water. And maybe a chocolate bar. She was hungry now, too.

Still, she didn't rush away from the garden and the small bit of peace she'd found.

All too soon, she'd be on her way back to the house and the difficult situation there. But hopefully, her time away from the house would give her the strength and clarity to keep going.

CHAPTER NINE

Zane watched his nieces and nephews as they clustered together, the older ones playing with the younger. They, more than anything else, showed the lapse of time he'd forgotten. Seeing Layla and Peyton as teenagers had been shocking. And then there were the babies who hadn't existed four years ago.

Along with Gareth and Aria's daughter, Janessa and Will's son, Liam, and Charli and Blake's son, Micah, were also two that he didn't remember. The three were already toddlers. All kids had grown up so much in the black hole years, as he was beginning to think of them.

Beyond his marriage to Kelsey, Zane had changed during those years, too.

In that time, he'd learned enough and gained enough experience that he'd been able to land the job in a top restaurant in Tampa.

He'd also abandoned his faith somewhere along the line.

And he'd apparently done something that had upset Sarah enough that she'd broken up with him. He wished he knew what that was.

It didn't make him feel very good that not all of the changes in his life had been for the better.

A light touch on his shoulder drew his attention from the kids. Glancing up, he saw Rori standing beside him, a concerned look on her face.

"Have you seen Kelsey?"

It took a moment for him to switch gears. Kelsey was not up-permost in his mind when he wasn't focused on her. He was still having a hard time believing she was his wife.

"No. I haven't." He glanced around. "The last time I saw her, she was carrying stuff out of the house."

Rori nodded, but the concerned look didn't ease from her face. "I can't find her."

"She's not in the house?" he asked. "Or in her room?"

"No. I checked." Her frown deepened. "She's not here."

Zane didn't know Kelsey well enough to have any idea of where she might have gone. "Is her car here?"

"I didn't check that." Turning, she went to where Lee was talk-ing with Blake and stood at his side, waiting for his attention.

Almost immediately, Lee slipped his arm around her and bent his head down. He listened for a moment, then the two of them made their way across the deck into the house.

Zane wondered if he should follow them to see if there was more he could do. He knew that as Kelsey's husband, he should be concerned. His lack of feelings for Kelsey was a constant strug-gle. Knowing he had a wife, but not remembering her or their love, left him confused, so he tried not to dwell on it too much.

Grabbing his crutches, he pushed to his feet, then tucked them under his arms and made his way to the back door.

"Where are you going, sweetheart?" his mom asked as he passed where she sat on a lawn chair.

"Just need to talk to Lee and Rori." He decided not to mention Kelsey to his mom. "I'll be back in a minute."

Inside the kitchen, he found the pair in conversation. They turned to face him as he joined them. "So what's up?"

"Her car's here," Rori said.

"So maybe she went for a walk."

"Without eating?" Rori asked. "Why would she do that?"

"Because she's not comfortable around us yet," Lee said. He crossed his arms as he leaned back against the counter. After regarding Zane for a long moment, he sighed. "This isn't going to work."

"What isn't?"

"The way you're choosing to approach the fact that you're married."

Zane scowled at his brother as he rested his weight on the crutches. "How am I supposed to approach it? I don't remember her."

"You need to spend time with her," Lee said. "You need to show that you care for her, if not as a wife, as a person who has lost someone very important to her. She's missing *you*. It can't be easy for her to see you every day—the man she loves—and for you not to act like that man."

"And that's my fault? She didn't have to come here."

Lee's gaze narrowed. "The way you are acting is not the way the Zane I know would act."

Zane felt his brother's words like a stab to his heart. Lee was right, and if the roles had been reversed, he would have lectured his brother about his attitude as well.

Lifting a hand to massage his forehead, he wished he could rub away the dull ache he seemed to be constantly dealing with. That ever-present ache had him on edge, and Zane knew that his patience was in short supply, and his tolerance was low.

"I'm not saying you have to jump into a relationship with her," Lee said. "But let her have some sort of role in your life while we wait to see what's going to happen with your memory."

"I think you'll regret the current course you're on if...when... you get your memory back," Rori said.

Lee nodded. "The way you spoke about Kelsey in the months prior to the accident made it clear how much you loved her. How much you cared for her. That Zane would be absolutely livid over the way you're treating her."

Zane knew that Lee was right about that, too. He needed to change his mindset, even without his memories.

"Okay," he said. "I get it."

"I hope so," Lee said. "I don't want to have to keep having this discussion with you."

"If you don't even try, there may come a point where Kelsey just walks away and starts her life over," Rori added. "And if you regain your memory after that happens, you'll have lost something that was very important to you."

Everything they said made sense, but he had a mental block where Kelsey was concerned. It was like he thought that if his memory didn't come back, he'd get to reset his life to four years ago. The problem with that was that four years ago, he was planning to marry Sarah.

"I'm going to call her," Rori said.

"Why didn't you do that to start with?" Zane asked.

"At first, I thought she'd just gone to her room, and I didn't want to make her feel like I was keeping track of her," Rori said. "But I'm worried. She's clearly left the house and has been gone for awhile. She also didn't eat anything before she left."

Rori looked at Lee, who nodded. She picked up her phone and tapped the screen, then held it in front of her. When he heard it ringing, Zane realized she'd put it on speakerphone.

"Hello?"

"Hi, Kelsey. It's Rori. Are you okay?"

"Yes. I'm fine," Kelsey said, and from the sound of her voice, Zane thought she was telling the truth. "I just decided to go for a walk."

"Where did you walk to?"

"I'm at a park."

Rori frowned. "A big park?"

"It seems like a big one. I'm currently sitting on a stone bench in a garden surrounded by lots of flowers."

"You've walked quite a ways."

Kelsey gave a soft laugh. "My feet definitely feel like I have."

"Let me come and get you so you don't have to walk all the way back."

"I'm not ready to leave the park just yet," Kelsey said.

"That's fine. Give me a call when you're ready."

There was a moment of silence before she said, "I don't want to interrupt the dinner."

"You won't be. It's not that formal of a thing."

"Okay. I'll call in a little bit."

"Sounds good."

"One thing," Kelsey said. "Could you bring me a bottle of water when you come? I'm parched."

Rori laughed. "Sure thing. I can do that."

After she hung up, she leaned into Lee, and he wrapped his arms around her, placing a kiss on the top of her head. Zane had to look away. Any time he saw the closeness of the couples in his family, his mind would go one of two places. He'd think about how he and Sarah had been as a couple. Or he'd wonder how he and Kelsey had interacted.

He pulled his phone out of his pocket and opened it. Out of the corner of his eye, he saw Lee and Rori leave the kitchen, leaving him alone. Staring at the icon for the app that would open his pictures, he knew he just had to pull the trigger.

Perhaps looking at the photos he'd taken would give him a glimpse of how he'd felt about Kelsey before the accident. He'd already considered doing that, but it had been easier to just procrastinate.

Maybe this was the push he needed to view the situation with Kelsey differently.

There was a shaking deep inside him that made Zane want to put his phone away. But if he was going to take the step forward that he'd told Lee he would, this was a good place to start. The pictures might give him a glimpse into who he'd been before the car accident that had robbed him of his memories.

He took a deep breath, then focused on the picture on the screen of his phone. It was the last picture he'd taken before his accident, just a couple of hours prior, according to the photo info, had been of food. Not a real surprise. Food had been his life, and it seemed that was still true.

Scrolling back, he found three more pictures of food. Finally, he found one that wasn't food. It was a picture of him and Kelsey laying together. She was kissing his cheek as he smiled at the camera. Their shoulders were bare, though they were covered by a blanket, giving it a very intimate feel. He looked... happy.

The next picture was of Kelsey sitting across the table from him. She had a forkful of pasta and was beaming at him. Was he smiling back at her with the same expression of love?

Zane soon discovered that his photo roll was filled with pictures of food, but more than that he had plenty of photos of Kelsey by herself, Kelsey with him, Kelsey eating. Every expression she wore was underpinned by the love in her eyes. There was no doubt that Kelsey had been important to him. And that he'd been important to her.

When he got to pictures of their wedding, he slowed, pausing on each one. Zooming in on his face. Zooming in on hers. Looking for something that might trigger a memory.

But there was nothing there. No memory, at least.

What he'd gained, however, was a curiosity. He'd clearly loved Kelsey. Zane could see that in his expression in the pictures. However, it was like he was looking at two strangers, one of whom looked like him. He couldn't reconcile the emotion he saw on his face for Kelsey with how he currently felt about Sarah.

His ribs gave a pulse of pain, reminding him that he was standing in the middle of the kitchen on his crutches. Tucking his phone into his pocket, he maneuvered himself over to the breakfast nook and sat down.

Alongside his photo app, the other things he hadn't opened on his phone were his social media accounts and text messages. Since he was alone in the kitchen, he tapped on the icon of the social media he remembered using the most.

It took a couple of minutes to sort out the password situation, but soon he had access to his account. He was slowly working his way through the levels of connection. The last thing he'd check would be the messages he and Kelsey had shared back and forth.

He'd put off doing all of that, and not just because of Kelsey. He had hoped that his memory would return on its own, especially the ones about his marriage. It was why he hadn't asked Kelsey for many details.

But after thinking it over, he'd realized that there was an innate connection to the memories he had that was lacking in what he was being told. So he'd know whether something in his mind was a real memory or one someone had told him.

Now, he just wanted to get his memory back however he could, and maybe the pictures and messages would help with that. He'd also put off looking through them because there was a fear that if he went through everything and it didn't trigger any memories, there would be nothing else to help him.

So he'd resisted taking that step, wanting to have it if all else failed. But now he was doing it for the sake of a woman and a relationship he couldn't remember.

After logging into one of his social media accounts, he scrolled through his posts. He'd posted something once every couple of days, and once again, a lot of the posts were of food. But then he saw one that was written a few days after their wedding.

Four days ago, I married the woman of my dreams. Kels, I knew pretty early on in our relationship that you were the one I wanted to spend the rest of my life with. Our wedding marked the start of our life together. It was a beautiful day. And you were beautiful, too.

Kelsey, thank you for taking a chance on me... on us... I am so thankful for you and can't wait to see where life takes us. I love you. Always and forever.

Zane's curiosity grew exponentially as he read the post and looked through the attached photos. They were the same ones he'd seen in the photo app, but he still paused on each one.

"Zane? Are you okay?"

Zane looked up from his phone as his mom slid into the seat across from him, concern on her face. It was a familiar sight since he'd woken up after the accident.

"I'm fine," he said, setting his phone down on the table. "Just looking through my phone and coming to some realizations."

"Oh? What are those?"

He hesitated, not sure how his mom was going to respond. "I need to spend some time with Kelsey. I need to learn more about her and our relationship."

The concern on his mom's face did not ease at his words. "I know that your relationship with her has been a stress."

"Well, I have to say that I don't believe it was stressful to me prior to the accident," he said. "I loved her very much." Picking his phone up, he found one of the pictures from the wedding and turned his phone to face his mom. "Look how happy we were."

His mom's gaze flooded with tears as she looked at the pictures. "I wish I knew why you didn't invite us to your wedding."

"Is that what all this is about?" he asked. "You're upset because we didn't invite you to the wedding?"

"It's not just that," she said. "But you know that weddings are a big deal in our family. We should have been there with you."

"And you think Kelsey's the reason you weren't invited?"

His mom shrugged. "I tried asking you, but you just said that it was what both of you had decided worked best. You didn't give any more details."

"I don't know my reasoning, but I know that I always questioned the need for big fancy weddings. When Charli and Blake had a fast engagement and a small wedding, I do remember thinking that made so much more sense."

"I didn't know you felt that way," his mom said, still staring at the picture on his phone.

"So you assumed that Kelsey was the one keeping everyone away?"

"Yeah. I guess I did. I thought for sure you'd want your family with you for such an important occasion."

"Maybe I'll be able to tell you more than that one day," Zane said. "But for now, just know that even if it was Kelsey's idea, I probably didn't object."

"Was her family there?"

"I don't remember," Zane said, reminding her that his memory was impaired. "But from looking at the pictures, I think only a couple of people were with us, and I don't think either of them were Kelsey's family."

"So, what are you going to do about your marriage?"

"I'm going to hope my memory comes back," Zane said. "And while I wait, I'm going to spend time with Kelsey."

"Make a go of the marriage?"

Zane shrugged. "I'm not committing to anything just yet. I feel like all I can do is take it a step at a time."

His mom nodded, the concern on her face having been exchanged for resignation. She might be accepting his relationship with Kelsey, but she still wasn't happy about it.

As Zane reached for his phone, the back door opened and Rori stepped into the kitchen. She headed for the door that led to the garage, then paused when she saw them sitting at the table.

"Kelsey called to say she was ready to come home," Rori said.

"Don't forget she wanted a bottle of water," Zane reminded her.

"Oh, right." Rori turned toward the fridge and got a bottle of water. "I'll be back in a few."

"Where's Kelsey?" his mom asked.

"At the park. She went for a walk."

"To the park? That's a bit of a walk."

"It is," Zane agreed. "That's why Rori offered to go pick her up."

They sat in silence for a moment, then his mom said, "I'd better get back outside. I think some were getting ready to leave."

The ones with young kids, most likely.

Sure enough, it wasn't long before there was a steady stream of people bringing dishes into the kitchen, then heading for the front door. Janessa and Will paused to talk for a few minutes, then left with their little guy.

His mom helped Lee put food away and load dishes into the dishwasher. They'd used paper plates and plastic ware, so there wasn't a lot to clean up.

They had just finished cleaning when he heard the garage door rumble. His stomach tightened at the thought of seeing Kelsey so soon after he'd made the decision to at least acknowledge what she was to him. What they had.

She followed Rori into the kitchen, pausing when she saw them all there. It was like a shutter dropped down over her face because her expression went completely blank.

Zane didn't blame her for wanting to keep a wall between herself and everyone there. Given how she'd been treated, it made sense.

Now that he'd made up his mind to focus more on her, Zane hoped that the atmosphere for Kelsey would change, and that it would become easier for her to be around them all.

No doubt the man he'd been when he married her would want to protect Kelsey and try to make things easier for her. So he'd try to do that as well, as much for Kelsey as for the man he'd been before the accident. Whether he'd ever be that man again or not, only time would tell. Right then, all he had was time.

At least until it was confirmed that his memory wasn't likely to return. Then he'd have to decide how he was going to move forward in his life.

CHAPTER TEN

When she saw the group—all of them members of her not-a-fan club—gathered in the kitchen, Kelsey wanted to turn right around and leave the house.

"We have plenty of food left from lunch," Rori said. "Let's get you a plate."

Kelsey wanted to protest, but honestly, she was hungry. The fact that seeing Zane and his parents there didn't rob her of her appetite hopefully meant that her resolve to make the situation work hadn't completely vanished in the face of reality.

Kelsey approached the counter where Cathy and Dan stood. Zane's mom moved over to sit at the breakfast nook with Zane, and her husband followed.

Lee bent to give Rori a kiss, then helped her get containers out of the fridge. Rori set an empty paper plate in front of Kelsey. "Take whatever you'd like. There's plenty."

Kelsey wasn't *that* hungry, but she still managed to fill her plate. It all looked good. She wondered what Zane had thought of the food. So far, he hadn't done any cooking that she'd seen since coming to Serenity.

That was a bit of a surprise because even though his job was to cook, he was rarely so tired of it that he refused to cook at home on his days off. In fact, most of the time he decided to cook in their apartment, he'd pull her into the kitchen with him and make her his sous chef. She had some great memories of those moments.

Rori placed a glass on the counter. "You can sit here."

Grateful that Rori hadn't sent her over to the breakfast nook, Kelsey sat down on one of the bar stools. She stared at her plate for a moment, willing her stomach to settle so she could eat what she'd taken.

"So you found our biggest and nicest park, huh?" Lee said.

"Quite by accident," Kelsey said as she took a sip of her water. "It's a beautiful place."

"It is," Lee agreed. "Hudson proposed to Kayleigh there."

"Really?" Kelsey hadn't heard that.

"Yep."

"How did Zane propose to you?" Rori asked.

Kelsey tensed, but then focused on her plate. "Over a meal he cooked for me for our six-month dating anniversary. He'd prepared my favorite meal, which included a chocolate souffle. As we were eating our dessert, he presented me with a ring."

She looked down at her fingers and the rings that Zane had placed there. They were looser on her than they had been before, but they were as beautiful as the day Zane had slid them onto her finger.

It felt a bit weird to be talking about Zane like he wasn't there, but unfortunately, in a sense, he wasn't. At least not the Zane who had chosen the engagement and wedding rings, then pledged his love to her.

"You were a very pretty bride."

Kelsey almost fell off her stool at Mrs. Halverson's words. Out of habit, she glanced at Zane, but there was no expression on his face. Looking back at the older woman, she said, "Thank you."

"Did you not want a larger wedding?" Cathy asked. "Rather than eloping?"

Kelsey wasn't sure where the conversation was headed, but all she could do was be honest about what had gone into that decision. "When we got engaged, Zane said he didn't want a long engagement. At that point, we were still thinking of just having a small wedding. But then, a few days later, he got the job offer in Tampa. He wanted me to go with him, so we decided to just elope."

"And you don't regret it?"

"No. We both agreed it was more important to move on to the marriage part of our relationship, rather than spend a lot of time and money on a fancy wedding. It seemed a waste of money when we needed to finance the move and setting up our new life in Tampa."

"And your family didn't mind that you eloped?" she asked.

Kelsey felt like the answers to these questions held weight, but she had no idea what the woman wanted her to say. "No. I'm not super close with my family, so it didn't really matter to them when we eloped."

"And did Zane say what his family might think?"

She glanced at Zane. But once again, he was no help. He was clearly listening to the conversation, but he didn't seem to have any comments himself.

"He didn't think you'd be happy to miss out on his wedding, but he said that there had been so many other family weddings that it wouldn't be a big deal if he didn't have an elaborate one himself."

"He really didn't want a big wedding," Lee added. "I spoke to him following their engagement, and the one thing he said was that he didn't want anything big."

Kelsey hoped that even if they didn't want to hear it from her, they'd accept it from Lee. She'd known that they weren't happy, but it seemed that Mrs. Halverson had taken offense at the fact they'd chosen to elope rather than have a wedding.

"Our weddings have all been a reflection of what we, as couples, wanted," Lee said. "It's not fair to hold it against Kelsey and Zane that they preferred to have something for just the two of them. If that's what they wanted, we need to respect that."

"What's done is done," Zane said, finally wading into the conversation. "It's not like we can go back and redo it. I might not remember the wedding, but I do know that in the past, I expressed a preference for a smaller wedding versus a larger one."

"I know you said that," Cathy said. "But I didn't realize that meant we wouldn't be there at all."

"I'm sorry that I can't tell you for certain why Zane made that decision," Kelsey told her. He had mentioned that getting his mom involved would most likely lead to a more complicated event than they wanted. However, she didn't say that out loud.

If this was going to be something Mrs. Halverson couldn't let go of, they'd never have a chance to develop any sort of relationship. Not that she felt like there was much of a chance to begin with.

"Let's just let the wedding go," Zane said. "Of all the issues facing me at the moment, the motivation behind why we eloped is not even on the list."

"You're right, of course, darling." Cathy rested her hand on Zane's arm. "It's not important."

"The fact they're *married* is important," Lee said. "Just not how they ended up that way."

Kelsey liked the reminder from Lee that he and Rori were there for her. So far, they were the only members of the family who had really warmed up to her. Not that the others had been rude or anything, they just hadn't shown much interest in getting to know her.

Which, if she was honest, wasn't a big deal. Especially considering the circumstances of Zane's accident.

It seemed like Mrs. Halverson was most upset at not being able to be a part of a special event in her son's life. But there was also still a feeling that she didn't think Kelsey was good enough for Zane.

Since she'd never had one, Kelsey didn't understand a protective parent. Her parents wouldn't have cared that she was getting married, with even less interest in who she was marrying. But she thought that having over-protective parents would be better than ones who were focused on things other than the children they'd birthed.

"We should probably head home," Mr. Halverson said, getting to his feet. "I think there's still time for a nap."

There were a couple of snickers, and at least one muttered mention of *old folks*. Kelsey would have to side with the *old folks* in this regard because she was ready for a nap herself. Her long walk was definitely catching up with her.

Both of the Halverson parents made sure to say goodbye to Kelsey, which made her equal parts grateful and suspicious. Though she did her best not to reveal the suspicions she harbored over their sudden warming up, Kelsey suspected that she might not have succeeded.

Once they were gone, a quiet settled over the house. Leaning against the counter, Lee took Rori in his arms. She relaxed back against him, and the tension melted from her face.

Witnessing that interaction, Kelsey knew that Lee was Rori's home. He was her safe place. Her protection from the world.

Zane had been that for her, but that wasn't the case anymore. Now, what she needed protection from the most was him. Or rather, her love for him because if he never remembered her, the heartbreak would be immense.

"I think we're just going to hang out in our room," Lee said after he and Zane had a brief conversation about something that had evidently been brought up earlier with their siblings.

"See you in a bit," Rori said with a smile as she took Lee's hand when he held it out to her.

A weighty silence settled over the kitchen in their absence, and as much as she'd once have loved to hang out with Zane, Kelsey was filled with a strong desire to leave. She took her nearly empty paper plate to the garbage, then picked up her glass.

"Do you think we could talk for a bit?"

It was a good thing she hadn't taken a drink of her water, or she would have choked on it. Instead, she clutched the glass between her hands and turned to face Zane.

"Uh... sure."

On legs that trembled just a bit, Kelsey made her way to the breakfast nook, fearful of what Zane might have to say to her. Had his parents been nice to her earlier because they knew she was on her way out?

Once she was seated, she lifted her glass to take a sip of water. Just to have something to do.

Zane looked down at his hands as he turned his phone over and over, making Kelsey's stomach twist. Just when she'd resolved to stay strong, she was being presented with a situation that threatened to break her down.

"I want to apologize for my attitude toward you since the accident." Kelsey could only stare at Zane in shock, his words having rendered her speechless. "I know it doesn't reflect well on me, but honestly, I've just wanted to put my head in the sand when it comes to our relationship. It felt like the easiest thing to do."

"I understand," she said, though she didn't, really.

"You shouldn't have to, but I appreciate it." Zane gave a familiar sigh, and if it still signified the same thing, it meant he was frustrated with himself. "I think we need to have a conversation about how we're going to approach this."

"Would you like me to leave?" she asked, needing to tear the bandage off.

He stared at her for a long moment. Unfortunately, Kelsey had zero confidence in her ability to read his expressions anymore, so she had no idea what he was thinking.

"Though that is tempting, simply because it would be the easiest thing for me, it's not the right thing." Zane's brow furrowed as he hesitated. "From what Lee has said, the me before the accident would be absolutely livid if I didn't give you... us... a chance."

Kelsey agreed, but she didn't let him know that. It felt important to really get a feel for what he was thinking before she revealed her own thoughts about their situation.

"So, I want to give us a chance," he continued. "I'm just not sure what that will look like."

Kelsey hadn't given it a lot of thought, but a few things came to mind. "Maybe I could drive you to your doctor's appointments. And instead of avoiding each other, we need to accept that we're sharing space here."

Zane nodded. "My parents will most likely want to go with me, but you could probably come."

"I'd like that." Even if she had to put up with awkward moments with Zane's parents.

Zane regarded her for a moment, his brown eyes serious. "How did we meet?"

"We both worked at the same restaurant in Chicago," she said. "You'd been working there for a couple of months already when I was hired."

"Did we start dating right away?"

Kelsey shook her head. "Rumor had it that you weren't giving any woman the time of day romantically, so even though I thought you were attractive and a nice guy, I didn't flirt with you or anything like that. Instead, we became friends."

"Why did things change?" Zane asked.

"It wasn't intentional."

"So, how did it happen?"

Kelsey couldn't help but smile as she thought back to that time. "We had planned to meet for dinner with some other friends from the restaurant on our night off. Everyone else cancelled at the last minute, which meant it was just you and me at the restaurant we'd agreed to meet at. I kind of thought you'd bail too, but we decided to go ahead and eat there like we'd planned."

"And that was it?"

"Sort of," she said. "We ended up talking for hours. We stayed until the restaurant closed, then moved on to a twenty-four-hour place. We stayed there until around three in the morning. Though we both tried to pass it off as us just getting closer as friends, that didn't last too long, especially since we parted ways with a hug."

"Who made the first move to take it beyond friendship?"

Kelsey took a drink of her water. "That was you."

His brows lifted. "Really?"

She nodded. "There was no way that I was going to put myself out there when everything I'd heard was that you didn't want a relationship."

"But you wanted one?"

"Yes. But I also wasn't in the market for a broken heart."

"What did I say to change your mind?"

"It wasn't so much what you said as what you did."

"Which was?"

Kelsey thought of that moment, and her heart ached with the memory. "At one point, as we were waiting to cross the street, you grabbed my hand. And you just never let go."

Until recently, anyway.

"What was our favorite date?"

"Well, it didn't start out as a date, but eventually, it became one because we did it every week." She missed those evenings so much right then. "You'd make us dinner, then we'd watch one of those reality cooking shows. While we watched, you'd tell me what you thought of the food they were cooking and how you'd do things differently. You were pretty good at predicting what the judges were going to say, and who was going to end up at the top and at the bottom."

"And you enjoyed that?" Zane didn't sound convinced.

"I did. Part of it was just because I got to hang out with you. Part of it was the great food you always prepared. Part of it was getting to know more about you through something you were so passionate about."

"Did I teach you anything about cooking?"

"A little. We'd do some cooking together on our days off, but I was limited to chopping and, occasionally, stirring."

Zane seemed to mull over what she'd shared with him. She had no idea what he planned to do with the information. Even if she wanted to jump ahead to getting their relationship back on track, she knew it couldn't happen that way.

At this point, he either needed to regain his memory, or they had to take their time getting to know each other again. This conversation was just step one in that process, and unfortunately, she knew there was no guarantee that he'd fall in love with her a second time.

It had happened so organically the first time around, which had helped Zane overcome his reluctance to be in a relationship. And it had helped her be willing to take a chance on love with him.

This time, Zane was stuck in the past at a point where he thought he was in love with another woman, and there was a possibility he wouldn't be willing to let go of it.

"Thank you for sharing all that with me," Zane said.

"You're welcome. Feel free to ask me anything about our relationship."

Zane nodded. "I'll do that."

Kelsey wanted to demand to know if he was really going to give them a chance, but she held her tongue. This conversation was more than she'd expected, so she would take it for now. Maybe in the future, she'd be able to ask some questions of her own.

When Zane lifted his hand to rub his forehead, she said, "Headache?"

He glanced at her. "Yeah. But that's nothing new."

"Really?"

"My head aches to some degree for a good chunk of most days. Sometimes it's worse than others."

"I guess that's maybe to be expected because of the concussion, right?"

"That's what they tell me," he muttered as he ran a hand through his hair. "Doesn't make it any easier, though."

Though Kelsey didn't want this time to end, she didn't object when he said he needed to go lay down. She hoped that this conversation was the start of more to come.

After he'd left her alone in the kitchen, Kelsey sat by herself for a few minutes, trying to decide if she should get excited or maintain her reserve.

In the end, she decided to be excited in the moment, but reserved in the future. And she needed to keep herself from building up expectations for what was to come.

Zane had promised her nothing. *This* Zane had promised her nothing.

Her Zane had promised her everything.

And she wanted that everything more than ever.

Her mind might be cautious, but her heart loved and missed Zane so much that it didn't even want to consider not sticking this out. No matter how difficult it might be.

CHAPTER ELEVEN

Though he would have liked to stay in his room, Zane forced himself out of bed and pulled on a pair of loose gym shorts and a T-shirt. He needed to take a shower at some point that day, but it required more energy than he had at that moment.

He dragged a hand through his hair, then stood for a moment in the darkened room to brace himself for the world beyond his door. It had been a long week, and he would have much rather stayed in bed.

Despite the conversation with Kelsey on Sunday, things hadn't magically become easier between them. He hadn't gone out of his way to avoid her, though, and it didn't seem that she had tried to avoid him either. That hadn't made their interactions any less awkward. If anything, they might have gotten more so.

It was a Friday, so no surprise, the house was quiet. He made his way to the stairs and carefully maneuvered himself down them to the main floor. It was only then he heard movement and became aware of the aromas in the air.

When he moved through the entryway to the kitchen, he spotted Kelsey standing at the counter. She had a mug in one hand and was staring down at her phone in the other. There was an electric griddle on the counter in front of her with circles of pancake batter on it.

Looking up, she regarded him for a long moment before she said, "Coffee and some pancakes?"

He nodded as he slowly crutched his way over to the counter and sank down on a bar stool there. He appreciated that she hadn't asked how he was doing, but that probably meant he looked as bad as he felt. Or worse.

When she set a large mug of coffee in front of him, Zane lifted it and took a sip. Perfect. It was then he realized that she'd doctored the coffee exactly how he liked it.

As he watched, she pulled some containers of berries from the fridge, along with a can of whipped cream. She got a couple of plates from the cupboard and set them on the counter.

He wondered if this was a breakfast she'd made them before. So far, she was getting out all the things he liked with his pancakes.

Music played in the background, so there wasn't a heavy silence when they didn't talk. He was glad she didn't press for conversation because he wasn't sure that he wouldn't be a little snappy with his replies.

She used a spatula to move three perfectly formed pancakes from the griddle to one of the plates. After adding some blueberries and cutting up some strawberries, she squirted a healthy dose of whipped cream on the pancakes.

"It says it's made from real whipping cream," she said when he eyed the can. "I forgot to buy cream to whip myself."

He looked up to find her watching him with slightly narrowed eyes. "I'm sure it will be fine."

She carefully slid the plate across to him, then opened up the silverware drawer and took out a couple of forks and knives. Handing him one of each, she set the others down on the second plate, then poured more pancake batter onto the grill.

Zane watched her for a moment, then bowed his head to thank God for the meal that Kelsey had prepared for him. He took a bite of pancake with berries and whipped cream and hummed in appreciation.

"Tastes good," Zane said.

"I'm not surprised you think that," Kelsey replied as she lifted her mug to take a sip. "It's your recipe."

Zane looked down at his pancakes, then back at her. "Did I teach you how to make them?"

"Yep. I wanted to learn how to make something you liked, and together we decided that this recipe was simple enough that I wasn't likely to mess it up."

"Well, apparently, we made a good decision because you didn't mess this up at all. Even with canned whipped cream."

The headache was still there, but the food and Kelsey were giving him something else to focus on. Elsa came over to him then and sat looking up at him.

"I can give her berries, right?" he asked.

"Yes, but probably not too many. We wouldn't want to make her sick, even if her dad is a vet."

Thinking of Lee as a dad to a dog led Zane to thinking of him as a dad to a kid. Lee had always hoped to have a family. However, when Lee's relationship prior to Rori had ended because the woman had rejected him over his unknown past, Zane hadn't been sure Lee would be willing to try for another. At least not without more answers about his past.

Now, however, Zane could see how children would fit into his brother's life so easily. His career was stable, and he was married to a woman who would make a wonderful mom.

Zane could see Rori's mothering tendencies already in how she cared for Kelsey and for him. She was a bit like a mother hen, worrying over both of them.

And then there was the house. Big enough for a whole lot of children.

Kelsey flipped the pancakes, then went to pour more coffee into her mug. "Did you want more?"

"I think I'm good for now. Thanks."

"Do you want more pancakes?" she asked as she removed hers from the griddle.

"I'm pretty full, so no more for me at the moment," Zane told her. "But they were great."

"I'm going to cook the rest of the batter up, anyway." She ladled more circles of batter onto the griddle. "I figure we can heat them up if we want more later."

"What were our days like in Tampa?" he asked.

She glanced up at him, then turned her attention back to the berries she was scooping onto her pancakes. "We were fortunate that our jobs had similar hours. Your days were longer than mine, though. You left before me and got home after me."

"Sounds about right for a sous chef in a restaurant of that caliber."

Kelsey nodded. "They worked you hard there, but you loved it."

"I'm sure I was more than happy to do whatever the job required."

"You were," Kelsey agreed. "But you always made sure that we had time for each other. Sometimes that was making breakfast together. That's when you taught me how to make these pancakes."

It was so easy to picture what she was describing... for someone else. But he still had a hard time imagining it being his life.

"I'd always wait up until you got home, then we'd have supper together, hang out for awhile and go to bed."

"Did we have friends in Tampa?"

"Not really," Kelsey said as she flipped the pancakes she'd poured onto the griddle. "We each had people at our workplaces that we got along well with, but we hadn't forged any real friendships yet."

That didn't really surprise Zane. He'd never made friends super easily, and if he was working hard at a new job, building friendships would have definitely taken a back burner. Especially if he had a wife to spend time with.

Zane was glad to hear that he'd made his relationship with Kelsey a priority. He still struggled with the idea of being married to anyone other than Sarah, but it was good that he had taken his marriage to Kelsey seriously.

Kelsey began to clear up the dishes she'd used to make their breakfast, as well as his plate. He took her offer of a refresh of his coffee, and once again, she'd fixed it just the way he liked it.

He felt like they were getting closer. Like these moments together were promoting natural growth between them. It was probably the best way for things to unfold. It helped to make things feel less forced.

Still, he hadn't read their personal text messages yet. It almost seemed wrong to read them when the people conversing were essentially strangers to him.

"I have a question," Zane said as Kelsey bent to put their plates into the dishwasher.

She slowly straightened and seemed to take a deep breath before looking at him. "What's that?"

"So, when I got my new phone, I loaded everything from the backup," he said. "I've looked through the pictures and read some of the stuff on my social media."

"Okay?" She was frowning, but didn't seem upset.

"What I haven't read is the text messages between you and... well... me."

"Why not?" she asked, picking up a dish towel to wipe her hands.

"I guess I assumed they might be pretty personal."

She didn't answer right away, as if she was thinking back through all they'd written to each other. "Our messages were a mix of practical and intimate, I suppose."

"That's why I didn't feel right reading them."

Kelsey looked away from him, blinking rapidly. "Yeah. It might be best to wait."

He was glad he'd decided not to read the messages, and also to ask Kelsey about them. It did make him more curious, though. He thought there might be a reason to read them in the future.

But it definitely wasn't that time yet.

"I'm heading out in a bit," she said once everything had been tidied up. "Do you need anything at the store?"

Zane had never really enjoyed shopping, unless it was at a specialty food store, but he felt like he'd been cooped up forever.

"Would you mind some company?"

Kelsey hesitated for a moment, then shrugged. "Nope. Not at all."

"Let me just go up to my room and grab my wallet."

"Okay. We'll leave in fifteen minutes."

Zane was glad she'd given him plenty of time because, once he got to his room, he decided his mother would be greatly disappointed in him if he didn't brush his hair before going out. He also swapped his T-shirt for one that wasn't quite so worn looking.

He spritzed a little cologne on, then found his wallet and phone and slipped them into the pocket of his shorts. Normally, he would have put jeans or nicer shorts on, but the long gym shorts were the easiest to put on over the cast and were the most comfortable.

When he made it back downstairs, Kelsey had her purse and was standing near the front door. She opened the door, then waited for him to make his way out onto the porch.

Her car was parked at the curb in front of the house, so it took him a few minutes to get to it and get settled in the front seat. As he buckled himself in, Zane glanced around the car.

It was an older model, with lots of wear and tear. He knew that the car he'd been driving when the accident happened had only been a couple of years old. Why didn't Kelsey have a newer car, too?

"How old is this car?" he asked as she pulled away from the curb.

"Twelve years."

"Why do you drive such an old vehicle?"

"It was what I could afford," she said with a shrug. "And it's still running fine, so there's been no need for me to spend money on another one."

"So you're happy with it?"

"Sure. It gets me where I need to go and hasn't left me stranded yet. So yeah, I guess I'm happy with it."

He noticed there was a little teddy bear hanging from the mirror. He reached out to touch it. "Stuffed animal?"

"It's an air freshener," she said. "You... Zane..." She sighed. "You bought it for me. You said it was so that something from you would always be along for the ride."

Zane stared at it, trying to imagine himself picking out the small bear. He had a bit of a struggle doing that.

"I guess I'm going to have to get another car," he said.

"Are you able to drive now?"

"Since it's my left leg that's broken, I should be able to. I'm not sure if there's any sort of restriction because of my concussion. No one has really said anything about my ability to drive. Most likely because I don't currently have a car."

"Do you think you'll have trouble driving?"

Zane considered her question for a bit before he answered. "I don't know. I think I'll be okay. It wasn't like it was my driving that resulted in the accident."

From what he'd been told, the guy who'd hit him had been drunk, and there was nothing Zane could have done to avoid the accident, short of leaving the restaurant earlier or later.

When they reached the store, Kelsey said, "Do you want me to drop you off at the door?"

"No. I need the exercise." Plus, to have a woman drop him off went against everything he'd been taught growing up, even if he was injured.

She found a parking spot fairly close to the entrance, then they climbed out of the car and made their way into the building. Kelsey found a cart, and together, they walked into the main part of the store.

"Did you want to go through the rest of the store before we hit the food section?" Kelsey asked.

"I wouldn't mind checking the shoes. I'd like to get a pair that's a little easier to put on."

"Sure." She looked out over the store, then gestured to the back. "I think shoes are over there."

It took longer than he would have liked to get to the shoe section. His mobility was definitely something he really missed. He was an active person by nature, and his career required him to be on his feet for long periods of time.

He couldn't wait until he could move around with ease once again.

"Do you want slides?" Kelsey asked as she headed down the aisle of men's shoes.

"Ugh."

Kelsey chuckled as she glanced his way, her eyes sparkling. "Yeah. You've never liked them."

"Well, it's good to know I didn't lose my sense of style in the past few years."

He sat down on one of the stools available for people to use when they tried on shoes. Though he probably should have searched for the shoes he wanted, as soon as he sat down, Kelsey began to pull shoes off the rack for his consideration.

For the next little while, he managed to put the complexities of their situation aside and just be in the moment. It was still hard to imagine that Sarah was out of his life, and he was married to someone else. But right then, he focused on being with Kelsey and tuned out thoughts and memories of Sarah.

"How about these?" Kelsey asked, showing him a pair of dark brown loafer style shoes. "They might be easy to slip on."

Zane took them from her and set them on the floor. He bent forward to take his runner off, then tried to put the new one on. His foot slid in easy enough without a lot of effort, and he realized that she'd known his size without even asking.

It was moments like that that seemed to be solid proof of the relationship he'd been told they had. She held so much knowledge about him, but he didn't have the same knowledge about her. It felt very unbalanced.

"These fit pretty good," he told her.

"They have black," she said, turning back to the shelves. "But I know you prefer brown."

Yes, he did prefer brown.

"Are you hoping to wear these after you get the cast off, or are they just for now?"

"I'm not sure," he said, staring down at the shoe he had on. "Why?"

"If you plan to wear them later, you'll need more than just them working for the moment. If you don't like the look of them—even if they're easy to put on—you won't wear them again."

"I think I'd probably wear these again. They're comfortable, which would be a bonus when I'm back in the kitchen."

Zane tried on a few more pairs, but none were as comfortable as the first ones Kelsey had brought him.

"So you want these?" she asked as she stood next to the cart with the shoes in hand.

"Yep. I do." He grabbed his crutches from where he'd leaned them against the shelves. "And now that I'm here, can we check out the gym shorts? I seem to be living in them these days, so I could use a few more pair."

They left the shoe section and wandered over to the men's section. Kelsey led the way, though she kept her pace even with his slow steps.

"Do you just want black or dark blue?" she asked when they reached a rack of gym shorts. Right away, she began to sort through them. "Here's a nice pair."

She held out a pair of dark blue shorts in his size. It made him wonder if they'd shopped together for clothes a lot.

He took the hanger she held out toward him. After checking the shorts over and holding them up against his waist, he put them in the cart.

"Here's another pair." She handed him a pair of black ones. They weren't silky like the other pair, but the soft cotton felt nice. "How many pairs did you want?"

"Maybe two more," he said. "I don't want to have to be doing laundry every day."

"Okay." She gave him two other pairs, both of which worked for him. "Did you want more T-shirts?"

"Yeah. Maybe a couple."

He hadn't planned to do a major shop when he'd asked to tag along, but now that he was in the store, it made sense to pick up a few things.

"I like this color on you," Kelsey said, holding up a lavender colored T-shirt.

He stared at it a moment, then frowned. "Uh..."

"You don't want to look like a flower."

"Yes. That. Exactly."

"You never have liked to wear this color," Kelsey said as she put the T-shirt back. "Even though I do think with your coloring, it would look really nice on you."

Zane rested his weight on his crutches and watched Kelsey as she sorted through the T-shirts. She pulled out a couple in colors that were more in line with what he liked to wear. Again, the size was correct.

"These are a softer cotton," Kelsey said as she turned to him. "But they're a little more expensive."

"I'll go with softer," Zane told her as he took one of the shirts. "Always."

After a brief discussion about colors, his choices were added to the cart.

"What next?" Kelsey asked. "Do you need any toiletries?"

He thought of the meticulously organized bag of toiletries he'd found when he'd gone through everything that Kelsey had packed from their apartment. "I think I'm good."

"I need to get a couple of things from the personal care section and then some groceries. Are you okay to keep going, or do you want to find a seat somewhere?"

"I'm fine," he said. The pain was still there, but he was getting better at ignoring it when he had something to distract him.

In the toiletry section, she went to the hair care products and looked through the shampoos and conditioners. As he watched her smell some of them, Zane wondered what sort of scents she preferred. He should know.

He'd known what Sarah had preferred for perfume, and her hair had always smelled lightly floral. If he'd known that about a girlfriend, he had hopefully known it about a wife.

After smelling one particular bottle, she glanced in his direction, then set it in the cart.

It wasn't long before she'd gotten the other items she needed and set them in the cart. "Now, off to get a few groceries."

As they neared the aisles of food, she said, "You want to pick up some meat to make a meal?"

Zane scoffed, then realized that there was a bit of humor in Kelsey's expression. "You know that I'm not a fan of the meat at stores like this."

"Yes. I do. You've made that very clear." She pushed the cart into the fruit and vegetable section. "Is there a store here in Serenity that has the type of meat you like to cook with?"

"I'm not sure about now, but there was a butcher here at one point. It took some convincing to get my folks to buy meat there, since it was more expensive, and they had a lot of mouths to feed."

"Pretty sure you've been eating meals made with food from here," Kelsey said as she stopped next to a bunch of bananas. "I don't think Rori and Lee shop anywhere too bougie."

"No. You're right. They don't."

Kelsey put a few bananas into a bag and then set them in the cart. "You want some grapefruit? I thought I'd pick up some bagels and cream cheese as well."

The casual question and comment again revealed that she knew his preferences.

"Though I know you'd probably rather not have the bagels from here."

"I would like some grapefruit," he said. "And I'll put up with the bagels from here for now."

After Kelsey had picked up some bagels and cream cheese, she went to the freezer aisle and stood in front of the ice cream.

"You like ice cream?" he asked.

"I do," she said without looking at him.

"I like it too," he told her, then realized that revelation was unnecessary when she said, "I know."

He found it interesting that she didn't ask him if he wanted some. She ended up choosing a container of fancy flavored ice cream, then after a brief hesitation she led him to another aisle where she picked up mini marshmallows, some nuts, and some chocolate syrup. And then there was a bag of cookies.

He knew better than to comment on a woman's junk food choices, so he kept his mouth shut about Kelsey's questionable food choices. Sarah got mad at him when he made any observations about her food cravings. Or rather, she *used* to get mad at him when he did that.

A pulse of pain went through him, and he turned away from Kelsey.

"Zane Halverson?" He glanced over to see Will's mom approaching them with a smile. "How are you doing, sweetheart?"

She leaned in to give him a quick hug, slipping her arms around him without too much hassle despite the crutches. Perhaps her experience with Will when he'd been injured helped her with that.

"I'm doing better," he said. "Every day is a step forward."

"Yep. That's how it was with Will, too. It's such a blessing to see you up and about." She turned to Kelsey, giving her a warm smile. "And you must be Kelsey."

"I am."

"I'm Alice Kennedy," Alice said as she held out her hand to Kelsey. "Will's mom."

Kelsey smiled as she shook her hand. "It's nice to meet you."

"We've been praying so much for both of you," Alice said, continuing to hold Kelsey's hand, now clasped between both of hers.

"Thank you. I very much appreciate that."

"We're grateful that God protected Zane, and despite the circumstances, we're happy to see you both here in Serenity."

She let go of Kelsey's hand and turned back to Zane. "Do you think you'll be staying here long term?"

Zane hadn't looked much beyond twenty-four hours into the future since the accident. At that moment, he couldn't see how he could stay in Serenity. But only time would tell which direction his life would take.

Their life together would take.

CHAPTER TWELVE

Kelsey watched as Alice Kennedy walked away, then said, "She seems really sweet."

"She is," Zane agreed. "That whole family is, really. Well, except for Reese. She's more like kettle corn."

"Kettle corn?" Kelsey asked as they made their way to the registers at the front.

"She *can* be sweet, but often, she's salty. You never know which one you're going to get, and it drives her brothers bonkers."

Thankfully, they didn't have to stand in line too long, and soon she was able to unload her items onto the conveyor belt. After all of her stuff was out of the cart, she set the divider down and started to work on Zane's.

It pained her a bit to have their items separate, but he probably wouldn't even think to pay for her things too. Even though they had kept most of their finances separate, whenever they went shopping together, he would pay for whatever they got. He'd also pay whenever they went out to eat. And that didn't even include the *just because* items he'd buy for her like a new candle or a new set of cozy pajamas.

But that had been when she'd been first his girlfriend, and then his wife. However, he no longer viewed her as someone important to him.

That thought hurt her to her very core.

She shouldn't have bought half of what she had. But it was that time of the month, so her emotions—which were already battered and bruised—were in upheaval. Ice cream and chocolate held a lot of appeal that day.

Once her items were through, she paid the bill, then transferred the bags to the cart. Zane took her place at the till, then paid for his stuff.

After it was all bagged and loaded into the cart, they left the store.

"Was there anywhere else you wanted to go before we head home?" Kelsey asked as she lifted the bags into the trunk of her car.

"Well, we can't dawdle too much, or your ice cream will melt," Zane said.

"Yeah. It is a bit warm for it to sit for too long in the car."

"Let's just head home." Zane moved to the passenger door and opened it.

Kelsey took the cart to the cart return, then went back to the car and got in.

Though a part of her had enjoyed spending time with Zane, she was ready for a little bit of space. The toll it took on her to spend time with Zane when he didn't have any emotional connection to her was intense.

"Thanks for letting me tag along," Zane said after they were home and Kelsey had put away her groceries. "It was nice to get out of the house for a bit."

"You're welcome." She picked up his bags. "I'll carry these up for you."

"It feels wrong to let you do that, but I don't have much choice."

"It's fine. I'm going upstairs, anyway."

They went up to the second floor, and Kelsey set the bags down just inside Zane's door, then went to her own room. She'd left the ice cream for later, but she'd grabbed her favorite candy bar at the till, and it was in the bag with her shampoo and conditioner.

It had been awhile since she'd eaten her feelings the way she wanted to right then. But she figured that she was entitled to it.

Her life was anything but the happy and stable place it had been not that long ago.

Her husband had feeling for his ex, who he'd woken up thinking was still his girlfriend.

She still had no job, and her money was running out.

All of that combined to make her feel incredibly sad and like she'd never have love and joy in her life again.

Alice Kennedy's words came to mind. *We've been praying so much for the both of you.* Would those prayers make any difference?

Kelsey went to put her newly purchased shampoo and conditioner bottles in the shower in her attached bathroom, then took her chocolate bar to the chair near the bay window. With a sigh, she sank into it and stared out the window.

Serenity was actually a nice little town, and in different circumstances, she might have loved to live there. She hadn't really considered it because in all the time she'd known Zane, he'd always made it very clear he'd never live in his hometown.

Even now, she knew it was only a temporary home.

If Zane didn't remember her and things didn't work out between them, she'd be leaving on her own.

And if he did get his memory back, he wouldn't want to stay there, so they'd both be leaving.

The second option was preferable, but she had a feeling that wasn't going to be the one she got.

Unwrapping her candy bar, she broke off a piece and popped it into her mouth. The delicious melt of the chocolate gave her a momentary burst of pleasure. Her appetite still wasn't what it had once been, but she always had room for chocolate.

There had been talk the evening before about some of the Halverson siblings coming over for a Friday night dinner. Kelsey wasn't all that keen on hanging out with them. She felt very much like she was being tolerated, and she'd already had enough of that in her lifetime.

When she'd visited at Christmas time with Zane, she hadn't really given much thought to whether they wanted her there or not. They'd been polite toward her, which seemed appropriate considering they were meeting her for the first time. It wasn't until they'd gotten married that the family's feelings about her had become more apparent.

Being in Serenity now, when *her* Zane wasn't there to stand at her side and be a buffer, made being with the Halversons difficult. Rori was about the only person—well, and Lee—who made Kelsey feel welcome and like she belonged there.

No one went out of their way to snub her, but none of them really sought her out for conversation. It made her feel like they blamed her in some way for what had happened to Zane. Or worse, that they didn't think he was going to remember her, so it wasn't worth their time to get to know her since she'd be leaving, eventually.

Granted, she knew that his siblings were all busy with their careers and their families, so she didn't expect them to take the time out of their schedule to spend with her. But it still hurt, especially since she was aware they'd known, and apparently liked, Zane's Sarah.

When her chocolate bar was gone, Kelsey frowned down at the empty wrapper. She crumpled it in her hand, then got up and went to drop it into the garbage can. While she was up, she went to the small desk in the room and picked up her tablet.

She was still planning to take the nursing exam, so she'd looked up the nearest place offering it. Turned out, she'd likely have to go to Spokane, which was over an hour away.

Knowing that, she still tried to spend time each day studying. Thankfully, it was a good way to pass the time once she'd done her daily check for jobs in the area.

She had to keep some purpose in her life, or she was going to lose her mind. If she couldn't have a relationship or a job, she'd at least continue on her path to becoming a nurse.

It might take a little longer, but if she ended up leaving Serenity, at least she'd be in a position of having what she needed to apply for nursing jobs. Hopefully.

From the moment she'd decided to pursue nursing, she'd kept her plans to herself, doing her best to juggle her classes and practicum with her shifts at the restaurant. She had only let Zane in on her plans after they'd been dating for around three months. When she'd asked him not to tell anyone about it until she'd passed the NCLEX, he'd agreed, though he'd thought his family would be supportive of her efforts.

Unfortunately, so often in her life, her attempts to strive for more than just the bare minimum had been dismissed and even discouraged. She'd learned to present things as a done deal, knowing that she'd have no support for the journey to her goals.

Zane had been supportive of her efforts, and he'd respected his promise not to share her news. But now he didn't remember what she'd told him, so no one knew.

After a couple of hours of distracted studying, there was a knock on Kelsey's door. Setting her tablet aside, she got to her feet and went to answer it.

"Hey, Kelsey," Rori said with a big smile. "How was your day?"

Kelsey stepped back so Rori could come in. "It was fine. How was yours?"

"Someone dropped off another litter of cats today, so we had to deal with them. They are so cute."

"Did you bring one home?" Kelsey asked.

"Nope. Lee still says absolutely not." Rori glanced around. "You could have a cat here if you wanted."

"Really?" Kelsey was surprised at that.

"As long as the cat stayed in your room, it would probably be okay."

"I don't think I should get any pets until things are a bit more settled." Though there was something appealing about having something to cuddle with, that needed her care and attention.

"I guess that's probably a good idea. But if you change your mind, you know who to come to."

Kelsey smiled. "I'll definitely keep that in mind."

"Anyway, I came up to let you know dinner will be in about an hour."

"I'm not going to be there," Kelsey said.

Rori's brows rose, and she crossed her arms. "Why not?"

"To be honest, I don't feel comfortable in a group setting with this family."

Rori frowned. "I know it can be difficult to get to know so many people. It was a bit overwhelming for me, too."

"But you had Lee," Kelsey said.

Rori's gaze dropped for a moment, then she looked back at Kelsey with a nod. "Yes. I did."

"I don't have that connection. A reason to be part of these gatherings."

"I understand that, but you'll never connect with them if you don't try," Rori said. "And I'll be there too. I can be your connection. We're friends, right?"

Kelsey didn't mean to hesitate, but she did, and her hesitation brought a look of hurt to Rori's face. "Yes. We're friends."

"Are you sure?"

"I am," Kelsey said. "It's just I don't have a lot of friends, and my best friend got mad at me when Zane and I eloped and then decided to move to Tampa. I agreed to all of that without discussing it with her, and it made her mad, and she's stopped talking to me."

"I haven't had a lot of friends either," Rori said. "I've made a few good ones since coming here, but I know that friendship can be a tricky thing. Just know I've got your back."

"Thank you. I appreciate that. I've got your back too."

"So come to dinner, and we'll stick together. If you can't be there as Zane's wife, you can be there as my friend."

Kelsey considered it. Going would give her the opportunity to spend more time around Zane. But if he ignored her, that would hurt. Every time she stepped foot into a situation where Zane was present, the potential for pain was high.

It had been fine earlier at the store, but that didn't guarantee the evening would be as well.

"Please come, Kelsey," Rori said. "You need to show the Halversons that you're willing to endure awkward situations for Zane's sake. For the sake of your marriage. I know it's not easy, but I think it's necessary."

Kelsey knew that Rori was right. But after so much hurt, it was hard to keep putting herself out there. Plus, though she hadn't mentioned it to Rori, it hurt to be around happy, affectionate couples. It was a painful reminder of what she'd had and lost, and what she might never have again.

"Okay. I'll be down in a few minutes."

Rori smiled broadly, then gave Kelsey a quick hug. "I'm happy you're coming. See you in a few."

Kelsey closed the door, then stood there for a moment, hoping she hadn't made a mistake. But she couldn't back out now, so she spent the time as she was getting ready psyching herself up for dinner with the in-laws.

After a brief debate with herself, Kelsey decided to change her clothes. She'd dressed for comfort earlier, but now it felt like she needed to dress to impress.

She took a few minutes to look through her clothes before settling on a sundress, since it was a warm day. It was a dress that she'd bought when Zane had gone shopping with her. He'd made comments on each of the outfits she'd tried on, and finally, he'd declared that one to be his favorite.

It was a light, flowy dress with a fitted bodice, a sweetheart neckline, and wide shoulder straps. The skirt floated just above her knees, and Zane had said that shade of light blue had looked good with her eyes.

Was she hoping to jog Zane's memory by showing up in a dress he'd had a hand in choosing? Sure. But also, she had only ever had positive memories in this dress. Zane had complimented her every time she'd worn it, telling her how beautiful she looked.

After putting it on, she realized it was a little looser than the last time she'd worn it. However, if she kept eating chocolate bars and ice cream, she'd probably have the opposite problem soon.

But that was a problem for future Kelsey.

Brushing her hair up into a high ponytail, Kelsey left a sweep of her bangs across her forehead, then she chose a pair of earrings that Zane had given her, along with its matching necklace. She slid her feet into a pair of strappy flat sandals, then left the room.

As she reached the main floor, Kelsey heard muffled conversation and smelled the aroma of food cooking. Wanting to help with dinner like she'd said, Kelsey quickly made her way into the kitchen.

Rori and Lee were there, talking softly at the counter. They turned in her direction, and when Rori saw her, her face lit up.

"What can I help with?" Kelsey asked as she approached them.

"You and I can set the table," Rori said. "Lee is in charge of the chicken."

"What kind of chicken are we having?" Kelsey asked, taking a stack of plates from Rori.

"Marinated and then cooked on the barbecue," Lee said. "Simple but tasty. I also did some baked. Chicken a couple of different ways, I guess."

Rori loaded the silverware onto a tray. "The others are bringing the rest of the meal."

Kelsey trailed Rori into the dining room. "Who all is coming?"

"This has turned out to be an evening for the childless couples."

That still meant that there would be four Halverson siblings that evening—including Zane and Lee.

But there were ten plates to set out. "Who are the two other plates for?"

Rori glanced at her. "Oh, that's for Jackson and Carisa."

"Have I met them?" Kelsey asked.

"I don't think so, though they might have been around at Christmas when you were here."

"I don't remember."

"Well, Jackson is a good friend of Gareth's. Carisa met him when she became friends with me and Lee. We went to her house to help her dog deliver her puppies."

Kelsey wondered if Carisa's presence would distract Rori since they were already friends. Well, it was too late to change her mind about attending.

Once the plates were set, Kelsey got the glasses. They had just finished setting the table when people started to arrive.

The first to show up were Wilder and Lexi. Kelsey had gotten to know Wilder a little while they'd been in Tampa, but she still didn't feel entirely comfortable with him. Plus, his wife, Lexi, was a bit aloof. Rori had assured her that Lexi was that way with most people and to not take it personally.

"Hi, Kelsey," Wilder said when he spotted her. "How's it going?"

"Good. How about with you?"

"It's going real good," he said, then looked around. "Where's Zane?"

"I assume he's up in his room if he's not down here."

Wilder nodded. "I'm going to go check on him."

Wilder didn't wait for her response before he headed for the stairs, pausing only briefly to say something to Lexi. He also called out a greeting to someone in the foyer before disappearing in the direction of the stairs.

A couple Kelsey didn't know appeared in the entryway to the kitchen. She assumed they were Jackson and Carisa, an assumption proven true when Lee called out a greeting to them by name.

Rori hurried over to give each of them a hug. Then she looped her arm through Carisa's and guided her over to where Kelsey stood.

"Cari, I want you to meet Kelsey, Zane's wife," Rori said. "Kelsey, this is Carisa."

"Nice to meet you," Kelsey said as she held out her hand.

"You, too." Carisa's smile was warm and friendly. "We've been praying for you and Zane."

"Thank you."

"So how are you finding Serenity?" Carisa asked as Rori moved off to talk to Lexi.

"It's a nice town," Kelsey said.

Carisa smiled. "It's a nice *small* town."

"Yeah. It's a bit smaller than I'm used to," Kelsey said. "I grew up in a big city."

"So did I."

"How did you end up here?"

"My dad brought my mom and I here when my mom was having some mental and physical health problems, and we ended up staying permanently. My mom is doing a lot better, and of course, I fell in love with Jackson, who was firmly entrenched in this place."

"So you're happy here?"

"Definitely. Even if I wasn't married to the love of my life, I think I would have been happy to stay here with my parents."

At that moment, Wilder reappeared, with Zane trailing behind him. For a heartbeat, Kelsey waited for him to search the room for her in the way he usually did.

Except he didn't. His attention went to Jackson, who he greeted with a smile. Would there ever come a point where she didn't anticipate Zane acting the way he had pre-accident? It would be great if she could reach that point soon and spare herself the pain she felt each time she expected something that didn't happen.

"It must be difficult."

Kelsey turned to see Carisa watching her with concern. She'd thought it would be pity, but that's not what she got from the woman. "It is."

"I wish I had some words of wisdom for you," Carisa said as she slipped her arm around Kelsey's shoulders and gave her a squeeze. "But all I can say is that I'm sorry this has happened to you."

Carisa might be a gorgeous woman, but it appeared that she was also very kind.

"It's not something you ever think you're going to have to deal with," Kelsey said. "Not in a million years."

"Yes, that's true. None of us start a relationship or get married imagining something like this happening. We're praying very hard that Zane's memory will return soon."

Kayleigh and Hudson arrived then, and soon, they were putting the food on the table. When they all sat down, Kelsey was surprised that Zane actually ended up sitting beside her. Unfortunately, it hadn't been because of his own actions, but rather the maneuvering of Rori, Lee, Jackson, and Carisa.

For a moment, though, Kelsey didn't feel so alone. There were others who wanted things to work out between her and Zane.

Conversation was plentiful around the table, and Zane was the most talkative he'd been since the accident.

"How's the house going?" Rori asked Carisa as they passed platters and bowls of food around.

"Pretty good. We're in the home stretch now, so I've got more to do."

"Carisa and Jackson flip houses, and Carisa also does staging for people who need to sell an empty house."

"That sounds interesting," Kelsey said. "Do you enjoy it?"

"I do." Carisa picked up her knife to spread butter on her dinner roll. "It wasn't what I intended to do when I completed college, but I discovered I had a bit of a knack for it after Jackson and I started dating."

"Carisa is also pregnant," Rori told her. "They just let us all know about a month ago."

"Congratulations," Kelsey told her. "How has the pregnancy been going?"

"Really well. I've had a few crazy cravings, but Jackson has been an absolute dream in dealing with them."

"He's so excited about becoming a dad." Rori grinned. "You're going to have two kids on your hands, I think."

Carisa laughed. "Jackson's youthful approach to life is one of the things I love about him. Makes our age difference not be so much of a big deal."

Kelsey wondered if there was any chance of her and Zane ever having kids. They'd talked about it in passing. Just enough to know it was something they both wanted, but they'd agreed to wait a couple of years before talking seriously about it.

Now, however, kids seemed a far off possibility.

Zane focused most of his attention on Wilder, who was seated to his right, and had barely acknowledged Kelsey beyond a quick smile as they'd taken their seats.

It was a harsh reminder that her role in his life was not uppermost in his mind the way it had been pre-accident. Back then, if they'd been sitting next to each other—even if he was talking to someone else—they'd have still had physical contact. Whether it was them holding hands, Zach's arm around her, or just a hand on a leg, there would have been some sort of contact.

Now, there was nothing. And Kelsey was at a complete loss as to how to help Zane regain his memory, or if not that, to help him fall in love with her again.

He'd fallen in love with her once, so one would think he could do it again. But unfortunately, he wasn't in the same state of mind—or state of heart—as when he'd fallen in love with her the first time. Because of the memories he'd lost, this time around, another woman held his heart and mind.

Kelsey feared that despite her best efforts, there would be no way to overcome that.

CHAPTER THIRTEEN

"How are you really doing?"

Zane glanced at Kayleigh, then stared back into the flames danc-ing in the firepit where Lee had lit a fire a few minutes earlier. "Still getting some headaches, especially if I'm in bright light or if I'm overly tired. My leg feels better, though, and I'm hoping Gareth will agree to put me in a walking boot soon."

"And your memory?"

Zane frowned at the flickering flames. That was the question he hated the most, though he understood why people asked it of him. "Still nothing."

"How are things with you and Kelsey?"

"They're okay, I guess."

"So you're spending some time getting to know her?"

Zane thought back to the time they'd spent at the store earlier that day. Had he learned anything new about her? Well, he'd dis-covered how much she knew about *him*. And also, that she apparently loved ice cream. But other than that, he hadn't really gotten to know her any better.

"We went to the store together this morning," he said.

Kayleigh gave a slow nod. "But are you spending time together? Like on a date?"

"A date feels..." *Wrong*. It felt wrong to go on a date with Kelsey when his heart and feelings were still tied up in someone else.

"I think a date is necessary." Kayleigh said. "I know you feel like Sarah is the woman you should be with, but she's not an option. You need to accept that and do what you can to make your mar-riage to Kelsey a priority."

"That's easier said than done," Zane said, glancing over to where Kelsey sat at the picnic table with Rori and Carisa.

They'd moved out to the back deck after dinner, and were also enjoying the fire Lee had lit since the evening was cool now that the sun had gone down.

"I feel like I have no closure on things with Sarah. I don't know why we broke up. I don't understand what happened to derail our relationship."

"Are you thinking about contacting her and having a conversation?"

"I've thought about it." A *lot,* if he was honest. But so far, something had held him in check, and he hadn't attempted to actually reach out to her.

What if she was available and wanted to try again? The temptation would be huge, but he was married to another woman.

"It's possible that if you don't regain your memory, you'll need a conversation with her in order to get closure."

He hadn't found any contact for her on his phone, and he hadn't been able to find her on any of the social media sites, which meant she'd probably blocked him. That didn't bode well for him getting the answers he wanted.

The best-case scenario in their current situation was that he'd make contact with Sarah, and she'd be married or in a serious relationship. He'd get the answers to his questions, and then hopefully be able to move on with his life.

And yet, he also didn't want her to be married.

Zane lifted his hands and dragged his fingers through his hair, then massaged his forehead. The tug of war between wanting to be with the woman he still loved and wanting to do the right thing as a Christian man was intense. It was a battle he'd never imagined having to fight.

Kayleigh shifted her chair over to sit right next to him. She hooked her hand through his arm and rested her head on his shoulder. "You were happy when you called to tell us you'd eloped with Kelsey. You were so excited about the future you were going to have together."

"But no one else was happy for us." He didn't remember that, but he'd been told about the family's reaction.

"We were confused," Kayleigh said. "When you and Sarah broke up, you were devastated. It was rough to see you in that state. You were so hurt, and you said that you were going to just focus on your career. No more relationships. You were adamant that it was going to be years before you dated again. Then I think it wasn't even a year, and you suddenly started dating Kelsey. You brought her home for Christmas, and then *boom*, six months later you tell us you'd gotten married. It was... perplexing, to be honest."

"I wish I could tell you why it happened that way, but I have no idea. Feeling how I do about Sarah, I can't believe I was able to move on like that. I think that's why I'm struggling with it myself," he confessed. "And I don't know what to do."

They sat quietly for a couple of minutes, with the sounds of the fire popping and murmured conversation filling the night air. Normally, he would have liked the atmosphere, but that wasn't possible when his personal life was such a mess.

"I think you need to talk to Kelsey about all of this."

"Nope." That was a hard no for Zane. "Can you imagine that conversation? Telling her I need to talk with the woman I love to get some closure? I'm not sure that would go over very well."

Kayleigh sighed. "Yeah, that might not be the best way to approach it."

"Definitely not."

"How about the two of you going to counseling?" she suggested. "It might be that you need some professional guidance through this."

That wasn't the worst idea, but Zane just wasn't sure he was ready to take that step. But if he wasn't, what was he waiting for? He just didn't know.

Yes, he was waiting to see if his memory returned, which would solve a lot of the issues he was facing. But how long did he wait before moving in a different direction?

And did he want to move in the direction of counseling and trying to force feelings for a woman he didn't know?

There was a small part of him that wished Kelsey would just give up on him and walk away. That was a cop-out, though. While that would be easier for him, he knew it wouldn't be easier for Kelsey.

"I wish we knew Kelsey better," Kayleigh said. "And I wish we had witnessed your relationship more."

"Why?" Zane asked.

"Because then we could share our perspective on what you had with her. Kelsey's emotions are so tied up in what's happening that it's hard for her to be able to talk about how things were between you without it hurting her more. If we could tell you what we saw between you two and what we knew of Kelsey, it might help encourage you to give her a chance."

What she said made sense, but there was no changing it now. For whatever reason, he and Kelsey hadn't shared their lives with his family. Whether that was by choice or because they lived away from Serenity, he didn't know. Maybe that was something he needed to ask Kelsey.

The idea of another conversation like that with Kelsey made him feel a little sick to his stomach. Because of his lingering feelings for Sarah, in some ways, his personal conversations with Kelsey felt a bit like he was cheating on her. Which was ridiculous.

The craziness of the situation made his head hurt, and his heart hurt even more.

He needed to talk to Sarah. It seemed that having her tell him that she had moved on and there was no hope for them would be the first step in moving forward himself.

Zane sighed deeply, and Kayleigh echoed him.

"We're all praying for you," Kayleigh said. "And I believe God will work things out for you if you truly trust Him and seek His will for you and Kelsey."

Kayleigh's words made him wonder again how he'd drifted away from the faith he'd once embraced.

So many questions. So few answers.

It had seemed that his life was following a fairly straightforward path with regards to his career and his romantic relationship. But something had happened in the past few years that had changed the direction of that path in all areas of his life.

Once again, his gaze drifted to where Kelsey sat with Rori and Carisa. She'd changed out of the pretty dress she'd been wearing earlier, into clothes that were more appropriate for sitting outside in the cooling night air.

Nothing was going to be accomplished that night. He wasn't in the right mood to pursue another conversation with her. Frankly, he wasn't ever really in the right mood, but he needed to put that mindset aside. But not that night.

Later, his head ached terribly as he prepared for bed, and Zane wanted to rail against everything. Absolutely everything. It felt a bit like a vicious cycle. The pain made him angry and on edge and being angry and on edge increased the pain.

Though he was exhausted, Zane made the effort to cover his cast completely, then took a long hot shower, hoping the water would help to ease the pain. Only, just like every other shower he'd taken, it didn't do anything except exhaust him.

Finally, he left the shower, dried off, and got dressed in a pair of sleep shorts and a T-shirt. Slumping down on the edge of his bed, with only the bedside lamp lighting the room, Zane concentrated on calming himself, trying to quiet his emotions before climbing under the covers.

Please, God, help me.

He didn't even know what help he wanted. If he was honest with himself, he was a little worried about what he'd discover if his memories returned.

Rather than continue his prayer, Zane settled onto the bed and dragged the comforter over him. He reached out to turn off the light, plunging the room into darkness.

Finally, he felt his body relax.

There was no one watching him. No one judging him for his reactions. No one trying to sort out the mess his life was currently in.

And thanks to the darkness, even *he* wasn't able to see himself. Which was what he needed in order to fall asleep.

Oblivion, sweet oblivion.

It ended up being a limited time oblivion, which was pretty much the norm these days. Zane woke several times in the night, so when his alarm went off in the morning, he was still tired. But he couldn't linger in bed that morning, so he dragged himself out from under the covers and stumbled into the bathroom.

After washing his face and brushing his hair into some semblance of order, Zane pulled on a pair of shorts. He chose one of his nicer T-shirts since he was going to be seeing non-family members that day.

When he walked into the kitchen a short time later, Kelsey was already there, sitting at the breakfast nook with a cup of coffee on the table in front of her. Her hands were cupped around it as she stared out the window beside her.

He wasn't silent in his movements thanks to the crutches, so as soon as he walked into the kitchen, she looked in his direction.

"Good morning," she said, then let go of her mug and got to her feet. "Want some breakfast and coffee?"

He hated having to be dependent on others. But since it was a challenge to do stuff for himself while on crutches, he had no choice. "A bagel and coffee would be nice. Please."

Kelsey made quick work of toasting a bagel and slathering cream cheese on it, then she filled a large mug with coffee, doctored it, before carrying both to the breakfast nook. He'd taken the seat across from her, so she put the mug and plate down in front of him.

"Thank you," he said. "I appreciate you making this for me."

"You're welcome." She sat back down and wrapped her hands around her mug again. "You've made enough meals for me, so it's only fair I make some for you when I have the opportunity."

"Are you still up to driving me to my scan and appointment this morning?"

She'd offered to drive him to his appointments once he'd moved to the house. Before that, his parents had been taking him. He'd thought they'd still want to do that, but he decided that maybe it would be better if he and Kelsey went on their own this time.

"Yep. I'd planned on it."

He had to go to Coeur d'Alene for his appointments with the specialist and to get any scans that he needed done. It was a bit of a pain he couldn't just have Gareth take care of his medical needs.

"I guess we'll need to leave in about forty-five minutes."

Kelsey nodded as she lifted her mug and took a sip of her coffee. "Will they have the results from your scan right away?"

"I'm not sure. But probably not," Zane said. "I'll still see the doctor today, though, He'll probably just get in contact with me if there are concerns from the scan."

"How have the headaches been?"

Zane was honest with her about how he was feeling physically. His mental and emotional state, however, he kept to himself.

As an awkward silence filled the space between them, Zane couldn't help but remember how easy communication with Sarah had been. He knew it wasn't fair to compare the two situations—especially when he didn't remember how things had been between him and Kelsey previously—but it was still hard not to.

After they'd finished eating, he went back upstairs to get the file of information he'd compiled so far, while Kelsey cleaned up their breakfast, then they met back in the front hall.

Once they were in the car, Zane braced himself for a long, silent car ride. He knew he should make more of an effort to carry the conversation, but he didn't know what topic to pick.

That morning, especially, he felt drained and exhausted by everything going on in his life. It didn't seem to be getting any better. Well, his mental state wasn't, anyway. His leg seemed to be improving as it should, but he didn't feel the same could be said for his head.

As they drove, Kelsey asked him questions about growing up in Serenity. It was a safe enough topic of conversation, and it helped pass the time. From the questions Kelsey had, it seemed that he hadn't shared much about his growing-up years. Did he know about hers?

"Where did you grow up?" he asked when there was about fifteen minutes left in the drive.

She glanced at him, then said, "Everywhere. My dad was military, but we ended up in Chicago when he retired."

"Oh, really?" For some reason, he'd assumed she'd had a childhood similar to his. "Did I know your family well?"

"No." For a moment, he didn't think she was going to expand on that. "Since we're estranged, you never met them."

"I'm sorry to hear that. Do you have siblings?"

"Yes. Two sisters."

"Are your parents still together?"

"As far as I know, they are," she said. "Unfortunately."

"Unfortunately?"

"They're not great people, and they seem to bring out the worst in each other."

Zane wondered if that worst had been turned on Kelsey and her sisters. Though he wanted to know, he didn't ask the question. That felt like probing a bit further than he was comfortable doing. And he suspected it was beyond what she would want to share.

"If you looked up dysfunctional in the dictionary, you'd see a picture of my family."

Zane wasn't sure how to respond to that. Had he known all this when they'd gotten married?

His life with the Halversons had been idyllic compared to some people's. However, his birth family must have had issues, or he wouldn't have ended up in foster care and then been adopted. He felt bad that Kelsey hadn't had the chance to have a good family like he had.

"Where do you fall in line with your sisters?"

"I'm the youngest."

"And you're not in contact with them either?" Though he'd had issues with his siblings at times, he couldn't imagine not having them in his life.

"No. As soon as they each turned eighteen, they left and never looked back."

As they neared Coeur d'Alene, their conversation shifted to finding the place where Zane was scheduled to have his scan. Once they arrived, Kelsey let him out at the door, then went to park. By the time she joined him inside, Zane had checked in with the receptionist and found a couple of seats for them.

Since he'd had several scans already, he wasn't nervous about it. It was a hassle, more than anything. But a necessary hassle. He just hoped that it didn't show that anything was getting worse, though perhaps it might give him some idea of why he still had frequent headaches.

When they called his name, he turned to Kelsey and said, "See you in a bit."

"I'll be here." The smile she gave him was brief, but it stayed with him as he followed the person down the hallway to the room where he was to be scanned.

The scan took longer than he'd thought it would, and when he rejoined Kelsey in the waiting room, she was reading something on her phone. They left the building together and got back in her car. The neurologist's office wasn't too far away, so they made it there in time for his appointment.

They found seats together in the waiting room, and Zane leaned back in his chair, resting his head against the wall. He closed his eyes, trying to block out the world, since his head was aching. Again. Still.

He thought Kelsey might try to talk to him, but she remained silent. He did feel her shift at one point, her arm pressing more firmly against his.

Turning his head, he cracked an eye to see what was going on. He spotted a man sitting in the chair right next to Kelsey, even though there were other seats he could have chosen that had empty spaces on either side. The man smiled at Kelsey, and she shifted even closer to Zane.

Ignoring the pain in his head, Zane leaned forward, sliding his arm around the back of Kelsey's chair, and stared at the man. "Can we help you?"

The man looked from Zane to where the back of his hand now pressed against the man's shoulder. "Just wanted to say hi."

"To my wife?" It was the first time he'd said the words, at least that he remembered, but it felt like a good time for it. "Does she know you?"

"Not yet."

"Not ever," Kelsey said. "You're coming on a bit strong, especially since I'm a married woman."

Before the man could say anything, Zane's name was called. Though he'd planned to just go in by himself, he wasn't going to leave Kelsey to deal with that guy. He seemed a little weird and perhaps unpredictable.

"That's us," Zane said as he reached for his crutches. Once he was on his feet, he looked at Kelsey and nodded toward the person who had called his name.

He could see hesitation on her face, but she got to her feet and walked with him to where the woman waited for them.

Once they were in the small office, the woman said, "The doctor will be with you shortly."

There were two chairs in the office, and Kelsey settled in the one furthest from the small desk. She moved her chair over a bit, giving Zane space for his cast and crutches.

"That was weird," Zane said when it was just the two of them. "That guy."

Kelsey shifted in her chair, then crossed her legs, wrapping her arms across her waist. "Thanks for deflecting him."

"Of course." Zane rubbed the heel of his hand against the thigh of his broken leg, trying to ease the achy tightness there that sometimes cropped up occasionally. "I've never understood why guys think it's okay to act that way around women."

"He's not the first, and probably won't be the last." Kelsey's foot tapped the air. "At least I won't make the mistake of dating him."

"Have you done that before?"

Her foot tapped the air more rapidly. "Yes. I have."

"It wasn't me, I hope."

Her foot paused, and she glanced at him. "No. Of course not."

"Whew. I didn't think I'd act that way, but since I can't remember the past few years, who knows?"

"*You* know," Kelsey said. "You aren't *that* different from the person I fell in... the person I married."

"I'm glad to hear that."

There was a light knock on the office door, then it swung open to reveal a middle-aged man with a fringe of white hair circling his head and a warm smile.

"Zane," he said as he held out his hand. "Good to see you again."

"You as well," Zane said as he shook his hand.

"And this is?" the doctor asked, turning to Kelsey with an extended hand.

Silence filled the air for a moment before Zane said, "This is Kelsey. My wife."

"Nice to meet you, Kelsey." They shook hands, then the doctor took his seat at the small desk. "I'm glad you've joined us today."

For the next little while, the doctor asked him questions about how he was feeling. Zane answered them all, and then asked a few of his own.

He was a bit surprised when the doctor turned his attention to Kelsey. When he asked her something, Kelsey turned to Zane, as if asking his permission to become an active participant in the conversation.

Though he wasn't completely sure about it, Zane gave a nod.

Zane hadn't mentioned that he didn't remember his wife during the previous appointment he'd had with the man, so the doctor was surprised when that fact came up.

"You didn't know him four years ago," the doctor clarified.

"No. So he has no memory of me, even from before we got married."

The doctor's brow furrowed. "How are the two of you handling that?"

Not well.

Zane didn't say that, however. He glanced at Kelsey to see her head bent.

"It's not been easy," Zane admitted. "We're just taking it one day at a time."

"And if you never get your memory back?"

Zane cleared his throat. "We haven't figured that out quite yet."

The doctor's gaze bounced between the two of them. "You were strangers once and fell in love. There's no reason it can't happen again if you are open to it."

There was a big reason, but Zane wasn't going to bring it up. He hadn't had a direct conversation with Kelsey about Sarah and his feelings for her. But he was sure she'd figured it out, thanks to conversations about it that had been held in her presence.

The doctor seemed to realize it wasn't a subject they were comfortable with and moved on to sharing with Kelsey the things she should look out for when she was dealing with Zane. It was similar to what he'd told Zane and his folks at his initial appointment.

"Once we've had a chance to review the scan from today, I'll give you a call to let you know the results."

After making another follow-up appointment at the front desk, they left the building and went back to the car. It was a quiet ride home, and Zane spent a lot of it with his eyes closed, head propped against the window.

He wished he could sleep, but his thoughts were too caught up in the situation with his feelings for Sarah and his marriage to Kelsey.

Please, God, give me back my memories.

CHAPTER FOURTEEN

"Come hang with us," Rori said as Kelsey stepped into the kitchen when she returned from studying in the library. She'd desperately needed a change of scenery. "We're just eating, watching TV and playing games."

Kelsey needed the distraction, but she wasn't sure she wanted to hang out with Zane. She was so discouraged with life, and it made her just want to retreat from everyone and everything.

She *needed* a job, and yet, she hadn't managed to find one. She'd applied to all the restaurants in town, to no avail. Now she'd moved on to applying at places where she probably didn't have the necessary experience.

Her savings were rapidly depleting, even though she tried to be careful with how she spent her money. She was just lucky that Rori and Lee weren't charging her rent. If she'd had to pay for a place to stay, she would have been homeless at this point.

"Wilder and Lexi are bringing some East Indian food for all of us."

"Who else is coming?" Kelsey asked, though it wouldn't determine whether she hung out with them or not.

"Wilder and Lexi, Carisa and Jackson, and Janessa and Will."

"Okay. I'll join you."

"That's great!" Rori said with a broad smile. "We'll probably eat in about half an hour."

"I'm just going to run up to my room."

She climbed the stairs, then headed for her room. They'd spent the earlier part of day doing yard work, and she hadn't showered before heading to the library. She took a quick shower and washed her hair, then got dressed in a pair of soft cotton shorts and a T-shirt. If they were going to be lounging around, she wanted to be comfortable.

By the time she got back downstairs, the food had arrived, along with the rest of the people Rori had named. They were busy setting different dishes of food on the counter, and it all smelled delicious.

Indian food was something that she and Zane had eaten fairly regularly when he was too tired to cook a meal for them. Her favorite was butter chicken, along with rice and naan bread. She hoped that they'd ordered plenty of everything.

"Hi, Kels," Carisa said as she headed toward her. After giving Kelsey a tight hug, she pulled her toward the others. "Come get some food."

Once they were gathered around the island counter, Lee prayed for the meal. when he said *amen*, Rori handed out plates. Kelsey glanced at Zane, then took two.

Over the past few days, they'd had a couple of brief conversations about the state of things between them. The doctor had been right that they could fall in love again... if only Zane wasn't in love with someone else.

Still, she'd been helping Zane when she could. It was a way to soothe her need to be with him and to take care of him. She wanted it to be a reminder for Zane of the relationship that existed between them.

Without even thinking, after she'd taken what she wanted, she began to fill Zane's plate with the stuff he always ordered when they had that type of food.

She happened to glance at Zane and found him watching her with a lifted brow. "We had Indian food fairly regularly. This is what you always wanted. Has that changed?"

Zane shook his head. "Nope. That's what I like."

Kelsey quickly finished loading his plate, then carried both down to the basement. Soon, the others joined them. Wilder and

Janessa were having an argument, apparently disagreeing on the best version of a show that had several different options.

"You're crazy," Janessa said. "He wasn't the best lead of the three series."

"What are you talking about?" Lee asked.

Wilder named two TV shows that were connected. "We don't agree on which cast was the best."

"You siblings find the weirdest things to argue over," Jackson said as he settled on one of the loveseats with Carisa.

"Wasn't one of those the show that Sarah was an extra in?" Lee asked.

"Yeah." Zane cleared his throat. "She had a small role in one episode of the medical one."

Kelsey's stomach clenched, and any desire to eat fled. She recalled that when they'd been trying to find a show to stream, he had quickly squashed her suggestion to watch that show, saying he wasn't interested in medical drama. Now, though, she was thinking that he probably hadn't wanted to watch it with her because he would have seen his ex.

He could have just told her why he didn't want to watch it. But the problem was, he'd never told her about Sarah. They'd briefly touched on previous relationships, but they'd both said that they hadn't had any super serious ones. Zane had lied. She knew that now, and it was hard to be reminded of that fact.

Stubbornly, she clung to the belief that, despite concealing his previous relationship with Sarah, he truly had loved her. But there were moments when it was really hard to keep that belief alive.

Rather than react to the comments about Sarah, Kelsey put a forkful of food into her mouth. She was glad that she'd always been able to hide her emotions, thanks to her parents.

The irony was that being more open about her emotions was something she'd been working on with Zane. Now she was having to regress in order to protect herself from him.

"Well, we're not watching a TV show tonight," Rori announced. "Let's discuss what movie we should watch."

Kelsey suspected that Rori was saying that as a way to change the subject, and she appreciated it more than words could say.

Everyone seemed to be making the assumption that Kelsey was aware of Zane's previous relationship with Sarah, and she'd never corrected them. She didn't want them to know that perhaps her relationship with Zane hadn't been quite as strong or as transparent as she'd thought it was.

As the discussion went on around her, Kelsey ate her food, though it was the last thing she wanted to do.

The only ones there with a kid were Will and Janessa, and they said that since they'd probably have to leave the soonest, they'd rather play games. In the end, they decided to leave the movie for later and play some games first, once they were done eating.

When they'd finished eating, she helped Rori gather up the dirty plates. Zane had fallen quiet after the conversation about the TV show, and he remained slumped in the corner of the couch. She wouldn't be surprised if he decided to bail on the whole evening.

It's what she wanted to do.

But Zane didn't bail, so neither did Kelsey.

Instead, she helped Rori and Lee carry down cups of coffee and some cookies. While they'd been upstairs, someone had set up an easel with a big white flip chart on it.

"Oh no," Lee groused. "They've decided on Pictionary. I'm doomed."

"You can't draw?" Kelsey asked.

"Not very well."

They ended up dividing into couples, which, to Kelsey's mind, put her and Zane at a disadvantage. Neither of them seemed to have much enthusiasm, and they didn't have the connection they once had that would have allowed them to communicate as easily as the other couples could.

Will and Janessa were up first. Will tossed out guesses as Janessa drew, and their son jumped between them, yelling out whatever Will said. It was actually kind of funny to watch the couple and their son. Kelsey thought that Will was intentionally making bad guesses in order to wind his wife up. And when Timmy would reinforce that bad guess at the top of his lungs, Janessa's frustration with her husband would double.

Just before their time ran out, Will made the right guess, resulting in Janessa giving him a fierce look. "You did that on purpose."

"I got it right," Will said with a shrug.

"The goal is to get as many as possible in our allotted time." Janessa plopped down on the floor. "That's how we always play it."

"Next time," Will promised.

Timothy climbed onto Janessa's lap and patted her cheek. "Next time, Mama."

Janessa sighed. "Promise, baby?"

"Promise." Everyone laughed as both Will and Timmy responded to Janessa.

Will leaned forward to grab a couple of cookies from the plate on the coffee table and gave them to Janessa and Timmy.

"We're next," Carisa said, popping up from the couch with surprising ease, then turning to offer Jackson her hand. He grinned as he took her hand, but instead of letting her pull him up, Jackson tugged her into his lap. Carisa let out a laugh. "Babe, come on. I want to win."

"Alright." Jackson set Carisa up on her feet, then got off the loveseat himself. Rubbing his hands together, he said, "Let's show them how it's done."

As Kelsey expected, the pair's turn was hilarious. Jackson apparently didn't share his wife's desire to win, because his guesses as she drew were as crazy as Will's. Even so, they didn't do as badly as Will and Janessa had and ended their turn with three correct guesses. And Carisa wasn't anywhere near as upset with Jackson as Janessa had been with Will.

When they were done, Lexi and Wilder took a turn. Wilder was drawing, and Lexi did a much better job of guessing, which meant they were ahead with four correct guesses.

Rori and Lee took the lead after their turn, with Lee getting six correct.

"Kels and Zane, it's your turn now," Rori announced.

Zane groaned. "I've never liked this game."

Kelsey wasn't surprised that Zane wasn't keen to play. His mood throughout the week had swung between subdued and testy. He hadn't been happy, so it stood to reason he wasn't excited to play the game the way his siblings were.

"I'm actually happy to just observe," Kelsey said, no more eager than Zane to have to participate.

Rori frowned at them. "I guess you can sit this out."

"Thank you," Kelsey said, relaxing back into the cushions of the couch.

Thankfully, her and Zane's refusal to take part didn't put a damper on the evening. It appeared that the siblings were well used to keeping the party going, even if one of them wasn't in the party mood.

Would she and Zane have been active participants if they lived closer? Or would the family's opinion of her have kept them from being invited?

Since no one had been outright hateful to her—and Zane's parents had actually tried to speak with her—Kelsey was beginning to wonder about the whole estrangement. Was it possible that Zane was the one who hadn't wanted them to be around her?

Already, his siblings had let things slip about Sarah, and they had clearly thought that Zane would marry her. Since he hadn't told her about Sarah, he might have been worried they would spill the beans.

That revelation left her in an emotional downward spiral. Even if Zane had loved her before the accident, it clearly hadn't been as much as he loved Sarah.

Even though she'd decided to stick it out with Zane, the idea of leaving was getting more and more appealing. But she had to know she'd given it her all.

The next morning, Kelsey contemplated skipping church. It was a struggle to be around people when she felt the way she did. She didn't even want to be around Zane.

But still, she crawled out of bed and got ready to go. Zane was waiting in the front hall when she got down there.

"Good morning," she said.

"I wasn't sure you were going to go this morning," Zane said after greeting her.

"I wasn't sure either." She glanced at him. "I wasn't sure you would be going either."

Zane shrugged as he leaned forward on his crutches. "Habit, I guess."

It certainly hadn't been his habit prior to the accident. But she had come to realize that at some point early on in his adult life, his faith had been hugely important to him.

"What's your reason for going?" Zane asked.

"I don't know, to be honest. I don't really have anywhere else to be, I guess."

She had slept in and had no time for breakfast or coffee, so she hoped that her stomach didn't start growling during the service.

"Do you want to go in my car?" she asked. "Or wait to go with Rori and Lee?"

"We can go in your car," he said. "And then we can leave more quickly after the service is done."

"Sounds like a plan." She pulled her keys from her purse. "Off we go."

"I'll text Lee once we're in the car to let them know."

Together, they left the house and climbed into her car.

A couple of minutes into the drive, Zane said, "Lee texted back that they wouldn't take it personally."

Kelsey chuckled. "If they weren't running late, we would have been at church already."

Once they got to the church, Kelsey let Zane off at the front doors, then went to park the car. When she returned, she found him still waiting outside the doors for her.

"Don't assume anything," she murmured to herself before she came into earshot.

As she approached him, he turned, and together they made their way up to the doors. Kelsey opened one of them and waited for Zane to go into the foyer before following him.

They greeted a few people as they made their way across the foyer to the sanctuary. Zane paused at the back of the sanctuary, and Kelsey thought perhaps they'd take seats in one of the rear rows. Instead, he led her to an outside aisle, then to a row midway down where Carisa and Jackson were seated.

Kelsey scooted into the row to sit beside Carisa, while Zane followed her.

"Good morning!" Carisa greeted them with a big smile. "How are you today?"

"I'm fine." And technically, she was. As long as she didn't think about the mess her life was currently in. "How're you?"

They talked for a few minutes, then Lee and Rori joined them, sliding into the row beside Zane just as the worship team began to play.

Kelsey was getting used to the format of the service now, and even some of the songs were becoming familiar. She enjoyed listening to Will's dad's sermons. What he said made a lot of sense and wasn't confusing to her, even though she didn't have a background in religious messages.

"My sermon this morning is inspired by personal events," Pastor Kennedy said after he'd greeted them from his place behind the podium. "Today is my thirty-fifth anniversary with my lovely, beautiful, amazing wife, Alice. This whole week, I've thought a lot about the past thirty-five years and the ups and downs we have experienced. This morning, I want to share what I've learned about relationships during that time. The romantic one I have with Alice, as well as the ones I have with my children, my family, fellow Christians, and other people in the world."

Kelsey wondered if she and Zane would be together in thirty-five years. Prior to the accident, she would have said yes, they'd make it. Now, however, she wasn't even sure they'd make it to their first anniversary.

"The one thing I have found is that love must be the foundation of the interactions we have," Pastor Kennedy said. "There are many types of love, but when we look at the Bible's definition of love, it can be applied to all of them."

Words appeared on the screen at the front of the sanctuary. Kelsey read through them, feeling the words challenge her heart.

Love is patient.
Love is kind.
Love doesn't envy.
Love doesn't boast.
Love is not proud.
Love is not rude.
Love is not selfish.
Love is not easily angered.
Love keeps no record of wrongs.
Love doesn't rejoice in evil.
Love rejoices in the truth.
Love bears all things,

believes all things,
hopes all things,
endures all things.
LOVE NEVER FAILS.

The words, every single one of them, pressed against the wall she'd placed around her love for Zane. Especially the last two lines. *Love endures all things,* and *love never fails.*

In contemplating walking away from Zane, she wasn't enduring all things. A terrible thing had happened—there was no denying that—and it would demand a lot of her to stay, but it seemed that was what God wanted.

But did she care what God wanted?

Never before had she thought about whether the decisions she made were what God would want her to make. She'd made her choices based on what worked best for her in fulfilling the plans she had for her life.

Was she willing to now give God more significance in her life?

As the pastor spoke, he shared personal experiences he'd had with love and even confessing to the areas where he'd failed. Like being as patient as he should have been.

"The love talked about in first Corinthians can seem too extreme. Too impossible a standard to achieve, but if we allow God to love through us, it becomes possible."

The whole concept was foreign to her. The idea of trusting God to help her love better.

"God set an example for us when He sent His Son to die for our sins. He did that out of His love for us. If He's willing to do that, why wouldn't He want us to succeed in loving others the way He has loved them?"

Kelsey glanced over at Zane, thinking she might find him dozing off. But rather, Zane was focused on the pastor, his expression serious as he seemed to be paying attention to what the man was saying.

She wished she could read his mind, but there was no chance of that. Given what she'd learned over the past few weeks, she was beginning to wish that she could have read Zane's mind pre-accident so that she could have known what he thought about Sarah and how he really felt about her.

It was hard not feeling like she was his second choice. That if he had the opportunity, he'd rather be with Sarah. From what she'd picked up from things his family had said, Sarah had been the one to end the relationship, and she'd left Zane heartbroken.

Could she love Zane the way the Bible said she should, even knowing all of that?

The question lingered in her mind even after the service had ended.

"Ready to head out?" she asked Zane once the service was over. "Or did you want to hang around and catch a ride with Lee and Rori?"

"Nope. I'd rather go with you."

With that plan in place, they made their way out of the sanctuary, following behind Lee, Rori, Jackson, and Carisa. As it turned out, Lee and Rori were ready to leave right away, too. People were coming by the house for a barbecue, so they needed to get home to prepare for that.

As usual, her first instinct was to opt out of it. However, Kelsey knew she couldn't. So when they got to the house, she immediately jumped in to help Rori and Lee prepare for the meal.

"Are you sticking around this time?" Rori asked as she handed Kelsey a stack of paper plates to put on a large tray.

"Yes."

"Good." Rori set a plastic bag with napkins in it on the tray. "I think people are warming up to you."

Lee and Zane had gone out onto the deck to start up the barbecue, so while it was just her and Rori in the kitchen, Kelsey said, "Do you think Zane needs to see Sarah?"

Rori's eyebrows rose, and she faced Kelsey over the expanse of the island counter. "What do you think that would accomplish?"

"Closure for him?" Kelsey paused. "Maybe?"

"I suppose you could suggest it to him. It could be he's thought the same thing, but hasn't been sure how to bring it up."

"Actually, I think it might be better if Lee suggested it to him."

"But he may need to hear it from you."

Kelsey sighed. "I'm not sure I'm capable of encouraging him to contact a woman he's had a serious relationship with."

"I understand that," Rori said. "But I really do think Zane needs to hear this suggestion from you."

"What do I need to hear from Kelsey?"

Kelsey turned toward the back door, realizing that they'd been so focused on their conversation that they hadn't heard Zane come in. She'd just assumed that he'd stay outside since, because of his crutches, there wasn't much he could do inside.

"Perhaps you should have a conversation," Rori said. "Just the two of you."

"Now?" Zane asked, his brow furrowed.

"After lunch," Kelsey said, needing time to prepare herself for this particular conversation.

"Am I going to like this conversation?"

Kelsey shrugged. "I don't know."

Zane stared hard at Kelsey, looking like he was going to press her for more information. But before he could say anything else, Janessa and Will arrived with their son.

"Later," Zane said, then turned to greet his sister.

A mass of nerves took up residence in Kelsey's stomach, but she tried to ignore it as she pitched in to help get the meal ready.

That day, for the first time, Zane's siblings all took a few minutes to speak with her. It was encouraging. Maybe they were warming up to her and becoming more accepting of her in Zane's life.

It might all be for nothing though, if Zane didn't get his memory back, and he decided he didn't want to continue their marriage.

CHAPTER FIFTEEN

Zane shifted in his seat, trying to keep his attention on the conversation Jay and Will were having about the upcoming basketball season at the high school. Though their youngest brother, Cole, hadn't been in high school for several years, and, in fact, was now playing professionally, Jay continued to coach the high school team.

His son, Peyton, was getting ready to start high school and, from the sound of things, he was going to be trying out for the basketball team. Zane had no idea if he'd still be around to go to any of the games, but he suspected he might be.

He looked toward where Kelsey was sitting, wondering again what she wanted to talk about. Was she going to tell him that she wanted to end their marriage and leave Serenity?

The idea left him a little unsettled. But would it leave him so unsettled that he'd ask her not to go? He didn't know.

He just wanted to have the conversation, so he knew what was going on. There was already too much uncertainty in his life.

It seemed to take forever for everyone to eat and leave. As much as he loved his siblings, he was relieved to see them go. Kelsey helped Rori clean up the kitchen, making Zane feel like as eager as he was to have the conversation, she was the opposite.

"Why don't you go on?" Rori said. "We're pretty much done here."

"Are you sure?" Kelsey asked as she hung up the dish towel she'd been using.

"Positive." Rori came and gave her a hug. "We'll be praying for you."

"Thanks."

"Want to chat upstairs?" Zane asked. He didn't want to be interrupted, even though there was no one but Rori and Lee in the house. Still, his family could be unpredictable, and it was possible someone would pop back in for one reason or another.

"Sure."

Together, they made their way up the stairs to the sitting area on the landing. There was overstuffed furniture in front of the fireplace, which hadn't been used while he'd been there.

And they wouldn't be using it right then, either. Cooler days were ahead, but it wasn't fireplace and sweater weather just yet.

Zane sat down on the couch while Kelsey chose one of the armchairs. She didn't relax back into it, however. She sat with a ramrod straight spine, her hands tightly clasped in her lap.

As he waited for her to speak, he saw her twist her wedding ring. Was she going to ask him for a divorce?

When she looked up, he could see turmoil on her face. "I think you should contact Sarah."

Of all the things she could have said, that hadn't even crossed his mind. In fact, her words rendered him momentarily speechless. He just sat and stared at her, dumbfounded and uncertain of how to respond.

"I don't think we can move forward without you having some type of closure with her," Kelsey said when he remained silent.

"Closure?" His first reaction was that he didn't want closure, but that wasn't a good response. It wasn't the right one, given that he was married to Kelsey.

"Or not," she said, her voice soft. "If things have changed for her, maybe you'd rather try to work things out." She sighed. "I just need to know."

Clearly, the unknown was weighing on her, too. "I don't know what to say..."

"I've given it some thought, and if your memory never returns, we don't have a hope if you can't or don't want to move on from Sarah... with me." Her gaze dropped to her hands, and she fiddled with her wedding ring. "Of course I don't know for sure that contact with her will help, but it feels like it can't hurt the situation. It'll hurt me if you decide to go back to her, but at least I'll know and can move forward in my life without you."

Zane frowned. For some reason, that didn't sit well with him.

The wary expression on Kelsey's face, her shoulders hunching forward, the way she twisted the rings on her finger—the rings he'd given her—all of it showed how difficult this suggestion was for her.

Could he do it? Was contacting Sarah the right decision? Ever since Kayleigh had suggested it, the thought had lingered more strongly in his mind. And now, here was Kelsey suggesting it.

There was definitely a part of him that longed to see Sarah again. But if she'd moved on with her life, did he want to have her reject him again?

"I think this is the only thing we can do now," Kelsey said. "Whether or not I like it, I don't think you'll be able to move forward without having a conversation with her."

The unfortunate circumstances they'd found themselves in were rare enough that there was no road map or guideline for how to move forward. No matter which direction they took, it seemed pain was inevitable for one or the other of them. Maybe even both.

Zane sat forward, resting his elbows on his knees. This felt like a monumental decision that he wasn't sure he was capable of making. And he was strangely reluctant to do anything to hurt Kelsey. At least more than he already had.

But this might be what was needed to move them forward.

Part of him understood that he shouldn't need to see Sarah to gain closure. He should be strong enough to accept—even without remembering—that they had broken up, and he, and presumably Sarah, had moved on.

But a larger part of him needed to understand what had happened. What had driven them apart when they'd talked about getting married one day? What had changed his commitment to his faith? What had seemed to switch in his outlook for his career?

"Please do it," Kelsey urged, her gaze holding his steadily. "I feel like there's no hope otherwise. Especially if you don't regain your memory."

For the most part, Zane tried not to dwell on the fact that his memory was still missing. But it was aggravating, especially considering he knew not all brain injuries resulted in memory loss. Why had his?

"I'm sorry," Zane said. "I'm sorry that I'm not the man you married. That I'm not the man you knew."

Kelsey grimaced, then sighed. "Honestly, I'm not sure I knew you all that well."

"What do you mean?"

After a brief hesitation, she said, "Even though we had a few conversations about previous relationships, you never told me about Sarah."

That surprised Zane. "Really? I never said *anything* about her?"

Kelsey shook her head. "The first time I heard her name was in your hospital room when you asked where she was."

Zane wished he could tell Kelsey why he'd kept that to himself, but he didn't know. "I'm sorry. I don't know why I didn't tell you."

"I was thinking I should just leave," Kelsey said. "And let you get on with your life."

"No," he said quickly, surprising himself with his protest. "That's not fair to you."

Kelsey slumped back in her seat, like the fight had just gone out of her. "None of this is fair to either of us."

Zane couldn't argue with her there. "I'm still sorry for how this has impacted you."

"I miss you..." The words were spoken softly, and she didn't look at him as she said them.

He had no idea how to respond to that. Saying that he missed her too would be a lie, and they'd both know it. Still, he was tempted to say the words, just to ease her pain.

The silence between them was heavy, weighed down by the memories and experiences they no longer shared.

"If you're sure about me contacting Sarah, I'll do it."

Kelsey looked up at him, her beautiful eyes sad. "I'm sure."

He wasn't totally convinced he bought that, but he wasn't going to argue with her. He wanted answers only Sarah could give him.

Pushing up from her seat, Kelsey got to her feet. "I'm going to my room."

Zane maneuvered himself up off the couch and braced himself on the crutches. "Thank you for the talk."

Kelsey nodded, but didn't smile or say anything more before she turned and headed for the door to her room. Even after she'd disappeared inside her room, Zane stayed where he was, staring at her closed door.

He needed to talk this over with someone. Pulling his phone out of his pocket, he sent a text off to Lee.

Do you have a few minutes to talk?

His reply came back without delay.

Lee: *Sure thing. Are you upstairs?*

Yes.

Lee: *brt*

As he waited for his brother, Zane stared blankly at the empty fireplace, thoughts tumbling through his mind.

When Lee joined Zane on the landing, he sat down in the chair that Kelsey had vacated.

"So what are you going to do?" Lee asked as he relaxed back, stretching his legs out in front of him.

"Did Rori tell you what Kelsey wanted?"

"She did."

"What do you think?"

Lee didn't say anything right away, which told Zane he probably wasn't going to like what he had to say.

Finally, Lee took a deep breath and said, "I think it's too bad that Kelsey has gotten to the point where she feels that this is the best option."

"What do you mean?"

"Do you think that any woman wants the man she loves—and is *married* to—to make contact with a woman he once loved, still loves, in your case, and was planning a future with? She knows there's a high risk that this is going to hurt her. And still, she's doing it."

"I haven't decided what I'm going to do yet."

"Don't lie to yourself," Lee said. "Even if you're going to lie to me."

Zane glared at Lee. "I'm not lying."

"You are. You called me up here hoping I would validate your decision to contact Sarah."

Sometimes Zane hated how well his siblings knew him. Especially Lee. Though his brother was always fairly level-headed, he could also be blunt with his observations.

"So what would you say I should do?"

"Let Sarah go. Accept that she ended things between you for a reason that was valid to her, and move on. You have a wife who needs you."

"I don't remember her at all."

"Then date her and ask God to give you love for her."

Kayleigh had said something similar, leaving Zane to wonder if his siblings had been having conversations about his situation. He mentally scoffed. Of course they were. Was the pastor in on it too? Because his sermon lined up with what Lee was saying.

"I think if I'm able to talk to Sarah, it will make doing that easier."

"Like I said. You've already made up your mind." Lee regarded him for a long moment. "I'll be praying that you're not headed down a road that will leave you with nothing."

"Nothing?"

"If you don't get the closure you want from Sarah and can't move forward, you're going to lose Kelsey. Or if you discover Sarah is single and decide you want to try with her again, you'll also lose Kelsey."

"But I'll gain Sarah."

"Without God's blessing."

Zane winced at that. But had it even been God's will for him to be with Kelsey? After all, Kelsey wasn't a Christian, and it seemed he hadn't been living a Christian life either.

"I know the family wasn't too keen on how things unfolded with Kelsey and you, and how quickly you got married," Lee said. "But I think most of us have come to realize that she's really a sweet woman. Rori adores her, and so does Carisa."

Zane had seen that too, but it was a more abstract observation for him. Which he knew wasn't a good thing.

The hardest part was that while his family had been his anchor for a long time, Sarah had also been an anchor for him. She'd been a huge part of his life. His anchor. His cheerleader. His companion. The love of his life.

"Are you willing to consider another option?" Lee's question interrupted his thoughts.

"Maybe? Depends on the option."

"Let me contact Sarah and have a conversation with her. See where she's at and tell her what's happened."

"Why would that be better?"

"I think it would be better for her *and* you," Lee said. "It would give me a chance to gauge how best to approach the situation for you and Kelsey."

Zane's first reaction to that was to say no. *He* wanted to be the one to speak to Sarah, but he knew that Lee's suggestion was probably better for everyone. And since he was being selfish enough as it was, wanting to contact Sarah, he should probably be considerate where he could be.

"She was a friend of mine too," Lee reminded him. "So me contacting her wouldn't be like a stranger was calling her up out of the blue."

Perhaps it was the best compromise. However, it would require him to trust Lee to actually want to help him gain some sort of closure, and it was clear that he wasn't keen for Zane to reconnect with Sarah.

"Will you be honest with me about what she says?"

"Of course," Lee said. "I'll be honest with her *and* with you."

"Okay. Then I guess I'll let you do it," Zane said. "But don't put it off."

"I won't."

Zane wanted to believe him. But knowing how his brother really felt about the situation, he wasn't sure they'd agree on the best way for Lee to handle contacting Sarah. But it was out of his hands now.

"Have you tracked down any information on her yet?" Lee asked.

"I don't have any contact info for her on my phone, and I couldn't find her social media, so maybe she's blocked me." Which was probably for the best. He hadn't wanted to see pictures that would indicate she'd moved on with her life.

"Okay. I'll see what I can find."

"You'll let me know right away?"

Lee gave him a long look, then nodded. Slapping his hands on his thighs, he pushed up to stand. "I'll talk to you later."

Alone again, Zane stayed on the couch, mulling over everything. Imagining all the different ways the situation with Sarah could unfold. The jumble of thoughts made his head ache, so he got up and crutched his way to his room.

Though he wanted to go to wherever Lee was, Zane instead went to his bed and laid down. He covered his eyes with his arm, trying to calm his thoughts.

Trust in the Lord with all your heart and lean not on your own understanding.

The verse flitted through his thoughts. He'd memorized it as a child, and he'd heard many sermons about the verse, where pastors had used it as a reminder that God's ways were not always easily understood. But even when he didn't understand, he should still trust that God had a plan and would work things out for His honor and glory.

Zane realized in that moment that it wouldn't bring honor or glory to God if he chose to abandon Kelsey, especially if he did so to reunite with Sarah. He'd known that—in his heart, he'd known it—but feeling so disconnected from the present had made him desperate for something that was familiar.

Zane knew he should tell Lee not to bother contacting Sarah, but he didn't move. His head pounded, and all he wanted in that moment was to fall asleep and wake up with his memories intact. That would make everything so much easier.

He could get his job back, or at least, another job of equal importance, since he'd regain all the knowledge and experience he'd forgotten from the past few years.

But more importantly, he'd once again be past all the feelings he had for Sarah. He'd remember Kelsey and all the reasons he'd had for marrying her so quickly.

They could pick up the pieces of their lives and move forward.

If only his memory would just return.

He must have dozed off at some point because a knock on the door jerked him awake. "Come in."

The door opened, and Lee stepped into the room. "Sorry. Did I wake you?"

"Yeah, but it's okay." Zane pushed himself up to sit propped against the headboard. He leaned down to scratch along the top of his cast, wishing he could reach inside and scratch where it really itched.

Lee came in and spun the chair from the desk around and sat down on it. "I've been in contact with Sarah."

Zane frowned. "Already? How long was I asleep?"

"About an hour or so."

"And you found her that quickly?"

"It wasn't overly hard," Lee said. "We still had some mutual friends on social media, and they were able to give me contact information for her. I was able to get hold of her, and we had a brief chat."

Zane's stomach twisted with nerves. "And?"

"She's willing to talk with you," Lee said. "Actually, she's willing to come here to Serenity."

"Really?" Zane felt a rush of excitement, though he tried to tamp it down.

"Yes. But she's not coming alone. She's married."

And just like that, hope died. Stabbed through the heart. "Married?"

"Yes. And her husband will be coming with her. If you're okay with that."

Zane didn't want to meet the man who had captured Sarah's heart and gotten her to marry him when Zane hadn't managed to do it. But even if the guy didn't come, he wouldn't cease to exist. If his goal was to get closure with Sarah, Zane knew he needed to meet the man.

"I'm okay with that."

Lee gave a nod, as if he approved of that response. "They said if you want them to come, they'd be able to come on the weekend."

That was so close, and yet so far away. "Where are they coming from?"

"Seattle."

"Wow. They're not that far away."

"Nope."

"Did she say anything else?"

"Not really. Just that she was sorry to hear what had happened to you, and she was happy to come speak with you."

"Thanks for doing that."

"I was happy to," Lee said. "I just hope that it helps you move forward."

Zane hoped that it did, too. If his memory wasn't going to return, talking with Sarah felt like the only way to get past where he was currently stuck in his life.

He just hoped that it worked out that way.

CHAPTER SIXTEEN

Kelsey paced around her room, pausing in front of the mirror to cast a critical eye at the outfit she'd chosen. A good portion of her wardrobe now lay tossed across her bed from her frenzied try-on earlier.

In the end, she'd chosen a white denim skirt that ended just above her knees, and she'd paired it with a baby blue blouse with puffed sleeves and a fitted bodice. The necklace and matching earrings she wore had been given to her by Zane for her birthday a couple of weeks before they'd gotten married.

She'd even put on makeup and curled her hair. Because though she'd never seen a picture of Sarah, Kelsey was sure that she wasn't going to measure up to her. She just knew it, deep in her gut.

There was a light rap on her door. Kelsey turned from the mirror, pressing a hand to her stomach. "Come in."

"It's just me," Rori said as she poked her head around the doorway. Stepping into the room, she smiled. "You look very nice."

"Thanks."

"I just came to let you know that Lee got a text from Sarah that they'll be here in about ten minutes."

"Do I have to be there?"

"Yes. You need to be a part of this." Rori came to stand in front of her. "This will affect your life, too."

That's what Kelsey was afraid of.

Rori reached out and took her hands. "Let me pray for you." She waited until Kelsey nodded before she closed her eyes and bowed her head. "Heavenly Father, we come before you today asking that Your hand be upon Kelsey, Zane, and Sarah as they meet together. You know better than anyone else how Kelsey is feeling about this meeting. I pray that You will place Your hand upon her and calm the nerves she might be feeling in this moment."

Rori's hands tightened around Kelsey's. "I've come to love Kelsey like a sister, Lord, and I so want this to go well and provide a path forward for her and Zane. Above all, we want what brings You the most glory. Fill Kelsey with the assurance that she is not alone and with peace about whatever unfolds. In Jesus' name, amen."

Emotion clogged Kelsey's throat, and she clung to Rori's hands. Ever since they'd received the news that Sarah would be coming, Rori had been a steady rock for Kelsey. Zane had been broody and on edge, though Kelsey didn't know if that was because of Sarah's impending visit or his head injury.

From her own research and from what the doctor had said, the head injury he'd sustained in the accident could lead to mood swings and bouts of anger and frustration. She'd seen more of both from him over the past few days, though none of it had ever been directed at her.

In the midst of all the turmoil of the pending visit, however, Kelsey had managed to land herself a job stocking shelves at the big box store. It wasn't a job she'd ever aspired to have, but it hadn't turned out to be so bad. Working at night meant she wasn't interacting with many people at the store, and the physical activity of stocking shelves helped tire her out, so she slept better.

Getting home after seven in the morning meant she spent a good chunk of the day sleeping, so there were only a few hours when she and Zane were both awake and interacting.

She missed Zane—*her* Zane—so much. But having him look at her without any of the love and affection she was used to seeing from him had become torture. So, while she would have loved to spend all her time with him, pain kept her from doing that, and now her job gave her an excuse to put a more distance between them.

"Let's go do this," Rori said, giving her hands a squeeze before releasing them. "I think it will be okay."

Kelsey tried to take strength from Rori's words, but it felt nearly impossible. Still, her nerves had settled a bit.

This was a crossroads for her. Even if Zane got closure with Sarah, there was no guarantee that he would want to try to work things out with her. If that was the case, she would leave.

As long as she kept her focus on the fact that soon she'd have a definite direction to move in, it helped her not feel like she was preparing to walk off the edge of a cliff.

Downstairs, they found Lee and Zane in the living room. Lee was seated on the couch, while Zane sat in an armchair. He wore a light blue polo shirt and a pair of black pleated shorts with a belt. It was the most dressed up she'd seen him in ages.

Tears stung her eyes for a moment, but she blinked them back. Tears could be shed later. First, she just needed to get through this meeting with Sarah.

Both men glanced toward them as they walked in, and Lee immediately got up and approached them. He smiled at Rori, then turned to Kelsey.

"I think this is going to go better than you think," he said. "Just hang in there."

Kelsey appreciated his words, but she had no idea how he could speak with such confidence. It was certainly nothing she'd felt since the night of Zane's accident. And when it came to her relationship, she felt like she'd never have confidence again.

Because even if Zane got his memory back, there would still be obstacles to overcome.

The doorbell rang, which made Kelsey's pulse jump, and her heart began to pound. As Lee went to answer it, Rori put her hand on Kelsey's arm and guided her further into the living room.

Kelsey moved to sit down, but then straightened. She'd only have to get back up again when she was introduced to Sarah.

She glanced over at Zane and saw that he was staring at the floor. It surprised her that he wasn't watching the entrance to the living room. She'd assumed he'd be eager to catch a glimpse of his former love... current love.

He lifted his head and looked in her direction. Their gazes met and held for a long moment, and Kelsey only looked away when she caught movement out of the corner of her eye.

Kelsey turned and saw Lee walking into the living room with a tall, slender, *beautiful* blonde woman and a slightly taller man, who, in her estimation, wasn't nearly as handsome as Zane.

Lee led them to where Kelsey and Rori stood. "Sarah, this is my wife, Rori, and this is Kelsey. Ladies, this is Sarah and her husband, Ross Talbot."

Their attention first went to Rori, and Ross shook her hand, then he offered it to Kelsey.

"Nice to meet you, Kelsey," Ross said with a smile that lit up his blue eyes, transforming his face from average to attractive.

"Nice to meet you, too." And she meant it. If Sarah had to come and talk to Zane, Kelsey was glad her husband had come along too.

"Kelsey." Sarah's voice was warm and her expression friendly as she focused on Kelsey. Instead of just holding out one hand, she held out both. When Kelsey took them, unsure what else to do, Sarah said, "I'm so, so glad to meet you. Zane told me so much about you that I feel like I know you."

Zane had spoken to Sarah about her? Why hadn't he also done the reverse?

Sarah let go of her hands and turned toward Zane. Moving with graceful steps across the room, Sarah approached Zane, who now stood with his crutches supporting him, while Ross followed more slowly.

"Zane." Sarah reached out and briefly touched Zane's arm. "I was so sorry to hear what happened. How are you doing?"

"I'm about as well as can be expected."

"Well, you're alive, so that's a blessing."

"Hey, Zane," Ross said. "Good to see you again."

"Again? We've met?"

"Yes," Sarah replied. "Why don't we all sit down so I can answer any questions you might have?"

"Would you like something to drink?" Rori asked. "Coffee? Water?"

"Water would be great," Sarah said. "For both of us."

Rori left the living room as the rest of them took their seats. Kelsey chose to sit on the couch with Lee, leaving the middle cushion open for Rori. Zane settled back into the armchair, while Ross and Sarah sat together on the love seat.

When Rori returned, she had a tray holding more than just glasses and a large pitcher of water. She also had a plate with cookies and brownies.

"You and Ross met a couple of months ago," Sarah said once they'd all gotten the drinks and food they wanted.

"I met with you guys?" Zane said, his brow furrowed. "I... well, obviously, I don't remember."

Sympathy filled Sarah's expression. "Yes. You came to see us because we were getting ready to make the move to Seattle. This was after we had reconnected a couple of weeks earlier."

"Why did we break up?" Zane asked, apparently deciding to jump right in. "I just can't come up with a reason."

"Our paths began to move in different directions," Sarah said. "I was feeling drawn to ministry, and you definitely... weren't."

"But you're a teacher," Zane said. "You were going to teach school, and I was going to start up my own restaurant."

Sarah nodded. "That's how our plans started off, but then I really felt the Lord was leading me to teach at a missionary school. We fought more about it until finally, I just said we needed to end our relationship. You were very, very unhappy about that."

Zane didn't respond right away. His gaze was lowered as Sarah spoke.

"About six months after we broke up, I met Ross, and we started dating. You found out about it, and you contacted me, furious that I'd moved on. I explained that it wasn't a reflection on you that I had fallen in love again, but that God had brought me someone whose direction in life aligned with mine. You didn't like that explanation at all." She pressed a hand to her chest. "It really hurt that we hadn't been able to continue on our separate paths while still remaining friends. Or at least amicable."

Zane looked up. "So, how did we end up talking again?"

Sarah smiled as she glanced at Kelsey. "You got my number from a mutual friend, and sent me a voice note, apologizing and saying you understood why I'd moved on because you'd fallen in love with someone unexpectedly. At first, I wasn't sure if you were just saying that in hopes of hurting me, or if it was true."

"I encouraged her to respond to you," Ross said. "Because I knew she was hurt by how things had ended between you."

"So I phoned you, and we arranged to meet for coffee." Sarah turned to look at Kelsey, giving her a smile. "And all he could talk about was you."

Her words filled Kelsey with warmth and helped to lessen the uneasiness that had filled her since Zane had woken up in the hospital asking for Sarah and not remembering her.

"You brought him so much joy," Sarah said. "And he was excited about the future you were going to have together. He let me know that you were getting married and moving to Tampa."

"Why didn't he ever talk to me about you?" Kelsey asked. It was the one thing that didn't make sense to her.

"I don't know," Sarah replied. "I did tell him that I hoped I could meet you at some point, not realizing that he'd never told you about me."

"What did he say in response to that?"

"He agreed, but then it didn't work out before you moved to Tampa, and we moved to Seattle."

"Why did he say I didn't come with him when he met with you and Ross?"

"Just that your schedule didn't work for the time that worked for me and Ross."

That made sense because, at that time, she'd been working at the restaurant and doing her nursing practicum. Though Kelsey had hoped that Sarah would have some answers for her and some closure for Zane, she had no idea if this visit was going to accomplish either.

She wanted to believe that Zane had truly been as in love with her as he'd once been with Sarah. But Sarah's existence, which had been unknown to her until recently, made her wonder.

"Kelsey, I truly believe that Zane loves you," Sarah said, her expression earnest. "He spoke so glowingly about you, and I know him well enough to know when he's not being honest. I felt he was very honest in the conversations we had about you."

Kelsey wanted to accept that. But it was a struggle. Especially since the Zane Sarah had had those conversations with wasn't currently present. And might never be again.

Sarah turned her attention back to Zane. "You need to figure out how to make your marriage work. I know you don't remember it, but you love Kelsey. She's very important to you. Important enough that you married her because you couldn't imagine life without her."

But not important enough to mention his previous relationship with Sarah.

Kelsey didn't like that she had moments when she resented Zane. She hadn't held his memory loss against him, and though it was hard, she'd accepted that he might never get it back. But discovering there were things he'd never shared with her—important things—made her feel like she couldn't truly trust what they'd had.

And if he never regained his memory, she would never get the answers she wanted.

How were they supposed to move forward?

For the first time, a sense of hopelessness filled Kelsey. She gripped her hands together as she stared at the floor.

Sarah continued to talk to Zane, answering more questions he had about everything that had transpired. His family had been able to answer some of his questions, but Sarah clearly had more answers that Zane needed.

"Why don't I show you guys to your room," Lee suggested when Zane finally fell silent. "We have some family coming to join us for dinner. Hopefully, you don't mind that."

Sarah smiled. "Not at all. I've always enjoyed your family."

Kelsey got up when the others did, then helped Rori carry the dishes back to the kitchen while Sarah and Ross went upstairs with Lee, after Ross retrieved their bags from the foyer.

Zane remained in the living room, leaving Kelsey to wonder what he thought about what Sarah had shared with them. Though they hadn't talked about Sarah's impending visit once the plans were set, Kelsey was sure that he'd had high expectations for what he hoped Sarah would tell him. The reality was probably not what he'd hoped for.

Suddenly, Kelsey found herself wrapped in a hug. She let out a sigh and, for a moment, just let Rori hold her. The woman had become a great friend. Her best friend, if Kelsey was honest. Rori's support had made Kelsey's time in Serenity bearable, even when everything else made her want to run away.

"Are you okay?" Rori asked as she stepped back.

Kelsey gave her a small smile. "I'm okay. My expectations for this weren't too high."

Rori's expression saddened. "I don't know what more we can do. We're praying so hard that Zane's memory comes back."

"But if it doesn't, we need to be prepared."

"Have you thought about what you'll do if that ends up being the case?"

Kelsey had thought of nothing else, but she just shrugged. "I don't know for sure."

"I hope you stay here," Rori said. "I know it's not ideal for you, but I'd hate to see you go."

The smile that came as a result of Rori's words felt more genuine. "I'd hate to leave, but I'm not sure that Zane will stay, even if his memory comes back."

The doorbell rang before Rori replied, and then they heard the front door open.

"Hello!" Wilder called out, then he and Lexi appeared in the doorway to the kitchen. "Hey, you two. Where is everyone else?"

"You're the first ones to arrive," Rori said. "Lee is upstairs with Sarah and her husband. Zane is in the living room."

"Okay. I'm gonna go talk to him."

Wilder disappeared while Lexi came further into the kitchen to take a seat at the island counter.

"How's skating going?" Rori asked her sister-in-law.

"It's going well. Amelia is signed up for a couple of competitions this fall, so we've been working hard to prepare her for that."

"I can't wait to see her compete," Rori said. "I never competed in anything, so this is going to be a lot of fun."

Kelsey had never competed either, and though she knew how to ice skate, it had never been at the level that Lexi had reached. Kelsey's skill was limited to being able to stay on her feet, and, if she was feeling adventurous, skating backwards.

When she heard voices, she braced herself for seeing Sarah again.

Soon she came into the kitchen with Lee and Ross, though there was still no sign of Zane and Wilder. Another ring of the doorbell brought Kayleigh and Hudson to the party. Soon Charli and Blake, and Janessa and Will arrived, though they didn't have any of their children with them.

Everyone greeted Sarah and Ross warmly, and Kelsey's heart-break deepened as she was faced once again with a reminder that Sarah had been their first choice for Zane.

"Where do you want the food, Rori?" Charli asked as she set a bag on the counter.

At Rori's direction, they all pitched in to get the dinner on the table. When they finally sat down, Kelsey found herself once again between Zane and Rori. Sarah and Ross were seated across the table from them.

Lee said a prayer for the food, then they began to pass the platters and bowls around the table. With so many people present, Kelsey didn't feel pressed to make conversation. Zane was also quiet, and he kept rubbing his forehead, making her think he was battling another headache.

Kelsey hadn't been sure why Lee had invited practically his whole family for dinner. But as the conversation flowed around the table, it dawned on her that this was an opportunity for Sarah and Ross to share their plans for missionary service.

"I'll talk to my dad," Will said. "He's the pastor of the church we all attend. I'm sure he would let you give a short presentation."

"That would be great," Ross said. "If he's willing to have us speak, just let me know how much time we have."

As she listened to these people rally around Sarah and Ross, Kelsey wondered if there was something about her that rubbed people the wrong way. Her parents. Her best friend. Her in-laws. Rori and Carisa were the only ones who had shown care and concern for her. It was why the loss of Zane's love had hit her so deeply, and she was beginning to think she had lost that forever.

When it was time for dessert, Kelsey helped clear the table and then she stayed in the kitchen, loading the dishwasher while Rori and Charli carried coffee and cake into the dining room. She wondered how long it would be until she could retreat to the solace of her room.

"Are you going to come have some dessert?" Rori asked as she returned with a couple more dishes.

"I'm not really hungry for dessert."

Rori regarded her for a moment, then nodded. "You're not the only one wanting to escape. Zane excused himself and went up to his room."

"Really?"

"Yep. So if you feel the need to leave as well, we'll understand. You don't even need to say anything. I'll make your excuses."

"You will?"

"I will. So if you want to go..." Rori made a shooing motion with her hands. "We'll talk tomorrow."

Kelsey dried her hands on the towel, then went to give Rori a hug. "Thank you."

Before anyone else came into the kitchen, Kelsey hurried from the room and up the stairs. It was too bad that she didn't have to work that night. She could have used the distraction.

Unfortunately, she only worked three shifts per week, and she wasn't scheduled for that night.

As Kelsey sat on the edge of her bed, she allowed herself to feel all the emotions that the predicament she found herself in had produced. Hurt. Anger. Disappointment. Frustration. Along with the overwhelming desire to run away and just leave it all behind.

But she wouldn't. Not yet anyway. She would see how Zane approached things now that he'd had this conversation with Sarah.

And then, if necessary, she'd walk away.

CHAPTER SEVENTEEN

Zane carefully made his way around people in the foyer as he followed Lee, Rori, and Kelsey to their seats in the sanctuary. Sarah and Ross had come earlier to meet with the pastor, and Zane spotted them standing next to the front row, speaking with Will's parents, along with a couple of other leaders from the church.

He still wasn't sure how he felt about everything that had transpired over the past twenty-four hours. Even though he'd known that Sarah was married, he'd wanted to see her, hoping for closure. But the reality was, he didn't immediately stop having feelings for her.

She was clearly in love with her husband and happy with the direction of her life, and though it hurt to see her that way with someone else, Zane was glad she was thriving. Now if he could only figure out how to thrive in his current life.

When Lee scooted into a row with enough space for them, Zane followed Kelsey into it and sat down beside her, leaning his crutches next to him at the end of the row.

"Hi, Zane." Looking up, Zane saw a friend of his parents standing in the aisle next to him. He moved to get to his feet, but the man rested his hand on Zane's shoulder, keeping him in place. "It's good to see you this morning with your lovely wife."

The man's wife gave them both a warm smile. "How are you feeling these days, Zane?"

"I'm hoping to get the cast off soon," he said, choosing to focus on the injury they could see. "Gareth says my leg is healing very well, so I appreciate your prayers."

"We've definitely been praying fervently for you since we heard about your accident. I know your parents are glad to have you back, though I know the circumstances aren't ideal."

"We'll continue to pray for you both," the man said. "Keep your head up."

"Thank you."

With a last squeeze of his shoulder, the pair moved further down the aisle. Zane appreciated the care and concern of the people who had known him his whole life, but it really didn't seem like their prayers were being answered when it came to his more serious injury.

Kelsey shifted on the pew beside him, her hands gripping her purse in her lap. Someone had started to play the piano, and announcements were cycling through on the large screens on either side of the stage at the front.

The familiarity of the church and its services was a balm for the turmoil in his spirit. He hadn't wanted to come that morning, but he'd known that church was precisely the place he needed to be.

It was a bit of a surprise that Kelsey continued to attend church with them, especially considering that she'd said that they'd never gone during their time together. He hadn't had a conversation about her attending with them now, to see if she had questions, but maybe he needed to.

His head throbbed dully, and he hoped the pills he'd taken before leaving the house would kick in soon. If the pain got any worse, he'd have a hard time focusing.

Gareth joined the worship team as they took their places on the platform, while the assistant pastor stepped up to the podium to welcome them. The service quickly got underway, and after all the usual parts, Pastor Kennedy got up and greeted the congregation.

"We have a special presentation this morning," he said, smiling warmly. "Will contacted me yesterday to see if we'd have room in the service for some friends of the Halverson family to share about their ministry. We are always happy to highlight mission ministries here, and after I spoke to them this morning, I knew this was a timely presentation, with school starting soon. Sarah and Ross, why don't you join me up here?"

Sarah and Ross stood up, and Zane felt his stomach clench when he saw Ross lay his hand on Sarah's back as they climbed the stairs to the stage. Pastor Kennedy shook hands with them, then stepped aside so they could take his place behind the podium.

"Thank you for allowing Sarah and I to share with you this morning where the Lord is leading us," Ross said, an engaging smile lighting up his face. "But first of all, we'd like to give you a little background on us. I was raised as a missionary kid in Malaysia, where my parents were serving as church planters. I returned to Chicago upon graduating from the missionary boarding school to attend college, and it was in Chicago where I met Sarah. I'll let her tell you a bit about herself."

"As Ross said, thank you for allowing us to share this morning," Sarah said with a familiar smile. "Unlike Ross, I was raised here in the States. I grew up in a Christian home just outside of Chicago and ended up moving there for college. Once I graduated, I found a job in a Christian school. During that time, I felt drawn to overseas ministry, but I wasn't sure what exactly that would look like for me. While teaching at the school, I met Ross, abnd he was able to assist me in thinking through this calling, and in the process, we fell in love."

Zane frowned, wondering if she'd already known Ross before she'd broken up with him. From what she'd said, he'd gotten upset because she'd started dating within six months of their breakup. Her knowing Ross already could help explain how she'd moved on so quickly.

"I'm a high school science teacher, while Sarah teaches elementary," Ross said. "During our time getting to know each other, we realized that we were both seeking to follow the Lord's leading into overseas ministry. After much prayer as a couple and individually, we felt God was leading us to teach at a missionary boarding school."

Ross gave some information about the school they hoped to serve at and also the mission they were going with. "We're now in the process of raising support. It had been our hope to be there in time to start this school year, but the timing hasn't worked out. In the meantime, we will be teaching at a school in Seattle, where we just recently moved. It is our hope to be in a position to go to our assignment next summer, and we'd sure appreciate your prayers as we plan toward that."

"We'd love to have you as partners as we minister to missionary children," Sarah said. "Supporting them as their parents work in their own ministries."

Pastor Kennedy stepped up to the podium and rested his hand on Ross's shoulder. "There's a table set up in the foyer with more information about Sarah and Ross's ministry. Right now, I'd like to ask our elders to come forward to pray for Sarah and Ross."

The piano played softly as several people—including Zane's dad—joined the pastor at the front of the sanctuary. The group gathered around the couple, laying hands on them as Pastor Kennedy prayed for them and their ministry.

As Zane listened to the pastor pray, he mulled over what Sarah had shared and the passion she had for the direction of her life with Ross. It wasn't a passion they'd ever had for the future they'd talked about.

He hadn't wanted to accept that anyone but him could have made Sarah happy. However, proof to the contrary was right in front of him. And more than just happy, she looked to be at peace.

Once the prayer was over, Sarah and Ross shook hands with the people who had prayed with them, then took their seats in the front row. Pastor Kennedy returned to his spot at the podium.

"Sarah and Ross being here to share about their ministry and the journey they've been on as they move toward where God is leading them, is timely. As you heard, their plan was to originally be at their assignment for the start of this school year, but that isn't how things have worked out for them. That does not mean, however, that this is not God's plan for them. It just means that His timing is different than what they might have thought it would be.

"I'm sure we've all experienced things not working out in varying degrees throughout our lives. Proverbs sixteen verse nine says *a man's heart plans his way, but the Lord directs his steps.* There is nothing wrong with making plans, even if we're not entirely sure they're what God would want for us. The important thing is to hold onto them loosely. Make your plan, but then be open to God moving you in a different direction or at a different speed."

Getting in a car accident and losing his memory had definitely *not* been his plan for his life. If it was God's plan, it sure didn't make much sense. Was God wanting to move him in a new direction?

Zane didn't know what had led him to marry Kelsey and make the move to Tampa, beyond it being the best move for his career. But given what Kelsey had said about his lack of faith, Zane doubted that he'd sought God's guidance regarding the move.

Conviction settled heavily in his heart. He didn't know if it had been God's will that he marry Kelsey. But the fact of the matter was... they were married. It was time he fully accepted that and do what he could to make the marriage work. Whether he loved Kelsey or not was irrelevant.

Please, God, direct my steps. I can't do this on my own. Take away my feelings for Sarah, and give me love for Kelsey. Help me make this work.

As Pastor Kennedy shared other Bible stories of people who had made plans, and then had them redirected by God, Zane realized he needed to completely rethink the direction of his life. For a long time, his career had been his focus. Being the best that he could be. Going for the dream of owning his own restaurant.

But it was all for naught now. He'd lost the experience and training he'd gained in the past few years, and he was no better than a chef barely out of culinary school. It was humbling, and one of the reasons he'd resisted cooking much so far.

Maybe there wasn't a way to have a ministry as a chef, but he could have a ministry in other areas of his life. Was he willing to sacrifice his big dreams for the plan God might have for him?

Right then, he felt like he didn't have a choice. His dream was farther out of reach than it had ever been, and he didn't know if he'd ever be able to get it back.

"If we want to have peace and joy in our lives, trusting God and obeying His direction is the best way to achieve that." Pastor Kennedy paused, then said, "I want you to take these verses with you this morning, and if you've memorized them, please say them with me. Proverbs three, verses five and six. *Trust in the Lord with all your heart, and lean not on your own understanding; In all your ways acknowledge Him, and He shall direct your paths.*"

Zane murmured the words along with others in the congregation, finding it interesting that the verse that had come to his mind a few days earlier was being brought to his attention again.

Pastor Kennedy closed his Bible and smiled out at the congregation. "Trust in God, seek His will, and glorify Him in all you do."

Rather than the whole worship team getting up as Pastor Kennedy stepped back, just the song leader took his place at the podium as the piano played. It was a familiar hymn that tied right into the sermon.

When we walk with the Lord,
In the light of His Word,
What a glory He sheds on our way!
While we do His good will,
He abides with us still,

And with all who will trust and obey.

Trust and obey,
For there's no other way
To be happy in Jesus,
But to trust and obey.

Not a burden we bear,
Not a sorrow we share,
But our toil He doth richly repay;
Not a grief or a loss,
Not a frown or a cross,
But is blessed if we trust and obey.

But we never can prove
The delights of His love
Until all on the altar we lay;
For the favor He shows,
For the joy He bestows,
Are for them who will trust and obey.

Then in fellowship sweet
We will sit at His feet.
Or we'll walk by His side in the way.
What He says we will do,
Where He sends we will go;
Never fear, only trust and obey.

The words resonated deeply with Zane, and reinforced within him the need to turn his focus from inward to upward.

He should have been able to come to this point sooner. He shouldn't have needed Sarah to come and give him closure. To shut the door on what they'd once had.

Now that he'd opened his heart to what he knew was right and was considering what God would want, the guilt of so many things weighed heavily on Zane.

When the service ended, Zane grabbed his crutches and got to his feet. He waited for a break in the people heading up the aisle, then maneuvered his way out of the row, moving back so that Kelsey and the others could exit. He was slow moving, so he always brought up the rear.

In the foyer, his parents found them, and his mom gave everyone hugs, even Kelsey. Zane could see that surprised her, and honestly, he was a bit surprised himself. Perhaps his mom was warming up to Kelsey. Or at least she was trying to treat her better than she had initially.

"How are you feeling, sweetheart?" his mom asked him. "I was so glad to hear that your scan showed that everything is healing well."

"Yes. The doctor was pleased with the results." Zane wished his brain felt like everything was doing well. The headaches were a pain. Literally.

"Nothing on the memory front?"

It was the question he hated the most those days. Like he wouldn't make a huge announcement on the family group chat if he started to recall things...

"Nope. No memories coming back."

"We'll continue to pray."

Zane had no idea when he was supposed to accept that this was just how things were going to be. When should he give up the hope that his memory would be restored? He doubted that anyone could give him a definite answer on that.

But he was coming to realize that he couldn't put his life—and Kelsey's life—on hold indefinitely. Once he was physically healed and no longer dealing with a leg cast, he was going to have to make some decisions.

He wasn't sure yet what direction he would choose in his career. It was a big decision, and it made his head ache if he thought too much about it.

"It was lovely to hear Sarah and her husband share," his mom said. "I'm glad Pastor Kennedy could fit them in."

Zane glanced over to where Sarah and Ross had set up their table. Several people stood there with them, so it was apparent that their presentation had resonated with some who'd heard it. He told himself that he was happy for them. And he was... mostly.

Turning to Kelsey as his parents spoke to Lee and Rori, Zane kept his voice low as he said, "Are you ready to go?"

She glanced around with a frown. "You don't want to wait for the others?"

"Not unless you do."

She hesitated a moment, but then shook her head. "We can go."

Shifting around to face Lee, Zane said, "We're headed out."

"You're leaving already?" his mom asked, her brow furrowed.

"Yes. I'm tired and have a bit of a headache."

His mom moved closer and gave him a hug. "Well, go get some rest."

"We'll be home shortly," Lee said. "We're not doing a barbecue for lunch since we had everyone over last night. Just leftovers."

"Sounds good. See you at home."

As he and Kelsey made their way to the doors of the church, he nodded at the people who greeted him, but he didn't stop to talk to anyone.

"I'll go get the car," Kelsey said.

"You don't have to do that," Zane told her. "I'll walk with you if you don't mind a slower pace."

"No. That's fine."

Neither of them spoke as they walked to where Kelsey had parked earlier. Zane wondered what Kelsey was thinking. She was hard to read.

Without remembering the dynamics of their relationship, Zane had no idea if she had been a person to share her thoughts readily.

Or had they been close enough that he could read her moods easily?

Her silence right then didn't seem to indicate that she was upset or angry. More like she was keeping her thoughts and emotions under tight wrap. And if that was the case, he couldn't exactly blame her.

"Has it been difficult?" Kelsey asked as they left the church parking lot.

Zane looked at her, wondering if she thought his brain injury had left him with the ability to read minds. There was so much that question could apply to in his life at the moment. "Has what been difficult?"

Kelsey kept her gaze forward, gripping the steering wheel with both hands. "Seeing Sarah again. With her husband."

The question didn't surprise Zane, but he wasn't sure how to answer it. The emotions he had surrounding Sarah were so complex and messy.

"Are you super hungry?"

"What?" She glanced at him, a question in her blue-green eyes. "Not really."

"Pull in up here for a second," Zane said, motioning to the diner that was just ahead. As she parked, he angled himself to reach his wallet in his back pocket. He pulled out his debit card and handed it to her. "Would you mind going in and ordering a frozen lemonade and a large fries for me? And get whatever you want as well. On me. I would recommend the lemonade and fries."

She stared at the card, then reached out and took it from him. "Okay. I'll be right back."

Zane watched as she walked to the entrance of the diner and disappeared inside. While he waited for her to come back, he sent a text to Lee.

Kelsey and I won't be around for lunch. See you a bit later.

Lee sent back a thumbs up without requiring any further information, though Zane was sure that Rori was pestering him with questions. Zane appreciated that about Lee. Though he might ask questions later, right in the moment, he didn't demand to know what was going on.

A few minutes later, Kelsey reappeared with a drink tray in one hand and a large paper bag in the other. He leaned across the console to open her door, and she bent over to hand him the drink tray and the bag. After she'd settled back in her seat, she held out the debit card.

"Do you mind if we go to the park?"

"Uh. Sure." She pulled out of the parking spot and turned in the direction of the park. "What part of the park did you want to go?"

"Anywhere with an available picnic table in the shade."

Kelsey nodded but remained silent until they were driving through the park. "How about that spot?"

Zane looked at where she was pointing. "That looks perfect."

After she'd parked the car, she got out, then took the drink tray and food bag from Zane, waiting until he was out with his crutches before walking with him across the grass to the picnic table. As they walked, Zane tried to get his thoughts in order for what he wanted to say to her.

Once at the picnic table, Kelsey set everything down, then sat down opposite Zane. While he worked the drinks free from the tray, she lifted out two covered containers and handed one to him.

Zane took a sip of his drink, appreciating the perfect blend of sweet and tart that they always seemed to get just right at the diner. "Did you decide on the frozen lemonade, too?"

Kelsey nodded. "It seemed like a good option on a day like today."

"Do I know your food preferences well?" he asked.

"Yes. You quizzed me pretty hard about the foods I liked when we first started dating."

"Did I encourage you to expand your food preferences?"

A small smile briefly curved the corners of her mouth as she lifted a fry from her container. "Oh yes. Once every couple of weeks, you'd make me a food I'd never had before."

"And how did that go?"

"I liked a lot of what you made, but not everything," she said. "There was nothing you could do to make me like okra or asparagus."

"Not even asparagus wrapped in bacon?"

"Not even."

Zane felt some of the emotional upheaval from earlier settle. He knew what God would have him do regarding Kelsey, so it was good to find these small things to connect over.

Though he didn't want to admit it, he was well aware that his attitude and approach to Kelsey going forward would determine how successful he might be in trying to figure his future out. All he could do was pray that God would give him the strength and wisdom that, thus far, he hadn't wanted.

Zane just hoped that he hadn't waited until it was too late.

CHAPTER EIGHTEEN

Kelsey had no idea why she was sitting with Zane at a picnic table in the park, eating fries and drinking frozen lemonade. Not that she was complaining. However, there was some uneasiness inside her that Zane had not answered her question about how he was feeling about Sarah.

"What was your favorite meal that I made for you?"

Kelsey took a sip of her lemonade as she considered her answer. "You made a lot of meals that I like, but I'm a bit of a pasta and chicken girl, so I always liked it when you made chicken parm with angel hair."

Zane nodded. "That's a dish I enjoy making."

It was weird to be having this conversation with him, but Kelsey supposed she should be happy that he was asking questions about her and about their relationship.

"I'm not ignoring your question about Sarah," Zane said. "Though I suppose it seems like I am."

Kelsey didn't respond to that, because he was right. Waiting for him to continue, she ate another fry.

"The truth is... it was very difficult to see her with someone else. But at the same time, I needed to witness it, and I needed to have her tell me what happened between us that ended things. I just couldn't fathom what would have led to that, since we were on track to get engaged and married."

Though she didn't like to hear that, Kelsey could understand his need to know, given his memory loss. It was a struggle, but she had to separate *her* Zane from *this* Zane, because she was coming to realize that they were two different people. The most obvious difference being that one loved her and the other didn't even know her.

"I wish I could have just accepted what people told me about what had happened with her, but I couldn't." Staring at his cup, Zane turned it between his hands. "The biggest stumbling block was that I couldn't imagine a scenario where it hadn't worked out for us."

"Can you imagine it now?" Kelsey asked.

"Yes. Now that I've spoken with Sarah, it... makes more senses." Zane paused before continuing. "It wasn't easy to wake up thinking I'm in love with someone, only to be told that no, that's not the case. That we broke up, and she doesn't love me anymore. And if that wasn't hard enough, to go on to learn she had actually married someone else. It felt so unbelievable to me."

"I can understand that," Kelsey said, because she could. "It also wasn't easy for me to have the man I love and am married to wake up and be in love with someone else. In some ways, we were in similar boats. The person I love loves someone else, just like the person you love loves someone else. So I understand where you're at. It hurts."

Zane stared at her for a long moment, then nodded. "I know that I shouldn't have needed to talk to her to accept what had happened. And I apologize for making a difficult situation even more challenging through my actions."

Kelsey's unease grew with his words. Was his apology leading up to him saying that he thought they should go their separate ways?

"What do we do now?"

It probably wasn't a good idea to push him for a decision, because it might result in something that would devastate her. But the truth was that she was so very tired of the uncertainty in her life.

Zane gazed off towards a group who were tossing a football around. Finally, he looked back at her, his expression unreadable. "What do you want?"

There were so many things she wanted. To be back in his arms again. To have him look at her with love in his eyes. To have their life together back.

But she couldn't say any of that, and she knew that saying she wanted his memory back was futile. That was definitely out of their control. "I guess I want whatever you want. It won't benefit either of us if you want us to go our separate ways, and I don't. If you do what I want, you're just going to be unhappy."

He was slow to answer, and Kelsey's heart thumped painfully in her chest. It felt like they were at a crossroads, and the trajectory of her life was going to change forever.

And she wasn't prepared for it.

When she'd woken that morning, she hadn't had any inkling that they'd be having such an intense conversation. One that had the power to completely change the direction of her life.

It wasn't like she'd never had moments like these before. However, this one had the potential to hurt more than all the other times she'd been rejected and sent off on her own.

Her appetite had vanished, but her mouth suddenly felt like the Sahara, so she picked up her cup and took a sip of her lemonade.

"I think we need to try."

His words made her heart skip a beat. "Try?"

"I think we need to spend some time getting to know each other. You're a stranger to me. To put it bluntly," he said. "And honestly, I'm a stranger to you. The person I am now is not the person you married. I don't know that person, and I struggle to understand how I became him."

"In what ways do you feel you're different?" Kelsey asked. "Aside from loving Sarah."

Zane ate a couple of fries as he seemed to contemplate his answer. "My faith, or lack thereof. My decision to leave Chicago."

"I don't know anything about why your faith is different now, but I know you considered the move to Tampa to be a step forward in your career."

"Had I talked to you about opening my own restaurant?"

Kelsey thought back over all their discussions about their careers and couldn't remember an in-depth conversation about it. "Only in passing."

"Really?" Kelsey nodded. "I wish I knew what changed my focus. I mean, I have a savings account with a ton of money in it, so I must have continued to save up."

That was news to Kelsey. They hadn't really discussed much about their finances beyond how they each would contribute to the running of the household. "I'm afraid I have no answers about that."

Zane's brow furrowed. "I'm beginning to think that I didn't do a great job of sharing myself with you."

Kelsey was beginning to think that, too.

"This is why I think it's important that we go back to the basics of getting to know each other," Zane said.

"And hope that we end up feeling the same way we did the first time around?" The more she discovered she didn't know about the Zane she'd married, the more she worried that their relationship might not survive the return of his memories.

Zane nodded. "Should we put a time limit on how long we try?"

Kelsey didn't have an answer to that. There was a part of her that wanted to try forever, but realistically, she knew that wouldn't be a good thing. To live in a weird limbo.

"We could do that," Kelsey agreed. "Or maybe we just need to be honest with each other. If one of us gets to the point where we just can't go on, then we tell the other person."

"Okay. We can agree to be honest," Zane said. "I think that's important in a relationship, anyway."

Kelsey was glad he felt that way about honesty now. But why hadn't he felt like that previously?

She did wonder what being honest meant exactly. Was she supposed to tell him everything about herself all at once? Or did she share it over time the way she had when they'd been dating? Like how she hadn't told him about going to nursing school right away. He said he'd understood why she hadn't revealed it sooner, but would this Zane be as understanding?

The hope flickering inside her was tempered by the reality that this Zane might never fall in love with her. Her love for him still filled her heart. It hadn't gone away just because she had some questions about the things he hadn't told her. There was still the potential for heartbreak for her.

"Let's start by asking each other one question," Zane said after they'd sat in silence for a long moment. He'd probably been trying to digest the agreement they'd just made, just like she was.

"A question?"

"Yes." He stared at her for a moment. "Is there something you'd like to ask me? Or do you want me to go first and ask you something?"

Kelsey wasn't entirely comfortable with either option, but she decided to go with him asking her a question first, figuring she could change the subject by asking him her question if she got too uncomfortable.

"You can go ahead."

"Tell me about your family," Zane said.

That had been something her Zane had asked early on in their relationship too. She realized later it was because his own family was important to him, and he liked to talk about them. Unfortunately, that wasn't the same for her.

"That's not a question," Kelsey said, trying to either stall or distract him. She wasn't sure which.

He narrowed his eyes at her for a moment, a move so familiar that her heart skipped a beat. "So it's going to be like that, huh?"

"They're your rules," she pointed out. "A *question*."

Zane moved his food to the side, then rested his arms on the picnic table and gave her his full attention. "Okay. Will you please tell me about your family?"

Kelsey decided she needed to offer up some information, hoping she wouldn't have to delve too deeply into her past in order to satisfy Zane's curiosity.

"I'm the youngest of three. I have two older sisters," Kelsey said, though it had been years since she'd felt like she had a sibling. She'd told him that already, so she doubted he'd accept that as an answer. "We were a military family, so we moved around a lot."

"Are you close to your sisters?"

"That's two questions," Kelsey told him. However, she knew she owed him an answer with new info, since her previous one hadn't contained any. "But I'll answer it. No, we aren't close. They both left home at eighteen and never looked back. I have no idea where they went."

Zane's brows lifted. "Why did they leave like that?"

Third question, but Kelsey was okay with talking a bit about her sisters. "They both had conflicts with our parents, and they didn't get along, so they parted ways as soon as they were able."

"That's a shame," he said.

Kelsey shrugged. "The house got a lot calmer as each one left, but I worried about them a lot, especially at first."

She could tell he wanted to ask more questions, but she'd allowed him some extra ones already. "My turn."

Zane sighed. "Okay. Your turn."

"What type of restaurant do you want to open?" she asked.

She hadn't been sure if that was still his plan, but she took a chance. And from the way his face lit up, she knew that it was.

"I would love to open a restaurant that serves haute cuisine that appeals to adults but is also child friendly. I think good food should be accessible to everyone. So I want to make it fun and inviting."

"You think kids want to eat snails?"

Zane laughed, and Kelsey felt a wash of emotion at the familiar sound. "Question two."

She let that emotion guide her as she playfully rolled her eyes. "I let you ask two extra questions, so I'm still ahead."

"Well, to answer your question, I don't think *all* kids want to eat snails, but some definitely would."

"Is it going to be an expensive restaurant?"

"Not as expensive as it might be if it catered to just adults and was more exclusive. I'm not going for exclusivity. I want kids exposed to fine dining in a setting that's family friendly."

"I've never heard of something like that before," Kelsey said. "Would you open it here or somewhere else?"

Kelsey knew she'd moved past the number of questions he'd asked her, but he seemed to enjoy talking about his dream.

"It had never been my plan to return here," Zane said. "I always assumed I'd open the restaurant in Chicago. I'm not sure there's much of a market here for what I want. And I don't know if Kayleigh would approve of me competing with the restaurants at the resort."

If they stayed in Serenity, there would be no opportunities for her to continue her nursing career unless she wanted to drive to Coeur d'Alene or Spokane to work at a hospital. Either place would necessitate a commute of over an hour one way.

"It's not something I need to think too much about at the moment, since I don't think it's going to happen anytime soon."

More questions were on the tip of her tongue, but she held them back, allowing silence to settle between them, interrupted only by the sound of people enjoying their Sunday afternoon.

The contrast to that first evening they'd ended up together was clear to Kelsey, and it pained her. Things between them had flowed so easily. They'd talked for hours, only going their separate ways when it was nearly four in the morning.

They had talked about all kinds of things. There had been plenty of questions. From the serious—like where they saw them-selves in five years—to the more lighthearted, like their favorite movie genre. It had been the first time she'd been that interested in a guy, and surprisingly, he'd returned that interest.

There at the picnic table, sitting across from the man she loved with everything in her, a hope for their future grew. For the first time since the accident, she felt that maybe they had an actual shot of being together again. Maybe they could fall in love again.

However, Kelsey also knew she needed to keep her expecta-tions in check. This wasn't the same Zane she'd fallen in love with. He himself had said he'd changed. What if those changes were what had made Zane fall in love with her? Without them, would he find her attractive?

"Do you have to work tonight?" he asked, breaking the silence.

"Yes. Eleven to seven."

"Guess we should probably head home."

Kelsey hated to leave the park and end their time together. But hopefully, it wouldn't be the last time they spent time together, just the two of them.

She gathered up all their garbage and carried it to the metal can near the road. Zane went directly to the car and stood by the tail-gate.

"I'm sorry I'm not doing stuff like that," he said. "I promise I wouldn't make you do everything if I wasn't in this cast."

It appeared that was one thing that hadn't changed about Zane. He'd always taken care of her. "I know. Please don't worry about it."

There was more traffic rolling through the park, so she had to wait a couple of minutes before she could pull away from the curb. On the way home, Zane seemed more relaxed as he pointed out places of interest from his childhood.

When they reached the house, there was no sign of Ross and Sarah's car. Kelsey didn't think they'd left yet because she'd heard them say they were in Serenity until Monday morning.

The house was quiet when they walked in. That meant Lee and Rori either weren't home, or they were in their bedroom at the back of the house. Lee's vehicle wasn't sitting in the driveway, but it could be parked in the garage.

When Kelsey headed for the kitchen, she could hear Zane following her. She got a glass from the cupboard, then turned to Zane. "Want something to drink?"

"I'm good, thanks."

She filled her glass from the dispenser on the front of the fridge, then went to the counter, standing opposite Zane. They talked a bit about their schedules for the upcoming week. With Kelsey working nights, she sometimes wasn't awake during business hours when Zane would have his medical appointments.

She heard a door open and the murmur of voices. A moment later, Sarah appeared in the doorway. The other woman paused, her gaze moving between Kelsey and Zane.

"Are we interrupting?" she asked.

Kelsey glanced at Zane, letting him respond to that. She didn't have a huge issue with Sarah and Ross joining them. It had more to do with Zane's comfort level.

"Nope. We're just talking about our schedules for next week."

As she and Ross approached them, Sarah gave Kelsey a warm smile before turning her attention to Zane. "Do you have a lot of doctor's appointments?"

"More than I want," Zane replied. "But less than I might have had. If the circumstances had been different."

"Will there be any charges against the driver of the other vehicle?" Ross asked.

Zane nodded. "His blood alcohol level was twice the legal limit, and unfortunately, this was not his first offense. Thankfully, they don't need anything from me, since I don't remember the accident."

"I just can't understand why people don't learn the dangers of drinking and driving," Sarah said. "Will it take killing someone for it to sink in?"

"Sad to say, that's often the case," Ross said.

Kelsey didn't sense any awkwardness between the trio, but she didn't assume that Zane was magically over his feelings for Sarah. It was hard to accept that, but she didn't have much choice. For now, she had to be content with the knowledge that he was going to at least try to move past them for her sake.

"Did you hang around the church?" Zane asked.

"For a bit," Sarah said. "But then we went for dinner with Pastor Kennedy and his wife and some of the elders."

"It sounds like the church might consider supporting us on a monthly basis," Ross added. "Which would be a real answer to prayer."

"That would be great," Zane said. "And not too surprising. It has always been a mission minded church."

"We did have several people sign up for our newsletter and take the information pamphlets we had there."

"I'm glad it wasn't a wasted trip for you," Zane said.

"Zane," Sarah said, a slight rebuke in her tone. "Even without that response, it wouldn't have been a waste. I think it was important for me to answer the questions you had. Especially since I was the only one who could tell you what happened between us."

"I do appreciate you and Ross making the time to come here."

"Thankfully, it was a shorter drive than if we'd still been in Chicago," Ross said with a laugh.

"That's true," Zane agreed.

"Do you have anything else you need answers for?" Sarah asked. "Before we leave tomorrow?"

"I don't think so," Zane said. "I mostly needed to understand what had happened."

"And do you?" she asked.

Zane nodded. "I understand why we're not together anymore, though I do still have a hard time reconciling in my mind how our paths diverged."

"You had as difficult a time accepting it then as you have understanding it now. So it's not like it made perfect sense to you at the time, either. When we spoke a few months ago, however, you said it made more sense."

Kelsey wished, once again, that Zane had been more honest with her about his relationship with Sarah. While it might not have changed things about their current situation, it would have meant she wasn't so shocked to learn about it when he no longer remembered or loved her.

At some point, Lee appeared, followed a few minutes later by Rori and Elsa. The dog made quick work of greeting them all, then wandered over to her bowls to lap up some water.

Rori gave Kelsey a quick one-arm hug before going to the counter to turn on the kettle. Kelsey was still getting used to the physical affection. Rori had asked her if she minded, sharing that she'd been deprived of physical affection for much of her life because she hadn't been close to her parents. Because of that, she loved offering affection to those she cared for.

Kelsey told her that she understood because of her own relationship with her parents, and she was glad someone thought she was worthy of affection, especially when she wasn't receiving any from her husband.

"Why don't we go sit outside?" Rori suggested. "Enjoy the nice warm days while we can. Fall is just around the corner."

"And I can't wait," Sarah said as they headed for the back door.

Kelsey was torn between joining them or going for a nap. In the end, she decided it was more important to hang out with this group of people. She could nap later.

CHAPTER NINETEEN

"Can't you please just cut the cast off, let me itch my leg, then put it back on again?"

When Gareth rolled his eyes at him, Zane felt like he was five years old and fighting the urge to punch his older brother.

"You have a couple more weeks," Gareth said. "Then we'll see how it's going."

Zane frowned, hoping Gareth could read his displeasure with that response. He was in a constant state of agitation these days. If his leg wasn't itching, his head was aching. And vice versa. He was also bored out of his mind.

It was so bad, he actually envied Kelsey going to her job stocking shelves. At least she got out of the house and had something to fill her time.

He had nothing, and it was driving him crazy. He'd started to do a bit of cooking at the house. But even then, he really had to be in the mood. Sometimes, being in the kitchen was just a reminder of what he'd lost. Both remembered and forgotten.

"What am I supposed to do with my time?" Zane asked. "I can't read books or watch screens for very long because I get a headache, or my headache gets worse. I can't do yard work because it's nearly impossible to manage crutches and a rake. I'm at a complete loss as to how to fill my time."

Gareth's expression turned sympathetic as he leaned back in the chair at his desk. "I understand that you're not used to sitting around doing nothing. But right now, the best thing you can do is just rest and let your brain continue to heal."

"I don't think I even care about getting my memory back anymore."

"Well, healing is needed for more than just your memory. The fact that you're dealing with headaches is a sign your brain still needs to recover from its injury."

"Will I ever not have headaches?" Zane asked.

"Hopefully. But it will take some time. Even your hard head wasn't enough to protect your brain from the knock around it got in that accident. It wasn't just a light tap on the noggin."

"It will help a lot to get this cast off, so I don't feel so helpless and useless."

"How are things with Kelsey?"

"As good as can be expected, given the circumstances."

"Have you talked at all about how you see your future?"

Zane nodded. "We talked and made the decision that we are going to give things a shot, even though I don't have my memory at the moment."

"That's good," Gareth said. "I think that's the best thing you can do. I know it's not easy for you since you have no memory of her and your marriage."

"Yeah. Talking to Sarah helped, not just because she could tell me why we broke up, but she also could share with me what I'd told her about Kelsey. Since the rest of you didn't really know Kelsey, it was good that Sarah had some insight."

"Is that why you decided to try to make it work?"

"Yeah. Partly. I felt like I owed it to Kelsey and to the man I was when I married her to stick it out and try."

"That's a good outlook," Gareth said. "I admire you for getting to this point."

"I just hope I'm not wasting our time, assuming I'll come to feel for her the way I did prior to the accident."

"You won't know if you don't try. We're definitely praying for both of you," Gareth assured him. "And if there's anything we can do, be sure to let us know."

There was a light knock on the door, then it swung open a crack and Janessa peeked her head through. "Your first afternoon patient is here." She smiled at Zane. "Or maybe it's your second."

"I guess that's my cue to head home," Zane said. "And try to find something to entertain myself."

"Are you bored?" Janessa asked as they walked toward the back of the clinic where he'd parked Kelsey's car, which she'd offered him the use of when she didn't need it. Currently, she was sleeping after working the night shift the previous night.

"A bit," he admitted. "It would be a lot easier if I didn't have this cast on my leg."

"Patience, little bro," Janessa said. "You need to give your body a chance to heal properly, or you'll have problems for much longer."

"I know." Zane sighed. "I'm just not used to having nothing to do."

"This will pass," Janessa told him, reaching out to give him a hug.

Zane hoped that was true. But honestly, sometimes he had a very difficult time imagining the future. That wasn't how it had previously been for him. He'd always had an idea of what his future would look like and the steps he needed to take to achieve his dreams.

Now, however, it seemed like he was staring into the distance, his vision obscured by the fog of memory loss.

After saying goodbye to Janessa, Zane left the clinic and climbed into Kelsey's car. Her small car wasn't the most comfortable or easy to get in and out of with his cast and crutches. Maybe he should spend his time doing some research for a new car since he would be receiving an insurance settlement for his other car, which had been totaled in the accident.

A glance at the dashboard showed him that the gas was just below a quarter tank. He thought he could pump gas, so instead of heading straight home, he went to a nearby gas station. There weren't a lot of things he could do for Kelsey, but he thought he could manage to fill the tank of her car.

It took a minute, but he finally got situated and started the pump. As he waited for it to finish, he leaned on his crutches and looked around. This was a newer gas station, and its main building also sold pizza and other gas station type fare.

Once the pump had finished, he got back into the car. As he drove home, Zane wondered again about how they'd dealt with finances in their marriage. It felt odd to give someone access to his money, but he'd always assumed that once he was married, he and his wife would combine their money. Truly become one in every way.

But could he become one with a stranger? Especially since it didn't appear that he'd given her access to his money, even when he had known her.

As he got back behind the wheel, Zane decided not to go home quite yet. Kelsey would probably sleep until around three, so there was no sense going home to an empty house.

Instead, he went for a bit of a drive. It had been awhile since he'd just toured around his hometown. There were some changes that had occurred over the years he'd been away. A new building for the library. New gas stations. A couple of new restaurants. An expansion of the high school.

He had good memories of his growing up years in Serenity.

At the time, he and his other adopted siblings had been part of a fairly small group of visible minorities. Thankfully, because they had many siblings around at school and their family was well known, they hadn't had bad experiences as a result of that. Still, he hadn't wanted to stick around in Serenity.

After he'd exhausted the town sights, Zane headed in the direction of the resort. He didn't plan to stop in, since he wasn't exactly dressed to visit a luxury resort.

He'd heard plenty about the new rink that Hudson's father had built, so he decided to take a drive past that. After looping past the rink, he headed for the hotel and pulled into the parking lot of The Steakhouse. He'd worked at the restaurants one summer as a bus boy between his junior and senior year.

Zane had wanted to work in the kitchen, but they hadn't had a spot for him there, though the chefs had been more than happy to answer any questions he had. And he'd been able to pick up a fair amount of information by just watching.

He wondered how they were staffed now. Perhaps he could get a job there until he had a better idea of where his life was going and what was happening with him and Kelsey.

Finally, he turned the car back towards the house. After parking at the curb, he made his way up the driveway and into the house. It was quiet, so he didn't think Kelsey was up yet.

In the kitchen, he surveyed the contents of the fridge, wondering what he should make for dinner. He still wasn't up for cooking more intricate dishes. The precise cutting and multiple ingredients required weren't interesting to him at the moment. Hopefully, that would change soon.

After a few minutes, he decided he'd make a Bolognese sauce and some pasta. Not freshly made because he didn't think Lee and Rori had a pasta maker.

Glancing at the clock, he figured Kelsey would be up soon, and having noticed that she liked a coffee when she got up, he started up the coffeemaker. Though his day was almost half over, hers was just beginning.

Zane had been working for a bit when he heard movement. Turning from the saucepan where he was browning some meat, he saw Kelsey walk into the kitchen. She wore a pair of loose shorts, an oversized T-shirt, and her hair was up in a messy bun.

"Good morning," he said.

She lifted her phone to look at the screen, then arched a brow at him. "Morning?"

"Your morning," he clarified. "Do you want some coffee?"

"Yes, but you don't need to get it for me."

"I think I can manage it." He lifted a mug from the mug tree and moved over to the coffee maker. He poured the coffee, then scooted it along the counter to where Kelsey had set her phone while she went to the fridge to get the cream she liked in her coffee.

"Thank you," she said as she poured a healthy dollop of cream into the mug, changing it from black to light brown.

Zane put a piece of sourdough bread in the toaster, then retrieved the butter from the fridge. Since committing himself to making an effort with Kelsey, he'd tried to pay close attention to the things she did and what she preferred.

It was why he now knew that she liked coffee and a piece of buttered toast when she woke up. He watched as she lifted her cup and took a sip of coffee, her eyes closing as she savored it.

Her slightly disheveled look appealed to him. He'd been taught young that he shouldn't focus on a person's outward appearance. But since Kelsey was technically his wife, he didn't think it was wrong to allow himself to appreciate her physical appeal.

It was weird to think that he'd been intimate with her but had no memory of it. If he thought about how much knowledge she had of him versus what he had of her, it left him feeling a little strange. He didn't dwell on that fact too much, but sometimes it was impossible to ignore.

"Here you go," Zane said as he placed the plate with toast on it in front of her.

"Thanks." The smile she gave him was warm, and, if he wasn't mistaken, held a bit of affection. "You don't need to do this for me, but I do appreciate it."

"You're welcome." Feeding people had always been something he enjoyed, and it seemed even more important that he do that for Kelsey. Even if it was just toast and coffee. "Are you working again tonight?"

"Yep. Even though I'm only part-time, I asked if they could give me my shifts in a row. It's difficult to keep going from working nights to being off. I know I could just keep the same schedule even when I'm off, but what am I going to do at night when everyone else is asleep? Thankfully, they were willing to make that adjustment for me."

"Are you hoping they'll give you full-time?"

She considered it for a moment, then said, "I don't know if I'm hoping or not, but I won't turn down extra shifts."

"If you could work another job, what would it be?"

Again, she was quiet for a moment as she took a bite of her toast before answering. "I've had different jobs, mainly in restaurants. Most recently, I worked as a hostess."

"And you enjoyed it?"

She nodded. "I did. And it was fun working in the same place you did."

"Was that the case in Tampa, as well?"

"No. They didn't need a hostess at your restaurant, so I got a job at a different one."

"And you still enjoyed it?"

"For the most part. Honestly, I hadn't worked there long before your accident. But the people there were nice, and the owners were so sympathetic when I let them know what had happened."

"Was there no hostess position around here?"

"Not that I found," she said. "And I wasn't keen on driving an hour or more to and from work each day for a job in Coeur d'Alene. I don't mind what I'm doing now. Keeps me physically active, and it doesn't require too much concentration."

Zane stirred the food in the pot on the stove. He wanted to ask her if she had any career aspirations beyond being a hostess, but he didn't want to offend her when they were just starting to figure things out.

"What are you making?" Kelsey asked as she lifted her mug and took a sip. "It smells good."

"Bolognese sauce and pasta."

"Are you making the pasta?"

"No. I don't have my pasta machine, and I don't think they have one here."

"You had one in Tampa. Did you want your things?" Kelsey asked, lowering her mug to the counter. "We could go to the storage unit and get what you want."

"My knives and everything?"

"Yep. Everything is there."

Though Zane wasn't sure he was ready to go into cooking full on, the thought of having his tools of the trade close at hand was appealing. "I think I'd like that."

"Tonight is my last shift for the next four days, so we could go whenever you want."

He knew that on the days she was shifting from working nights to her days off, she usually only slept until around noon. "Maybe we could go tomorrow afternoon."

"That works for me."

"What was the first thing I cooked for you?"

"This."

He glanced over at her. "Bolognese?"

"Yes. I told you that I liked spaghetti with a meat sauce, and you said that you could make something similar, but much better."

"And did I?"

"Yep. I'd never seen anyone make pasta before, so that was fun. And it all tasted delicious."

"So I made a good first impression?"

"Good first *cooking* impression," she said.

"Did I make other impressions? What was your very first impression of me?"

"I was told, even before I met you, that though you were handsome and super nice, you were off limits for anything but friendship."

Zane set the wooden spoon down and turned to face her. "Did they say why?"

"Just that you were very career focused, and every woman who'd tried to get your attention was rebuffed. I wouldn't have pursued you, regardless. So when we did meet, I just viewed you through the lens of a co-worker. And later, a friend."

"And your impression of me as a friend?"

"You were super nice, but also very intense when it came to cooking and your career. There were times you yelled at people, but everyone would say it was deserved. I don't know how you were at your new restaurant, though, since I wasn't there with you."

"Sometimes the only way to get people to listen in a busy kitchen is to yell at them," Zane said as he turned his attention to the sauce. "Hopefully, I never yelled at you."

"Nope. You never did."

"Did we argue?"

"Not really. Probably our most intense discussions came around our elopement and the move to Tampa. Not that we disagreed about either, but more along the lines of discussing how we were going to carry it all out."

Zane wanted to know everything. To understand the dynamics they'd had between them. What they had now was still awkward and, at times, tense. This was never how he'd envisioned a relationship being.

He filled a large pot with water, then slid it along the counter to the stove, where he set it on a burner. Though he would have liked to have had some sort of garlic bread with the meal, he wasn't much of a baker. Especially when it came to yeast products.

"Is there anything you want me to do?"

"You're my sous-chef, right?" he asked.

"Sometimes. Are we having a salad? That's my forte, after all."

Zane chuckled. "Sure. I think we have the stuff for a garden salad."

For the next little while, Kelsey cut up vegetables for the salad, then set the table. Shortly after five, Lee and Rori arrived home from the vet clinic.

"I have to say, I'm really seeing the appeal of having a personal chef," Rori said when she walked into the kitchen. She took a deep breath, then exhaled with a satisfied look on her face. "It smells delicious."

"It tastes delicious too," Zane said with a smile.

"Well, let us go get cleaned up and changed," Lee said. "We'll be back in a few minutes."

Once they'd left, with Elsa trailing after them, Zane put the pasta into the boiling water, to which he'd added some oil and salt. Kelsey got a pitcher of water from the fridge and set it on the table.

She ended up having to help him drain the pasta once it was done, since he couldn't manage to lift the pot off the stove on his own. Sliding it along the counter when it was filled with hot water didn't seem like the smartest move.

By the time Lee and Rori reappeared, everything was ready.

As the four of them ate dinner, Zane found himself enjoying the evening. He'd never spent any significant time in Serenity as an adult. Once he'd left to get his degree in Culinary Arts, he'd only been home for a few days around the holidays each year or if there was a wedding.

So being in Serenity—if he ignored how he'd ended up there—was actually enjoyable. He'd always been closest to Lee, and since they'd both spent time in Chicago, they'd also been roommates for awhile. Now they were roommates again, but this time, with wives.

He enjoyed hanging out with his whole family. But the quiet times when it was just the four of them, he enjoyed even more.

He'd never imagined living in Serenity as an adult—and he still wasn't sure he could—but at least it wasn't as bad as he'd thought it would be. Especially since he was living with Lee. If he'd continued to live with his parents and without Kelsey, he probably wouldn't have enjoyed it as much.

He loved his parents and appreciated all they'd done for him. But now he needed to focus on Kelsey, and he couldn't have done that very well if they'd still been living separately. And he was pretty sure that Kelsey wouldn't have wanted to live with his parents, at least not initially.

Making the move to Lee's seemed to have set him on the right path, especially where Kelsey was concerned. And now he was back to doing some cooking.

He still wasn't sure what the future held, but at least he felt like he'd taken some proactive steps forward. He just prayed that God would give him clear guidance in the days and weeks ahead.

CHAPTER TWENTY

Kelsey woke with her alarm at noon the next day. She hit the snooze and turned onto her back, but stayed under the covers, wishing for more than four hours of sleep. She couldn't stay in bed too long, though. She and Zane were headed into Coeur d'Alene and the place where she'd arranged to have their belongings stored.

After her alarm went again, she tapped the screen to silence it, then flung her blanket off and swung her feet over the side of the bed. She sat for a moment before heading to the bathroom to get ready for her day.

A check of the weather showed that it was a cloudy, cooler-than-usual day, but thankfully, there was no rain in the forecast. With that in mind, she pulled on a pair of skinny jeans and a long sleeve T-shirt. If they were digging through boxes and stuff, she wanted to be comfortable.

She brushed her hair back into a ponytail, then glanced down at her hand. She'd gotten into the habit of removing her wedding and engagement rings before she went to work, then she'd put them back on once she was home. The last few times she'd put the rings back on, it had been with some reluctance.

That day, she decided to leave them off completely. It wasn't that she was rejecting her marriage to Zane. But it didn't feel right to wear the outward sign of their love when they weren't acting like a married couple. Zane also wasn't wearing his ring. He'd never even asked about it.

Going to the high dresser in the bedroom, she opened the top drawer and lifted out the small jewelry box that contained Zane's ring. After a moment's hesitation, she laid her two rings next to his, then she stared at them before snapping the lid shut.

Please, God, let there come a day when we once again place these rings on each other's fingers as a sign of our love and commitment to each other.

Kelsey had no idea if God would answer her prayer, but she was pretty sure that she wasn't the only one praying that things would work out for her and Zane. Though she did wonder what Zane's prayer for their situation was.

Did he pray that things would work out for them?

Or had he suggested trying so that when he eventually walked away from her, he could say that he'd given it a good effort?

It was hard not to consider that, because aside from spending time together like they had the previous day, just talking, they didn't do anything else together. He didn't take her on any dates or try to arrange for them to hang out, just the two of them. Any time they spent together was purely incidental.

Even going to the storage unit together wasn't because he wanted to spend time with her. It was because he wanted something from there, and she could help him get it.

She thought that perhaps they might be becoming friends, but more than that? She just didn't know.

With a sigh, Kelsey picked up her purse, phone, and keys and left the bedroom.

Once downstairs, she headed for the kitchen, drawn by the aroma of coffee. Zane was there, leaning on his crutches at the counter.

He looked up at her and said, "Good morning."

"Good morning."

"The coffee is fresh. Do you want it here or in a travel mug to go?"

"Maybe in a travel mug," she said.

He got a couple of tall travel mugs down from the cupboard, then filled them from the coffee carafe. Kelsey went to the fridge to get cream.

"Do you want toast before we go?"

She wasn't terribly hungry right then, so she said, "No. I'll be fine for now."

"We can stop for a late lunch after we're done at the storage place."

"That'll work."

Once their coffees were ready, Kelsey looped her purse over her shoulder, then picked up both travel mugs since Zane couldn't handle his with the crutches.

"Fall's coming," Zane said as they stepped out on the porch.

"I bet it's beautiful around here with the turning colors."

"It is. And we have some fall activities here in Serenity that make it a fun time of year."

"When does school start?"

"Usually after Labor Day. So in about a week."

Kelsey tucked one mug in the crook of her arm and fished her keys out of her pocket to click the fob to unlock the car doors. While Zane got in the passenger seat, she circled around the car to the driver's side. Opening the door, she leaned in and put the mugs in the cup holder, then slid behind the wheel.

As she pulled away from the curb, Zane asked, "Did you like going back to school?"

"Not really," Kelsey said. "Especially if we'd ended up moving because it meant I was starting at a new school."

"Oh, yeah. That wouldn't be fun."

"No. It wasn't fun at all."

"I graduated with a few people who had been with me since kindergarten."

"I can't even imagine that," Kelsey said, wondering how her life might have been different if she'd had that kind of stability in her life.

It probably wouldn't have made her strong enough to deal with the situation she'd found herself in when Zane woke up without his memories of her and their marriage. Her whole life had been one unexpected event after another. She'd had to learn how to weather those times, and it had given her the ability to keep moving forward, even when all she wanted to do was run away and hide.

"Were you a good student?" he asked.

"I wasn't brilliant or anything, but with hard work, I got pretty good grades." It hadn't mattered much to her parents, but she'd figured out she would need good grades if she wanted to go to college because she'd have to rely on scholarships and financial aid.

In the end, it hadn't mattered. She'd had to do a lot of her college education without scholarships, and she hadn't wanted to go into too much debt, which is why it had taken her so long to get to the point of taking the nursing exam. Working and going to school had been tough.

"How about you?"

She did already know how *her* Zane had felt about school, but it felt like she should ask him questions that were relevant just so it wasn't all one-sided. Plus, she wondered if she'd get different responses from this Zane than she had from hers.

"I liked school for the most part," he said. "I think one of my favorite subjects was science, especially once I saw parts of cooking as a form of science."

That was basically what Zane had told her the first time around. "Did you take cooking in high school?"

"No, they didn't offer anything like that. I would find recipes online and then persuade my mom to buy the ingredients."

"Were all the recipes a success?"

Zane gave a bark of laughter. "Nope. Especially not at the start. But after I'd been cooking for about a year, I had way more hits than misses."

"At least you persevered," she said. "And your family kept letting you try, even after you had disasters."

That would *not* have been the case with her family. Plus, their meals had been made from whatever was cheapest and/or whatever they had on hand.

"My parents have been pretty good at letting each of us find our own paths, and doing what they can to support us."

"Did Gareth not feel pressured to become a doctor?"

"Not that I'm aware of. He was helping at the clinic while in high school. None of the rest of us, aside from Janessa, were as interested in the medical side of things. Well, I guess Lee was, but he preferred to work on animals."

"Is there a sibling that has surprised you with their career choice?"

Zane was quiet for a moment, then said, "Cole. Not so much his career choice, but that he's actually achieving his dream of playing professionally."

For the remainder of the trip, they talked about his family. He shared more with her than he had previously. She'd realized that though he wasn't technically estranged from his family, he'd gotten distant from them. This Zane wasn't, and it was apparent in how he talked about them.

She had a slight inkling that him distancing himself from his family had something to do with Sarah. It seemed the demise of that relationship had really done a number on him. Especially his faith.

It was possible that his lack of faith had meant he kept distant from his family so they wouldn't know. She'd seen how important faith was to his family, so if he wasn't acting like they expected, it would have been a challenge for him to remain close to them.

Now, however, he was back in the mindset of having a strong and committed faith. Kelsey still wasn't sure about that with regards to herself, but she wasn't opposed to learning more about the faith that was so important to Zane and his family.

When they reached their storage unit, Kelsey parked in front of the building, then got out to open it. Zane approached her as she stood in the large open doorway.

"Wow. Lots of stuff."

"Yep. It's everything from our apartment, except for our clothes. Well, I think our winter clothes are here."

"We should probably dig those out while we're here too," Zane said as he moved into the unit. "Save us making a trip back in a few weeks."

"I'm not sure where everything is in here." She stepped past Zane and looked around. "They just unloaded the truck and shoved it in."

"Hopefully, stuff is labelled."

"It should be. I'll check this side, and you can check that one. Your knives and other tools should be in a box labeled from the kitchen."

"This says Zane bedroom. What does that mean?"

"That has stuff from your nightstand and any non-clothing items from your dresser."

Kelsey helped lift the box down to where he stood. He pulled a box cutter from his pocket and sliced the tape on it.

While he looked through the box, Kelsey returned to her search for the boxes from the kitchen. She should have thought about him wanting his knives and set them aside when they were packing up the apartment.

"Did I read a lot?" Zane asked as he held up two paperbacks.

"Not a lot," she said. "But we were working our way through the Dean Koontz book."

"Working our way?"

"Two or three times a week, we would take turns reading it aloud."

He angled the Dean Koontz book to look at the top of it where a bookmark was sticking up. "We must have just started it."

"Yes. We'd only been reading it for a couple of weeks before your accident."

He returned the books to the box, then folded the flaps over to seal it. "I think I want to take this box with us as well."

Kelsey went to open the back hatch of her car, then walked to where Zane stood with the box. "I'll put it in the back of the car."

"Thanks."

They probably had room for four or five boxes if they put some of them on the back seat. She tried to think if there was something else that he might want.

"Were there any boxes that I hadn't unpacked from the move to Tampa yet?" Zane asked.

Kelsey thought back. "Yeah. I think you had two totes that you brought to Tampa that you said were just keepsakes and stuff."

"I think I'd like to take those back as well."

It took about twenty minutes to shift furniture and boxes around to locate the totes, and in the process, they found the boxes containing his knives and other kitchen tools along with their winter clothes. Kelsey slid the totes into the back seat, then put the other boxes into the trunk.

Once they were back in the car, Kelsey said, "Where do you want to go for food?"

"What are you in the mood for?" he asked.

"I hate to tell you this, but I'm in the mood for breakfast."

Zane chuckled. "Why would you hate to tell me that?"

"You never liked going out to eat for breakfast once it wasn't morning anymore."

"Why?"

"You said it was because of the type of restaurant we had to go to in order to get me what I wanted."

"Ahhhh. Well, I still sort of feel that way, but I don't mind if we go somewhere that serves an all-day breakfast."

After a short discussion and consulting their phones, they made their decision and left the storage place. It didn't take too long to get to the restaurant, and soon they were seated at a booth.

It wasn't too busy in the restaurant, likely because it was just after two in the afternoon. Zane took longer than her to peruse the menu, but when their waitress returned with their drinks, they were both ready to order.

Zane ended up opting for a burger and fries, while Kelsey got pancakes, scrambled eggs, and bacon. She was really hungry, so she hoped they didn't take too long to bring them their food.

"Do you mind that we're staying with Lee and Rori?" Zane asked.

The question came so out of the blue that Kelsey just stared at him for a moment. "Why would I mind?"

"I know that this is not exactly what you would have chosen," Zane said. "I just want to make sure you're comfortable staying there still."

"I'm fine," she told him. "But I'll let you know if that changes."

"Seeing all the furniture and boxes in that storage unit reminded me that we once had a whole apartment. That we lived together, on our own."

"Yeah, but I don't mind staying with Lee and Rori. They've both been great. I'm more worried that they might not want us sticking around."

"They're fine with it," Zane said. "I think Rori would actually be upset if we left. She's taken a liking to you."

"I really like her too," Kelsey told him. "But are you okay living there?"

Zane nodded. "Which is good, because I don't think it would make much sense to rent an apartment here."

And she doubted that he wanted to be alone in an apartment with her. It would probably be a bit awkward.

She missed their apartment in Tampa. Or rather, she missed what they had together in that apartment. She missed *them*.

When the food arrived, Kelsey realized that this was how they'd spent the second half of their first evening together. Because they hadn't wanted their time together to end when the restaurant closed, they'd found a twenty-four-hour restaurant, and she'd had breakfast that night too. And Zane had ordered a burger and fries.

Without even realizing it, they'd recreated that time. She decided not to tell Zane about it, though she wasn't sure why.

However, unlike that evening, this time their conversation had lapses and silences that felt heavy. She knew it was partly because of Zane's injury. Though he didn't say anything, she could tell that his head was hurting because he frequently touched his temple and forehead as he ate.

When the waitress brought the bill, Kelsey wasn't sure what to do. Previously, Zane would have picked up the bill. However, this was an odd situation.

Zane reached out and picked up the bill before she could decide what to do.

"How much is mine?" she asked as she pulled her wallet out of her purse.

Zane frowned at her. "I'll take care of the bill."

"But—"

"No buts. I'm taking care of it."

"Thank you."

"You're welcome."

Once the bill had been paid, they left the restaurant and got back in the car.

"Sorry I'm lousy company," Zane said after they'd been driving in silence for several minutes. "My head is hurting again."

"Feel free to close your eyes and rest," Kelsey told him. "You don't need to entertain me."

"I think I'll take you up on that."

Zane reclined the seat a bit, then settled back, closing his eyes. Kelsey wished he didn't get the headaches, not just because Zane was in pain, but because it made her think that his brain wasn't healing as fast as they would have liked.

His breathing slowly evened out, and for the remainder of the drive, Kelsey allowed herself to just appreciate being in the moment. Zane might not have his memories of her and their marriage, but he was still alive, and there was still an ember of hope that things would work out between them.

When she pulled to a stop in front of the house, Zane groggily straightened in his seat and looked around.

"Go on into the house," Kelsey said. "I'll bring the boxes in."

Zane frowned. "I wish I could help you with that."

"It's fine. They aren't that heavy."

"Still," he grumped. "I can't wait until this cast is off."

They got out of the car, then Zane went ahead to open the front door. Kelsey wrangled each of the boxes out of the car and carried them into the house. She took the totes right up to Zane's bedroom, along with the box of his stuff from their apartment in Tampa. The boxes that contained his knives and other cooking tools, she left in the kitchen, then she set the winter clothes box at the bottom of the stairs to take to her room to sort later.

"Did you want to go through these boxes?" Kelsey asked, gesturing to the ones sitting on the floor in the kitchen.

"Sure. Might as well see what I had."

Kelsey ended up being the one to unpack the boxes, taking out each of the items and setting them on the counter for Zane to look over.

"I guess I bought myself a new set of knives," he said as he unrolled the bag containing them.

"I bought those for you as a wedding gift," she told him.

He looked at her with raised brows. "Really? These are great knives. How did you know what to get?"

"I talked to the head chef at the restaurant where we both worked. He told me what knives you'd like."

Zane ran his hand over the knives. "These are beautiful. Thank you."

"You're welcome." Zane's reaction to the knives this time was much lower key than when she'd given them to him following their wedding.

"What did I get you?"

The reality was, Zane hadn't given her anything on the day of the wedding. It had hurt at the time, but she'd shoved that hurt down, knowing that he'd had a lot of things going on around that time. He couldn't be blamed for not thinking about a gift for her for their wedding. Plus, he'd spent money on her rings, so she chose to consider them her wedding gift from him.

"Did I not get you anything?" Zane asked when she didn't answer right away.

"You bought me my rings."

His gaze dropped to her hand, his brow furrowing. "Why aren't you wearing them? You were wearing them before."

Kelsey flexed the fingers on her left hand before making a fist. "I decided I wasn't comfortable wearing them, considering our circumstances."

"We're still legally married," Zane said.

"True. But you're not sure you want to be married to me," Kelsey said, managing to get the words out, even though they hurt to say. "So, I thought it would probably be best to keep them off until we make a decision one way or the other."

Zane's frown deepened at her words, but he didn't respond to what she'd said.

"And anyway, you're not wearing your ring either."

He looked down at his hand. "I didn't know I had one. Where is it?"

"It's in a box with my rings. They gave it to me at the hospital after your accident."

Zane sat in silence for a long moment, staring at his hand.

Kelsey hadn't planned to have this conversation with him. If she'd known that it was a possibility, triggered by her not having her rings on, she might not have left them off.

"Would you prefer that I wear my rings?" Kelsey asked.

"I don't know," he said. At least he was honest.

"I don't know either."

"I think I'd rather that we did wear them, because we're going to get a lot of questions if you don't. But if you're not comfortable with it, I'm not going to force the issue."

Her shoulders slumped as she rested her hands on the counter. All of this was uncharted territory for them. She'd never heard of anyone else being in the position they were in, though she supposed that if some existed, they might not be making it public. After all, she and Zane hadn't exactly gone public with their situation.

Kelsey turned her attention back to the boxes and pulled out more items. The discussion about this wasn't over, but she had no idea what more to say. She wanted him to want them to wear their rings because of what they represented, not just to avoid questions.

Her heart hurt as she finished putting the contents of the box on the counter. Zane seemed troubled, though she was sure he wasn't feeling the hurt she was.

She really hoped she was strong enough to carry this through to wherever it was headed. Right then, it felt like they were in a tenuous position, but she wasn't going to give up until Zane said the word.

CHAPTER TWENTY-ONE

Zane pulled the casserole dish out of the oven and set it on a cooling rack on the counter. It pained him to be making a casserole, but it was the easiest thing to make given the food available to him.

Thankfully, he knew how to make it taste good, and the people who would be eating it were always appreciative. Especially Rori, who was glad to not have to be doing the cooking herself.

That night, his parents were joining them for dinner. He wished that wasn't the case because things were still tense between him and Kelsey after their conversation the previous day.

Who would have thought that a quick trip to retrieve his cooking tools would lead to the tension they'd ended up with?

Not him. He'd just thought it would be nice to get some of his stuff—hoping it might jar some memories loose—and also for them to spend a bit of time together.

Instead, they wandered into a difficult conversation, with him discovering that for whatever reason, he'd not given Kelsey a wedding gift when she'd given him an expensive set of knives. She'd said that her rings were a gift from him, but in his mind, he should have given her more.

Her expression had closed down during their discussion about it, so he hadn't been able to tell if the memory had made her mad or sad. But the fact that she hadn't revealed how she felt told him that she hadn't been happy about it. And she shouldn't have been. He should have gotten her a necklace or something to commemorate their special day, especially considering they'd eloped.

His disappointment in himself was only topped by his disappointment that Kelsey had decided not to wear her rings. It wasn't disappointment in Kelsey. He was just disappointed in the circumstances that had made her feel like taking them off was a good idea.

But he could hardly complain since he wasn't wearing his either. It hadn't even crossed his mind to ask where his ring was, or to ask for it back.

It just felt like she didn't believe that he was committed to giving their marriage a genuine shot. He needed to figure out how to prove that to her.

"I'm short a fork," Kelsey said as she came into the kitchen from setting the table in the dining room.

There were only six of them there for the meal, but the breakfast nook felt like it would be a bit crowded for them. He didn't want it to end up being an awkward meal, but the chances were high. Things were still tense between him and Kelsey, but he hoped that it wasn't too apparent. Especially to his mom.

Kelsey grabbed a fork from the drawer, then went to check out the chicken broccoli cheese casserole that was sitting on the counter. "Smells good."

"Here's hoping it tastes good."

She looked at him with raised brows. "Is there a chance it won't? Because if that's the case, we might have some deaths around here tonight."

"What do you mean?"

"Well, when you cook great, it tastes amazing," she said. "So I can only assume that when you cook bad, it's lethal."

That got a huff of laughter out of Zane, and he felt a little of the tension he'd been carrying ease. "It won't kill anyone. I promise."

"Then I'm sure it will taste fine."

As she disappeared, the door to the garage opened. Rori and Lee came in with smiles, but they didn't linger before heading to their room to change out of their scrubs, since dinner was almost ready to be served.

Zane had placed some rolls in the oven, so he checked the timer and saw that they still had a couple of minutes left. He hadn't made them himself. The store had had frozen unbaked rolls, so he'd added them to the grocery order he'd placed for delivery earlier that day.

The doorbell rang, and he looked toward the entrance to the kitchen, listening to hear if whoever it was let themselves in.

"Hello!" his mom called out.

"In here, Mom."

A moment later, his parents appeared in the doorway of the kitchen.

"It smells delicious, darling," his mom said as she approached him and gave him a hug. "Better than anything I could ever make."

"I think it's been established that that's a fairly low bar," Zane said with a laugh.

His dad also chuckled as he gave Zane a hug. "Did you make enough so there'll be leftovers? If so, I'll gladly take them off your hands."

"I might fight you for them," Lee said as he walked in with Rori.

"Hello, darlings." His mom gave them both a hug, then bent to greet Elsa, who had followed them into the kitchen. She gave the dog all the attention she'd probably give a grandchild, if any were present.

Kelsey quietly joined them, making no effort to insert herself into the conversation. Zane knew she was still uncomfortable around his parents, but all of them were trying to interact with her a bit more.

"Can someone please carry this to the table?" Zane asked as he gestured to the casserole dish on the counter.

Lee stepped up to take it, while Zane pulled the pan of rolls out. He slid them out onto the cooling racks on the counter beside the oven, waiting as Kelsey moved past him to the fridge, then he got the basket he'd set out for the rolls earlier.

"I'll take those," Rori offered once he'd transferred them to the basket.

Zane handed them over, then they all moved to the dining room and took seats around the table. They'd shrunk it down to its smallest size, since they hadn't wanted to have everyone clustered around one end of the expanded table. There was still lots of room around it, though.

Lee said a prayer before they began to eat. In addition to the casserole and rolls, Kelsey had made a salad. It wasn't a meal Zane would ever serve in a restaurant, but the majority of his family preferred more down to earth, hearty comfort food style meals. So, he gave them what they wanted.

"This tastes as delicious as it smells," his mom said after she took a bite.

"Thanks, Mom."

"Are you a good cook, Kelsey?" his mom asked.

"When measured against Zane, I'd say no," Kelsey said. "But if I compare myself to non-chef people, I'd say I do okay. Never poisoned myself or anyone else, so I figure that's a win."

"You're fortunate to be married to someone who likes to cook," his mom said with a smile. "Neither Dan nor I are very good cooks, but we get by."

"I love having Zane here to help with the cooking," Rori said. "I'm hoping he never leaves."

Zane wanted to groan at Rori's words because he just knew his mom was going to jump on them.

"I hope he never leaves too," his mom said, right on cue.

He glanced at Kelsey and found her watching him, perhaps waiting for his response to that, since it pertained to their future.

"I'm not sure that's possible, Mom," Zane said. "You know that."

His mom nodded. "I know, but a mom can always dream."

"You should propose your restaurant idea to Kayleigh and Hudson," Lee said. "Maybe you could open it at the resort."

"Kayleigh knows about my idea," Zane told him. "So, if it was a possibility, I'm sure she would have said something already."

He had a hard time thinking about a future in Serenity because he'd never considered it before. But right then, he had a hard time thinking about a future anywhere. Uncertainty surrounding his health and his marriage made it a challenge to envision his future beyond the next day or so.

"Maybe I should talk to Alexander," his mom said. "Parent to parent."

"Mom. Please don't do that," Zane protested. "I have no idea what my memory is going to do, so I need to focus on getting healthy before I consider opening a restaurant."

"That's true," his dad said. "You have time to figure it out."

Zane didn't necessarily feel that was the case, but he didn't voice that.

"How is your job going, Kelsey?" his mom asked.

"It's going well," Kelsey said.

"Do you enjoy working nights?"

"I'm not sure if *enjoy* is the word I'd use. But I've worked evenings before, so having a job with hours different from the norm isn't unusual for me."

"I remember when Dan and I were both doing our ER residency, and there were times we worked opposite shifts and hardly ever saw each other. It was terrible."

"In Chicago, Zane and I were fortunate that we worked similar hours at the same restaurant."

"It wasn't like that in Tampa?" his mom asked.

Kelsey shook her head. "We were working at two different places. Zane's restaurant didn't need a hostess, so I got a job somewhere else."

"Was that difficult?"

"It was an adjustment, but we made it work. Zane's days were longer than mine, but I always stayed up until he got home."

"So you were waiting for him the night of the accident?"

Kelsey nodded, emotion crossing her face. "It was the worst few hours of my life as I was trying to figure out what had happened. I was in denial at first. Telling myself that he was just working late, even though his phone showed he'd left the restaurant already."

"You had tracking on him?" his dad asked.

Kelsey hesitated a moment before answering. "Our phones were set up to show our locations to each other."

It was a bit weird to listen to Kelsey talk about him. It felt like they were talking about another person who had the same name as him. It was rather surreal.

Zane was still trying to figure out what kind of man he'd become, and he wasn't entirely sure he was happy with all the changes. It made him not want to regain his memories because he didn't know what would happen to him. Would he revert to who he'd been, or would this experience bring his priorities back to where they should be?

Obviously, he wanted to regain his memories and experience where it related to his career, but in all other areas, he wasn't sure he wanted to remember. If he was going to make a marriage with Kelsey work, he wanted to do it as the man he was when he married her, not the one he'd become.

"Do you have a... uh... career?" his mom asked.

Zane had wondered himself if Kelsey had any career aspirations beyond restaurant hostess. If her goal had been to be a wife and a mother, he could respect that. But she hadn't mentioned that they'd been planning for a family right away.

"I've enjoyed being in the hospitality business," Kelsey said. "But I have other interests, too. They just haven't solidified into anything yet."

Zane sensed there was something more there, but he wasn't going to press her for answers in front of his family. He found that he wanted to know things about her before his family did. In their current situation, that felt like how things should unfold.

"I'm grateful that even though I wasn't able to pursue education beyond high school, I've ended up with a job I really love," Rori said, clearly trying to take the focus off Kelsey and her career aspirations.

"And you do a great job at it," Lee said, giving her an affectionate smile.

"Who would have known that I'd love working in an animal clinic?"

"Might have something to do with your husband also working there," Zane said.

Rori smiled at Lee. "It definitely has something to do with that."

The conversation drifted away from Kelsey, and Zane was relieved. He was never sure how to take his mom's questions when they were directed at Kelsey. He thought she was just making an attempt to get to know Kelsey better. However, some of the questions seem to wander into areas that Kelsey wasn't comfortable discussing.

Zane felt like there was still so much he didn't know about his relationship with Kelsey, but he didn't know how to delve deeper into it. Would it matter if he never discovered everything about their relationship, especially if he didn't get his memory back?

She needed to learn who he was now, and he needed to learn about her from scratch. They were making some progress on that, he thought, but it felt a bit like one step forward, two back at times.

"We're having ice cream sundaes for dessert," Rori announced as they finished the meal. "So let me know if there's something specific you want to have on your sundae."

Kelsey got up to help Rori and Lee clear the table.

When they disappeared into the kitchen, his mom said, "How are things going with you and Kelsey?"

"They're going well," he said, though perhaps that was a bit of a stretch. "We've been spending more time together."

"Do you think it's going to work?"

"We're trying, Mom," he said. "That's all I can say. We both want to get to a good place in our marriage, so the best thing you can do to help us is to continue to pray for us and support us."

"We *are* praying for you both," his dad assured him.

"Thank you."

Lee came back in with a carafe of coffee and set it on the table. There were mugs and bowls with spoons in them already set out on the buffet against the wall, so he moved them over to the table. Kelsey and Rori returned with trays holding the ice cream and all the options for their sundaes.

"Do you think you have enough ice cream?" his dad asked as Rori set out three containers of different flavors.

"Yep. Unless you don't like any of the flavors," Rori said. "In which case, we have failed."

"I told her which flavors our family seems to prefer, so we should be okay."

Lee scooped out the ice cream requests, then took the containers back into the kitchen once he was done. Zane watched what Kelsey chose for her sundae, wondering if this was something they'd shared before.

She chose the mini marshmallows, walnuts, bananas, and chocolate syrup. He also liked the marshmallows, walnuts, and chocolate syrup, but he passed on the bananas and chose a brownie instead.

"We leave in a week for the hospital ship," his mom said as they ate their dessert. "We had already planned to join them before your accident. I wanted to put off going, but your dad said we should still go."

"You should," Zane encouraged her. "There's no reason for you to stay here. I'm doing fine, and if we need you, we can contact you."

"It's just hard to leave when you're still not one hundred percent."

"I know, but Gareth is keeping tabs on me, so you don't have to worry."

"It'll be fine," his dad said, putting his arm around Zane's mom. We know that God will be with you, just like He'll be with us."

"We'll take care of him," Rori said. "And make sure he does what the doctor tells him."

"Well, we'll try at least," Lee added with a chuckle. "Zane is nothing if not a little stubborn."

"Zane is sitting right here," Zane pointed out. "Do not disparage my character."

That got another laugh out of Lee, and Rori joined in. If there was one person who didn't take him too seriously, it was Lee.

"I'll expect regular updates," his mom said. "That will help me focus on what we're supposed to be doing on the ship."

"When are you coming back?" Lee asked.

"We had planned to be back for Thanksgiving," his dad said. "But they asked if we'd be willing to extend to the middle of December, and we agreed."

That his parents had agreed to leave Serenity was a sign to Zane that he really was on the right path to recovery. There was no way his mom would leave his side if he wasn't doing okay.

When they finished the meal, they visited a little longer, but then his parents decided it was time to go. They gave hugs and said goodnight before leaving the house.

Zane went into the kitchen and settled on one of the barstools at the counter. Lee worked to put the food away while Kelsey and Rori finished clearing the table and putting the dishes in the dishwasher. He'd tried to put away a lot of what he'd used in the meal prep, so there wasn't too much else to clean up.

"That casserole was delicious," Kelsey said. "Thanks for making it."

"Yes," Rori agreed. "It was very yummy. You'll have to make it again."

"I'm actually surprised you made a casserole." Kelsey wiped the counter in front of him. "You told me once that you hated making them."

"I do," he agreed. "But my family likes them, and they're fairly easy for me to make, especially being on crutches."

"How are you feeling?" Lee asked as he took a seat on one of the other stools at the counter. "You didn't overdo it, did you?"

"No. I'm not doing enough in a day to overdo it by making a simple meal."

"Once you get your cast off, you might have to go to physio to strengthen your leg muscles again."

Zane nodded. "Yeah. Gareth told me that might be necessary. I suppose it would give me something more to do while everyone is working or sleeping."

"We need to go for a double date," Rori announced, completely veering off-topic. "What do you think?"

Zane glanced at Kelsey, but she didn't respond, apparently leaving the decision up to him.

"What are you thinking?" he asked. "Keeping in mind that I'm not up for anything too athletic."

"Maybe dinner and a movie? We could see if there's anything on at the theater in Coeur d'Alene."

"We can talk more about it tomorrow," Lee said. "I'm ready to wind down now."

Soon, Lee and Rori retreated to their bedroom, leaving Zane with Kelsey.

"I guess I need to get ready for work," Kelsey said. "They asked me to come in a little early tonight."

"Is that a good or bad thing?"

"I think it's for an employee meeting, so I don't know if it's a good or bad thing. Hopefully, they're not laying us all off. I haven't heard anything about that, but I guess you never know."

"I'll pray that it's nothing like that."

Kelsey hesitated a moment before she said, "Thank you."

Left alone once Kelsey had left for work, Zane's thoughts went to the totes up in his room. He'd gone through them the night before, discovering his old set of knives, among other things. At the bottom of one of them, he'd also discovered a box that contained the remnants of his relationship with Sarah.

He'd found a journal, which had surprised him, since he wasn't given to journaling. Reading the first page had revealed that he'd started writing his thoughts and emotions down because he felt there was no other outlet for them. Everyone—including his family—had urged him to move forward and just let Sarah get on with her life.

His pain over the end of their relationship had been splashed all over the pages, though he'd stopped reading after five or six entries. It was clear that he had struggled greatly with the breakup. But that wasn't too surprising, considering he was still struggling with the knowledge that he'd not only lost Sarah, but she'd gone on to marry someone else.

The anguish in his words had been too much for Zane the previous night. It wouldn't help him move forward if he allowed himself to wallow in the pain he'd experienced already several years in the past.

Maybe he needed to read the last entries he'd written to see the state of his mind when he'd finally stopped writing them. Maybe he'd even mentioned Kelsey.

A thought had been lingering in his mind since they'd decided to try to make their marriage work that he needed to talk to someone. To get some advice from someone outside the situation. The person who came to mind was Pastor Kennedy.

He pulled out his phone and sent a text off to Will, asking for his dad's phone number.

Will: *He's probably in bed, if you're planning to call him, but you could probably send a text, and he'll get back to you in the morning.*

Zane thanked him for the number, appreciative of the fact that Will didn't ask why he wanted it.

After a brief hesitation, he typed out a message to the pastor.

Hi, Pastor Kennedy. This is Zane. I was wondering if I'd be able to stop by for a chat tomorrow. I find myself in need of some counsel.

Zane couldn't remember a time in his life when Pastor Kennedy hadn't been part of it, so he knew that he could trust the man to give him thoughtful yet straightforward advice. He wasn't sure that he would get that from his parents. Their love for him would probably overshadow their ability to give him good guidance that didn't favor him over Kelsey.

He needed someone who would look out for Kelsey's interests as well as his own, and he thought Will's dad could be that person.

CHAPTER TWENTY-TWO

"You're up early," Lee said when Zane crutched his way into the kitchen the next morning. It was just after seven o'clock, which was a time he rarely saw if he could help it.

"Couldn't sleep." Zane made it to the coffeemaker, got himself a mug from the mug tree, and filled it with coffee.

"Everything okay?" Lee asked as he leaned a hip against the counter. He lifted the mug he held to take a sip.

"Nope." If there was one person Zane felt he could be mostly honest with, it was Lee. "Been awhile since I felt like anything was even remotely okay."

Zane slid his mug along the counter, while using his crutches to get to a barstool. Lee reached out and picked the mug up, then set it in front of the seat Zane usually chose.

Sinking down onto the barstool, Zane said, "Thank you."

"Want something to eat?"

"Not at the moment."

"Anything in particular that's bothering you?"

"Stuff with Kelsey," he said. "I just don't know how to navigate it."

Lee nodded, but he didn't say anything.

"I'm going to talk to Pastor Kennedy today, hopefully. I messaged him to ask if he'd have time for me."

"That's a good idea," Lee said. "He's a good one to talk to."

"I just need some guidance and maybe some insight into how to handle everything."

He heard the front door open, and a moment later, Kelsey appeared in the doorway. When their gazes met, her steps came to a halt. Just for a moment, however, then she walked further into the kitchen.

"Good morning," Zane said.

"Good morning." She gave him a brief smile. "You're not usually up this early."

"Yeah. Couldn't sleep so decided to get up. How was work? Was the meeting okay?"

"It was fine. They just wanted to reinforce what they expect from the overnight shift. Apparently, some people think that since there's not as much oversight that they don't have to do as much work."

"I'm sure that didn't apply to you," Zane said.

She turned from where she'd filled her glass with water. "No. I try to do my best, even if it's not my favorite job."

Zane could see that she looked tired, and he wondered if the weird hours were wearing her out. She'd said that their previous life had been lived with odd hours, but not this odd.

"Morning," Rori said as she joined them in the kitchen. "Wow. You're up early, Zane."

"Decided to see what it was like in these early morning hours."

"Well, now we're busted," Rori said. "Zane's going to find out how exciting it is to be up this early. It's just a party every day."

While they'd been talking, Lee had gone to the stove and put a frying pan on a burner. As it heated, he went to the fridge and pulled out the eggs and butter.

Kelsey sat down beside Zane and took a drink of her water. Rori poured herself a cup of coffee, then watched as Lee cracked several eggs into the pan and salt and peppered them.

As the eggs cooked, Lee put a couple of English muffins into the four-slot toaster. When the eggs were done, Lee assembled them with the English muffins and put one on each plate and set one in front of Kelsey and one in front of Rori.

"Thank you," Kelsey said. "I'm starving."

Had Lee been feeding Kelsey every morning? If Zane had known she ate when she got home, he might have made more of an effort to get out of bed and make her some food. For some reason, he'd assumed she came home and went right to bed.

"Want an egg muffin, bro?" Lee asked as he went back to the pan and added a little more butter.

"Sure. That would be great."

It wasn't too long before he had an egg muffin of his own. "Thank you."

As they ate, Lee and Rori chatted about the day ahead of them at the clinic. Zane wasn't quite awake enough to contribute meaningfully to the conversation, and Kelsey seemed like she was too tired to talk very much.

Zane's text alert went off as he took his last bite, and when he picked his phone up, he saw that Pastor Kennedy had replied to him.

P. Kennedy: *I'd love to meet with you. Would ten work?*
That would be fine.

P. Kennedy: *Will you need a ride?*
Nope. I can drive since my injured leg is my left leg.

P. Kennedy: *Then I'll see you at ten.*
Looking forward to it.

As Zane lowered his phone, Kelsey got to her feet and took her plate and glass to the dishwasher.

"Want me to put yours in the dishwasher, Zane?" she asked.

"Sure. That would be great."

Kelsey took his plate and mug and added them to the dishwasher, and Lee and Rori did the same with theirs.

"Well, we're off," Lee said as Rori retrieved their lunch bags from the fridge. "See you both later."

"Have a good day," Kelsey told them.

Elsa trotted after them, but she returned pretty quickly when the door to the garage closed.

"I'm going to sleep," Kelsey said once it was just the two of them. "I'm beat."

"You're still working tonight?"

"Yep. One more night."

"Have they offered you more hours yet?"

"No, but I'm okay with that."

"That's good."

"Well, I'll see you in a few hours."

"Sleep well."

She gave him a nod, then left the kitchen. Quiet settled over the large house, and Zane stayed in the kitchen for a few more minutes. He still hadn't gotten into the habit of looking through social media, but he liked to check on the news.

There was a lot that had happened in the world during the years he no longer remembered. It had taken him awhile to get caught up on that.

After a few minutes, he got to his feet and grabbed his crutches to make his way upstairs. Though it was a pain, he took a shower before his meeting, since he had the time.

It took longer than it used to, specifically prepping for the shower, since he had to make sure that his cast stayed dry.

By the time nine-thirty rolled around, he was ready to go. Kelsey had taken to leaving the keys for her car in the bowl on the small table by the front door, so he made his way down the stairs and picked them up.

He had plenty of time, so he didn't rush as he made his way to the car and then drove to the church. The sun was shining brightly, and it promised to be a warm day. Maybe he'd have time to enjoy it later.

Rather than go through the big doors that led to the foyer, he circled around and entered the door that led to the offices of the church. It was cool and quiet as he stepped inside, and the carpet muffled his steps as he used his crutches to move along the carpeted hall to where the pastor's office was located.

"Hi, Mrs. Kennedy," Zane said as he spotted Will's mom behind the desk outside the pastor's office.

"Zane!" The older woman got up and came around the desk to hug him. "How are you doing?"

"I'm doing alright. How are you?"

"Just great." She pointed to the open door of the pastor's office. "You can go on in. He's waiting for you."

"Thank you."

As Zane approached the pastor's office, the man appeared in the doorway and greeted Zane with a smile and a handshake.

"C'mon in." He stepped back to allow Zane to enter his office, then gestured to a cluster of chairs near a large window.

Zane chose a comfortable-looking armchair and sank down onto it, then leaned his crutches against the chair beside him, while Pastor Kennedy took the seat opposite him.

"It's good to see you, Zane," the older man said. "I know you're back under not the greatest of circumstances, but it's been good to see you home in Serenity again."

"It hasn't been as bad as I'd thought it would be," Zane said. "I never imagined that I'd be back for an extended period of time as an adult. But here I am."

"Well, before we start, why don't we pray?"

Zane nodded and bowed his head, listening as the pastor prayed for wisdom, clarity, and understanding for their conversation.

"So, how have things been going?"

Zane took a deep breath. He'd been thinking a lot about what to tell Pastor Kennedy, and he'd finally decided that if he wanted sound advice, he needed to tell him everything. So he did.

He told him what it was like waking up to discover that he'd forgotten several years of his life. Of how shocking it had been to learn he had a wife, and it wasn't Sarah. Of the difficult situation he'd found himself in with regards to having feelings for a woman who wasn't his wife. Of the physical challenges he faced with his mobility issues and the headaches that still plagued him.

It was a bit like throwing up all the emotions he'd gone through since first regaining consciousness in a world that differed from what he remembered. Emotions he hadn't even known he was suppressing bubbled up and out, leaving him a mess. It was like lancing a boil.

Throughout all of it, Pastor Kennedy just listened. His expression was encouraging and sympathetic.

Zane was more honest with him than he'd been with anyone since waking up in the hospital. He knew that he could trust Pastor Kennedy with all of it.

"You've definitely been going through a lot," Pastor Kennedy said when Zane finally fell silent. "What are you struggling with the most at the moment?"

His response came without hesitation. "My marriage."

"I can see that it's been tremendously hard for you to be married to a stranger, especially when your feelings are still caught up in Sarah."

"I want to do what's right, but I struggle with what that is."

"Do you think the right thing is to divorce Kelsey?"

"No." Once again, his response was quick. "If I regained my memory and learned I'd divorced the woman I loved, I would be devastated."

"Then your decision is to love Kelsey and to respect your wedding vows."

"I guess... yes. But I don't know how to do that. The love part. I know how to respect my vows."

"It might not be easy, but I believe that because this is the God-honoring thing to do, He will guide you and give you the wisdom and ability to love Kelsey."

The pastor picked up his Bible from where it lay on a small table next to his chair. It was large, with a worn leather cover. When he flipped it open, Zane could see that passages were highlighted and there were scribbles in the margins.

"I'm sure you know the verses where God commands us to love, right?"

Zane nodded. "Love your neighbor as yourself."

"Yep. That one, but He also commands us to love our enemies."

"Kelsey's not my enemy."

"No, she's not," Pastor Kennedy agreed. "But most of us would struggle to love our enemies if it were not for God's help. So if He can give us love for someone we would normally find unlovable, then surely He can give you love for your wife."

"I've been praying for that, but it doesn't seem to be working."

"It might not happen overnight, but if you give it time and care, I believe that it will. God wants your marriage to succeed. Have you been taking steps to try to encourage that?"

"I'm trying to spend time with her," Zane said. "So I can get to know her better."

"That's a good start. But I think you also need to begin to tell yourself that you love her. Because, with God's help, you will."

It was hard for Zane to imagine. It felt like a weird way to fall in love with someone, let alone his wife. Forcing himself to have feelings went against everything he'd ever thought about love.

"Let's not forget that the Bible tells husbands to love their wives," Pastor Kennedy said. "So you are honoring that command in seeking to love Kelsey."

"I don't think she's a Christian," Zane told him. "It seems that I had walked away from the Lord in the years I've forgotten."

"That means, along with love for Kelsey, we need to pray for her to come to love the Lord."

It seemed like a lot to pray for. A lot to expect God to do for him.

"You mustn't be discouraged," Pastor Kennedy said. "You're not alone. We will be praying for you and Kelsey. Just remember that Satan will not want your desire to honor God in this way to succeed, but don't give up."

"What if she decides she doesn't want to stay in the marriage?" She hadn't said anything like that yet, but he knew it could still happen.

"I realize that's a possibility, so we'll just have to pray that God will grant her patience and a willingness to give you both time to adjust to your new normal."

Zane had always had an unwavering faith in God and that He could answer prayer. His struggle at that moment, however, was to believe that God would answer these prayers. They seemed so lofty and unattainable.

"Don't give up hope," Pastor Kennedy said. "Commit this to the Lord and trust Him to guide you and Kelsey."

Zane nodded. "Also, I could use some advice or insight with regards to my parents."

Pastor Kennedy's brows rose at that. "What's happened?"

"They're not happy about my marriage to Kelsey."

"Ah." Pastor Kennedy nodded. "I don't think it's that they're unhappy. More that they're concerned."

"I feel like there's a conflict within me because I never imagined they'd be upset about who I married. And from what I've seen, Kelsey seems to be a perfectly nice woman. But sometimes, it doesn't feel like I have their support in trying to make this marriage with her work."

"I think you do," Pastor Kennedy said. "It's natural for parents to be concerned, especially when they're not sure what's going on. Your marriage to Kelsey certainly took them off-guard."

"But I brought her home to meet them," Zane said. "Didn't that show them I was serious about her?"

"I think they expected more notice before the wedding, and that they'd be included. Everything happened so quickly that it's probably left them feeling a little unsettled. Give them time. I'm confident they're praying for you and Kelsey."

They talked for a bit longer, then Pastor Kennedy challenged him to find ways to share God's love with Kelsey until he could also confidently show her his own.

Finally, they spent some time in prayer, both of them praying this time, and when their time together was over, Zane felt lighter and like he had a bit more clarity on how he should move forward.

Though it still felt a bit like he was walking in a dense fog, now he didn't feel so alone.

"You know you're always welcome to come back for another chat," Pastor Kennedy said as he exited the office.

"Thank you. I appreciate that."

Mrs. Kennedy got up and came to give him another hug. "You take care of yourself."

"I'll try." He gave the couple a smile as Pastor Kennedy joined his wife, slipping an arm around her. "You take care of yourselves, too."

After saying goodbye, Zane made his way out of the church and around to where he'd parked Kelsey's car. Once behind the wheel, he let out a long sigh.

His plan had been to go back home, but Pastor Kennedy's encouragement to find ways to show Kelsey love, even if he didn't feel it yet, lingered in his mind.

Sarah had been his most serious girlfriend, so his romantic experience with women was rather limited. But didn't all women like flowers and chocolate?

He tried to think about what else might appeal to Kelsey, but he didn't know her well enough to have any ideas that would be specific to her. Well, he knew what flavor of ice cream she liked, and he'd seen her grab a chocolate bar when they'd gone to the store together, so he could buy her that.

It was nearly noon, so he still had time before Kelsey would be up. He planned to be home in time to make her coffee and some toast.

But first, he had a couple of stops to make.

CHAPTER TWENTY-THREE

Kelsey woke when her alarm went off, but she was slow to get out of bed. Her heart felt heavy, though, and she wasn't sure she was ready to face the world. Or more specifically, Zane.

It had been odd to see him up when she'd gotten home from work. He'd looked like he'd just rolled out of bed, and it had stirred up a lot of memories for her.

She missed her Zane *so* much. She missed the conversations they shared before falling asleep. And how he held her as they laid together. The kisses they'd shared. The closeness that she'd never imagined having with someone.

The affection Zane offered her had been something new, and she'd soaked it up like a sponge. It had taken her awhile to feel confident in approaching Zane with affection of her own, trusting that he wouldn't reject it. Or tell her that it was too much.

But now that closeness was gone again, and she no longer had any right to give him affection, and he certainly wasn't offering her any.

Tears pricked her eyes again. She was sure they were puffy from the tears she'd shed before falling asleep earlier, and though she'd slept okay, she still felt emotionally drained.

How long was she supposed to do this?

She felt like she was on a road to nowhere. Each day, she was putting one foot in front of the other, but had no idea where she was actually headed. It felt like at any moment she was going to reach a dead end and be forced in a new direction.

A new direction that would entail a whole lot of pain and heart-ache.

Curling on her side, Kelsey tried to find the motivation to get up. Even though she had a different shift than everyone else, she attempted to keep to a schedule, depending on if she was working or not. And she needed to stick to it.

With a sigh, she flipped back the blanket and sat up. She was very grateful that she had a room with an attached bathroom. In fact, she was very grateful that Rori and Lee had given her a room in their home. It was a beautiful space. Nicer than anything she'd had prior to marrying Zane.

Pushing up from the bed, she went into the bathroom to go through her morning routine. When she was done, she changed into a pair of shorts and a T-shirt, then left her room.

Zane was usually downstairs when she went to the kitchen, and it seemed that would be the case that day too. The aroma of coffee reached her even as she stepped out of her room.

Bracing herself to see her husband, Kelsey gripped the smooth surface of the banister and made her way down to the main floor. When she walked into the kitchen, she immediately spotted Zane at the counter with a couple of mugs in front of him.

He looked up and smiled at her, his brown gaze warm. For a moment, she thought maybe his memory had returned. However, all he said was, "Good morning."

Swallowing, Kelsey said, "Good morning."

"Coffee?"

"Please."

As she approached the counter, she noticed a large bouquet in a vase. It hadn't been there earlier, so either Lee had asked him to pick up flowers for Rori, or he'd picked them up for her himself. Maybe as a thank you for opening her home to them.

"Here you go," he said, sliding the mug across to her along with the cream she usually put in her coffee. "How did you sleep?"

She poured some cream into her mug. "Not too bad."

Her eyes were puffy—she'd seen that in the mirror—but she hoped he wrote it off as her still being sleepy. She watched as he moved to put a couple of pieces of bread in the toaster.

Once the toast was out and buttered, he handed her the plate. "Thank you. How has your day been?"

"It's been good," he said as he picked up his mug and took a sip. "I went to talk to Pastor Kennedy."

"Will's dad?"

Zane nodded. "Yeah. I needed someone to talk to."

"Is he like a therapist or something?"

"Yeah. Something like that. Most pastors also counsel members of their congregation as needed."

Kelsey had so many questions, but she wasn't sure he'd go into detail about his conversation with the pastor. "I hope it went well."

"It went pretty good. Sometimes it's nice to talk to someone who is outside the family circle."

"But isn't he part of the family since Janessa is married to his son?"

"I suppose, but he's been my pastor longer than he's been my brother-in-law's father."

Kelsey kind of wished she had someone to talk to about everything, but her best friend—former best friend?—was apparently still mad at her, because she hadn't replied to any of the messages Kelsey had sent her. So, she was left with no one to confide in.

Rori had ended up being a good friend, but she was still part of Zane's family. Carisa might be a good option, but the woman seemed to have it all together, and Kelsey wasn't sure that she'd understand what Kelsey was struggling with.

"After spending time with Pastor Kennedy, I went to the store and picked up a few things. Including these." He gestured to the flowers. "Which are for you."

Kelsey slowly lowered her mug to the counter. "For me?"

"Yes. I thought maybe you'd... like some flowers?"

She shifted off her seat and moved closer to the flowers. Leaning in, she took a sniff of them. "Oh, Zane, these are very beautiful." She looked up at him. "Thank you."

He smiled. "You're welcome."

As she slid back to where her toast and coffee were, she pulled the vase closer too, wanting to enjoy the bouquet. She had no idea what to think about Zane buying her flowers.

He'd done that a couple of times while they'd been dating, but these flowers were even more beautiful than any of those had been.

But that didn't mean anything, of course. He didn't remember anything about those previous bouquets, so he couldn't have chosen this bouquet because it was nicer than those ones.

She needed to stop comparing what Zane did now to what he'd done prior to the accident. With him not having any memories of what had happened between them in the past, he was only working with their present circumstances.

Until he got his memory back, she had to stop the comparisons. And if that never happened, then she'd just have to get used to this Zane. If he still wanted her around.

The desire to get up and hug Zane to thank him for the flowers was strong, but Kelsey resisted. Not that they'd waited for their first hug at the beginning of their relationship. When they'd gone their separate ways that very first night, they'd hugged as they'd said goodbye.

Right then, though, she was afraid to initiate a hug, for fear he'd reject her. It felt like they taken a large step forward, and the last thing she wanted was to do anything to jeopardize that.

"Do you have plans for your afternoon?"

"Not really."

Though she did plan to call and see about taking the nursing exam. It was time. She'd studied so much, and she'd taken the practice test and done okay. The authorization to test she'd received was also due to expire soon, so she wanted to get it done.

If things didn't work out with Zane, she wanted to have the exam out of the way. Hopefully, she'd pass it on the first go, so she wouldn't have to take it again.

"I do have to make a phone call, but other than that, I don't have any big plans."

"Do you want to help me with dinner?"

"Uh, sure." It wasn't the first time she'd done that. She was usually in charge of the salad. "I can make the salad again."

"No. This time, I want help with the main meal."

"Oh? What are we having?"

"Chicken parm."

"Yum. But you don't need my help with that."

"I thought it might be nice to have it, anyway."

Kelsey wasn't going to turn his idea down. "Are you going to make the pasta?"

"*We're* going to make the pasta."

Zane had never really taken the time to teach her how to cook. When they were at home and he would make their food, she usually just watched or helped out with the simpler things.

But make pasta? That was definitely not something she'd done before.

"I'm going to go take care of something, then I'll be back."

"Sounds good."

Kelsey left the flowers on the counter, wanting to show them to Rori when she got home. Upstairs in her room, she sat down at the small desk to make her appointment. It didn't take too long, and then she headed back downstairs to join Zane in the kitchen.

"We have plenty of time before we need to start on the pasta, since we don't have to cook it until right before we're to eat."

Kelsey wondered if he was taking the time to teach her now because he wasn't devoting so much of his day to cooking. Whatever the reason, she was going to roll with it. If things ended up not working out, she wanted to know that she had taken every opportunity to try.

For the next couple of hours, Zane walked her through how he made her favorite dish. He didn't move too quickly—he literally couldn't, thanks to the crutches—and he patiently answered all her questions.

When it came time to make the pasta, he told her to prepare to get her hands messy. Under his instruction, she combined flour, oil, salt, and eggs until it all came together into a smooth dough.

While it was resting, Kelsey quickly set the table in the breakfast nook, since it was going to be just the four of them. As she finished, she glanced over at Zane and saw him frowning down at his phone.

She froze, wondering what he'd say if she asked what he was looking at. As she approached the counter, he looked up as he slid his phone into the pocket of his shorts.

"Ready to make the noodles?" he asked.

"Yep."

Once again, he led her through the steps, sticking close as he showed her how to work his pasta machine. Their arms bumped as he showed her how to feed the dough into the machine.

Partway through, Lee and Rori arrived home. Rori came to a stop, her eyes wide as she looked from where Kelsey and Zane stood together at the pasta machine to the large bouquet of flowers.

"Are we... interrupting?" Rori asked.

"Nope," Zane said as he swung around on his crutches to lean back against the counter. "I decided to teach Kelsey how to make pasta."

"Oh. Fun!" Rori ventured further into the room, a smile on her face. "I can't wait to try it."

"Let's go get changed, love," Lee said. "How long until dinner's ready?"

"Probably about twenty minutes."

Lee placed a hand on his wife's back and guided her toward the entrance of the kitchen. "Sounds good."

As they left the kitchen, Zane swung back around. "Okay. Let's get this meal finished up."

Kelsey tucked each of their moments of closeness into her heart to cherish, still not sure what had prompted Zane to spend this time with her. Though they had spent time together in the more recent days since his accident, this felt a lot more intentional.

Would this be a one and done thing?

She really hoped it wasn't the last time they spent time together in the kitchen. It wasn't a space that they'd shared a lot at their apartment in Tampa. At least not working together like they were right then.

Since he always moved so quickly and confidently, it probably wouldn't have been enjoyable for either of them. He had an intensity in the kitchen that he didn't quite lose, even when he was cooking at home.

This leisurely version of Zane was something she'd never seen before, and she was enjoying being allowed into this part of his life. For however long he let her be there.

"Great job," Zane said when they got to the point of adding the pasta to the pot of boiling water.

"This has been fun," Kelsey said, reaching for a cloth on the counter and taking a moment to fold it. "Thank you for teaching me. I appreciate it."

"I've enjoyed it too."

She glanced at him out of the corner of her eye. "Maybe we could do it again sometime...?"

"Sure. I could use a sous chef."

Kelsey gave a huff of laughter. "You must be desperate."

"Hey. You did a good job today. Are you sure you haven't helped me in the kitchen before? You followed directions really well."

If there was one thing she knew how to do, it was to do what she was told. Her parents had drilled that into her early on. Now, she might question things she was told to do, but if it made sense—or if she didn't know any better—she usually did as instructed.

And apparently that was a good thing when it came to working in the kitchen with Zane.

Kelsey tried to keep her smile under control, when all she wanted was to beam at him. It was probably the best time they'd had together since the accident.

It wasn't enough to fill her with total confidence that things were going to work out, but it grew her hope just a little.

When Friday rolled around a couple of days later, they were back in the kitchen. This time, they were making dinner for the four of them, as well as Carisa and Jackson.

Zane had decided that he'd treat for steak. They'd talked about the menu the night before, and he shared how he came up with the side dishes he'd serve once he chose the main part of the meal.

Kelsey wasn't sure she'd ever use the information, but she wasn't going to turn down the opportunity to learn about something that was important to Zane. It was more than she'd ever learned from him before.

Though she knew that this Zane was different, Kelsey hadn't really realized exactly how different he was. And she didn't really know how to process the differences. She loved *her* Zane, but there were things she really liked about *this* Zane, too.

"Can you carry this pan out to the barbecue for me?" Zane asked, gesturing to the large baking pan where he'd put the six steaks.

"Yep." Kelsey picked it up, then headed for the back door that led out to the deck. Once out there, she set the pan next to the barbecue.

"Thanks," Zane said as he approached her and leaned over to check the temperature of the barbecue. "I think it's hot enough."

It was a fancier barbecue than Kelsey had ever seen, but Zane seemed to know what to do with it. "Everything else is ready, right?"

"It is," he said with a nod.

"I'll go finish setting the table, then."

Back inside, Kelsey carried the glasses to the table in the dining room. The last time they'd eaten there had been with Zane's parents. Hopefully, this evening would be a little more relaxed.

The Halverson parents had stopped by the previous afternoon to say goodbye, and Kelsey had seen that they were continuing to try to interact with her more. She knew that if she wanted things to not be awkward when around Zane's family, she had to meet them halfway.

She did want them all to get along, so even though it might end up being for nothing if things didn't work out with Zane, she was trying to respond with a friendliness of her own. She had a feeling that this Zane would like her to get along with his family, even though *her* Zane hadn't really seemed to care about that.

Rori and Lee had just arrived home from work when the doorbell chimed. Lee answered it as he and Rori headed for the bedroom.

"Kelsey!" Carisa greeted her with a big smile and a hug. "How are you doing?"

After they exchanged greetings, Jackson headed for the back door to join Zane at the barbecue.

"How are things between you and Zane?" Carisa asked, perching on a bar stool at the counter.

"They're going... better," Kelsey said. "He brought me flowers the other day. A beautiful bouquet."

"Really?" Carisa's eyes lit up. "That's amazing."

Kelsey nodded. "It was a surprise. I didn't expect anything like that from him."

"Did he used to bring you flowers?"

"Occasionally, yes." Kelsey went to the fridge to get a pitcher of water. "But I didn't expect anything like that right now."

"It's definitely a step in the right direction."

"As long as he did it because he wanted to and not because he feels like he has to. I have no expectations of him," Kelsey said. "So, I'd rather our interactions be genuine and not because of feelings of obligation."

"Have you told him that?"

Before Kelsey could answer, Lee and Rori came into the kitchen, though Lee continued on through to the back door.

"So," Carisa prompted once it was just them and Rori. "Have you told him that?"

"Told who what?" Rori asked, looking from Carisa to Kelsey. "What did I miss?"

"Zane brought her flowers," Carisa said.

"I didn't miss that," Rori told her. "They're beautiful."

"Kelsey says she wants the stuff Zane does to be organic and not out of obligation."

"Oh." Rori's brows lifted as she considered Carisa's words. "That makes sense."

"Do you think Zane is doing things out of obligation?" Carisa asked.

Rori's brief hesitation was like a stab to Kelsey's heart. If anyone would know that, it would be Rori or Lee. She stared at her friend, her heart aching.

"I don't think he feels an obligation, per se," Rori clarified. "I think he wants to do things for you that will help him view you as someone he loves."

"Even if he doesn't really love me?" Kelsey asked, a bit perplexed at the idea.

"As Christians, we believe that sometimes we have to choose to love someone, even if, at first, we don't have those feelings," Carisa said. "I believe Zane is choosing to love you, knowing that you are someone he has loved in the past, even if he doesn't remember it."

Kelsey wasn't sure how she felt about that. It was a foreign concept to her, and it felt like it meant that Zane would force himself to love her. She didn't want that.

"I think it will all work out," Rori said as she gave Kelsey a hug. "We're all praying toward that end, and I think Zane is as well."

After feeling so high, Kelsey was suddenly back down on planet reality. She wasn't mad at Rori and Carisa for what they'd said. She much preferred for them to be honest with her. It was important to be realistic.

And a big part of that was to not read too much into what Zane said or did. She would accept anything he did, but she wouldn't assume that it came from his heart.

The back door opened, putting an end to their conversation. However, it didn't put an end to it in her head.

"Everything ready?" Kelsey asked as Lee slid the platter of steaks onto the counter, while Jackson carried the baking pan they'd taken the meat out on.

"We'll leave the steaks to rest while we get everything else on the table," Zane said.

It wasn't long before they were seated at the table, ready to dig into the meal. After saying grace, they began to eat, conversation flowing easily among the six of them.

Well, there wasn't much flowing out of Kelsey because her thoughts weren't anything she wanted to share. But she tried to participate in some of the discussions so that Rori and Carisa didn't think she was upset by their earlier conversation.

She wished she could experience again how things had been when she and Zane had been falling in love for the first time. But that didn't seem to be how things were going to unfold this time around.

Whether she liked it or not.

CHAPTER TWENTY-FOUR

Zane gave his brother a hard stare. "You're not teasing me, are you?"

"Nope. The x-ray shows that the fracture is healing well, so we can move you to a walking boot."

"And no more crutches?"

"Continue to use them for the rest of the week, then try short periods without them and see how it feels."

"This is great news," he said as he patted the new boot he sported. "How long am I going to be in the boot?"

"Let's give it a week, then see how it's going."

Zane had a hard time believing that five weeks had passed since his accident. This was a step in the right direction, physically. However, his headaches and lack of memory were still a worry.

"Any other concerns?" Gareth asked as he leaned back in his chair at the small desk in the exam room.

Zane's appointments were usually the last one of the mornings, so Gareth didn't need to rush off to another patient.

"No. I think physically I'm feeling fairly well. The headaches are still a nuisance, but I'm learning what triggers them and try to avoid that if possible."

"Does it work all the time?"

Zane shook his head. "No. Unfortunately, I can avoid the triggers and still end up with a headache, but at least I'm having fewer of them."

"It will take time," Gareth said. "But the healing will come."

"I hope so. I need to make some decisions about my future."

"How are things with you and Kelsey?"

Zane thought about the question for a moment. "I think we're doing better. I've been trying to spend more time with her. It seems to be going well."

"So, you're committed to making the marriage work?"

"Yes. I went to talk to Pastor Kennedy last week, and he challenged me to choose to love Kelsey. He said it would be what was most honoring to God."

"How do you feel about that?" Gareth asked. "It's not the usual way we start relationships."

Zane nodded. "That's true. But I'm trying to... court Kelsey, for lack of a better word, in order to keep the focus in my mind on building a relationship with her."

"How is Kelsey responding?"

That was the question of the hour. He thought they were getting closer, the more time they spent together. However, he also got the feeling that she was holding a part of herself back. He wasn't sure what to do about that, or how to overcome the distance she still kept between them.

"She's receptive, but she also seems cautious."

"That makes sense. You're not the man she married. Or at least not completely." Gareth paused, then said, "How are your feelings for Sarah?"

Again, Zane took his time answering. He was trying his best to be honest with himself and others as he navigated this new life path.

"I've accepted that there is no hope with her," he said. "She's not dominating my thoughts like she did right after I woke up from the accident. There are times I wonder what might have been, but I can see now that the direction in which God was moving her wasn't compatible with the direction I was moving with my career. That has helped me to accept where I am now a little better."

"I'm glad to hear that."

"But I can't just sit around forever. I need to figure out what I'm going to do next."

"Have you talked to Kelsey about it?"

"Not yet, but I will. I know I need her input since my decision will impact her, too."

"You could always stay here," Gareth suggested with a grin.

"I don't know about that."

"Open up a restaurant, and you and Kelsey can work there."

"Not sure that will work," Zane said. "But I'm not closing the door on anything at the moment."

"That's good. Who knows where God might lead you and Kelsey?"

Zane hoped that God would be very clear about His direction because he still didn't have a clear view on where his future might take him.

"Are you joining us at the gym tonight?" Gareth asked. "I think Jay said we have it starting at six-thirty."

"I might. I can't exactly do anything, though. I'd only be a spectator."

"We aren't all going to be playing at the same time," Gareth said. "We're just hanging out."

"I'll see."

"I think the ladies and the younger kids are hanging out at Charli and Blake's."

"Are they?" Zane said. He hadn't heard all the plans for the evening aside from Jay texting him earlier to invite him to the high school gym to play volleyball. Or, in his case, watch them play volleyball.

"That's what Aria said."

"Okay. I'll think about it."

Zane pushed up to his feet and turned for the crutches. "Can't wait until I'm completely done with these."

"You're closer than ever," Gareth said as he stood up. "Just don't overdo it, or it'll take you longer to be completely free of the boot."

Zane hoped that wouldn't be the case, but he had already de-cided that he wasn't going to push himself, realizing that to do so would be counterproductive. He had to take the time now, in order to benefit later. And that included his relationship with Kelsey.

He positioned the crutches under his arms, then took a couple of tentative steps to see how different it felt from the hard cast he'd been wearing for weeks.

Gareth chuckled as he walked with him to the back door of the clinic. "Hop-along-son."

"Haha."

"Hope to see you later," Gareth said once they reached the back door. "Call if your leg gives you any problems."

"Will do."

Out at Kelsey's car, Zane put the crutches in the back seat, then slid behind the wheel, maneuvering his new boot into the wheel well of the small car. He'd been doing research into his next vehi-cle, but he still hadn't made up his mind. So far, Kelsey didn't seem to mind sharing her car with him, but he really should get his own.

Zane swung through a drive-thru and picked up some coffee for him and Kelsey. Over the past couple of weeks, he'd learned how she liked her coffee, and that occasionally, she enjoyed a fancy one. So, he picked up two lattes, along with a couple of chocolate crois-sants.

When he got home, it took him a minute to figure out how to get everything into the house. He ended up using just one crutch while he held the bag and the drinks in his free hand.

He found Kelsey in the kitchen with a mug of coffee in her hand. When he greeted her with a smile, she returned it.

"I brought you a latte," Zane said, lifting the drink tray a bit. "And a pastry."

"Oh, well, I'm almost done with this coffee, so you're right on time."

He walked over to the counter. Or rather, he limped over to the counter.

"Oh, wow!" Kelsey exclaimed. "You're only using one crutch." She leaned over and looked at his leg. "And you're out of your cast."

"Yep. Gareth put me in a boot because the x-ray showed that the break has healed well."

"I'm sure you're relieved about that."

"It is a step in the right direction," Zane said as he sat down on a stool. He worked one of the drinks free of the drink tray, then held it out to her. "Here you go."

Her fingers brushed his as she took the cup from him. "Thank you."

She lifted the mug and took a sip, humming in appreciation. Zane had always preferred regular coffee with just a little cream and sugar. But since he'd learned that Kelsey occasionally liked a fancy drink, he'd taken to getting one himself whenever he got one for her.

"So no work tonight?" he asked, removing the pastries from the bag.

"Nope. I'm done for the next few days."

"I hear the ladies are meeting at Charli's tonight."

After a brief hesitation, Kelsey said, "Rori mentioned it."

"Are you going?"

"I don't think so."

"Why not?" Zane asked, although he wasn't all that surprised.

"I think I'd rather just stick close to home."

"The guys are all getting together with the older kids at the high school gym to play some volleyball."

"Are you joining them?"

"I haven't decided yet." He tore off a piece of his chocolate croissant. "I'd be going as a spectator, and that's not really fun unless I'm cheering for a favorite team."

"Would you play volleyball if you were able?"

"Probably." He took a sip of his coffee. "So, what do you plan to do with your evening?"

"I think I'm going to make some popcorn and watch a movie."

"Want some company?" he asked.

Her brows lifted slightly as she regarded him for a moment. "Sure."

"Do you have a movie in mind?"

"Yep. I like disaster movies, especially the B movie ones, and there's a new one out that looks rather crazy."

"I like those types of movies as well." He tilted his head. "Did you know that?"

She nodded. "We were making our way through all the disaster movies, even the bad ones."

"I think some of those have been my favorite."

"I guess you've forgotten all the ones from the past four years. You have some catching up to do."

"Are you up for re-watching some?"

Her smile grew. "Sure. Sometimes you have to watch them more than once in order to enjoy the true cheesiness of them."

"Sounds like a plan."

"Why don't you choose one you think you'd like to watch?" Kelsey suggested. "I'm good to watch or re-watch anything."

"Should we get takeout for dinner?"

"That would be nice," Kelsey said. "I had planned to just have a sandwich or something light."

"Let's get some Chinese," he said. "I'm kind of in the mood for it. Though I'm up for anything, if you want something different."

"Chinese is fine."

Zane grinned. "Chinese and disaster movies. Sounds like a great plan."

She seemed to relax right in front of his eyes, and her smile lingered as they discussed what they wanted to order. A quick search on his phone revealed that the restaurant the family had always used was still in business.

They didn't have to rush to place the order, since it was still early afternoon. As they finished their coffee and pastries, they continued to chat, then Kelsey went upstairs to get changed.

When she came back downstairs, she was wearing a pair of leggings and a thin, light green sweater. Though she was blonde like Sarah, Kelsey's style was a little more relaxed. She was also shorter and had a slightly fuller figure.

He was aware that, as a married couple, they had been physically intimate. But right then, he didn't know how to even take the initial step of holding her hand or hugging her. But for the first time, he found himself wanting to figure that out.

While he sat at the counter, Kelsey unloaded the dishwasher, then loaded it again with the few dishes that were sitting on the counter. She wiped down the counters, then went to the laundry room and returned with a basket of clothes.

As she folded the dishtowels, Zane wondered what their home had been like in Tampa. He hadn't had a chance to see it before it was all packed up.

"I'm sure Rori doesn't expect you to do the laundry," he said.

"I know, but I like to feel like I'm contributing to household chores. Especially since they don't take rent from me."

"Tell me about our life in Tampa," he said.

She glanced up at him, her eyes wide. "What exactly do you want to know?"

"I don't know. Just how we lived. Our schedules. Stuff like that."

Pulling a towel out of the basket, she laid it out on the counter and began to fold it. "Well, your restaurant in Tampa was different from the one in Chicago. It had three seatings, starting at six, then eight, then ten. It was rare that you were out of there before midnight. Because of that, our days started later than most people's."

"How late?"

"Since we didn't usually go to bed until three-thirty or so, we would wake up around noon."

"Oh wow. Yeah, that is late."

"We'd usually stay up for a few hours after you got home from work. We both really liked that time." She set the folded towel on top of the others, then pulled out another one. "We enjoyed the peace and quiet of those hours. There were no phone calls or text messages demanding our attention. We could just eat together, talk about our day, and sometimes we'd watch TV or a movie. It was wonderful."

Zane found what Kelsey had described to be very appealing.

Sarah had always been more social than him, and because he worked evenings, while she worked days, she often went out with her friends while he was working. When he'd had his days off in the week, he'd preferred to stay home, but Sarah had liked for them to go out and socialize with friends. Sometimes he'd agreed, but sometimes, he just wanted to stay home and decompress from a busy week at work.

On occasion, it had been a bone of contention between them.

From the sound of things, he'd ended up with a life that suited him well, and with a woman who seemed to appreciate many of the same things he did.

"Did we have friends that we spent time with?"

"Not really. We each had people at work we were friendly with, but none that we really socialized with." She set the folded towel on the pile and reached for another one. "Technically, we were still newlyweds, and we hadn't really had the chance to take a honeymoon, so we were happy to just spend time together."

"Did we explore Tampa at all?"

"Not much yet. But on one of our days off, we'd gone to the beach."

"Did you enjoy it?"

Kelsey wrinkled her nose as she plucked a facecloth from the basket. "No. I got a sunburn and ended up with sand in so many places sand shouldn't be. Plus, I have to say, I've never really been comfortable around nearly naked strangers."

Zane chuckled. "Actually, I was surprised to hear that I ended up in Florida. I've never been a big fan of beaches, the heat, or hurricanes."

"Yes. You did mention that."

"So why did I accept a job there?"

"The Michelin star."

She said it like that explained everything, and it probably did.

"Was I happy there?"

"Yes." Kelsey placed the stack of folded towels into the basket. "You said it was so inspiring working for a chef who had attained such a lofty position in the restaurant world. You would talk about some of the incredible dishes the chef had developed, and the people who came to the restaurant to try them."

It was odd, because as he listened to Kelsey describe what he'd been like working at such a prestigious place, it really felt like she was talking about another person. A person he wasn't anymore. Though a part of that life really appealed to him, his desire to work for prestige had never been that strong.

He'd only wanted enough prestige to be able to dictate the type of restaurant he could open. But he'd never viewed a Michelin star rating as the pinnacle of his career, though, of course, he'd never turn it down.

"Would you be surprised if I said that I'm not sure I'll try for a position like that again?"

Kelsey frowned. "You mean at a Michelin star restaurant?"

"Yeah."

"Maybe?" Her brow furrowed. "But you worked really hard to get that position."

"And now I've forgotten all the work that I did."

Kelsey nodded. "That's true."

"Back at the start of my training, I dreamed of having a Michelin star restaurant," Zane said. "But as time went on, my perspective shifted, and I began to dream of a restaurant that made high concept food accessible to all ages."

"How did you come up with that idea?"

"Mainly my family," Zane said with a laugh. "Aside from Kayleigh, none of them really like the more haute cuisine. All they care about is that food tastes good, and I know that there are a lot of people who feel that way. It made me think about how to make haute cuisine more appealing to people like my brothers."

"You really think you can do that?"

"I think so. I have journals filled with recipes that I developed over the years. The ones I remember doing were my first attempts at that. As I reviewed the recipes I'd worked on over the past couple of years, that has definitely changed."

Kelsey nodded. "By the time I met you, you definitely were working to attain the highest position you could. Which is what led you to Tampa."

"And you were okay uprooting your life in order for me to follow my dreams?"

"I had no problem with that," she said. "I can get a job anywhere."

"Do you like moving around?" Zane asked. "Or did the way you grew up make that difficult?"

"I prefer to stay in one place, but I was willing to make the move in order to be with you."

"And then you had to pick up and move again," he said.

She nodded. "But circumstances aside, it hasn't been a horrible move."

"Do you like Serenity?"

"It seems like a nice place, from what I've seen."

"Not someplace you probably ever thought you'd live, huh?"

Kelsey shrugged. "I don't know that I ever really thought about where I wanted to live. Chicago had been home for quite awhile, so I guess I just assumed I'd always live there."

Zane was in the unique position of knowing where certain decisions had led him, and he wasn't interested in repeating them. The two things he'd been most disappointed in learning about who he had become were how he'd distanced himself from his family and from his faith.

It felt like he had the opportunity to reset his life's direction. Or perhaps it was a forced reset. One that might have been impossible to make without a change of heart.

In his case, it had taken a drastic, life-threatening event in order for him to take a hard look at where he'd been headed. It wouldn't be a good thing if he wasted this opportunity. Which was why he was trying not to rush into anything.

He needed to take the time to pray about what God wanted for his career, Kelsey, and their marriage. It was his hope and prayer that Kelsey was also open to taking some time before they dove into whatever they decided for their future.

But for the time being, they were going to eat some Chinese food and watch a movie about a disaster that wasn't their current life.

CHAPTER TWENTY-FIVE

Kelsey settled back on the couch, pulling her legs up to cross them. She held a plate in her hands, and her drink sat on the end table. "This smells so good."

"It does, and I'm starving."

Zane limped over to sit on the couch with her. She waited for him to say grace. Once he had, Kelsey started up the movie.

When Rori had told her that the ladies were getting together while the guys went for dinner, then played some volleyball, Kelsey knew she'd wanted her to join them. The problem was, it was at Charli's, and since it was a gathering of Zane's family, she would have felt more comfortable attending if the invite had come from a family member.

Though she was getting more at ease with a few of the Halverson family members, it was mainly the men. Connecting with the women seemed a little more challenging. Also, she still wasn't sure about investing her emotions into relationships that she might not be able to keep if things didn't work out with her and Zane.

Kelsey hoped Rori would continue to be her friend, but she was prepared for that not to happen. Friends came and went. She'd learned that early on in her life.

"Why aren't they boiling their water?" Zane asked, interrupting her thoughts. He pointed his fork at the screen. "Everyone should know that when the world has ended, and they're having to scrounge for food, you boil any water you find if you don't have any other way to purify it."

Kelsey chuckled. "Yep. Always boil the water."

"Do you do anything to prepare for disaster?" Zane asked.

Finishing the bite she had in her mouth, Kelsey shook her head. "We talked about it, of course, living in a hurricane zone, but we didn't have the room to stock up a lot. We did have hiking backpacks with emergency supplies. A couple of changes of clothes, socks, shoes, flashlights, cash, some bottles of water, a couple of boxes of granola and protein bars, a charging block, charger cords, and our important papers in a small fireproof safe. Just some things that would give us a decent start if we needed to evacuate."

"Sounds like a good plan, except we should have had a portable water filter."

Kelsey chuckled. "True. Sometimes I wondered if we should do more, but I didn't put too much thought into it. We hadn't been through a hurricane yet, so I don't know if it would have been enough." She scooped up a forkful of chow mein. "How do you feel about stocking up?"

"I didn't tell you how I felt?" Zane asked.

"Well, yes, you told me how you felt as the person you were pre-accident. But maybe four years ago, you felt differently."

Zane nodded. "I always made sure I was prepared for winter, keeping things in my trunk that would help me if I got stranded."

"Yeah. I had stuff like that too."

"But these people that build bunkers underground?" Zane stared at the screen. "I'm not sure I could justify the cost."

"Maybe you could open a bunker restaurant."

Zane grinned as he laughed. "That would be something."

"Just think of all the rich people who'd like to come to something so unique. It would be the hottest place in Idaho."

"I can't imagine the cost of building something like that underground. I'd definitely have to bring in Alexander as a partner."

Something happened on the screen, drawing their attention. As they finished eating, they watched the rest of the movie.

When they'd gone to pick up the food, they'd stopped at the grocery store and Kelsey had run in to grab some dessert. Zane had asked for ice cream and brownies, so she'd picked that up for them.

When the first movie was over, they made themselves bowls of ice cream and brownies and started up another one.

For a moment, she was able to put aside everything that had happened over the past few weeks and pretend that they were back before the accident, spending time together. The only difference was that they usually didn't sit on opposite ends of the couch. Cuddling up together had been part of what she'd enjoyed about their times spent watching movies.

These times were a reminder of what she'd lost, but they also gave her hope. At least, the man she loved was still with her. The accident could have had a very different result, and she'd be grieving the complete loss of her husband. Until he said differently, there was hope for them.

As the movie continued, Zane shifted his body so that his legs were stretched out in her direction and sank further back into the couch. Pre-accident, she would have curled up with him, stretching out along his side, with his arms around her.

Though she still had hope, her patience wasn't as plentiful. She wanted to be further along in this new relationship they were trying to piece together. They might have only been married for six weeks, but it had been enough time for her to get used to loving and being loved by Zane.

She desperately wanted that back. They'd now been apart for the same amount of time that they'd been married, and it really sucked.

It was almost ten when the second movie drew to a close. They cleaned up their food, taking the leftovers upstairs to the kitchen.

As they were transferring the remainder of the Chinese food into containers, Rori and Lee arrived home.

"You had Chinese?" Lee asked. "Any leftovers?"

"You're hungry?" Rori frowned at her husband. "Didn't you have dinner with the guys?"

"Sure. We went to the diner before the gym, but then I played a bunch of volleyball and burned it all off. I'm hungry again."

The lids came back off the containers—they'd really ordered far too much—and soon all of them were seated at the breakfast nook with plates of food.

"How did volleyball go?" Zane asked.

"It was good. Peyton is really excelling at both basketball and volleyball. He held his own against us. The girls decided to stay with the women, so Peyton was the only kid there with us."

"It was good that Amelia and Layla stayed with us," Rori said. "They helped take care of the little ones."

"Did you two enjoy your evening?" Lee asked.

"Yep," Zane said. "We watched some cheesy disaster movies."

"That's not exactly my idea of a good time," Rori said.

Zane chuckled. "Yeah. I know that it's not the most popular genre, but I like it, and so does Kelsey."

"Bonding over disasters," Lee said.

"That seems appropriate," Zane replied. "Since we're trying to make our way out of one."

They continued to chat until it was almost midnight. Kelsey could hardly contain her yawns, since she'd only had about four hours of sleep coming off her night shift.

When she and Zane reached the landing of the second floor, Zane paused. "Thanks for a great evening. I really enjoyed it."

"I enjoyed it too. I'm glad we were able to hang out."

She wished they didn't have to go their separate ways. But while she missed having him close to her as they slept, he didn't remember having that closeness with her. Her heart ached a bit as they said goodnight and went to their separate rooms.

As she got ready for bed, however, Kelsey realized that even though she wanted to be physically close with Zane again, she didn't know if she could embrace that closeness with *this* Zane. At least not yet.

Each day, she reminded herself that she had to keep moving forward. And moving forward meant accepting that she might never get her version of Zane back again. Somehow, she had to reconcile the two in her mind and allow herself to feel love for *this* Zane, just like she had the pre-accident Zane.

It was easy to say she loved Zane, but each time she thought about it, those feelings were directed toward her version of Zane. How she was supposed to mesh the two in her mind and heart was something she was still trying to figure out.

She wasn't ready to give up just yet.

Over the next few days, Kelsey did some last-minute cramming. The date of her exam had arrived quickly, and now she was nervous.

She still hadn't told anyone she was going to take the exam. Maybe once she'd taken it and passed, she would tell them. If she didn't pass, she didn't want anyone to know. And she'd pick herself up and try again as soon as she was allowed to.

The night before her exam, Kelsey had let the others know she would be gone for a good chunk of the next day. She'd have over an hour's drive to get to Spokane, and they said she should allow five hours to take the exam, including breaks. Then the drive back would be another hour or so.

Her plan was to leave around six-fifteen, so she'd have plenty of time to find where she needed to be and get herself signed in.

She had already put all her stuff together and laid out her clothes. She planned to wear a comfortable pair of jeans and a light-weight sweater, just in case the testing room was cold. It was light enough that she wouldn't be too hot as long as the room temperature wasn't set to boiling.

"Where are you going?" Rori asked.

"To Spokane," Kelsey told her. "I have some personal stuff I need to take care of. I've kind of been putting it off since I got here, but now I just want to get it done."

"Do you want company?" Zane asked.

Kelsey had been afraid that he'd offer that. She didn't want to turn him down, but he couldn't come with her.

"I appreciate the offer, but I think I'd better just go on my own this time."

Zane nodded. "It's probably for the best. With my leg, I probably wouldn't be able to keep up with you."

"Maybe next time," she said. "When I don't have to spend so much time taking care of things."

Kelsey could see the curiosity on the faces of the other three, but she resisted giving more details.

Would they offer her support and encouragement? Most likely.

Would she want them to know if she failed? Definitely not. Especially not Zane.

Since she was going to be up earlier than usual, she said good-night around eight and went upstairs to take a shower and get to bed. Her stomach was churning with nerves, and she hoped that she'd be able to sleep because she wanted to go into the exam well-rested.

She resisted the urge to look over her notes and test exams one last time. If she didn't know the subject already, she wasn't going to learn it through last-minute cramming.

When her alarm went off at five-thirty the next morning, Kelsey crawled out of bed, surprisingly refreshed. Though she'd tossed and turned for a bit before falling asleep, once she was out, she'd stayed out.

After dressing in the clothes she'd laid out, she braided her hair, leaving a small chunk free at the front to keep her appearance from being too stark. The occasion didn't call for a lot of makeup, so she applied just enough to even out her skin tone, then swept on a layer of mascara.

Just after six, she left her room, planning to get some coffee before she hit the road. The aroma of coffee that greeted her surprised Kelsey, as she didn't think anyone ever got up that early.

Hurrying down the stairs, she approached the kitchen. Her heart skipped a beat at the sight of Zane sitting at the counter. He looked up and smiled, his tousled appearance making her heart continue its wild gallop.

"You're up super early," she said as she walked closer and set her bag on the counter.

"When you said how early you were planning to leave, I thought I'd get up and make sure you had some coffee for your drive."

Kelsey retrieved her travel mug from the cupboard. "Thank you. I really appreciate you doing that."

"Are you sure you don't want company?" he asked. "I would just have to brush my hair and get my shoes."

Kelsey glanced over as she removed the carafe of coffee, almost wishing that he hadn't gotten up because she didn't want to have to turn him down again. But the ingrained need to keep potential failures to herself kicked in.

"I'm sure," she said. "I need to tackle this stuff by myself. I should have done it sooner, but with everything that's been going on, it hasn't been possible. Finally, I decided I just needed to get it done."

"Well, if you run into any trouble, call me, and we'll come rescue you."

"I'll keep that in mind," she said with a smile. "But I hope I don't have to."

She poured coffee into her mug, then added some cream and sugar. After stirring it, she put the lid on.

"I wasn't sure if you wanted to eat before you left."

Kelsey considered it, but then shook her head. The nerves in her stomach had completely robbed her of her appetite. Instead, she said, "I'm just going to grab a couple of granola bars to eat later."

"You should take an apple or banana too," he suggested.

Kelsey nodded and went to the fruit basket on the counter to choose a banana. "If only I could take some chocolate syrup to dip it in."

Zane chuckled. "You need a portable chocolate fondue."

"That would be great." She put the food into her large tote bag. "I'd better get going. Gotta be there for my first appointment by seven-thirty."

"Well, hope everything goes smoothly," Zane said, getting to his feet. He followed her to the front door, using one crutch as he walked. "Drive safely. If you want, you could text me when you get there."

She turned to look at him, and when she saw that he was actually serious, she nodded. "I will."

Stepping out onto the porch, she continued to the steps leading to the decorative stone path that took her to where her car was parked. She climbed behind the wheel of her car and started it up.

As she put it in gear to pull away from the curb, she glanced at the house, surprised to see Zane still standing in the doorway, leaning a shoulder against the jamb. Kelsey lifted a hand to wave at him, which he returned, then she turned her attention to the road as she drove away.

Christian music drifted from her car's speakers. The first time Zane had used her car, he'd tuned the radio to a Christian station. She'd just left it there, since she didn't feel strongly enough about any genre of music to change it.

After she'd been on the road for about fifteen minutes, the radio station switched from music to a podcast. As the intro music faded, a man with a lovely mellow voice began to talk.

"Hello. My name is Jonathon Anders. Welcome to *On This Journey,* a podcast where I talk to Christians from all walks of life to hear their stories and learn how God has worked in their lives. Today, I have two people with me, one of whom I have a history with that stretches back years and across continents. It is my absolute joy to have Danae and Brock Peterson with me today. Welcome."

A woman and man responded, thanking him for having them.

"As regular listeners of this show know, I was raised as a missionary kid in Asia, and a lot of those experiences have shaped my outlook on God, faith, and the world around me. Danae was one of the people who shared some of those experiences with me. We attended the same MK boarding school, and I knew her first husband. We were all in the same grade, and William and I played on the school's basketball team through our high school years.

"Everyone knew that Danae and William were going to get married. They were just that couple in high school, having started dating in our freshman year. A few years after graduation, I heard that they'd gotten married and had some kids. It seemed they were well on their way to their happily ever after. But Danae's story didn't end there."

"No, it certainly didn't," Danae agreed.

"Do you want to share with us where your journey has taken you since we graduated?"

"Sure. It's a story that never gets easier to tell, but I also feel it's important to share and to show how God works in even the most terrible of circumstances. Like Jordan mentioned, William and I were high school sweethearts. William planned to go to college to become an engineer. My dream, however, was to be a wife and a mother. We married not long after graduation—to the dismay of our parents—though they still supported us."

"Your parents were all friends, right?" Jordan asked.

"Yes. We were all part of the same mission, and I'd known William from when we were very young. Us getting married felt like joining two families who were already super close."

"So your parents already had a really good idea of who their child was marrying."

"Yep. Which was part of the reason why they hadn't objected too strongly to us marrying so young."

"How did those early years of marriage unfold?"

Danae softly cleared her throat. "At first, they were easy. William was in school and working, I was working part time, and the rest of the time, I was at home, trying to create an environment that I thought would make our marriage flourish. However, it wasn't long before I got pregnant, and once I had our first child, I was determined to be a stay-at-home mom."

Kelsey found herself totally caught up in the story the woman was sharing. In fact, she felt a bit of a knot in her stomach as the story unfolded, knowing something catastrophic must have happened because she was there with a man who wasn't her first husband.

"By the time our third child was born, we were both overwhelmed. William had dropped out of school by that point in order to work full time and support our family. Though our marriage was struggling and parenting was taxing our ability to model love and patience to our children, we tried our best to hide our struggles from everyone."

Kelsey understood why. They were failing and didn't want people to know.

"One Saturday, William said he'd give me a break, and he took the kids out for breakfast at McDonalds. Only, they never came home. A drunk truck driver made sure of that. It was an absolutely horrible time. The grief and guilt were overwhelming, and I couldn't understand why God had taken all of them and left me."

As Kelsey listened to Danae share how she struggled to survive mentally and emotionally in the days, weeks, months, and years that followed, Kelsey marveled that she had made it through. The strength she'd needed to do that was incredible.

Except that Danae made it clear she hadn't done it alone. That she believed God had been with her through that time, giving her what she needed to move forward.

Kelsey thought of her own situation. She felt a bit like she'd experienced the death of a loved one, with Zane having lost his memory of her and their marriage. Though it was possible it would return, the more time that passed without that happening, the less likely she thought it was that it would.

However, her loss was nothing compared to what Danae had experienced. And yet, even after the death of her family, Danae had found a way to keep going. From everything the couple shared about their journey, Kelsey knew that they had relied heavily on God.

Would she be able to more readily accept what had happened and move forward if she trusted in God?

Zane seemed to be trusting God with his situation, and from what Rori and Carisa had said, he was choosing to try to love her and work on their relationship because of God.

"I've had people ask me how I can be so trusting of God when He could have saved my family and yet didn't. I think that's a question a lot of people have when something bad happens."

"And do you have an answer to that?" Jonathon asked.

"Well, my first response is that I don't know the mind of God," she said. "But I know that's not the answer people want. All I can say is that I tried to cope with what had happened on my own, and I was contemplating suicide. When I turned to God and asked Him to help me, I was able to slowly, but surely, deal with the tremendous grief that dominated my life."

"How did you and Brock meet?"

Kelsey listened as the couple shared the journey they'd each taken to find the other and the things they'd had to overcome in order to have a future together. Brock had faced struggles, and he'd had challenges of his own that might have kept them apart. The journeys they'd taken seemed impossible and even improbable to someone like Kelsey.

"As Christians, we will only live our most God-honoring lives if we seek His will for us," Brock said. "Sometimes it can be hard to know what that will is. Sometimes the road seems rough and impassible, but God is faithful. Just like He helped Danae with her struggles, and me with mine, He will help those who seek Him and ask for His guidance."

Kelsey thought about everything she'd been struggling with. The loss of the man she loved. The uncertainty about her future. Her marriage. Her career.

She hadn't experienced what Danae and Brock had, but she was facing so much uncertainty that seeking God's will for her life was appealing. But she wasn't a Christian, and that seemed like something she had to change if she wanted God to direct her life.

Maybe Rori and Carisa would help her understand what that meant. The pastor had mentioned it a few times in the sermons she'd heard him preach, but she needed to know specifically what she had to do.

The podcast was ending as she pulled into the parking lot of the building where the test was taking place. She still had a few minutes before she had to go inside, so she stayed in the car, her thoughts full of everything she'd heard.

One upside to having been distracted by the podcast was she hadn't had time to worry about the looming exam. Remembering her promise to Zane that she'd let him know when she arrived in Spokane, she plucked her phone from the cup holder.

Arrived safe and sound.

She stared out the window as other cars joined her in the parking lot. It was almost time to go in, and the nerves that had faded away on the trip were coming back to life.

When her phone let her know that a text had arrived, she saw that Zane had replied.

Zane: *Wonderful! Hope everything goes smoothly there. Let me know when you're on your way home.*

Kelsey stared at the red heart he'd added at the end of the message. He seemed committed to their relationship, but if he didn't really have feelings for her, how long would that commitment last? She was scared of what the answer to that would mean for her.

But for now, she needed to focus on this exam to secure at least one part of her future.

CHAPTER TWENTY-SIX

Zane stood in front of the large living room window, staring out at the street as he watched for Kelsey. She'd sent him a message an hour earlier to let him know she was leaving Spokane, so she should be home in the next ten or fifteen minutes.

His curiosity about her day was high, but he wasn't going to press her for information. It was clear that she hadn't felt comfortable sharing her plans. Whatever they were.

If he had his memory, he probably would have bugged her until she told him. Or maybe he would have already known, just because they were married and sharing their lives. Maybe she would have even wanted him to go with her.

However, even though technically he was her husband, he didn't feel he had the right to question her further.

The house was quiet since Rori and Lee were both at work, meaning it was just him and Elsa hanging out together.

The day had dragged, which wasn't really unusual. But that day, it had felt super long. And a little bit lonely without the knowledge that Kelsey was in the house. Even though there were days when she slept most of the day, just knowing she was there made the house feel less empty.

He needed to find things to occupy his time.

In one of his totes, he'd discovered his collection of cookbooks. They had been an eclectic assortment. But then, his interest in food was also eclectic. Where some people zeroed in on one type of cuisine, his interest had been more broad.

He had a cookbook featuring recipes from Thomas Keller's *French Laundry* and *Per Se* restaurants, along with *The Silver*

Spoon, which was a cookbook jam packed with Italian recipes. There was also a copy of *The Professional Chef* by The Culinary Institute of America.

Early on in his career, he'd followed the recipes in those cookbooks to the letter. But recently—his recently—he'd taken what he'd learned while making those recipes and developed some of his own.

In the tote, he'd also found his leather-bound journals that contained all the recipes he'd tried, along with the notes he'd made about them. It had been interesting to read through the recipes he'd added during his amnesic gap. He'd definitely grown as a chef in that time.

Those journals had been as revealing as his breakup ones.

As he'd read through the recipes and the notes he'd made on them, he could see himself moving away from the focus he'd had on taking haute cuisine recipes and remaking them into dishes that would be enjoyable for kids and people who might think they don't like that type of food.

The recipes he'd filled the latter part of the journal with had been interesting, but they hadn't followed the dream he'd had for his restaurant. It was like he'd abandoned that dream after Sarah had broken up with him.

Even after that, though, he'd continued adding to his savings account. That money was originally to be used to start his restaurant, so he had no idea what he'd been saving it for. Maybe for another style of restaurant. One that might cost more to start.

There was nothing saying he couldn't switch it back, however. Looking through that journal had been inspiring, and it had reminded him of his passion.

He might not remember those missing years, but he was beginning to think that perhaps this was the reset he needed. And in reading those recipes and notes, he was also regaining a bit of the experience he'd lost. His forgotten self was still able to share some knowledge with him.

Maybe it was better he didn't remember that time. It seemed the only truly good thing that had happened during those years was that he'd continued to save money.

And... marrying Kelsey. Definitely marrying Kelsey had been a good thing.

Now that he'd changed how he looked at the marriage he didn't remember, he felt a hope for the future that he hadn't had initially. Where that future might lead him and Kelsey, he didn't yet know, but he wanted it to be fulfilling for them both.

Zane hoped that God would give them clear direction for where He would have them go. Or stay. He wasn't as opposed to staying around Serenity as he'd once been.

Leaving Serenity for the sake of his career had ended up distancing him from his family and his faith. That bothered him, and he didn't want that happening again.

When he saw Kelsey's car glide to a stop in front of the house, Zane smiled. He was still curious about what had taken her away from the house for so long, but he was just glad that she'd made it safely to Spokane and back home again.

Zane watched her walk up the sidewalk to the steps of the porch. She moved slowly, like she was exhausted, her bag hanging from her hand.

Concerned, Zane limped from the living room to the foyer, arriving just as she opened the door and stepped inside the house. When Kelsey looked up and spotted him, she gave him a small smile.

"How was your day?" he asked as she shut the door and toed off her shoes.

Though she looked tired, she said, "It went well. I'm glad to be home, though."

When Kelsey headed for the kitchen, he followed her. She set her bag on the counter, then went to the coffee maker. "Do you want coffee? Or should I just use one of the pods?"

"I'll have some," he said. "But let me make it. You sit down."

"You don't trust me to make good coffee?" Kelsey asked as she turned to him.

"Your coffee is just fine." He approached where she stood, then took her arms and gently urged her to move to the side. "You look tired."

She let out a sigh as she moved to sit on the barstool. "I am a bit."

"So everything went okay?" he asked as he prepped the coffee-maker.

"Yep."

"How did you find the drive?"

That got a smile out of her. "It was really nice, actually. A lot of beautiful scenery."

"The mountains are always a sight to see."

"I've never spent a lot of time in the mountains," Kelsey said. "My time here is the closest I've been to mountains for any length of time."

"Even moving around growing up, you never lived near mountains?"

"Not that I can remember. If we did, we certainly didn't go see them."

"After I'm free of my boot, we can go to the mountains," Zane said. "They are beautiful this time of year."

"I'd like that," Kelsey said, a soft smile on her face.

"Then it's a date." Zane chuckled. "Whenever we settle on the date."

As he waited for the carafe to fill, Zane took two mugs from the mug tree and set them on the counter. He got the cream from the fridge, finding it so much easier to move now that he was just in the boot, and he'd ditched the crutches.

Once the carafe was about half full, Zane pulled it out and filled their mugs. He quickly added cream and sugar to both, then stirred them before he slid one across the counter to Kelsey.

Searching for another topic to keep their conversation going, Zane asked, "Did I ever talk to you about being adopted?"

Lee had said something earlier about birth families, and Zane wondered if he and Kelsey had discussed the fact that he was adopted.

Kelsey looked at him from where she sat, her mug cupped in her hands. "You did talk about it a few times, but the only time we discussed it at length was in relation to Lee."

"What do you mean?"

"It was when Lee's girlfriend broke up with him because he didn't know about his birth family. I wasn't around when that happened, but you told me about it when you heard from Lee that he had started dating Rori."

"How did I feel about what had happened to Lee?" he asked. He'd remembered Lee telling him about his girlfriend not being happy with his lack of knowledge about his past, but he didn't recall their actual breakup.

"You thought he should have broken up with her right away when she first said she had an issue," Kelsey said. "And that you would never stay with a woman who had a problem with you being adopted."

"So, I'm assuming you didn't?"

Kelsey shook her head. "I didn't have a problem with that."

"Did I tell you why I never sought out information about my own birth parents?"

Kelsey lowered her mug to the counter. "You said that since the Halversons hadn't adopted you as a newborn, likely the circumstances of how you'd come to them had been bad. You didn't really want to know because you didn't think that information would bring anything good to your life."

That was what he'd always felt. Plus, he'd been happy with the Halversons and didn't feel like he'd needed another family. It didn't sound like he'd told Kelsey that, which was more proof of the distance he'd ended up with from his family in recent years.

"Is that how you feel about it now?" Kelsey's brow furrowed. "Or then?"

Zane knew what she was saying. "I do feel that way, and I've always viewed the Halversons as the only family I need."

"I don't blame you for feeling that way."

Zane lifted his brows. "You say that even though they haven't exactly been warm and welcoming to you?"

"I'm a stranger to them," she said with a shrug. "But even so, I can see how much they love and care for you."

"They're coming around," he told her, happy that she'd noticed his family's love for him.

"I can see that."

He still didn't one hundred percent understand his family's reaction to Kelsey. Nothing he'd learned about her seemed to warrant that reaction. Maybe it really had just been them being upset because they'd eloped.

Though he still didn't like it, at least they were making an effort. He was just glad that Kelsey and Rori had bonded the way they had, because at least she had someone in the family she felt comfortable with.

"Do you think much about the future?" Zane asked, lifting his mug to take a sip.

Kelsey froze. The only things on her body that moved were her eyelids as she blinked rapidly. After what felt like forever, she shifted the mug on the counter in front of her.

"Uh... I do think about it, yes."

"A lot?"

Kelsey shrugged. "I suppose. At least once a day."

"Would you like to have a conversation about it?"

"Is now really the time for that?" Kelsey asked with a frown.

"I think it is," Zane said, wondering why she wouldn't want to have the conversation. "We don't have to make definite plans, but I think it would be good to be aware of what we're each thinking."

She nodded. "So, what are you thinking, then?"

"I think we should probably stay here, maybe until the end of the year," he said, having given it some serious thought already. "And then, if I still don't have my memory back, we can start to make plans of where we want to go next."

"You always said that you weren't interested in living here," Kelsey said.

Zane nodded. "That's true. And I'm not saying that we have to live here long term."

"So you wouldn't consider staying here?"

That made him pause for a moment. "Would *you* want to stay here?"

Kelsey tilted her head as she stared down at her mug. "I don't know. It's not the worst place. Though I'm not sure I'd want to work full-time as a shelf stocker. Maybe I could find a different job here or drive to Coeur d'Alene."

Her willingness to consider staying in Serenity took Zane by surprise.

"You'd really want to stay this close to my family?"

"Like you said, they're getting more friendly," she said. "Plus, Rori and Carisa are here."

"Yes. They are." Zane smiled. "See? I'm glad we talked about this. It lets me know what options we have."

"So you would consider making this our permanent home?"

"Sure," he said, glancing around. "And we could probably keep living with Lee and Rori. As long as you don't mind that."

She paused for a moment before shaking her head. "I don't mind."

"I'm going to start looking into restaurant possibilities around here. That way, if we do decide to stick around, I'll have some ideas in mind."

"Will you talk to Kayleigh?"

"I'm not sure. I don't want her to feel obliged to hire me. I'm not really going to be in a position to work in a busy kitchen for awhile yet. Gareth said I can probably be walking without the boot soon, but he wants me to go for physio once it comes off."

"That's good." She smiled, and it lit up her eyes. "You're going to be so happy to be free of that and the crutches."

"I am," he agreed. "Want to go dancing?"

That got a laugh out of her. "Not a chance. I've never danced."

"Neither have I," he said. "Maybe we could take lessons."

"How about you get your leg strengthened up first," she told him, her smile growing. "Then we'll talk about dancing."

Zane felt their connection strengthen as they shared a laugh. He couldn't deny that something had settled inside him when Kelsey had arrived home earlier. As time passed, his desire to be around her grew.

Early on, he'd rarely thought of her, and he'd tried to avoid being around her—especially if it was just the two of them.

Now, he sought out her company and really enjoyed it when they hung out on their own. And he rarely thought of Sarah these days.

When he'd initially made the decision to stick it out with Kelsey, it had seemed like getting to this point would be nearly impossible. Now that he had, he knew that it could only be God working in his heart.

To no longer feel the pulse of heartache from losing Sarah this soon was a minor miracle. Zane had envisioned it taking longer, but he wasn't upset that it had happened sooner. There was a chance that if he'd taken too long to get to that point, they would have gone their separate ways.

So he was thankful that God was working in him, and hopefully, He was also working in Kelsey. There were still moments when he saw reservation in her gaze, and he knew she was still afraid to hope. Afraid to get hurt by him.

The last thing he wanted was to hurt her. He cared about how she felt now, in a way he hadn't really cared a few weeks ago.

He moved over to where a ceramic cookie jar sat on the counter. As he lifted the lid, he glanced over at Kelsey. "Want one?"

"Sure. Chocolate chip?"

"Yep. I tried my hand at making some earlier today."

He wasn't a huge sweets eater, but he'd definitely been eating more while he'd been in Serenity. And though he wasn't a baker, per se, he knew how to bake something relatively simple, like chocolate chip cookies.

"These are yum," Kelsey said. "Another winner from Chef Zane."

"I'm not really a baker, but I decided to give it a whirl."

"What's for supper?" she asked as they ate their cookies. "Something smells good."

"I've got a chicken stew in the crock pot."

"The crock pot?"

Zane grinned. "I think my family is rubbing off on me."

"No kidding. I'm not sure you've ever used a crock pot since I've known you. A pressure cooker, yes, but not a crock pot."

Some of the exhaustion Kelsey had had when she'd walked through the door had faded, and Zane was glad to see that. His curiosity was still there, but he didn't feel a pressing need to know what she'd been doing in Spokane.

She was back home, and she was smiling at him. Despite the wariness that he sometimes spotted in her eyes, he thought that she

was happy. Or as happy as she could be considering their circumstances.

He hoped that meant that she was willing to continue on this
journey together... slow though it might be. His hope was strong
that they were going to be able to make things work.

Their marriage might end up looking different from the one
they'd had prior to the accident and his memory loss, but he had
confidence that it would still be good. If they were both committed
to making it work, he was more certain than ever that things would
be fine between them.

He just had to keep doing his best to learn about Kelsey and the
things she liked, to make her feel like she was important to him.
Because, while that hadn't been the case when he woke up after
the accident, it had become that over time.

CHAPTER TWENTY-SEVEN

Kelsey followed Zane into the large gym at the high school. Others of the family were also there, many having already secured seats on the bleachers.

The sound of multiple basketballs hitting the floor echoed in the large space, but it couldn't quite block out the murmur of conversations from the people already gathered there.

It had been a long time since Kelsey had last been in a school gym. Even when she'd been in high school, she'd gone to the gym only under the duress of having to take physical education.

There certainly hadn't been nights when she'd gone with a group of friends to cheer on other friends as they played sports. If she'd made friends at all in a new school, they were definitely not a part of the cool kids group. More often than not, she hadn't had a close friend, so her Friday nights were spent working or at home.

There was a buzz in the air as people anticipated the first home game for the local high school basketball team. The Halversons were all there to support Jay as he coached the team and his son Peyton, who played on the team.

Kelsey hadn't been sure about attending the game, but when Zane had made it clear that he was going, she'd decided to go too. These days she was trying to spend what time she could with Zane, even if that included attending a basketball game for high schoolers.

As they approached the section where members of the family already sat, Zane slowly headed up the metal bleachers to the row in front of his sisters. Once they reached the row, Zane led the way into it, carefully maneuvering his booted leg.

He would be going to see Gareth next week to get an x-ray done to see if he still needed to continue to wear the boot. But things were looking promising, and Kelsey was sure that in a week's time he'd have it off.

"Hey, you two," Janessa said as they settled on the bleacher in front of her and Will.

"Where's the little man?" Zane asked as he turned toward Janessa.

"We left him with my folks," Will said. "They're having Grandma and Grandpa time with him."

Zane turned to Charli. "What about your kids?"

Charli gestured down at the court. "Layla and Amelia are hanging out with their friends, closer to the action. The younger ones are with a babysitter from church, having more fun with her than they'd have here."

"It's almost like date night for you," Zane said.

Blake nodded. "We take date night where we can."

"Where are Rori and Lee?" Charlie asked. "Are they not coming?"

"They were late getting home from work," Zane said. "They'll be here soon."

"How are you doing, Kelsey?" Janessa asked with a smile.

"I'm doing well. Thank you." Kelsey returned her smile. "How are you?"

"I'm doing great," Janessa said. "Glad it's the weekend."

"How were the first couple weeks of school, Will? Zane asked.

"It's going really well," Will replied. "The first week was a bit of an adjustment for everyone, as usual. But things have settled down this week."

"Do you miss not going back to school, Charli?" Zane asked his sister.

"Not so much anymore," she said. "The first year I didn't go back was the hardest. But now, I'm fine with not having to juggle the kids and daycare and teaching all at the same time."

"There's Lee and Rori," Will said as pointed to the entrance to the gym, then waved at them. Lee lifted a hand in response, before leading Rori through the crowd to reach them.

As the couple reached them, a loud buzzer pierced the air as the clock on the electronic board had hit zero.

Will grinned as he rubbed his hands together. "It's game time, folks."

The players on the floor gathered around their coaches and several teenage girls cartwheeled out onto the floor, yelling as they went.

"I would kill myself if I tried to do that," Rori said

"You and me both," Kelsey said. "I've never been that coordinated."

"Me either."

"Kayleigh used to be a cheerleader." Zane said.

Kelsey had a hard time imagining her polished, always put together, sister-in-law cartwheeling onto the floor and yelling the way these girls were. The picture that came to her mind made her smile a bit.

"So was Skylar," Janessa said. "And Layla used to love to dress up in her own little uniform and join them as a mini cheerleader when she was younger."

"Does Amelia not want to join them?" Zane asked

Charlie shook her head. "Nope. Her focus is strictly on ice-skating."

A whistle sounded then, and several boys from each team filed onto the court to begin their game. Jay stood on the sidelines, calling out encouragement as the ref spoke to the boys from both teams.

The noise factor in the gym rose considerably as the game got underway. Kelsey had a general idea of how the game was played, so she was able to follow the action fairly well.

Everyone around her was very into the game. Many jumped to their feet at different points of the game to yell encouragement at the players.

Lee had mentioned that since this was the first game of the season, the players would probably be a little rough around the edges. But if that was the case, Kelsey couldn't tell. They played better than she would have.

At half time, the score was close, and low, according to Zane, but the home team had a two-point advantage. As the players disappeared into the locker rooms, people around them stood up.

"We're going to get some food and drinks," Rori said. "Want to come with us?"

"Uh. Sure." Kelsey glanced at a Zane. "Did you want something?"

"I wouldn't mind a soda and a hotdog."

"Got it," Rori said. "We'll be back in a few."

Kelsey followed them out of the row, but Lee and Rori got a little ahead of her and a couple of people filed in between them. She kept her head down, making sure that she didn't trip on the metal steps.

As she neared the bottom with tentative steps, a hand appeared in front of her. She looked up, expecting it to be Lee, but it was another man. She didn't recognize him, but he was aiming a friendly smile her way.

Kelsey didn't want to take his hand, but she wasn't sure how to refuse him without being rude. As she reached out to take it, Kelsey wished so much that it was Zane's instead.

As she stepped onto the floor, the man gave her hand a squeeze but didn't let go right away. Kelsey pulled her hand from his and murmured, "Thank you."

She realized then that there was a definite benefit to wearing her wedding rings that she hadn't even considered.

"My name is Eric," the man said before she could move away from him.

"Hey." Rori stepped up beside Kelsey and threaded her arm through Kelsey's. "I thought we'd lost you."

"How's it going, Eric?" Lee said as he joined Rori.

"Good. Good. Can't complain." Eric's gaze darted between the three of them. "Is this beautiful lady a friend of yours?"

"A friend, yes," Lee said. "But also, a sister-in-law. She's Zane's wife."

Eric's brows drew together as his gaze dropped to Kelsey's left hand. "My apologies. I didn't know."

"No harm done," Lee told him with a grin. "Zane's still not out of the boot from his broken leg, so you could probably outrun him."

Eric chuckled. "Good to know."

"Well, we're gonna go get in line for food," Lee said. "See you around, man."

Eric nodded and smiled as they turned to leave.

"Well, that was awkward," Kelsey murmured as she and Rori followed Lee.

His large frame cut through the crowd of people, making it easier for Rori and Kelsey to move. Not far from the gym, they found a line of people at the high school canteen. As they stood in line, Lee checked his phone, confirming orders with the people still in the gym.

Kelsey wondered if Zane had caught the interaction she'd had with Eric. And if so, what he'd thought about it. Probably nothing.

Unfortunately, Zane had yet to seek out any sort of physical interaction with her, let alone offer her any physical affection. It was one of the hardest things for her, since she'd gotten used to being hugged and kissed and physically intimate with Zane. Right then, she'd settle for just holding his hand.

As they stood waiting in line, Lee slipped his arm around Rori's shoulders, and her friend tipped her head back to smile at her husband. Kelsey turned away, feeling a bit raw, and finding that their interaction only made her feel worse.

It didn't take long to reach the front of the line, and soon they were replacing orders for the food everyone wanted. The person working behind the counter knew Lee and chatted with him as they prepared the food, loading everything into a couple of boxes to make it easier for them to carry.

Kelsey tried to pay for hers, but Lee just waved her off. Rather than argue about it, Kelsey let him take charge of the payment.

As they made their way back into the gym, she saw that the cheerleaders were once again on the floor, this time performing a choreographed program set to music. She marveled anew at their ability to fling their bodies in all sorts of different directions all while smiling broadly.

As they passed Eric. He nodded at them, but didn't say anything more to Kelsey. She felt a little guilty because it was her not wearing a ring that had prompted him to approach her. She was sure of that.

But had he not seen her with Zane prior to walking down the steps? Or maybe he'd seen her and assumed she was just a friend of the family. She and Zane certainly didn't act like a married couple. And then when he'd noticed that she wasn't wearing any rings, considered her approachable.

Perhaps it was time to put her rings back on. Although it felt like it was for a really lousy reason. She wasn't at the point with Zane that she had hoped she'd be before putting them back on. And she had really hoped that Zane would be the one to put them back on her finger again as a sign of his love and commitment to her, just like he'd done the first time.

When they were back in their seats, all the attention was on handing out the food and drinks they'd picked up for everyone. Surprisingly, everything was correct.

Kelsey hadn't been hungry for a hotdog, so she'd settled for a bag of chips and a drink. Meanwhile, Zane tucked into his hot dog, looking like it was his favourite food ever, though she wasn't sure she'd ever actually seen him eat one before.

"Was that guy bugging you?" he asked.

"Bugging me?" Kelsey said. "Not really. He just gave me a hand down from the bleachers."

Zane glanced from her to Lee and back to Kelsey again. "As long as he wasn't bugging you."

"Lee knows him," Kelsey told him. "And he introduced me, letting him know that I was his sister-in-law."

Zane's gaze drifted down to where Eric still stood with a handful of people. Kelsey wished she could read his mind in that moment to see if he was upset with her because of what had happened.

He hadn't been pleased when she decided not to wear her rings. She knew that. So maybe he'd blame her for Eric's approach.

The thought left a pit in Kelsey's stomach because she'd once had a boyfriend who had blamed her any time a guy showed the slightest bit of interest in her, even if it was just as friends. That relationship hadn't lasted long because Kelsey didn't like being held responsible for something over which she had no control.

She had never acted flirtatiously with other men. It just wasn't who she was. And even if she was inclined to be that way, she certainly wouldn't flirt with a guy while she was in a relationship with someone else.

Kelsey could only hope that Zane would see that it had been a truly innocent interaction. She wasn't completely certain how her Zane would've acted, because they'd never really run into that situation.

"As long as you didn't feel harassed."

"Not harassed, really," she said as she peered into her chip bag. "Just kind of an awkward situation."

"Want me to have a word with him?"

Kelsey quickly shook her head. "It really was nothing. He just offered his help off the bleachers, and Lee stepped in to introduce me as his sister-in-law. It's all fine."

She really wanted to get past the interaction. It was a nothing encounter, and she just wanted to put it out of her mind. They'd been enjoying the evening, and she didn't want this to negatively impact it.

The second half started with the blow of a whistle, and for the remainder of the game, Kelsey tried her best not to dwell on what had happened with Eric.

When the final buzzer sounded, people stood and clapped for the home team's win. Jay gathered his players around him, high fiving each of them.

Charli and Blake left pretty quickly after saying goodbye, no doubt eager to pry the girls from their friends and get home to their other kids. Will and Janessa weren't far behind.

As she filed out of the row, Zane stayed close behind her as they made their way down. Thankfully, Eric was gone already when they reached the floor, and Kelsey was able to leave to step off the bleachers without any issue, even without a helping hand.

"Who was that guy making the moves on my wife, Lee?" Zane asked as the four of them left the gym.

"He wasn't necessarily making moves on Kelsey, bro," Lee replied. "He was offering her a hand."

"Who is he? I didn't recognize him."

"His name is Eric, and I know him because he's brought his dog into the clinic a couple of times. He's a nice guy."

"He needs to direct his niceness in another direction," Zane said.

Kelsey hadn't seen a jealous side of Zane before. And she wasn't entirely sure she was seeing it then, either. But it was odd that he felt the need to warn a guy off of being nice to her.

If only Zane understood that right then, the only man she wanted that type of attention from was him. She wanted *him* to offer her a hand. She wanted *him* to tell her she was beautiful.

But that wasn't what had happened that evening. A stranger had stepped in and done those things, and apparently, it had unsettled both her and Zane. What that meant, she had no idea.

"Are you sure that guy wasn't bugging you?" Zane asked once it was just the two of them in her car. "Even if Lee likes the guy, you can be honest."

"I was honest," she said. "He wasn't bugging me. He offered me a hand down off the last step, then asked Lee who the... beautiful lady was."

"He called you beautiful, too?" Zane asked.

Kelsey didn't want to be defending a stranger, so she just shrugged as she started up the car. It might not be the best thing to have told him that, but at the same time, she didn't want it to come out at another point and become a big deal because she hadn't told him.

"I don't want you to be subjected to unsolicited attention with stuff like that." Zane paused. "Maybe you should put your rings back on."

She'd considered that herself, but she had a question first. "Are you going to put yours back on?"

When he hesitated again, Kelsey's heart sank. Without waiting for his response, she said, "I'd rather wait until we're both ready to put our rings back on."

Zane didn't say anything to that, and silence filled the car. Thankfully, the drive home was short because it was definitely not a comfortable one.

Kelsey was left feeling like they'd just taken a massive step backwards, and she didn't know what to do about it. She'd been honest, and all it had done was bite her.

They arrived home at the same time as Lee and Rori, so there was no more awkward silence between them. Well, there was still an awkwardness between them, but it wasn't as obvious with the other two there.

Kelsey was still struggling with what had transpired. She wanted to believe that *her* Zane would have just laughed it off with her. They had been that secure in their feelings for each other.

Once they'd become serious—which had been rather quickly—she had never once questioned his loyalty to her. But, of course, she had come to find out that he had something in his past that probably would have made her a little less certain about things.

So who knew how they would have handled this situation back then?

"Do you have plans for tomorrow?" Rori asked as she got a couple of cookies out of the jar and handed one to Lee.

"I'm going to be doing some yard work," Lee said. "With fall arriving, it's time to start prepping things for winter."

"I'll help," Rori told him with a smile. "I like doing yard work with you."

"I probably can't be a lot of help," Zane said. "But I'm onboard with yard work if you need me."

Now that Kelsey didn't have her exam to study for, she didn't really have much to fill her time with. "I can help too."

"Perfect," Rori said. "We can have a late breakfast, then do some work. It's supposed to be cool and cloudy, but no rain. Perfect for doing sweaty work."

They chatted for a bit longer, then Kelsey excused herself to go up to her room. She was ready to call it a day.

"See you all in the morning."

Rori gave her a hug. "Goodnight, Kels. Sleep well."

"You too." Kelsey gave the guys a smile that she hoped didn't look as weak as it felt. "Goodnight."

She heard the murmur of conversation as she climbed the stairs and briefly wondered what they were talking about. But she wasn't curious enough to try to listen in.

When she reached her room, she went straight to the bathroom to prepare for bed. If she took a minute to sit down, her thoughts would circle around to her and Zane, and she didn't want that just yet.

But when she curled up in bed a short time later, there was no stopping the thoughts that swelled to take up all the space in her mind. She wanted to be mad at Eric, but honestly, he'd innocently wandered into a complex situation.

Still, Kelsey couldn't help but wish that he'd kept his hand and his compliment to himself.

CHAPTER TWENTY-EIGHT

Zane stared down at his leg and bent forward to give it a pat. "Welcome back, ol' chap!"

Gareth chuckled. "Missed it that much, huh?"

"I really have. You know I'm not one to sit around, and this bum leg has definitely been forcing me to do just that."

"Well, you're not going to be running a marathon anytime soon," Gareth reminded him. "You need to get some physio on that leg before you do that."

"Still not planning to run a marathon, but I'd love to be ready to get back into the kitchen sooner rather than later."

"I get that," Gareth said. "But wait for the go ahead from the physiotherapist."

"I'm not that close to getting back into the kitchen. But I want the option, if something should pop up."

"How're the headaches?"

"Better." And Zane was glad that was the truth. "They're not completely gone, but they're lessening in frequency and intensity. It seems like the healing is happening more quickly now. The difference from last week to today is marked."

"That's good," Gareth said. "Have you seen the neurologist recently?"

"I'm going back on Friday." And he hoped that, even though he could drive himself, Kelsey would be willing to go with him.

"How're things with you and Kelsey?"

Wasn't that the question of the hour? Again... "Things are a bit tense. Though maybe awkward is a better word."

Gareth frowned. "What did you do?"

Zane gave an indignant huff. "Why are you assuming I did something?"

"Kelsey has always struck me as all-in when it comes to your relationship," Gareth said. "You, on the other hand, have been more reluctant to fully commit."

"Well, honestly..." Zane paused, thinking what he was going to say.

He was going to tell Gareth that it hadn't had anything to do with his reluctance to fully commit, but that wasn't really true.

"Honestly?" Gareth prompted.

"Yeah. Okay. Maybe that's partly true."

His older brother leaned back in his chair and crossed his arms over his chest. "So what happened?"

"I may have overreacted on Friday night," Zane confessed.

"At the basketball game?"

After hesitating, Zane dove into the details.

"So, wait." Gareth sat forward. "You both decided to remove your rings until you were ready to fully commit, but you thought she should wear hers so guys wouldn't hit on her? But you didn't jump at the opportunity to put yours back on?"

"That pretty much sums it up."

"I think you already know that that was perhaps the wrong position to take."

"Yep. It feels like I've lost a lot of the progress I'd made with Kelsey."

"You haven't," Gareth told him. "Do you think I've never messed up with Aria? Oh boy, I have. I almost lost the best thing that's happened to me back when we were dating. I'm sure that every married man has had a misstep or two. It didn't mean the end of the relationship. It meant that we had to step up and do the hard work to make things right again."

"The hard work?"

"Well, for me, I had to apologize profusely for the way I reacted to something Aria hadn't revealed to us when she came to work at the clinic."

Zane nodded, remembering when he'd heard about all of that. "I do owe Kelsey an apology."

"What are you going to apologize for?"

He thought about it for a minute, then said, "I need to apologize for asking her to wear her ring when I wasn't willing to wear mine."

"That's a good place to start," Gareth agreed. "But have you thought about why you're not willing to make that commitment yet?"

Though he definitely had strong feelings for Kelsey, he didn't feel about her the way he remembered feeling about Sarah. That was the standard he was measuring his progress with Kelsey against. Was that wrong?

When he asked Gareth about it, his brother said, "Comparing two different relationships made up of two different people—because you are different now than when you dated Sarah—isn't a good idea. The reality is that you'll never love two people exactly the same way. If your feelings for Sarah have truly changed, then focus on loving Kelsey. Don't try to recreate what you felt with Sarah with Kelsey. She deserves her own version of your love. One that's just for her. No one else."

Zane had never really thought of it that way.

"I mean, would you like it if Kelsey told you she loved you just like she loved her last boyfriend? The one that turned out to be a dud?"

"No. I would want my own relationship with Kelsey."

"And she deserves her own with you."

"I'm not really thinking that much about Sarah anymore," he said.

"Maybe not, but your relationship with her is still popping up in how you deal with crucial moments with Kelsey. In the future, you need to take a step back when presented with situations that tempt you to compare things with your relationship with Sarah and really focus in on Kelsey."

Though Zane hadn't been super close to Gareth growing up, he appreciated his advice. He knew it was basically the same advice Lee would have given him if they'd had a conversation about what had happened. For some reason, he'd avoided having that conversation, and he wasn't sure why.

"Now I just have to figure out how to make things right with Kelsey."

"I have a feeling that a conversation—an honest conversation—would be a good place to start. Don't take her gifts as a way to apologize but avoid talking. You can take her flowers or whatever, but only as a way to get the conversation started."

"Thanks for the advice," Zane said, with total sincerity. "I really do appreciate it."

"I'm happy to share what I've learned." Gareth smiled at him "And the most important things I've learned are to take concerns to God in prayer, approach Aria with love, and always have open and honest conversations."

It was such basic advice for a married Christian, and yet, it seemed to be a struggle to put it into practice. At least for him.

As he sat there, he thought about each of his married siblings and their marriages. Zane knew that they'd all experienced some bumps in the road with their spouses, both before and after their marriages. And yet, they'd found the way to work through the issues that had arisen.

He was determined to do the same with Kelsey.

"I'd better go," he said, getting to his feet. It felt weird to not have the support of the boot, and for a moment, he felt uneasy putting weight on his leg. What if it hadn't healed the way it should have?

"You'll be fine," Gareth said, clearly reading his mind. He stood up and followed Zane out the door of the office, and together they walked to the back door.

"Thanks again."

Gareth reached out and pulled Zane into a tight hug. "I'm so proud of you, little brother." Moving back a bit, he gripped Zane's shoulders, his brown eyes warm with affection. "I know you're doing the right thing, and I can't wait to see how God leads you and Kelsey."

Zane felt emotion surge within him. He wasn't a stranger to encouragement like Gareth had voiced, but in the midst of his current struggle, it felt like so much more than just simple encouragement.

"Love you," Zane murmured past the tightness in his throat.

"I love you too."

"Can a sister get in on this, too?" Janessa asked as she swept in and wrapped her arms around them both.

"Sure thing," Gareth said with a laugh as he and Zane each wrapped an arm around her.

When Zane left a few minutes later, his heart felt lighter, and he knew it was now time to sort things out with Kelsey.

He wanted to say it was time to *try* to sort things out, but there was no *try* in this. Try meant there was an option for failure, and for the sake of his marriage, he couldn't fail. He didn't want to fail.

On the way home, he swung by the florist shop and bought a bouquet of beautiful autumnal flowers, then went by the coffee shop to pick up two coffees and some pastries. It wasn't anything unique, but he knew that she liked all of it, and that was what he wanted.

When he got home, the house was quiet. He'd thought she would be up since she usually was when coming off her nighttime shifts for the week.

After a moment's hesitation, Zane carried his purchases up the stairs and approached her door. Tucking the bouquet in the crook of his arm, he lifted his hand to knock lightly on the door.

It took a minute before Kelsey opened the door. She looked like she had just gotten out of bed, and her eyes looked a little puffy. Zane felt bad that he might have woken her.

Her eyes widened as she took in the items he held.

"Can I come in?" Zane asked.

Normally, he would never have asked to enter a woman's room, but she was his wife, and they'd already been intimate with each other in a way he'd never been with another woman.

Her eyes widened even further as her gaze met his, then she nodded and stepped back, giving him room to step through the doorway. He gave a quick look around the room, noticing the un-made bed as he headed for the small sitting area by the bay window.

After setting the coffee and pastry bag down on the small round table, he turned to hand her the flowers. Only... she wasn't there.

He noticed that the bathroom door was closed, so he sat down on the loveseat, leaving the other chair for her since it looked like that was her preferred seat. There was a blanket over the arm of the chair, and a notebook and a tablet were stacked on the edge of the table nearest the chair.

When he heard movement behind him, he turned to see Kelsey walking toward him. It looked like she'd brushed her hair, but she still wore the pair of leggings and oversized shirt she'd had on when she answered the door.

"How are you doing?" he asked, getting to his feet as she joined him at the chairs.

"I'm fine," she said.

As they settled into their seats, Zane said, "Well, I'm not."

Kelsey frowned at him. "What's wrong?"

"What's wrong is that I hurt and upset you, and I feel horrible about it," he told her. "I don't like this awkwardness between us. I want us to work this out. If that's what you want, too."

Emotion flooded Kelsey's face, and her eyes glistened with tears that didn't remain unshed for long. "I want that too." Her voice was barely above a whisper.

Zane knew then that he had to fight for this. Over the previous weeks, he'd come to see what had probably drawn his forgotten self to Kelsey. And there was no sense in denying what he felt for her while he waited for... something—he didn't even know what—to happen.

Dropping to his knees in front of her, Zane reached out and took her hands in his. He gazed up at her, taking in the misery in her gaze.

"I want this," Zane said, earnestly. "I want this marriage. I want to make things work between us. I want you, Kelsey."

As he said the words, a tightness he hadn't even known he carried suddenly loosened in his chest, and peace flooded him.

Tears fell unchecked down Kelsey's cheeks as she clung to his hands. Zane wished with all his heart that he could remember everything he knew of her, but he had accepted that those memories were lost to him.

It was time to build new ones with this woman who had been a stranger not that long ago. But now, there was love in his heart for her. More love than he'd realized until that moment.

"I don't know why I reacted the way I did at the basketball game," Zane said. "But I'm sorry for how it hurt you. I want to put my ring back on, and I want to put your rings back on your finger too."

"You do?"

He could see that she wasn't convinced, and he couldn't blame her for that.

"I do," he said. "I really do. I'm not sure you'll believe me yet, but I want you to know that I love you."

Kelsey's jaw went slack, and more tears slid down her cheeks. "I didn't think I'd ever hear you say those words again. I've missed us so much."

"I'm not the same man that you fell in love with," he cautioned. "Are you willing to accept that I may never regain my memories?"

"So much of you is still the same," she told him, lifting one hand to wipe the tears from her cheeks. "There are things I have some questions about. But I think, if you love me now, I'm happy to leave those things in the past."

"And focus on the future?"

She nodded as she once again gripped his hands with both of hers. "And focus on our future."

Straightening, Zane pulled Kelsey up from the seat and wrapped her in a hug. He knew that this wouldn't be their first hug in Kelsey's memory, but it was for him, and he cherished the feel of her in his arms.

He lowered his cheek to rest it on her head, getting a whiff of vanilla shampoo. "You smell like cookies."

For some reason, that seemed to trigger more tears for Kelsey. Zane worried he'd said something wrong.

"You always say that to me." She finally got the words out as she tipped her head back to look up at him.

"I'm not surprised." He gave her a wink. "You smell delicious."

For a long moment, they stared at each other, then Zane felt drawn, as if by something deep inside him, to lower his head and press his lips to Kelsey's. Maybe, if he had his memory, being wrapped in her arms would have felt like coming home.

Instead, all he felt in that moment was a sense of rightness. Like finally, after floundering for the past several weeks, he was where he belonged.

When their kiss ended, Zane rested his forehead against hers. "I honestly wasn't sure if I could ever feel this way, but you have my whole heart. All my love is yours, Kelsey. Only yours."

Kelsey's arms tightened around him as she buried her head in his shoulder. He could tell she was crying again, and he thought he knew why. It pained him to think he'd inflicted so much hurt on her when he'd first woken up after the accident loving another woman.

Now, though, it was so important that she knew his heart belonged to her and her alone.

Moving them around a bit, Zane sat down in the armchair, then settled Kelsey on his lap. His arm went around her waist, his hand resting on her hip as she kept her head on his shoulder.

"I want to thank you for being patient with me," he said. "I know that it was extremely difficult at some points, and no one would have blamed you if you walked away. I'm just so glad that you didn't."

"I needed to know that I'd done everything," she replied softly. "That I'd given us every chance before I left. You probably would have had to be the one to tell me that there was no way it was going to work out. Until you said it was done, there was hope."

"I may not have known what I was doing half the time, but once I started to come out of the fog of everything that had happened, I just couldn't pull the plug on our marriage. It might have started as me not wanting to lose you for the me who fell in love and married you, but soon, it was for my sake, too."

He hesitated for a moment, then said, "Is it wrong of me to not want to get my memory back?"

Kelsey straightened and stared at him. "You don't want to remember those years? You don't want to remember the relationship we had?"

Zane took a moment to formulate his response in his head before he answered her. "I don't like the man I'd become. I walked away from my faith, and I distanced myself from my family. I even switched up the dream I'd had for my future as a chef. The only good thing from that time that I can see is you. I want to love you as this me, and I want you to love this version of me."

"I do," Kelsey said. "I love the man you became, but I love who you are now, too. I admire your faith and even though I've had a rough start with your family, I love how you relate to them. I wouldn't want you to walk away from them or your faith again."

Zane took Kelsey's hand in his, staring down at her fingers for a moment before meeting her gaze again. "I'm glad to hear that because they're important to me. Just like you are."

"You're important to me, too," Kelsey said.

Though she smiled at him, he could see something in her eyes that seemed a little like sadness. "Is everything else okay? Your job?"

Her gaze dropped to where their hands were entwined, and her shoulders slumped. Letting go of his hand, she leaned forward and picked up an envelope that had been sitting on top of her tablet. She held it for a moment before handing it to him.

"What's this?" Zane asked as he took it. He read the return address, but he didn't recognize it. Glancing up, he saw a defeated look on Kelsey's face. "Sweetheart, what is this?"

"Remember that day I went to Spokane?"

Zane nodded as he tried to figure out what could have happened there to upset her. She'd seemed tired when she'd come home, but otherwise, she'd said she was fine.

"Are you having health problems?"

"No. I took the nursing exam," she said. "And I failed."

Zane stared at her for a moment. "I'm confused. You're a nurse?"

"Not yet, I'm not. It took me ages to get through nursing school, and I was just getting ready to take the exam in Tampa when you had your accident."

"Why didn't you say anything about this?" Zane asked, still confused.

Kelsey moved to get up off his lap, clearly distressed. Zane stopped her with a gentle hold, one she could break free of if she truly wanted to. He was relieved when she sank back onto his lap.

"I'm not mad," he said. "I'm just confused. Did I know about this before my accident?"

"Yes. I didn't tell you right away when we were dating, but I eventually did."

"Why wouldn't you tell me—us—now?"

"I didn't want people to know in case I failed." She gave a sad laugh. "And look at that. I failed."

"You only fail if you give up," Zane said, thinking of the countless times he'd failed with recipes over the years. "Are you going to take it again?"

"I guess so."

"Did you want to work at the clinic?"

Her eyes briefly widened before she shook her head. "No. And that's why I didn't say anything about being a nurse. I didn't want your family to think I was trying to get into the family business."

"I didn't tell them?"

"No. I asked you not to."

"You never have to hold stuff back from me for fear of failing," Zane said. "I'd rather know and be able to support you. You've had a *lot* on your plate for the past several weeks. Maybe it wasn't the best time to take an exam."

"I know, but I wanted to have it all done, so that if you sent me away, I would have a chance of getting a decent job."

Zane's heart hurt at the very idea of sending her away, but he put that aside for the moment. "Well, I want you to take the exam again as soon as you're comfortable doing so. If this is the career you want, then I want to support you as you work to attain it."

Tears once again slid down her cheeks. Uncertain what had prompted them, Zane reached up to wipe them away. "Explain these to me, sweetheart."

"You were the first person who truly believed in me unconditionally. My parents didn't care about anything I tried to do, and when I failed, I was ridiculed. I quickly figured out it was better for me to just keep my goals to myself. Even when I did manage to succeed at something, they didn't really care." She took a deep, shuddering breath. "When you lost your memory, in addition to everything else, I lost the first support I'd ever had. But now... now I feel like even without your memory, I'm getting that back."

"Of course you are," Zane said. "I'm going to be your biggest cheerleader! I can do a cartwheel and a backflip, and I'm sure Layla would teach me some cheers if you wanted that."

Even though her eyes were still damp with tears, Kelsey laughed, and Zane counted that a win, even as his heart skipped a beat at how beautiful she looked in that moment.

"You're beautiful," Zane said, needing to share that with her since he hadn't told her that yet. His old self probably had, but he had a whole bunch of catching up to do.

Kelsey cupped his face in her hands and leaned forward, her eyes free from the shadows of sadness that had been there earlier. "And you are so handsome. All the ladies at the restaurant used to tell me how lucky I was to have you. I always agreed, but not because of how you looked, but because you were—are—an amazing man."

Zane had had no expectation of how things would go when he got home from the clinic, but this was better than he might have imagined. But he still needed to talk to her about one more thing.

After they shared another kiss, they moved to sit on the loveseat and turned their attention to the pastries and the coffee that had cooled slightly.

"I've been wanting to ask you something else."

"What's that?" Kelsey asked as she lifted her coffee cup to take a sip.

"Do you have any questions about God or my faith?"

"Oh." A contemplative expression came over her face. "Well, actually, I do. I was planning to ask Rori and Carisa about it."

"Are you comfortable asking me your questions?" Zane asked. "As your husband, I'd love to help you with them."

Zane said a silent prayer that she'd feel comfortable with him because he wanted to help guide her into the faith in God that was so important to him.

"I want to know how to become a Christian," she said. "Pastor Kennedy talks about how Christians should live, but I don't have a clear understanding of how to become a Christian."

Zane smiled at her. "That I can help you with."

Nothing could have prepared Zane for how amazing it would feel to lead his wife to the Lord. To pray with her as she confessed her sins and accepted God's forgiveness and gift of eternal life.

He may have lost his memory of the past four years and all the chef's experience he'd gained during that time, but he had gained so much more. A return to his faith. A closer relationship with his family. But most of all, he'd gained Kelsey's love and a marriage he was willing to fight for.

EPILOGUE

Kelsey smiled at the woman who approached the desk, a large coffee cup in her hand. "How's it going, Eva?"

Eva covered her mouth as she yawned. "I'm still getting used to this shift."

"It'll be worth it once you do," Kelsey assured her. "I am so thankful I'm on the same shift hours as Zane."

Nodding, Eva sank down on the stool at the desk and took a sip of her coffee. "I like still having my evenings free with Dougie. I just have to get used to sleeping through the day. And I need to tell my mom not to call us until after three."

They chatted for a few more minutes, their conversation eventually turning to what had happened on Kelsey's shift. There were others also in the process of going off shift, so they each took their turn passing on any pertinent information about the residents of the care home where they all worked.

Once that was done, Kelsey clocked out and gathered up her stuff. After saying goodnight to the others, she headed out to her car. Sliding behind the wheel of her small SUV, she took a moment to just breathe.

It hadn't been the easiest shift. One of her residents had died. And though it had been expected, it had still been heartbreaking because he hadn't had family present when he passed.

Unfortunately, working where she did, accepting death had become part of her life. It didn't make it any easier, however.

After she'd experienced the death of one of her residents for the first time, Kelsey had questioned whether she wanted to continue on with the job, knowing it was probably just the first death of many. Zane had encouraged her to use her faith and love for people to make the days of the residents more enjoyable, whether they had many or few left.

So that had been her goal each day she went in to work. To show joy, love, gentleness, and caring to the residents, some of whom had no one come to visit them. The deaths hadn't gotten any easier, but she no longer struggled with them as she once had.

Finally, she put her car in gear and prepared for the thirty-minute drive home.

Once she'd passed the nursing exam, after taking it for the second time, Zane's family had offered her a position in the clinic. However, if she'd agreed to the job, she would never have seen Zane. She'd wanted hours as close to his as possible.

The closest hospital was in Coeur d'Alene, so she'd looked for other options since she didn't want to drive an hour to and from work. The care home she'd ended up getting a position at was in a town about halfway to Coeur d'Alene.

It had taken some getting used to making the drive in the dark since she got off at midnight, but now she did so in the comfort of the vehicle Zane had purchased for her. He hadn't been happy with the idea of her driving her little car on the winding roads at night, especially during winter.

Worship music played from the speakers as she drove, and as she sang along, Kelsey felt the stresses of the day fall away. As she neared Serenity, anticipation began to build.

In the year since that afternoon in her room, life had changed completely. Well, not completely. Zane still didn't have his memory back. They were still in Serenity and still living in the big house with Lee and Rori, who was soon to have their first child.

Job wise, she no longer stocked shelves, and Zane was back to work as a chef. But this time in his own restaurant, with Hudson and Kayleigh as silent partners.

Also, her relationship with Zane's family had improved greatly, for which she was very grateful. It had taken some work for them to get beyond their rocky start, but they'd built a relationship that Kelsey was thankful for.

As she pulled her car to a stop in front of the house several minutes later, she saw that Zane's car was already there. That wasn't unusual. Though the restaurant closed at eleven, he usually stayed until midnight doing the restaurant related business he didn't have a chance to do while it was open. His commute back and forth was much shorter, so he was always home before she was.

Their days had fallen into a similar pattern to what they'd had in Tampa, and she enjoyed it as much now as she had then. It also made sharing a home with Lee and Rori fairly easy. Because of their opposite schedules, each couple had plenty of alone time.

As she approached the front door, Zane swung it open, letting her know that, as usual, he'd been watching for her. She picked up her pace, eager to reach the man she loved.

Once she'd stepped into the foyer and he'd closed the door behind her, Zane drew her into a hug. Wrapping her arms around his waist, Kelsey leaned against him, grateful to be reunited.

After a couple of minutes, Kelsey lifted her head for his kiss, and Zane did not disappoint. Then, hand in hand, they made their way up to their room, where they showered together.

"Ready to eat?" Lee asked after they'd dressed in their pajamas.

"I am," she said. "I'm starving."

Unlike in Tampa, they usually ate their main meal together when they got home from work. Most nights, Zane brought food home from the restaurant, but there were times he made them something once he got home.

Because Lee and Rori's room wasn't close to the kitchen, they didn't need to worry about being too quiet as they set about plating the food that Zane had left to warm in the oven. Soon they were seated at the breakfast nook together.

Zane laid his hand on the table, palm up, and Kelsey didn't hesitate to put her hand on top of it. His fingers tightened around hers as he smiled at her, his brown eyes shining with love she hadn't been sure she'd ever see from him again.

"I love you," he said.

Kelsey never tired of hearing those words from him, unable to completely let go of the fear from those early days following the accident when she'd wondered if he'd ever say them to her again. "I love you too."

With a gentle squeeze of her fingers, he bent his head and said grace for their food.

"We're fully booked for the next week," Zane told her. "Unless we get some cancellations, from the moment we open on Wednesday, our tables will be full."

"That's wonderful!"

The restaurant had only been open for three months, but it was already doing extremely well, thanks to a famous actor who had shown up with his wife and four kids a month earlier. On Kayleigh's recommendation, they'd decided to give it a try.

The kids had loved the experience so much that the actor had shared his endorsement of the restaurant all over his social media. From that point on, the reservations had grown. It was a blessing after all the hard work Zane had put into it.

It had taken nine months for him to find a location around Serenity that would be suitable. There had still been plenty of work needed to create the welcoming, comfortable, yet elegant interior he'd envisioned.

Having their dreams unfolding at the same time had been a bit hectic, but Zane had resolved to always give their relationship precedence.

So, while he might have made more money if he'd been open seven days a week, he chose to close the restaurant on Mondays and Tuesdays. The care home had also been willing to give Kelsey those days off, so they spent that time together, unwinding from their busy careers.

"You still up to going to Mom and Dad's tomorrow for the barbecue?" he asked.

Kelsey nodded. "What's Labor Day weekend without a barbecue?"

Zane chuckled. "Exactly."

"Are you cooking for it?"

"Nope. Mom said that they were going to take care of everything."

"Can you imagine if Rori went into labor on Labor Day?" Kelsey said. "That would be hilarious."

"I don't think she wants that."

"No, that's true. She said she wanted to be able to enjoy the holiday, and *then* she could go into labor."

It was going to be odd to have a baby around all the time, but Kelsey was looking forward to it. Though she and Zane had both agreed they wanted to have kids, they weren't ready just yet. So, in the meantime, they'd enjoy being aunt and uncle to yet another niece or nephew.

Once they were done eating, they cleaned up their dishes, then locked up and turned off the lights on the main floor before going up to their room—formerly her room. Lee and Rori had given them free rein to change anything they wanted to in the room, so over the past year, they'd repainted and brought a few more of their things out of storage.

If someone had asked her if she'd be happy living with other people after getting married, she probably would have said no. But, for whatever reason, this worked out well for them. Plus, she enjoyed being close to her best friend. They had a lot of fun with Lee and Rori.

Maybe it was because, growing up, she'd lacked a community of supportive and loving people. Having found it there in Serenity, she was happy to keep those people close. One day, they'd move out on their own. But for now, she didn't want to mess with a good thing.

Since they had a full day ahead, they didn't stay up as late as they might have on other nights. Once they were ready for bed, Kelsey curled up against Zane and listened as he read a chapter of the Christian suspense book they were working their way through.

After he finished the chapter, they put their phones aside and turned off the lights before cuddling together and spending some time in prayer. It was her favorite time of the day, and the last things Kelsey did each night before sleeping was to thank God for sparing Zane's life that night in Tampa and bringing them even closer together.

It was something she would never take for granted.

~ * ~

Around one the next afternoon, Zane and Kelsey made their way out to the family home for the barbecue.

"I can't wait until the leaves are fully turned," Kelsey said. "And all the fall events start up."

"We might have to miss some of it this year because of our schedules," Zane told her.

Kelsey sighed. "Yeah. But hopefully there will be some activities that we can enjoy together. I'm just glad the ladies were willing to have our Bible study on Tuesday evenings."

Sundays were often exhausting for them as they got up early to go to church and then still had to go to work afterwards. They'd missed out on a few of the casual family get-togethers, but it was the price they had to pay for their careers.

That was why they always tried to attend any gathering that worked with their schedules.

"Whoa," Kelsey said as they drove up the winding driveway to the house, which was located about ten minutes outside of Serenity. "Are we late?"

"Nope."

"Well, it looks like everyone else is here already."

They were, but he let the comment slide as they got out of the car. Hand in hand, they walked up the porch and through the front door without knocking.

"Where is everyone?" Kelsey asked. "It's so quiet."

"Probably outside, since it's such a nice day." He was glad for that, because if it had been raining, his plans would have been a little difficult to pull off.

The kitchen held signs of the meal that was to come, but there was still no one around.

"This is weird." Kelsey glanced around. "Usually this place is bustling with activity when we all get together."

"We're not eating for a couple of hours, so there's no rush to get food ready just yet."

Butterflies came to life in his stomach as he approached the door that led out onto the large porch and the expansive multi-level deck. He hoped she liked what he had planned and wasn't mad that she hadn't had a say in the planning.

As they stepped out onto the porch, Kelsey came to a stop before taking a couple more steps. Zane stayed where he was, letting her hand slip from his.

"What is this?" she asked, staring out over their family and close friends who were all gathered there, smiling and cheering. Past the group, on the lowest deck, was a large arch covered in autumnal flowers and greenery.

While she was distracted, Zane lowered himself to one knee, grateful that his leg had regained its full strength after the accident. Then he waited for Kelsey to turn back toward him.

When she did, her eyes went wide as she spotted him. "Zane, what's going on?"

"I know we've done all of this already, but I don't remember it, and I want this memory. I really want to do it again, this time before

God and our family." He held out his hand to her. "Kelsey, would you renew our vows with me today?"

Tears flooded her eyes as she placed her hand in his. "Yes. Always yes."

The cheers and claps of his family and friends were raucous as Zane got to his feet and pulled Kelsey into his arms to kiss her.

"Save some of the kissing for later," Rori exclaimed as she came toward them, her belly leading the way. "We have a ceremony to get ready for!"

"Get ready?" Kelsey asked.

"Yep." Rori took her hand and pulled her toward the door. "We've got someone to help with hair and makeup, and we have dresses to change into."

When Kelsey glanced back over her shoulder at Zane as Rori led her away, he nodded, then blew her a kiss. He had his own preparations to make.

Since it wouldn't take as long for him to get ready, Zane stayed out in the backyard to make sure that everything was as he'd planned. He'd had to rely on his family to do the setup since he hadn't wanted to alert Kelsey that anything was going on, which is what his leaving the house without her would have done.

"Everything look like you wanted?" Kayleigh asked as she and Hudson approached him.

Zane glanced around, taking in the white folding chairs and the flowers and ribbons that they'd worked hard to put together. He'd given his sister the idea of what he wanted, along with a budget, and set her loose. She had not disappointed. In fact, he thought she may have exceeded what he'd had in mind.

"It looks wonderful. Perfect."

"We also have a photographer here. She's upstairs taking pictures of Kelsey, Rori, and Carisa as they get ready."

He'd thought of doing something super simple, but then he realized that part of why they'd gone so simple previously was because there hadn't been anyone they really wanted present. That wasn't the case any longer, so he wanted to share this moment with those closest to them.

Plus, he really did want the memory of committing to Kelsey before friends and family and slipping a ring on her finger.

Putting his arm around Kayleigh's shoulders, he said, "Thank you for everything you've done to pull this off. I really appreciate it."

"Anything for you, brother." She gave him a hug, then relinquished him to Lee, who took him into the house and down to the basement where the guys were getting ready.

Since he hadn't had a strong opinion on clothes for the wedding, he'd left that to Kayleigh as well. She was by far the most stylish of his siblings, though Lexi and Carisa were also pros when it came to fashion.

Kayleigh had taken responsibility for the men while Carisa had chosen the dresses for her, Rori, and Kelsey. He and the guys had had a chance to try on their outfits, but that hadn't been the case for Kelsey, so he hoped that her dress fit and that she was happy with it.

Gareth joined them a few minutes later, since he was also standing up with Zane. Though he could have picked any of his brothers, Zane had appreciated the input Gareth had given him when he and Kelsey were struggling and wanted him standing up with them as they renewed their vows.

It didn't take long for them to get dressed in the dark gray pleated slacks and white long-sleeved shirt that Kayleigh had chosen for them. Each of the men also wore a colored vest. Zane's was a deep dark green, while Gareth wore maroon, and Lee was in a burnt orange vest. The ladies who were standing up with Kelsey would match the men they were paired with.

"How are you gentlemen doing?" Pastor Kennedy asked as he joined them once they were dressed.

"We're ready to get this show on the road," Lee told him.

"Perfect!" The pastor rubbed his hands together. "How about we say a prayer together before we join the others?"

After a short prayer, the men left the basement and returned to the backyard. The photographer took a few pictures of them, along with his parents, then it was time for the ladies to join them.

Because it wasn't a traditional wedding, there wasn't going to be a giving away of the bride. Instead, the men lined up by the back door.

When the door opened and Carisa stepped out, Gareth offered her his arm and they walked up the aisle to the string quartet version of *Ode to Joy* that flowed out of Bluetooth speakers strategically placed around the yard. Next, Rori came out, her burgeoning belly filling out the front of her dress.

Lee rested his hand on her stomach briefly before offering her his arm. They moved more slowly than Carisa and Gareth had, with Lee carefully helping Rori carefully descend each level of the deck.

Finally, Zane turned his attention to the door in anticipation of Kelsey's appearance. When she stepped through the door, she took his breath away. Not because of the beautiful champagne colored dress she wore that fit her perfectly, or her flawless hair and makeup, or even the earrings and necklace he'd picked out for the occasion.

No, it was the expression on her face. Her beautiful smile and the light of love in her eyes when she saw him.

Approaching her, he said, "You look gorgeous."

She rested her hand on his chest. "And you, my love, are so handsome."

"Ready to do this?"

"Oh, yes."

She shifted her bouquet, which was made up of all her favorite fall flowers, and slipped her hand through his arm. The two of them took their time walking to where Pastor Kennedy now waited for them at the arch.

The ceremony didn't have many of the traditional elements of a wedding, but it did have a part for them to share their vows with each other. And then he had a ring for her.

After she handed off her bouquet to Rori, Zane took Kelsey's hands. Pastor Kennedy welcomed them and said a prayer before sharing a few words, then he turned it over to Zane and took a seat beside his wife in the front row.

As Zane gazed down at Kelsey, the rest of the world fell away, and it was just the two of them.

"Kelsey, I may not remember how things started for us, but I'm thankful for the person I was then for choosing you to marry. You are a strong, beautiful woman who has brought so much joy into my life. Every day, my love for you grows."

Feeling his emotions start to swell, he took a deep breath. "Thank you. Thank you for sticking with me through those first few months after the accident when I'd forgotten the most important things in my life. You and my love for you. You were faithful to our vows as you saw me through the worst, patiently loving me even though it hurt you.

"I'm thankful for how God has guided us through that dark time, and I know that He will see us through all the times ahead, both good and bad. Thank you for loving me when I wasn't very lovable. Thank you for being willing to walk into the future, hand in hand with me.

"Today, as we stand before God and those we love, I vow to love you, and I will strive to be the husband that God would have me be. One that cherishes our love and guards it against anything that might try to tear us apart. I want the love we share to reflect God's love for us.

"Kelsey, I love you more than I ever thought I could love some-one. You hold my whole heart in your hands." He cleared his throat. "I can't wait to see where God takes us. I love you."

Zane hadn't given much thought to what he was going to say since Kelsey wasn't going to have opportunity to prepare her vows ahead of time. So he just spoke from the heart.

"My turn?" Kelsey asked when he stopped talking. As he nod-ded, she took a deep breath. "I might have panicked about speaking publicly with no advance notice, but in this case, I have so much to say. I'll keep it short though, just in case Rori goes into labor."

There was laughter from their family, but they quickly quieted so Kelsey could speak.

"I never knew what love was until I met you. Even before we dated, I could see that you were a good man, treating everyone with respect. From the people bussing the tables to the head chef. And when you told me you loved me, I was sure I was the luckiest per-son in the world. I still feel that way. Blessed. Fortunate.

Her fingers tightened around his. "The day you woke up and didn't remember me or our love was the worst day of my life, be-cause it felt like I'd lost you. But I refused to give up hope, though. Even through the difficult weeks that followed, I held onto hope because if there was even a chance you might love me again, I couldn't walk away.

"When you told me you loved me for the first time after losing your memory, I knew all the heartache and struggles during those weeks had been worth it. Being loved by you is the most amazing thing. From that moment on, you've never given me a reason to doubt your love, and I'm thankful for that. And not only did you bring me into a physical family—who I've come to love—but also into a spiritual one. A true blessing.

"I'm so thankful for you teaching me what real love is and for your never-ending support. And thank you for loving me enough to point me to God. You hold my heart, now and forever. Through the good and bad. Through the ups and downs. Through all of it, I'll be there at your side, being the wife God would want me to be. I know we're going to make it. I love you so much."

As she finished speaking, Zane reached into his pocket and pulled out the simple band that he'd bought to compliment the two other rings she wore. "I don't remember when I gave you your rings for the first time, though I do recall the second time."

Kelsey's smile grew just a bit as he gave her a wink. They'd each returned the other's rings to their rightful place the night they came together again physically, which had been shortly after that conversation in her bedroom.

"I'm giving you this ring today as a promise that I will always love you, cherish you, and give you precedence over everyone in my life but God." He slid the ring on her finger to join it with the other two already there. "Always and forever."

"Always and forever," she echoed with a beautiful smile.

Moving close, he wrapped his arms around her and bent to kiss her.

More whoops and cheers erupted as they kissed, then Zane picked Kelsey up and spun around with her, his joy in the moment spilling over. Kelsey laughed as she locked her hands behind his neck.

"Before you take flight," Pastor Kennedy said as he joined them again. "Why don't you all gather round as we say a prayer for Zane and Kelsey?"

As his family and friends encircled them, Kelsey slipped her arms around his waist. She looked up at him with a smile, her gaze full of love. "Thank you for this. It's amazing, and such a surprise. I had no idea."

"That was the plan," he told her. "You're happy with everything?"

"I am." She went up on her toes to kiss him. "I'm so happy. Forever doesn't feel long enough to be with you."

Zane agreed.

The accident had been a devastating moment in their lives, but it had led to something wonderful. Though his body still bore the scars of that day, his heart was fully healed because of God and Kelsey's love for him. God had taken a tragedy and written a beautiful story for them, with many more chapters to come.

ABOUT THE AUTHOR

Kimberly Rae Jordan is a USA Today bestselling author of Christian romances. Many years ago, her love of reading Christian romance morphed into a desire to write stories of love, faith, and family, and thus began a journey that would lead her to places Kimberly never imagined she'd go.

In addition to being a writer, she is also a wife and mother, which means Kimberly spends her days straddling the line between real life in a house on the prairies of Canada and the imaginary world her characters live in. Though caring for her husband and four kids and working on her stories takes up a large portion of her day, Kimberly also enjoys reading and looking at craft ideas that she will likely never attempt to make.

As she continues to pen heartwarming stories of love, faith, and family, Kimberly hopes that readers of all ages will enjoy the journeys her characters take in each book. She has no plan to stop writing the stories God places on her heart and looks forward to where her journey will take her in the years to come.